FALLING

TOWARD

HEAVEN

FALLING

TOWARD

HEAVEN

JOHN BENNION

SIGNATURE BOOKS

SALT LAKE CITY

For Karla, Kent, Phillip, and the others who helped

COVER ILLUSTRATION: TREVOR SOUTHEY:
Into Thy Hands I Commend My Spirit, 60 X 51 INCHES,
ENGRAVED PLEXIGLASS OVER CHARCOAL ON PANEL, 1975.

COVER DESIGN: RON STUCKI

∞ *Falling Toward Heaven* was printed on acid-free
paper and was composed, printed, and bound in
the United States of America.

05   04   03   02   01   2000   6   5   4   3   2   I

LIBRARY OF CONGRESS CATALOGING-IN-PUBLICATION DATA
Bennion, John
    Falling toward heaven/by John Bennion.
      p. cm.
    ISBN I-56085-I40-6 (pap.)
    I. Mormons—Fiction. I. Title.
PS3552.E547564 B87 2000
813'.54—dc2I
             99-053298

I. Houston, Texas

*"By the rivers of Babylon, there we sat down,
yea, we wept, when we remembered Zion."*

—PSALMS 137:1

One

From his blanket on the hilltop above the outdoor theater, Elder Howard Rockwood scanned the crowd. Men and women baaed like sheep, gabbled like geese; they spread mats and blankets, opened bottles of wine and soda, lifted fried chicken and fat sandwiches from wicker baskets or grocery bags—a celebration almost like a rodeo or county fair back home in Utah. "A city which is set on a hill," Howard whispered, "cannot be hid." Despite his sense of carnival, his soul was in a waning phase, narrowing to a sliver. He felt isolated—in, but not of, the world—as if he sat on a hilltop on Mars or a planet near Kolob. The air was heavy, hot enough to make the Spanish moss sweat and droop from the branches of the live oaks.

Fifty yards below him, Peterson lumbered like a primeval hunter through the crowd. He chatted with a white-haired grandfather who held a white-blonde child on his lap. He accosted a man in a blue "Houston-Proud" T-shirt but passed by a woman in an orange halter top. He drifted down to the security guards who lounged between the motley crowd and the reserved seats, shaded by a high, rusted shell. Peterson's shoulders were heavy, his neck thick and long, a bear-like neck. Howard knew Peterson watched for a sign, bright as a settling dove, which marked the true-blooded children of Israel. Earlier that week they had been walking along a bayou, the Houston word for a canal with fetid water in the bottom, when Peterson had felt the Spirit hover above them, sweep toward downtown, and hesitate above an apartment building just inside the Loop. They knocked on every door but were invited in only once, by a man who proposed union in a revolutionary form of polygamy. Their failure proved nothing to Peterson; he had felt "a true motion of the Spirit in his bones."

Which was close to what Howard wanted—the certainty that his life wasn't passing like a dream. He had turned twenty-three the previous April and decided that his mission was like thermal underwear, useful for safety and warmth, but hampering his free movement, the flow of his life. With two months left, he wondered if any of the professions he had made throughout his mission were true. Could Christ actually redeem men and women from the lethargy of flesh? Once the body shut down, once chemical impulses stopped leaping the synapses in the brain, did an impossible spirit live on, or was the mass of cells, recycled, the resurrection? The thin, organic skin of the earth might be the only eternal life. He had thought that, because he was a doubter, he should leave his mission, but he knew that would break his mother's heart. He had decided to muddle through to the end.

His prayers seemed superficial, partly because of the irony of asking God if he existed, and partly because of Howard's longstanding fear of the Father of the Universe. God had always seemed to Howard to be a stern teacher, one focused on obedience to rules. His fear had intensified when, right after passing the mid-point of his mission, he started reading the Old Testament. Children were slaughtered by bears, cities destroyed by fire, water, or disease—all to serve the private interest of God's people. Howard had also become sensitive to contemporary evidence that God had departed or was not paying attention: the burgeoning abuse of children he saw in the headlines of newspapers, the battles so common they could hardly be called war, the gulf between the professors living around Rice University, many of them affluent and bigoted, and those blacks and Hispanics living only a few miles to the south and west, most of them impoverished and ignorant. If God is in charge, Howard thought, then he is unpredictable, arbitrary, even cruel—an abusive father. A simpler explanation was that the governing spirit of the cosmos was chaos. Still Howard's habit was faith, and he doubted even his doubts of God.

Most recently Howard had worried that what he had hoped for his whole mission would happen: that he would return from Texas swathed in glory, finish his last year of college (range management and European history), and gradually take over the ranch from his father; like Abraham, he would build herds and domain; like Joseph, he would heal his cantankerous family; like Moses, he would become a great leader in the church; and like King Solomon, he would engender posterity, not on a harem of women, but only on Belinda Jakeman, who had written him faithfully since the day he left her for God. His future, once fraught with hope, now appeared as the narrow hallway leading to a prison cell.

What next? How could he be Howard, when the universe had become unstable? He could wallow in despair, beset by his fear of God and impending death, or he could embrace life, treasure each second of awareness. On a mission, treasuring life seemed like trying to suck steak through a straw.

Peterson, who was only nineteen and had little fear of the rush of time, refused to take Howard's ramblings seriously. He said that the debate between faith and doubt was as old as the war in heaven, not merely Howard's discovery. He said that Howard suffered from Missionary Menopause, a stage he would pass through. Howard's response was to goad Peterson, saying, "God makes men peak in sexual energy in their late teens and early twenties and calls them to celibate missions. They either translate libido into religious fervor or go crazy." Then Peterson told him that his obsession with sex would drag him down to hell. Howard answered that he was obsessed not with sex, but with finding truth, and Peterson said he knew of several missionaries who had confused the two. Pondering later, Howard decided that Peterson might have stumbled onto something ("from the mouths of babes"), and he was not surprised when his dream of a full and vital life came to him as a longing for conversation with a beautiful, intelligent woman. He began indulging in a discreet rebellion—watching women.

Sitting alone on the hill above Miller Theater, Howard kept one eye on Peterson, conspicuous in white shirt and tie, and the other on the women near him. They wore Levis and tank tops or T-shirts, white shorts and iridescent bras, thin flowered dresses; one sported a green silk pantsuit and earrings which flashed like fishing lures. He glanced at each one and moved on, his gaze never ardent. He released each image of curved lip or swell of thigh before experiencing what he still felt to be soul-dulling lust. Their arms and legs were pale or tanned, ebony or brown; their faces were inviting or cold, each one different. Their voices tangled in the air, rising toward him like jazz riffs.

Suddenly, as if in answer to prayer, a tall woman appeared fifty yards below, one hand flat above her eyes as she scanned the hillside. She seemed endowed with light, an illusion certainly caused by the sun reflecting off her sleeveless, white blouse. A thick-bodied man behind her lugged a food basket. Peterson appeared at the woman's elbow, grinning and pointing up toward Howard. The woman nodded and Peterson led the way. Loose and confident, she ranged like a farm woman, not prim or artful with her arms and legs. She considered some problem, frowning, working her lower lip with her teeth. She wore a denim skirt, thigh length. "Thanks," she said to Peterson as they arrived. "From down below this hilltop looked full up." She lengthened her words, making them languid, a trace of East Texas accent. Her hair was deep brown, almost black; her face was hard. She saw Howard, glanced back at Peterson. "There's another one of you," she said. She looked again at Howard and smiled.

Then the man bumped her from behind and she lifted a plaid blanket from the top of the food basket. "Must be ten thousand people," she said. "By night they'll be thick as roaches in a sewer." The man, fastidious in his motions, helped her open their blanket over the triangle of grass. While she looked to be mid-twenties, he was perhaps forty.

"I told you it would be like this," he said softly. He wore a trim black beard.

"We could have come earlier." She flipped the blanket hard, yanking it out of the man's hands. Her eye was wild, as if she were a mare circling a corral, looking for a gate to bolt through. Howard felt he couldn't resist a trapped woman, and he savored again her lanky and rough-edged beauty. Neither wore wedding rings.

The man laid out the blanket, careful to keep a narrow border between his domain and the missionary's. He placed the basket in the center of his space, took out food and a bottle of wine. "Pastrami, ham, or turkey," he said. "All with cheese." The woman looked toward the theater, her mouth a moody line. Then she saw something—maybe the twin girls with flaming hair who played Go Fish on their blanket, maybe the large-bellied man who had covered his face with a cloth napkin, the corners peaking like the ears of a half-submerged hippo—and she smiled, flat and wry, hardly different from her frown. She took a can of beer from the basket, opened it, and Howard caught the thick odor. The man offered her a choice of two sandwiches, but she shoved her palm toward him. "Not hungry."

"I'm Elder Peterson." Peterson extended his hand, fingers wide, for the man to shake.

The man, still holding the sandwiches, stared at Peterson's hand, finally touching it briefly. He glanced across at Howard's name tag: "Elder Rockwood." "You're both named Elder?"

"It's a title," said Peterson, "a rank in the priesthood. We're from the Church of Jesus Christ of Latter-day Saints."

"The Mormons," said Howard.

"Oh," said the man. He looked as if he'd found a worm in his lettuce.

"Should be Younger," said the woman. "Out of honor to Brigham Young." She turned back to her drink. The man rummaged in the picnic basket for a plastic cup.

"And you are?" asked Peterson.

"Allison Warren. This is Eliot Stone."

"What's your work?" Peterson asked him.

"I teach psychology at the University of Houston. I research sexual dysfunction."

"Whew," said Peterson. "Heavy stuff, but I'll bet couples are grateful for your help."

"Eliot thinks he and my mother are going to be the next Masters and Johnson," said the woman. The man licked a drop of wine from the brim of his cup. "I write software for oil companies," she said to Peterson. "Freelance."

"She helps the rich get richer," said the man; Eliot, she'd called him.

"Not that much richer," she said. "The only industry with less margin than the oil business is academia." Touch and touch, they spar, thought Howard. What's the real fight?

"Ouch," said Peterson, smiling, friendly as a puppy.

"You're either a professional wrestler or a football player," said Allison to Peterson.

"We're professional wrestlers for God," said Howard. Allison gave him her scant smile, sly and reserved as the Mona Lisa. He looked at her long bare legs then glanced away, worried that she might catch him looking and take offense.

"I was a lineman for Brigham Young University before my mission," said Elder Peterson.

Allison raised her eyebrows at Howard.

"Me?" he said. "Peterson's body is a gift from God. Mine proves his fallibility." He wiped both hands down his face. Shut it, he thought.

"I play soccer," said Allison to Peterson.

"She's good," said Eliot. "Frustrates the hell out of those macho Mexicans."

"Not just the Mexicans," she said. She gripped her second beer.

"Where do you play?" asked Peterson, leaning forward.

"We play pickup games every Saturday at Memorial Park."

Peterson smiled and nodded.

"You're a native Texan," said Howard.

"We're an endangered species. The Warrens were here before the Indians and Mexicans."

"A Texan who can't stand Texas," said Eliot.

"Can't stand Houston," she said. "There's a difference. I'm half lone wolf and the city's finally got me down." Her voice was nearly as deep as a man's. She looked at Howard, and he shifted his gaze toward

Eliot. The stubble of his black beard against a pale face, the snide curl of his mouth irritated Howard.

The hippo man's wife had come, and he was telling her off, quietly. She chewed her hamburger in his face; her eyes didn't flicker. A woman and a dog played Frisbee between the guards and the crowd. A boy juggled two shoes and a pink hat. Allison clapped and whooped.

"You're both from Utah?" she asked.

"Santa Barbara," said Peterson. "California."

"And you?" She tucked her hair behind one ear.

"Rockwood, Utah," said Howard. "A hundred miles southwest of Salt Lake."

"A Rockwood from Rockwood," she said.

"He's the aristocracy," said Peterson.

"The city elder and the country elder," Allison said. "Such different birds."

Howard grinned.

"I'm curious. How does someone from the desert survive in Houston?"

Had he survived? "I go downtown and squint till my vision blurs. Then buildings look like bluffs and people's faces look like the faces of antelope."

"My parents and I drove through Phoenix and Zion National Park on our way to Yellowstone once," said Allison. "I thought it was Mars with all the red rock."

"Rockwood is farther north," said Howard. "Great Basin." Eliot pulled out a book and began reading; Howard couldn't see the cover.

"So how do you proselytize?" she asked.

"We go to Fourth of July concerts and wait until someone talks to us, and then we hit on them," Howard said.

"When would you like your first lesson?" said Peterson.

She laughed. "Before I was born my mother went to Utah as a graduate student to do research for the Kinsey report. She interviewed hundreds of college students. A few of them, more than a few, dozens of guys like you, filled with piety and integrity like you, refused to be interviewed. Some of them told her that she shouldn't go around polluting innocent college students with talk about sexuality. They tried to get her banned from campus."

"Narrow-minded prudes," said Eliot. He didn't lift his eyes from his book.

Peterson arched an eyebrow at Howard as if to say, "Hey, dude, we're in; this couple is not cold to Mormonism." He said, "So ever since then you've wondered if those few were characteristic of Mormons everywhere. Right?"

She didn't seem to hear. "My aunt married a Mormon," she said. "After seven years he became convinced he was one of the prophets described in the Book of Revelation. The bastard planned to throw his children off the spire of the Salt Lake temple, believed they would flame into angels as they fell. She barely escaped the city with them. He's in a psychiatric hospital in Utah."

"Crazies are everywhere," said Peterson.

"How does it feel living among fanatics?" said Allison.

"When I turned twelve," Howard said, "I went into the mountains and fasted for four days. On the last day magpies and ravens flew in and out of my campfire and an angel dressed in doeskin rode a white donkey down through the aspens."

"Smartass," she said, and he smiled at the prospect of four or five more hours of edgy talk. She seemed independent, even brazen—but still hampered by this weasel, Eliot.

"Are you two interested in archeology?" said Peterson. "In ancient America—."

"I have one more story," she said. "My mother helped organize the International Women's Year Conference here before I was born. Mormon women were bused in from all over."

"You sound critical," said Peterson. "Mormon women are politically active."

"In a manner of speaking. My mother talked to some of them, pure reactionaries. They had been organized and instructed by men. They were herded in to vote down every measure for the advancement of women. Puppets."

"Just because their leaders helped them get there," said Peterson, "doesn't mean those women were puppets."

"Right," said Howard. "Most would have voted like reactionaries without being herded."

She looked at him and laughed. Again, he thought. Do that again.

"You know, you're sarcastic about everything," she said. "I can't tell what you think."

"Neither can he," said Peterson. "He has a knee-jerk mouth. What I meant is that they probably didn't think of unlimited abortion and making women into men as advancements. Motherhood is a divine right and calling."

Allison leaned forward—either to speak or take a bite out of Peterson's face. Howard had only recently discovered that Peterson was a whole man, completely self-consistent. No stranger could decode such a mystery in five minutes.

Eliot placed one hand on her shoulder. She shook it off. "Feels like I'm caught in a time warp." Her flat smile showed again, hard and quick as a glove across the face.

"Not all Mormons are conservative," Howard said.

"Fetch," said Peterson. "Here we go again."

"My mother is the leader of all the women in our ward," Howard said. Allison frowned. "Congregation." He leaned toward her. "She's not suppressed, oppressed, repressed, or depressed. She organizes and teaches the women service and spirituality and if someone doesn't have enough to eat, she requests a food order from the bishop and they go shopping." Below them a boy carrying a fan of American flags groped with his free hand for change.

"Damn," said Allison. "I touched a nerve here."

"Look," said Eliot, "we're just not the types who would ever convert."

"It takes a special type to believe," said Howard, feeling weary. He thought with longing of his mother, whose faith seemed as effortless as breathing.

Peterson shrugged his shoulders, turned the other way, started talking to the parents of the red-haired twins. He always focused on the men, potential heads of household, and he had little patience when his quarry was a liberal intellectual, not that they had the opportunity to teach many people like that.

Allison added a can to her collection of empties and immediately opened another. Eliot poured one more cup of wine, capped the bottle, and put it back in the basket. He looked at the empty beer cans, then at Allison.

Howard examined her face, closed off, anger waiting just under the surface—not the person to welcome the Mormon story of modern angels visiting the earth. She had been drinking steadily and appeared to be in an unhappy relationship. Like Howard, maybe she was trapped by circumstance. The gospel could bless her life, expand it from narrowness. He had watched it happen before. Despite himself he felt the old rush, the hope of another conversion, which seemed to him as culture-bound as the fever of jumping a buck while hunting. Below them, a boy hawked six-foot balloons, twisted together like strands of DNA. On which gene is the code for propensity of faith, which for self-destruction? The musk of enclosed animals drifted across from the zoo. Howard hooked a finger behind the knot of his tie. He flapped the damp cloth of his white shirt, trying to get some air inside.

An artificial pond lay behind the theater. A duck flapped along the shore and children ran under a sprinkler which tap-tapped in a circle, spreading a sheen over their bodies as they leaped and touched hands. "That would sure feel good right now," said Howard. "In the evening back home, after it's dry all day, the air turns moist and cool."

"I thought Rockwood was in the desert," she said.

"The Russian olives are blooming, and if I sat on my back porch, I'd smell the sweet scent of alfalfa blossoms because my father hasn't cut the hay yet." Then he found himself blabbing on about how his father had changed, becoming weaker, and about his mother, strong as ever, and that he wished he could teleport his mother to the grassy hillside so that anyone who wanted could see that Mormon women were vital, strong, and unrepressed.

"You don't need to prove anything to me," Allison said.

Howard felt his face flush. He had forgotten that she was a stranger and that they were both bound. She turned toward Eliot, tickling his ear with a stem of grass. Eliot brushed her hand away, not pleased. Howard rested, hands behind his head, and watched Allison and Eliot through half-closed eyes. Their bickering proved their familiarity. She lay on her back; her face pensive and moody. Her hair, which seemed very fine, pooled around her head. Eliot sat cross-legged, his head still bent over his book—arch of back, tidy black hair, tight beard. He started reading out loud, and Howard recognized the beginning of *Walden*. Eliot reached to massage Allison's calf.

Howard numbered those whom the Holy Ghost had touched while he taught: Amy and Jack Henderson, married schoolteachers from the Heights; Jerry Candle, son of a rice farmer; the Salley family from East Houston; Andrew Bills, who'd just graduated from high school and didn't know what to do next; and Grace Montoya, ninety years old. Except for Grace, they had all grasped the gospel as if it were a life preserver; their previous lives had been one desperate strait after another. When they rose smiling out of the waters of baptism, their faces shone bright as pearls. Each time he had been surprised, feeling that he'd had little to do with their conversion. From the beginning of his mission, he had refused zealotry, but, at the same time, he had believed his lack of enthusiasm might anger an imperious and jealous God, one who wanted to devour his soul. Now he didn't know how to feel. That was putting a name to it—not knowing how to feel.

Allison frowned, pensive. Her face was tanned, made darker by the white of her shirt. As Howard watched, she rolled and lit a thin cigarette, dragged on it, and held the smoke in her lungs. She exhaled slowly and smiled at Eliot for the first time all night. "Here," she said. Eliot took the peace offering, puffed, and passed it back.

Howard closed his eyes, willing himself away from the sweltering hilltop. The memory was not solitary but one felt on his skin innumerable times. He was out west on his father's farm, his skin sweaty and dirty, covered with green dust from hauling hay or white clay from digging the wheat grass crowns from the bottom of a ditch or dried manure from castrating calves. The truck churned dust behind them as they dropped from Lookout Pass toward home in Rockwood and he smelled moist air under the dappling shade of cottonwoods and willows and all his senses were alive as he stood on his front lawn and looked up at the mountains curved around Rockwood town and felt the porcelain handle of the door in his palm and the natural cold inside the thick-walled adobe. The ranch and town and desert spread always in his head, but they were fifteen hundred miles away and the landscape in his mind was like the chapel of the Holy Grail, not a place he could travel to by moving his legs. Finally, he felt himself slipping toward sleep.

In the dream, he tumbled down an endless tunnel—narrow, soundless, and empty. Not even the eye of God watched him fall. He woke clutching at Peterson's shirt. It was dusk and the orchestra was tuning up. Eliot and the twin girls stared at him; Allison dozed across Eliot's lap.

"Are you gifted with the interpretation of dreams?" Howard said to Peterson. "It was a flying/falling dream."

"Flying dreams are dreams of sublimated sex," said Eliot, shifting his position.

Allison woke and sat up, moving slightly toward Howard and Peterson. "Freud was up in the night."

"My flying dreams feel like escape," said Peterson, "not sex."

"Interpret it. I flew and fell."

"In your case, escape from responsibility," said Peterson. "You're so trunked out you can't think of anything but the clear skies of Utah. Falling is a return to reality and duty."

"Everything was quiet," said Howard. "I couldn't see or hear."

"Sounds like one of those near-death experiences," said Peterson.

Howard looked at him, surprised. "It did feel like death. Like dying and falling through a tunnel—thick with darkness."

"As I said, the Freudian interpretation is clear," said Eliot.

"Both your interpretations are as vague as a horoscope," said Howard. "I want specifics."

"It's a message from your libido," said Eliot. Peterson frowned, staring up into the purplish Houston sky. "The long dark tunnel is a woman's va—"

"Maybe we'd better stay away from the Freudian," said Peterson, "innocent as we are."

"You're about as innocent as Lot," Howard said. "Give me *your* interpretation." The musicians quieted, waiting for the conductor.

"I need more context," said Peterson.

"I'm Nebuchadnezzar and you're Daniel. You don't need to know the whole dream."

"You were alone?"

"Totally alone. Cold and alone and unable to see."

"It's a message from God." Peterson glanced toward Eliot. "He was warning you what Outer Darkness is like. He wants you to know what it's like to deny the Holy Ghost and become a Son of Perdition. Kicked out of God's kingdom."

Howard rolled his neck on his shoulders. "Worse than being kicked out. Worse than death. Like consciousness stopping."

"Libido transformed into lust for death," said Eliot. "The French call sex the little death."

"You are fixated," said Allison, "and you don't even know it."

The conductor lifted his arms and the musicians began with the *William Tell Overture*. Trumpets and other horns multiplied, rising waves of bright blue. Allison slid back against Eliot, who wrapped his arms around her. She lit another cigarette, a joint this time, which she held above her head while Eliot pulled on it. Howard watched in the growing dark as Eliot trailed his fingertips across the inside of her knee. Patriotic music flowed over the hill. They turned forehead to forehead, trading the short cigarette and drinking the rest of her beer. She has to be bombed before she can stand him, thought Howard, resenting every intimacy.

Several times he and Belinda had spread a blanket under a juniper in the canyon, listening to the rustle of aspens, and sharing wet, soft kisses. Her fingertips had wandered the nape of his neck—much better than sitting on a hillside with a hulking Californian or a hard-face, hard-mouth Texan who was always looking for another beer.

Finally, the orchestra performed the *Star Spangled Banner*, and Allison struggled to her feet as the first fireworks showered blue, white, and red, lighting the faces of the crowd. She arched her back and looked at the sky, her forearms clasped across the top of her head. Suddenly, she stumbled down the dark side of the hill, moving unsteadily toward a cluster of trees on the street. "Excuse me," she said. "Not feeling well. Excuse me. Not well at all."

"Allison," said Eliot. "Allison, where are you going?" Her white shirt moved down the hill. "Allison!" he shouted.

"Be right back," she called, the thin voice of a child. Then she disappeared under the trees. Howard saw the headlights of cars passing, heard the sound of their tires and engines. He jumped to his feet and sprinted down the hill, leaping over the heads of people as they craned their necks to see the fireworks. He finally broke free of the crowd and ran between the trees.

Ahead he saw Allison, her shirt brilliant in the beam of headlights. She stepped down into the road, and he ran harder. Then his arms were around her, and he had pulled her back, hearing the whine and fade of the passing car. He lowered her to the grass, breathing an odd mix of smoke, alcohol, and musky perfume. "You shouldn't have drunk so much," he said. Eliot and Peterson moved toward them through the trees. Her hands twitched, and she sat, aided by Eliot. "She wasn't looking," said Howard. "I grabbed her just as she was stepping off." His wrists and palms tingled from touching her.

Eliot swore steadily and then laughed. "We'll need to go back and give CPR to some of those people you jumped over."

"I've never seen you move like that," said Peterson.

"I didn't think I'd get to her in time." Howard bent lower. "Are you all right?"

"Look." She pointed as fireworks spread across the sky. "Such bright flowers."

"Let's get you home," said Eliot, lifting her to her feet.

"Your stuff," said Peterson. Howard followed him up the hill to gather the baskets and blankets and beer cans; the fireworks streamed and popped above their heads. When they returned, she was leaning against Eliot. Howard smelled vomit, acrid and sweet.

"I think we got everything," said Peterson. Neither Eliot nor Allison looked up.

"I haven't drunk so much for a long time," she said. "I've been good."

"It's been a tough three weeks," said Eliot.

She pulled away from him and walked unsteadily to the verge of the street. She looked both ways this time.

Howard and Peterson followed as Eliot helped her to a car, a red Mustang convertible. "Can we drop you?" said Eliot. "Oh, your bikes."

"We rode the bus," said Howard. "Peterson had his bike stolen here at the Juneteenth concert."

"It was worth it," said Peterson. "We baptized the man we met."

The two missionaries climbed into the rear seat. Howard sat on the right, and, as Eliot drove, Allison lay back. Her hair fluttered toward Howard's face, and he leaned slightly forward and breathed. The tangled scent both invited and repulsed him.

Feeling Peterson's hand on his arm, he leaned back again. He believed that, like Allison, he was fretted by irremediable conditions. Like him, she was a capricious being desiring a clarity which might always evade her. He decided that somehow he would see her again, and his soul expanded, almost like the thrill of truth. Then an old woman —his grandmother, his grandmother's grandmother?—rasped in his ear, "Foolish, unwary child." Frightened, Howard leaned out the side of the convertible, filling his head with the smoky odor of the city.

Two

Perched on a chair in the dark, Howard
waited for the roaches to creep back to the middle of the kitchen floor.
Peterson, standing near the light switch, was a white shadow large as a
floating stove. Howard straightened each cramped knee and pondered
the subtleties of God's mind, or rather the cultural/genetic construction which he now believed was his image of God's mind. Several days
before, he had felt a rush of hope when he thought about converting
Allison, a woman mired in carnality and drunkenness. His philosophy
teacher at the University of Utah might claim that God's will and
Allison were the irresistible force and the immovable object. His
mother would tell him that the situation had all the markings of a divine test. He felt confounded by all the voices in his head. The strang-
est part of the evening had been the imagined voice, saying what his
sarcastic maternal grandmother would say, had she known about his
loss of faith: "Foolish child."

Despite that warning, all week when Howard couldn't sleep because the humidity stuck the bed sheet to his back, his mind had gone
to Allison. Her angular face, hard mouth, and eyes that could make the
devil back down—all reminded him of a woman he couldn't quite
place. He knew Peterson believed that men recognized their future
wives by deep memory from the pre-earth life when all humankind was

in heaven, brothers and sisters. If so, he could have covenanted before birth with Allison, not Belinda.

"Now," he called. Peterson flipped the light switch and Howard flung himself outward, pounding left and right with the rubber mallet. The record for the apartment had been set more than a year earlier by Elder Shepherdson, who had hung a white-pine plaque with nineteen roaches drawn in brown ink. Only accidental bait was legal.

"Eight," said Howard.

"That one's still moving," said Peterson. "Seven again."

"Soccer tomorrow? That woman at the concert gave us an opening." Allison was the kind of woman his senile grandfather had told him stories about—a man-eating pagan.

"Monday is P-day, not Saturday," said Peterson after a pause. "And soccer won't wash as contacting work and she's a flipping lascivious atheist humanist feminist drugheaded winebibbing psychologist."

"He was the psychologist."

"And they're not a legitimate family unit, never will become one. Look, suppose you're Noah looking for righteous people and they're the last man and woman on earth, do you think humanity would survive the Flood?" He and Howard traded places.

"Elder, are we so wealthy with contacts?"

"Did I ever tell you about the elders in Humble who tried to kill roaches with circles of gunpowder?" said Peterson. "One night they used too much and set fire to their apartment. The police thought they had discovered a cult of devil worshippers. Now!" Howard flicked the switch and Peterson flailed with the hammer. "Nine."

"She's a daughter of Abraham," Howard said. He crouched near the sink; Peterson shut off the light. "Or do you think God wouldn't give me an erotic sign?"

"Shut up," said Peterson. "This kind of talk is frightening the roaches."

Had there been a sign, a luminosity? No, he was foolish to imagine voices and signs, especially since they contradicted each other. The voice was his superego, sounding like his mother. The sign was his neurons, shorted out by the lift of Allison's breasts and the reach of her thighs, the slow movement of her hands, the way she put her head to one side as she talked, the curious edge to her words. She had stroked the back of Eliot's hand with her fingertips, and Howard's own skin had tingled. In the car he had nearly taken the weight of her hair in his hands.

Here we go again, he thought. His hormones were dragging him into another instant romance, the fourth of the past month. Early in June, the speakers in church had been the bishop's twin daughters, both philosophy majors with pale hair and startling red lips, who had just returned home from school in Utah. Howard had endured a week of sweet agony. His next sudden beloved was Lucy Gomez, whose skin was the color of ripe barley and who had washed her laundry the same place he and Peterson did theirs. They had eagerly tried to teach her, but she wanted conversation, not conversion. Then there was a woman on a bus, auburn hair and blue eyes and thin body. Her face had been lonely as she carried a small girl on her hip down the aisle. All these women had suddenly flared luminous as angels. His passion had little to do with intention; each time he was afflicted by rapture, as if with the flu.

Because he had found the habits of faith so difficult to shed, his first impulse was to blame God. Had the old rogue just let temptation flourish, testing whether Howard, like Job, could endure to the end of his two years of celibacy? Teetering in the dark, he felt that if, despite all his culture's sanctions, he buried himself in this woman's body, she might calm his skittish flesh. Following an old habit, he moved his lips in a hymn:

> *Lead Kindly Light amidst the encircling gloom,*
> *Lead Thou me on.*
> *The night is dark and I am far from home,*
> *Lead Thou me on.*

Lead kindly lust.

Someone pounded on the door and pushed it open. Peterson clicked the switch.

"And there was light," said Elder Francis, entering, his arms spread wide. Stocky and short, he wore tinted glasses even though it was night. His white shirt had been starched and pressed commercially. His companion followed, carrying a full grocery bag. Elder Bittner, the greenest of the four missionaries, was as tall as Peterson, but thin, a bristle-haired farm boy from Idaho. Francis and Bittner worked the section of Houston immediately south of Rice University.

"Hey, Elder dudes, I don't mean to pry," said Francis, "but what the fetch were you doing in here with the lights off?"

"Killing roaches," said Howard. "We decided to let the good times roll." Bittner was subdued; he sat at the table and looked around as if lost.

"Right on," said Francis. "What's the high score, Rockwood? Bet these chips I beat it."

"*Elder* Rockwood," said Peterson, "and you're outside your area."

"It's legit," said Francis. "Written permission from the zone leaders. Our house has been tented for termites. But you only get the pleasure of our company for tonight because we've got to get back to our area early in the morning."

"Hey, Bittner," Howard said, clapping his friend on the shoulder. They were both rancher stock.

"Hey, Rockwood." He didn't smile, didn't look up.

From the grocery bag Francis lifted two plastic bottles of root beer, a bag of tortilla chips, a bottle of salsa, and a container of sour cream. "With your permission, Elder Proper Peterson, let the party begin." The four missionaries sat around the kitchen table eating the food.

Francis stood on a chair and held his hands out for silence. "Today Bittner was *stricken* with tragedy."

Howard turned to Bittner, whose face had turned from sorrow to anger.

"Geez, Elder," said Bittner. "Let it alone."

"This morning Bittner received his Dear John."

"Rotten break," Howard said. Talking about Dear John letters made his stomach tight. He had feared all through his mission that Belinda would fall for some fool just before Howard came home. God would then arrange for him to marry a pious woman, someone for whom he felt no passion—like Evaline Stewart, an angel-faced neighbor back home.

Francis tried to take Bittner's face in his hands, but Bittner slapped them away. "Dude, unburden your *soul*."

"Francis, you've got such a compassionate nature," said Howard. "No wonder your companions love you so much." One had punched Francis in the eye, which was not really the offending organ.

"I'm like helping him out," said Francis. "A cheerful countenance driveth away wrath. Where's your Bible? This is just the thing for you, Bittner. It's what I sent my fiancée when she wrote me off." He swept aside some shirts and socks on the couch and found it. "Eureka." He turned the pages. "What kind of missionaries are you to *hide* your light under a bushel?" He held the book open, one finger tracing the lines. "'And when I received your epistle, I plucked out the hairs of my beard and sat down astonied.'"

"Astonied?" said Peterson. "What the flip is astonied?"

Howard took thick scoops of sauce on chip after chip, eating quickly until his throat and lips burned. "You'd think you'd have a kind word for your companion in his hour of need."

"I'll send her that scripture," said Bittner. "I'll tell her that I'm grateful she's gone because that clears the underbrush between me and another girl."

"Bittner, my bud," said Francis. "You've been keeping secrets from me. I didn't know you like had options."

"I don't *like* have options. I just want revenge."

"I knew an elder once who mailed his girl a dead cat in a Tupperware box after she wrote him off," said Peterson. "It was totally ripe when she opened the package."

"Dude," said Francis, clapping Peterson on the shoulder. "It's music to my ears to hear your lying voice. Your stories should be like recorded for posterity." He turned to Bittner. "You've joined an elite club. Raise your hand if you've had a Dear John." Both Peterson and Howard kept their hands in their laps. Belinda's most recent letter had a sketch of a wedding announcement—the two of them straddling a bareback horse. She had written, "For our honeymoon we can camp on Mt. Brigham and make love in a meadow."

"I knew about Rockwood's woman, light of his life, angel of his night dreams, but Peterson, you surprise me. You telling us that some woman's waiting for your bulky body?"

"I didn't say that. I cut all ties before I left. I didn't want anything distracting me from the work. I'll wait until I get home to worry about women."

"Eye single to the glory of God. Peterson, you are one rock solid dude. An inspiration to the mission. Speaking of inspirations, tell them how many hours we worked this week. Tell them, Bittner."

"Eighty hours."

"Inflation," said Howard.

"The honest truth," said Francis. "We like knocked on doors and set up a display and talked to people in a mall and used our priesthood to bless thirteen people in a hospital and our members referred three contacts to us this week. President Wister called to praise our hard work. So what do you have to report?"

"We met a psychologist and his lover," said Peterson. "They're not married."

"Tough," said Francis. "Real tough. Lay the law of chastity on them. That'll separate the sheep dudes from the goat dudes. Sex just about makes conversion impossible."

"She's a six-foot Texan," said Peterson. "Thin as a cattail."

"Yikes," said Francis. "But I was telling you about my Dear John."

"Thin as a fishing pole," said Howard. "Tall as an eel. Peterson knew a girl once who was so skinny that one day she slipped down a badger hole when they went for a walk in a meadow. The tragedy has made him shun all wiry women." Long-limbed Allison strode up the hill, sprawled on the grass. Belinda was shorter, more soft and rounded.

"Rockwood," said Francis. "Leave the stories to Peterson. Yours like *suck*."

"Peterson isn't as innocent as he seems. He has a woman on his mind—Susy Wister," Howard said.

Francis's head whipped toward Peterson, whose throat turned

mottled pink. Bittner laughed and slapped his leg. "The secret is out," he said.

The last missionary conference, late in May, Susy, the mission president's daughter, had sat back of the podium dressed in a polka-dot dress with a white lace yoke. She was a double major at Brigham Young University—home economics and early childhood development. Her father had stood and told the missionaries that he was grateful to have his family on the stand with him because he wanted to make visible the fruits of marriage to a good woman. The admiring gaze of a hundred fifty missionaries had swung toward Susy.

"But I was telling you what my woman wrote me," said Francis. He still frowned at Peterson. "I've memorized it." He pretended to hold up a page. "'I've done some deep thinking recently and decided that I can never reach your level of spirituality. If we were to get married, that difference would be an unbridgeable gulf between us. I'm settling for a lesser man, one who is more carnal-minded.'"

"Low and foul blow," said Howard. "Low and foul."

"I knew an elder once," said Peterson, and they all groaned, "who was so despondent after receiving a Dear John that his hormonal system shut down. He confessed to President Wister that he had no more interest in the feminine gender. As a cure, they sent him to a house of prostitution without purse or scrip. But it didn't do him any good because after a week the whole building lifted up to Heaven. He'd purified all those sisters."

"Can't you tell normal stories?" said Howard. "Sometimes I wish you'd be lifted up."

"It'll never happen. After prayers, just before I take my salt pill, I think one lascivious thought. It's all that's keeping me on earth."

"That and three hundred-odd pounds of flesh," said Francis, who immediately ran to the bathroom, locking himself inside. "I repent, Elder Dude," he called out, as Peterson beat the door with the flat of one large hand. "I misspoke myself. Forgive me. Forgive me. I'm such a fool."

"That's the first time in three months he's said the truth," said

Bittner quietly. Soon Francis returned, his arm up around Peterson's shoulder.

When the lights were out and the other missionaries' breathing had become slow and regular, Howard sneaked downstairs to the laundry room. Dwight, their pot-bellied landlord, was in his office, building a pagoda out of playing cards and eating canned artichoke hearts balanced on thin wheat crackers. "Sitting behind that desk," said Howard, "you remind me of my bishop back home."

"Think I just been insulted," said Dwight. "What you want?"

"Little cribbage."

"What about all that thumping earlier? You missionary boys cutting loose? Drugs, women, and booze?"

"Killing roaches. We have to do something since you're too cheap to spray."

"Swear I heard voices coming and going."

Howard grinned. "Voices? Just Bittner and Francis."

"You know what the contract says about overnight guests, but I'll overlook it if you keep that Francis away from *me*. Smartassed as a thirteen-year-old. Told me I was going to hell if I didn't listen to him."

"Well, he was half right," said Howard. "Now stop swearing and get out the board."

Dwight grinned. "I can always tell when we're going to have a little problem sleeping. My fingers start itching and walking toward that deck of cards. The time you get down here I have them shuffled."

"Stacked, you mean." Playing cribbage reminded him of his father and grandfather, who both loved the game. Every time he went out to the desert, they had played for hours. Like Peterson with his daily dirty thought, Howard had an unweeded patch which no rule could touch.

An hour later Peterson filled the doorway, his face filled with righteous indignation. Clearly he thought that Howard was a piss-poor team player, God an unsmiling football coach.

"Couldn't sleep?" said Howard.

"We're supposed to stay together."

"It's worse than being married," said Howard to Dwight.

"He's mostly safe here, Elder Pete," said Dwight. "Won't lose his soul, just a little pocket change."

"Goodnight, Dwight," said Howard, laying down his cards. "He's determined." He followed as Peterson lumbered up the stairs. He wondered again what it would be like to see with a whole and clear vision.

"It's midnight," said Peterson on the stairway. "Promise you won't go out again."

"Go to sleep. I promise. Soccer in the morning, right? All we can do is get whipped."

"I'll go with you. But it's a waste of time. Did you feel anything from either one? Neither soul spoke to my soul—our seeds fell on stony ground with those two."

"Sweet dreams, Elder Pete."

He lay on his back in bed, hands clasped behind his head. He was seven or eight and he and his father had been trying to get out west one snowy day to feed the cattle when one tire slipped a chain. One back wheel, Howard believed it was the left, dropped into the borrow pit and they were stuck. No, it had definitely been the right wheel. As soon as Howard's father turned off the engine, warmth had drained from the cab. The wind was blowing snow nearly horizontally, but as Howard followed his father, stepping in his father's tracks, he felt like it was a grand adventure. They had walked for hours toward his grandfather's cabin, shuffling through a wide fuzzy-walled tunnel whirled with confetti. His boots were heavy but he lugged them forward, step, step again, through the heavy whiteness. He could tell when they left the road because his feet dropped into the borrow pit, nearly twisting his ankles. In the dream he worried about the child following and turned to look back. The child (was it a boy or girl?) smiled a flat smile and said, "What a crock!" in a voice as deep as Allison's.

Then he and Belinda galloped a bareback horse together, she hanging on behind him. The motion of the ride, and the feeling of her arms around him and her breasts against his back, aroused him. He thought, I don't want to spoil this by waking, and immediately he opened his eyes. He was angry because what happened when he was asleep was not even God's business.

He had expected Belinda. After each flash of infatuation, she reasserted herself and he felt as fresh pain the shock of leaving her. His body buzzed, as if someone shot him up with drugs while he slept. He rolled out of bed and dressed, walking out the door and along the bayou.

He and Belinda had dated all through high school. Once, while the rest of the kids at church painted scenery for a one-act play, they had crept into the furnace room. "We'll have our own play," she said. But the adult leader had surprised them, and flashed the light on Howard trying to wrench his hand out of Belinda's bra. They each had several interviews with the bishop, who said certain acts were too sacred to perform outside the holy bonds of marriage. Fondling Belinda had seemed only a more exciting sport than soccer or rodeo, but after his interview Howard knew it was sacred sin, alluring and terrifying. Despite the bishop's warning, they often parked in the canyon, undressing but holding a blanket, limp protection, between them.

On the day Howard turned eighteen, Belinda shoved the blanket out the car window. "Happy birthday," she said, kissing him long and deep. The calluses on his palms had scratched against her skin as he caressed her shoulders and cradled her breasts. When they finished, she became unsteady, alternatively crying and laughing. Her strange reaction had frightened him.

When she told him it was time for her period, the wait became mortifying. He didn't want to see or talk to her, was unable to pray or read the scriptures, couldn't relax or eat or sleep well. His mother had asked him a dozen times what was wrong, but he hadn't been able to tell her.

"I'm having it," Belinda said finally.

"Way to go," he had said. "Way to go." After an hour of vigorous talk, with her dark eyes always on him, she had agreed that they wait to marry. One month later he had left for college.

Contrary to what he expected, they gradually drifted apart. School filled his mind. There were more books in the library than he could read in an eternity. His professors spoke revelations to him. Belinda, his mother wrote, had gone to Cedar City to school. That summer she worked at the Grand Canyon Lodge as a waitress, but he didn't write, even though he thought about her. His friends were leaving on missions, and Howard's mother and the bishop encouraged him to send in his papers. He put them off, afraid to confess what had happened between him and Belinda.

At school that fall, he was again surrounded by thousands of women, and he loved watching their motions. His observations were made poignant because of his one experience of sex with Belinda; he knew the pleasure women could give him. Women's breasts, thighs, and hips remained alive in his imagination, but whenever he began to feel close to someone, so that he wanted to talk to her, touch her, perhaps think of making love, he became suddenly frightened, guilty— and his interest died. He realized he was as sick as a porno addict—teasing himself with images but never touching or kissing anyone. He was a libertine in imagination, a Puritan in habit. Of the two possible solutions to his dilemma, he wanted to make himself completely a man of God. But he still couldn't bring himself to undergo a shameful confession.

So the time passed. He dated occasionally, but his serious love was studying the juncture between range plants and animals, and the motions of class history in Europe, which reminded him of plate tectonics. Then the fall of his junior year, his mother wrote him a long letter. Her older sister, Mary, had died and she wrote about the gift of peace, despite her sorrow, that she knew was a sign of God's love for her and her sister. "Sometimes it seemed that Mary's arm was around me. Can you imagine God's love for you, Howard? I have the feeling that you are stuck, that some little thing is blocking you." Reading the letter, he had wept. Before his old defenses could return, he called and made an appointment with his university bishop. Walking to the interview that Sunday, his body was heavy with anguish; after his confession, he had felt weightless, as if each cell brimmed with light.

His bishop had seized the opportunity to invite Howard onto a mission. They sent in the papers, and Howard sold his truck to pay at least part of the expenses. He was filled with the desire to bring others to the tree of life where they could taste the same white fruit he had eaten.

When he returned home the summer before his mission, he rediscovered Belinda, who had finished her second year at Southern Utah University. She was tanned and confident, fuller of body. They went to firesides and church together, quickly comfortable, as if there had been no interruption of their friendship. At first Howard had thought her return was a gift from God signifying that he would restore each of Howard's righteous sacrifices, but soon he felt a painful ambivalence toward his impending mission.

The Saturday before he left for Texas, they parked in front of the church. Main Street was deserted except for two cars driving slowly and parallel down the middle line. Two teenagers kissed through the back seat windows, reaching their mouths and arms across the gap between the cars. The voices of the drivers and the noise of their engines sounded in the empty street.

At her door, he had put his arms around her and kissed her. "I don't want to go," he said. "I want to stay here and marry you." Her hands had cradled the back of his neck, her lips had been warm. But she finally released him and stepped inside. "We were hasty before," she said through the screen door. "It would be safer if you let this be our good-bye. I love you, Howard. I want to have children with you. A month after your mission we'll be married."

Sitting on the bank of the bayou, Howard sweated. Leaving had petrified him; he believed that if he missed one step, God would take Belinda away again. He threw a rock into the stagnant water. All his mission he had acted with fear and caution; now he was tired. If God existed, he was as contradictory as Belinda. "Touch my breasts, taste my mouth, so that for two years of abstinence your body will be tortured with the memory of pleasure." God the trickster patriarch. Help me, Friend Jesus, Howard prayed. Talk to the Father for me. Get him to play me some slack.

Grace Montoya, their latest convert, was small, four and a half feet at the tallest. He and Peterson had tracted her out in the Heights, north of downtown Houston. "I've been expecting you," she had said when she answered the door. "I had a dream that two sweaty angels came to my house. You're very funny looking angels." She had seated him and Peterson on a swinging chair in her backyard and had fed them tamales wrapped in corn shucks, which they had washed down with water in which discs of ice floated. She had watched them eat and giggled. "I never thought that angels eat tamales. I never thought it."

"We're not angels," Howard had told her repeatedly. When they had asked if they could teach her, she had laughed heartily, bending forward at her small waist and reaching up to touch their hands and forearms. They had taught her all seven lessons in two days, and she had listened patiently, never drifting away, never looking bored. But their words had left her unchanged; she already possessed a perfect charity.

When the lessons were over, she said to Howard, "You are a seeker, *muy authenticia*. Much integrity."

"No," said Howard. "You have described yourself." She smiled and shook her head. God should be more like her.

Three

When Allison woke, she untangled her-
self from the sheet and rolled across Eliot toward the closet. He lay
half uncovered—black beard, thick down his throat, thighs and belly
heavier than sixteen months before when she'd first met him.

She walked into the bathroom, slammed down the toilet seat, and
sat. Nearly nine; soccer started at nine. Her head hurt. She walked back
into the bedroom. "You coming?"

Eliot pulled a pillow over his face and mumbled something about
STIV. He and Allison's mother called their therapeutic software package Sex Therapy on Interactive Video. The image of dysfunctional
men and women panting over computer monitors still made Allison
weak with laughter.

"I promised her I'd be there at nine-thirty," said Eliot.

"Who undressed me last night? You or those missionaries?"

Eliot peered out from under the pillow. "Whoever it was didn't
have a very good time."

She found some underwear and socks, pulled on her shorts, and
sat on the bed.

"I wish you'd just forget about the whole thing," he said quietly.

"Alaska?" She jiggled the bed as she laced her shoes. His finger followed the line of vertebrae up her back. "Eliot, we've both made up our

minds. We're just too chickenshit to make it verbal. You're scared to start over."

"At a fourth-rate university. I'd lose everything I've worked on for the past decade."

"Exaggeration." She turned to look at his face, which he held blank. "I'm frightened of keeping it up with freelance work." She stood, positioned her breasts inside a gray sports bra, then grabbed her black B. B. King T-shirt from the back of a chair. "I'm outta here," she said.

Within seconds, she was rolling down Bissonet toward the Loop with the top of her Mustang down—the hot, humid wind blowing into her face. Three weeks earlier all her stars had aligned, and she was given the hope of escaping Houston. A woman she had impressed at a computing convention had asked her to join a custom software company that did contract work in Anchorage. The money would be twice what she made in Houston, three times what Eliot made, and it would be constant income—without the fluctuations of freelance work. But Eliot wouldn't follow her to Alaska. What she wouldn't give for a tractable man. Her religious/feminist Aunt Jenny from Waco said, "Raise up a boy in the way he should go and when he is a man he will not depart from it."

She exited and wound through Memorial Park; some of the other players were late also, so she had time to stretch. She hooked her fingers in the net high over her head and pulled herself up and forward, feeling the burn in her thighs and calves as she rocked forward and back.

Two men on bikes rode into the parking lot—the missionaries, still ridiculous in their white shirts and ties. She watched, lips pursed, as they walked toward her. The sight of them nudged her memory: a carnival of people chattering on the hillside, beer slipping across her tongue, the ironic-innocent missionary who looked at her as if she were the first woman he'd seen. Ironic mouth and virginal eyes. His talk about the desert. Eliot reading *Walden* to her, his jealous voice tolling the syllables as if he chanted a mantra meant to win her back. The thin missionary had flushed red after talking about his mother. He was a handsome boy, with mahogany hair and a hawk nose. His long, thin face and wild hazel eyes gave him the look of a desert ascetic. He would probably be fun in bed, maybe inexperienced, but beauty made up for a multitude of sins. Next to him, Eliot had looked like a stodgy professor—which he was. The boy had a delicious, sinewy body, strong forearms, probably from milking all those cows. Corn-fed Mormon virgin. Taking him down would be like taking down a monk.

"You're over-dressed," she said as they stopped their bikes next to her.

Barefoot, Howard ranged mid-field, feeling in his bones the sweetness of being on a soccer field again. He hadn't played since his high school team took third in state. He watched Allison, who crouched in front of the opposite goal, knees bent, arms loose, glaring at him; he had three times received her kicks and fed the ball back to the attacking forwards. To his left, solid as a wall, stood Peterson, who had refused to take off even his tie. The opposing forwards still thought they could slip past him, but Peterson was surprisingly quick on his feet. He stole the ball once again and passed to Howard, with more force than accuracy. Howard held for a while, drawing toward him the defending player, an anglo with curly blond hair and immense thighs. When he charged, Howard kicked the ball to the receiving forward, a balding Hispanic man, who immediately shot on the goal—a sweet parabolic kick which dropped toward the high right corner. Allison turned and leaped, tipping the ball backward over the bar of the goal.

The Hispanic stood in the field and clapped. "Next time, muchacha."

"Next time my ass!" shouted Allison. "I ain't ya muchacha." Howard cringed when she swore. Most ranchers swore, his father included, but his mother never had. She had made him feel it was a low habit. He was surprised that his recent doubts did not sway his gut reactions to swearing and drinking.

The corner kick bounced off Allison's hands, but one of her team, a tall man with a German accent, kicked it against one of Howard's team and out of bounds. Allison set the ball at the corner of the box and boomed it upfield—a high floater.

Howard took the ball on his chest so it dropped neatly at his feet. He sprinted left around one defender and fed it back to the bald forward, who took it up the sideline. Instead of shooting at the goal, he fed the ball inside. A short man in a blue shirt twisted in the air and hooked it powerfully toward Allison's left. She dived and knocked the ball down, cradling it in her arms and rolling to her feet as the other forwards rushed her. She took three sprinting leaps and kicked it high again, this time over Howard's head.

By the end of the 4th of July concert, she had seemed thin, even frail, but now she loomed large as a force of nature. Would she consider it intrusive if he ran to embrace her? The pass dropped close to him, but he wasn't moving and couldn't get to it. Allison shouted at him, "Get your head in the game." Her speech was hard-edged, but her laugh bubbled out of a spring of good humor. Talking with her was like hearing the sudden buzz of a rattlesnake, dangerous and thrilling. A fallen angel had dropped her out of the sky, clouding his mind and confounding his purposes. He pictured Allison wearing not a black T-shirt but a long white dress as she descended into the waters of baptism. But her face was wrong, not pious but aggressive, her mouth twisted by sarcasm as she rose dripping from the font.

After the game the two missionaries hung around. The large one— Elder Peterson according to his name tag which he had worn even while playing—pulled three bottles of sports drink out of his backpack. "What happened to Eliot?" he asked. "I thought he ran with you." Elder Rockwood was distracted, frowning down at the pages of a letter.

"Occasionally." Alison wondered why he was interested in Eliot.

Peterson leaned forward with the false familiarity of a salesman: it did seem even hotter, if that were possible, he said, than the day of the concert. Yes, it was lucky we happened to be there, a stroke of fortune for us all. You don't remember a thing? A shame you missed the last songs—such a great concert—and the fireworks, they were great, too.

Was Eliot still opening new vistas in sex research? It's fine to record and unravel the tangles of today's perverse society. Modern life can be so confusing. Then he rambled on about the crisis of values in the United States, teenage pregnancy, drugs, divorce, gangs, sexual perversion, high taxes, and the deficit—a general fragmentation of family life— flinging out a net of words which she at first thought accidental. Howard glanced toward her and rolled his eyes. Then she realized that Elder Peterson wanted to catch a certain kind of fish—not her kind—and to repel all others. It was a conservative net. "Soon life will be as corrupt right here in the U.S.A. as it is in Europe."

Howard's feet were skinned and his slacks were streaked with grass stains. Tall and wiry, he had hair the color of mahogany. If it weren't for Peterson's zeal, she might find a way of asking him why he was so somber. He held the letter, which was written with a tidy feminine hand, open on his lap, but he was staring at the ground next to his foot. At the concert he had been hyped up, nervous and glib, and she wondered what was making him so blue. She had known that Mormons were polygamist, evangelical, with peculiar theology, but he was an unsteady mix of rational and mystic, innocence and worldliness, sarcasm and piety. Very curious.

Then Peterson used communism and feminism in the same sentence, and she couldn't take it anymore. What the hell was his first name? He said, "Many people are looking for a haven from the storm in this life and the next"—said it without interest, like something memorized. "Have you ever sorrowed over a loved one who has passed on? Have you thought of the pleasure of greeting them when you leave this life?"

She stood, furious at Peterson's aggressive questions. He was trying to manipulate her like a wrong-headed life insurance salesman, fishing for any private sorrow or unhappiness. "This whole thing is bullshit." A bead of sweat ran down Peterson's face and into his shirt collar.

"Fine," he said. "I know our message isn't for everyone."

She started to walk away and then turned back for her bag, picked it up, and slung it across her shoulder. She looked down at them. Her head was fuzzy with anger at Peterson. Her brother had been eighteen, she thirteen, when he killed himself trying to drive under a flooded underpass. Peterson leaned back against a tree, a false, half smile on his lips. The other one, Howard, stared up at her, angry and forlorn, a cross between James Dean and a Boy Scout, lovely to look at. "Don't let this guy talk you out of coming next week. I know he's going to try. Tell him you need the exercise. You need to get knocked on your butt once a week. Only next time, don't dress for church. It's damned embarrassing." She squatted to pick up the envelope which lay next to his knee; the return address was Rockwood, Utah. "Bad news?" He handed her the pages. "No," she said. "I don't want to read your mail."

He folded the pages and put them back in the envelope, thrusting it in her bag. "Read it," he said. "It's from my mother and I don't know what to do about it."

She wanted to fling the envelope to the ground, but something desperate in his face stopped her. Instead she turned and marched to her car. Still angry at the obnoxious questions, she took the ramp too fast and nearly ran into a semi as she pulled onto the Loop. The day Michael died, he had picked her up from school in a storm that had put down twelve inches in ten hours. The underpass seemed to have only a thin sheet of water covering the street, but as Michael gunned the car, water sprayed up heavily around them. "Stop, Michael!" she screamed. They hadn't quite reached the underpass when the car slipped sideways and then lifted, soon tumbling onto its side—still moving sideways toward the river like a foundering boat.

She had hung by her seat belt as the car turned again, tumbling faster and faster, filling with water. Her seat belt kept her inside as the water sloshed around her. Finally they hit something solid. She unfastened her belt and crawled out the window, clinging to the roof. The car had lodged against a tree on the edge of Buffalo Bayou. Michael seemed unconscious; the car was full of water. When she tried to help him, she slipped into the rushing stream, and barely caught herself by hanging on to the radio antenna. She didn't have the strength to pull herself back on top of the car. Finally a boat came for her—too late for Michael.

Losing him had been unbearable. Because of their parents' on-and-off-again marriage, she and Michael had been forced to rely heavily on each other. Nothing salved her sorrow, especially not the article her mother gave her which described the stages of grief. A librarian at school recommended *The Problem of Pain* by C. S. Lewis, which offered only distant comfort, and the Book of John, which moved her with its beautiful language. She tried to read *The Sickness Unto Death*, but couldn't figure out the sentences. Then she asked a Catholic friend to invite her to mass. The chanted ceremony had affected her deeply; she breathed the incense, a mystery as thick as marijuana smoke. She thought of Christ, the hero, who would descend under the water and return, carrying Michael in his arms. After a year she had changed her mind, believing that Michael was merely flesh rotting in the ground. Her belief in Christ had been like bayou mist and dissipated with the morning sun.

Back in her apartment, she sloughed her clothes off and dumped out her bag. The fat envelope fell out, and she became angry at what seemed to be another missionary trick. She was also curious about this woman who was not repressed, depressed, or suppressed, but who lived in a tiny Mormon, conservative desert town. She opened the letter and read:

Dear Elder Howie,

It's dry and the Russian olives blossomed early this year. Everywhere I went this week I smelled them. I know I'm not supposed to write what could make you homesick, but I thought you'd find comfort in knowing that the cycles are regular here, well almost regular. Your father cut first crop in June, but took so long to get it up that the new alfalfa had grown up into the windrows. Bishop Hansen finally helped him. Prepare yourself, he is slower than he used to be. I've been thinking about going back to college. But there's no money for it, unless we sold some land, and your father won't do that. I saw Belinda at the grocery last Monday. She said that she gets a letter from you every Friday or Saturday. Seems that on your end cycles are also regular.

I have a confession to make, more like a confusion. If Bishop Hansen ever finds out, it would certainly break his heart. Maybe he'd release me as Relief Society president, which would finally give me some relief. One of the Hamblin Feldsens moved into the

Johnson place just after you left. Anyway, Sister Feldsen told me last month that her marriage was breaking up. Her husband told her he didn't love her anymore, and, as soon as all their children were in college, he wanted a divorce. Their youngest is in kindergarten, for heaven's sake! What did he think she was going to do for fourteen more years, smile and be grateful for his forbearance? So she went to Bishop Hansen with her troubles. First off, he didn't believe that Tom Feldsen would say such a thing and then advised her that some of the sisters in the ward might be able to help her take better care of herself. As if her marriage is going to be saved by a makeover.

So she came to me. I told her Tom was the one needing a makeover, and that I had a two-by-four that might do the job. The worst of it is she'd given herself severe headaches by worrying that she was responsible for her husband's behavior. I told her that she needed to tell her husband that if he was leaving he'd better do it in fourteen minutes not fourteen years, and that he'd better deed the house over to her and send her $500 a month on which he'd already paid the income tax and tithing. But that if he couldn't make up his mind to do that, he should stay and she'd try to forgive him for being an idiot. She did what I told her. Well, I'm sure she didn't put it to him in those exact words, but in essence they're trying to struggle through their troubles.

She still had the headaches and the depression. I talked her into going to a doctor and then a specialist in Salt Lake, who said it was psychosomatic, as if that was telling her anything new. In short, she needs drugs to keep her balance, but her husband doesn't want her to have a crutch. So she came to me again. The way she looked when she walked in, her head must have felt like one of those cactuses which are ready to burst and send baby spiders flying everywhere. We'd done everything humanly possible, so I knew healing her headache was up to the Lord. I said I'd pray with her. We kneeled down and then I felt strong as anything that I could stand up and lay my hands on her head. I couldn't bless her through the priesthood because I didn't have it, so I blessed her through your father's priesthood. He hasn't used it since he blessed Nan to get over the Rocky Mountain Spotted Fever, and I thought that somebody might as well get some benefit from it. I felt warm when I laid my hands on her head and a power went out of me, just like is described in the Gospels. Afterward I felt funny doing something which all my life I'd seen only men do. But her headache disappeared that instant and hasn't returned to this day, two months later. How can good come from an evil act?

After that I blessed Liza Smith to get pregnant, and she did, Beatrice Hansen that she'd have more energy, and she does. I blessed someone I won't name that she could forgive herself for the unspeakable things her dead uncle did to her when she was little. Last week she broke a baseball bat over his headstone. I guess that counts as a partial healing. I blessed Holly Laffert that she would no longer have insomnia. She still can't sleep. But now she wakes her husband up and they talk or do whatever. I know I'm not supposed to involve a missionary in the mysteries, but I need to know what you think. I know it's not traditional for a woman to use her husband's priesthood.

I have another confession. Last weekend your father and I had a terrific argument and I had to get out of the house, out of town. I felt like I was carrying the weight of every woman in the ward on my back. I just started driving and five hours later I was in Ely. Before long the $20 in my purse was $300 at the blackjack tables. I kept thinking that God was leading me on so that he could teach me a lesson in the end, but he never did. I finally quit when I had $550. I called Alice Warner and asked her to take charge in Relief Society, and I rented a room in a fancy hotel and didn't wake up until 11:00. I don't know what got into me. Then I called your Aunt Effie. "I've been with you all weekend," I said to her. Slow Effie didn't catch my drift at first. Anyway, after that, I felt like I could face your father and my calling again. If I ever get feeling too desperate, I'll just tell Bishop Hansen I went off to Nevada and came back a wicked woman. He'd have to release me on the spot because I would no longer be a proper role model for the sisters in our ward. I'll just keep this story to myself, you excepting; it'll be my ace in the hole, so to speak. Funny thing is, we are a little short until your father sells the calves, and I couldn't figure where I was going to get the money for your missionary account this month. The Lord moves in a mysterious way. Howard, you were always our peacemaker. Now that you're gone, your father and I are at each other every day. We need you back! Your father says I have turned wacko on him. What kind of word is that to use for your wife?

Love,
Your Apostate Mother

Allison let the letter slip onto the bed. She pictured a Quaker woman laying her hands on the head of a blackjack dealer. "Hit me with the Spirit." Perplexing mother, perplexing son, both trapped in the prison of their beliefs. The voice which had been rising from the letter seemed to still hum in the room. "It's dry and the Russian olives blossomed early this year." That afternoon this woman's son had danced toward the ball, his black slacks flapping, the tail of his shirt flying. "The Lord moves in a mysterious way." When she had kicked the ball over his head, he forgot about the game and watched her, his face and body as pitiful as an orphan's.

She jumped up from the bed and yanked on the shower. The letter had focused her attention on this country boy, had made his motions precious, like in a movie when light strikes one face in a crowd of faces. Was she such a sucker for a forlorn man?

A week and a half later, sitting in her parents' beach house west of Galveston, Allison proofread the last few lines of computer code. She was finished with the part of STIV they'd had her write. Her mother and Eliot were painting the outside walls of the house and their words floated up to her through the open window—something about the irony of using sensate-focus in virtual reality therapy. For some reason she had no desire to tell them she had finished.

Sitting on the grass after their second soccer game, Howard's eyes had swung between her and Eliot, who had dragged himself out of bed. She knew Howard was attracted to her, but he was so swaddled in religion that he could only manage covert glances at her face or her bare legs. He was repressed, unsteady as a squirrel tempted by food in her hand.

She shook her head and double checked the parameters for fractal-generated human figures. Begin at XB and proceed to XY. For STIV her mother and Eliot assumed that sex is like the grammar in a language such as English or computer code: with acts and bodies as the words or variables, and with cultural attitudes as the syntax. If X is a sexual prompt, then Y is the female response—frigidity or sexual frustration. Event driven. Cause and effect.

She grinned, thinking that her Aunt Jenny would say the missionary was a gift—a man-child coming to Allison's need, just like a revelation. All she needed to do was seduce him and he'd go off to Anchorage with her. But Aunt Jenny's Mormon man-child had gone visionary. The first rule was never trust a religious man.

That was one problem with STIV—complexity. Too many variables. If X then Y unless Q equals R or P equals W. Perfectly rational.

Perfectly tangled. How could they possibly feed into a computer signs of attractiveness, courtship methods and rituals, gender roles, civil and religious taboos, instinctual behavior and the bad syntax learned from stereotypes in TV and romance novels—the convoluted language of eroticism? They could never explain why she was thinking about a Mormon boy with pleasure, his thin, mobile face, rich mahogany hair.

Eliot stuck his head in the window. "I was reading a nineteenth-century sex manual," he said. "Not a how-to book, of course. More like evolutionary goals—phrenology and survival of the fittest. Leafing through, I saw a picture of Brigham Young. It was given as a model of perfect manhood. And I thought of those missionaries."

"Perfect, how?" she said.

"Potency. Or nobility. I didn't read it carefully." He disappeared down the ladder.

She imagined the culture that had produced this lusty ascetic, or so she imagined him as Howard traced her body with his eyes. The same culture had produced his desert-feminist mother. Allison should have been offended by Howard's grimaces when she swore, his unhappiness when she came to the second game hung over, with sour wine on her breath. Somehow his Puritan traits affected her perversely. Allison, she thought, you're a fool for fundamentalists. Bobby, the wrestler who'd taught her sex, had told her that his favorite Bible story was Samson and that he always prayed before matches. "God gives me victory," he'd said. He'd call her Delilah and laugh like hell.

With the next religious boy, names were no joke. At a science fair, she'd met a rancher's son from Cut and Shoot. He was molds, she number crunching. They'd slipped naturally into talk about the intersection of their fields of interest. He had blue eyes and dimples. She was sixteen and romance still overwhelmed her; he seemed evening to her morning. But she was wrong: his mother was a Pentecostal minister. Instead of going to the awards banquet, they'd driven his pickup to a corner of the parking lot and grappled in back on a yellow raincoat he'd spread, fast and unsubtle sex, what he'd apparently learned by observing his father's bulls. Nothing like what she'd experienced with Bobby, a slow and sensitive wrestler. When they went indoors again, dessert was being served. She led the way to two empty chairs, but he sat across the room from her. He glowered while the awards were presented. Afterward she tried to talk to him. "Slut," he whispered. "Why did you tempt me?" She had looked into his insane face and the hair rose on the back of her neck. She finally decided that the names simply allowed him to return to his mama with an easy conscience.

The way Howard looked at her after that second game, could he possibly imagine that it was her conversion he wanted? Sometimes he stared at the ground, so focused on her that the air vibrated. If that was all he did, she might have slapped his repressed face, shocked him with some sweet vulgarity, or simply said good-bye, but he showed flashes of returning to the Howard of the first night on the hill above Miller Theater—his face bright with life, giving her back quick, quirky talk, fast as a tennis game. Also he was interested in *her*, wanting to know about her computer work, her dreams of Anchorage, her life as a child. He had even probed delicately enough that she had told them about Michael. His rebuke to Peterson afterward had been satisfying. She imagined that with a few nudges he would follow her anywhere, to Alaska if she asked, unlike Eliot, who was bound to his own past. Of course, it was just female fantasy; Howard, whom she barely knew, was also bound to a past. If Aunt Jenny had learned anything, it had been that it was impossible to train any man up in the way he should go. The dream of power over someone weaker was the male fantasy; women were too smart to buy into that. Men made Cinderella movies about flower girls, prostitutes, nurses, secretaries, child-brides, slaves, maids, nuns, rape victims, and princesses—all of them trapped by conditions inside conditions like magic boxes. Computers had no monopoly on virtual reality.

Allison's mother drifted inside, walked across the room to the table, lifted a gallon can of paint, and shook it. A strand of hair lay against her mother's neck. The form of her back and legs was familiar. As a child, Allison had read on the couch after school. Later her mother would come home, crossing that other room as she had just crossed this one, touching her own neck as she poured a drink from the cabinet or sat in the bay window reading the newspaper. "Hey, Ali," she might say. Perhaps touching Allison on the head. Perhaps not.

"I thought I'd have to paint it alone," her mother said.

Wanted to do it alone, Allison thought. Or else she would've told us, told Dad.

Eliot stepped up and painted the outer wall above the window.

"You could do that from inside," she said.

"Reaching out?" he said. "I'd fall."

Allison had met him nearly two years before. She had been debugging a program in her mother's office when Eliot had knocked on the door. "You're Lois's daughter, aren't you?" he said. "No," she said. "Just the hired help." He had looked at her strangely; she knew she had her mother's face and build. A month later they met again at a party in her parents' house. When he saw her, he did a double-take. "You lied," he said. She held up her glass. "This is molecular software. Affects the way my CPU reacts." They'd spent the evening talking about the evolution of the bra—from the bullet-shaped armor worn by Doris Day and Madonna to the filmy ones shown in current Victoria's Secret catalogs to the one she wasn't wearing. They had argued about whether U2 or Jimi Hendrix had a better version of "All Along the Watchtower," and they agreed that Jack Kerouac had gotten more mileage out of his liver than he should have.

That seemed long ago. Now she knew she couldn't hold him. She would drive to Alaska a lone wolf, like the yellow-eyed dream-wolf that had once bounded across snow under dark trees. Her totem.

Her mother painted the window sills with a three-inch brush. "We built this house before you were born," she said.

Eliot climbed down the ladder, then returned with a rag, rubbing something above the window. He smiled in at her and her mother, then disappeared again.

"He's a perfectionist," said her mother.

"Drives me crazy," said Allison.

"He refines my wild and fragmented ideas. I wouldn't know what to do without him."

Allison turned toward her mother.

"Ali, I've kept my mouth shut the last month," her mother said. "You can't blame me for his refusal to go with you."

"It doesn't matter. If it wasn't you and STIV keeping him here, it would be something else." She slammed the roller up and down, showering herself with droplets of white paint.

That night, after her mother had driven back to Houston, Allison walked to the beach. No one was there except a pickup and a tent far down the shore, and the lights of a shrimper miles out in the Gulf. She leaned against the railroad ties stuck upright in the sand, the boundary between the public and private beaches. Eliot slumped next to her; she felt his shoulder against hers. For most of her time with Eliot she had savored the tension before lovemaking—knowing that soon he would turn toward her, or she toward him. But now the prospect didn't move her.

She stood and walked down to the beach, knowing he was probably arousing himself by looking at her. Suddenly she was angry again, wanting to jerk free of the tether of his sight. She imagined the ways he might have viewed her during the past two years: Student lover? Fresh skin for seasoned hands? Friend? Little sister? Mystery? Her mother, but younger, less of a bitch?

"Allison," he said.

"I want to move out of this skin," she called back. "Like a snake."

Later she watched the breeze blow the curtains inward—curling, softly snapping ghosts. Eliot knelt above her, his face a pale blotch. She found herself picturing Howard—wide-eyed, virginal—looking down at her on the bed. "Anger," her mother told her when Allison was a raving teenager, "only means you stand to lose something." She wanted to roll back time to when she and Eliot were like left and right hands and she had felt no confusion when they coupled. She lifted herself on her elbows and pressed her mouth against his, biting his lips.

To Howard's delight, after their third game of soccer Peterson fell asleep against the trunk of a great tree, legs crossed, hands laid across his knees, palms up. Soon his breathing turned heavy, regular as waves. Peterson could sleep standing in the shower.

"I keep running," Allison said. She was talking again about her plan to relocate in Alaska. "Anybody stands still, entropy sets in." She looked at Peterson. "Sleeping Buddha. Sleeping Bubba. I don't keep moving, soon I'm stymied and can't budge. Now you, you're nothing like me. You lie through your teeth when you say you're frightened of going back, having your dreams. Really you're more frightened of moving on. You'll slide right back into the same old Utah skin you've always worn."

He was silent. "The desert is like no skin *you've* ever worn," he said finally, and she laughed. "If you ever went there, you'd change your mind."

"Is the desert worth going back to Utah culture?"

"*Jeopardy*," he said. "The answer is Rockwood, Rockwood, Rockwood." Sleep on, Peterson, he thought, you're a big boy and you need your rest.

"What is the roll call at one of your town meetings?" She laid her head on her own shoulder, watching him. He looked into her eyes and neither of them looked away. Swallowed by her amber-flecked eyes.

"Close," he managed to say. "Next guess."

"What is a cheer at your high school cow-chip tossing contests?"

"Have some respect. Give up?"

"Yes," she said.

"Where did I wreck my parents' car?"

"That's Rockwood."

"No," he said.

"You wrecked their car three times?"

"Not the same car. Once I wasn't even driving. I was backing the tractor around our new Buick and the front-end loader smashed the windshield and roof. Another time I tail-ended a guy who was stopped at a red light on Main Street."

"Rockwood has a stop light?"

"Had. They took it out after the accident. Once I slipped off the dam at midnight and dropped my father's pickup into the reservoir."

"What were you doing at the dam at midnight?"

"That's what my parents asked."

"Chappaquiddick?"

"No," he said. "She pulled me to shore."

She laughed once, a cough like the bark of a hyena. "But that would be Rockwood, Rockwood dam."

"Close to what my father said." He pointed, nearly touching her lips with his fingertip. "Your turn." He picked up a magazine she had taken from her bag, only to drop it on the grass between them. He stared at the address label, and memorized it.

She flipped her hair back and laid her hand on his knee. "You're going home soon. Marry a few docile Mormon women?"

He glanced at Peterson and stood, sat again, slightly farther away from her. He couldn't puzzle out why, when his mind had shucked off tradition, physical habit forced him away from a woman who wanted him. He should rip off his tie and stomp on it. He grinned because that was the deepest liberation his imagination allowed.

"You're looking forward to it," she said. "Molly Monday, Tammy Tuesday, Wanda—."

"Polygamy is out," he said. "And Mormon women are not docile."

Allison raised one eyebrow.

"You doubt me?" he said. "Once, driving home from Hamblin, my mother saw four teenagers beating up a Mexican sheepherder. She stopped and faced them down, made three of them stop. One was still down on the guy's chest, slugging him, so she took a short board out of the truck. Whopped him across the back. Then she said, 'Have I got your attention now?'"

"You're looking forward to it," said Allison.

"It's true. The boy stood up and broke her nose."

"You can't move your lips without lying." Then she stopped grinning. "I want to meet this woman. That letter was astonishing. Your mother seems familiar to me already." She leaned forward. "*Jeopardy.* The offspring of a pomegranate and a beehive."

"I give up."

"What is your head?" She leaned forward. "You say you want me to convert. To what?"

To me, he thought. I want to freeze time, keep you talking on this lawn forever. He finally said, "To the gospel."

"Triple liar. You look at me like a starving man. How can you imagine that would have no effect on me?" She reached across and took his hand so tightly he couldn't pull free.

Peterson jerked upright. "Baptism and sealings for the dead," he said, rubbing his face.

"He's doing *Jeopardy*," she said. "What is the dream life of a Mormon missionary?"

He lumbered to his feet and stared down at their hands. "I must have drifted off."

As they ate lunch, Howard felt ashamed and frightened that Peterson would tell the mission president that he had held Allison's hand. He had a longing to talk to Belinda, whose voice he hadn't heard for nearly two years, but who was so far away he could never touch her. While Peterson took his customary short nap after lunch, Howard walked downstairs and phoned Utah. Dwight, who had been fingering the cribbage cards, pretended to read a newspaper. After the embarrassment of talking to her mother, who preached to him that phoning was certainly a breach of mission rules, he finally got Belinda on the phone. "Howard?" she said. "I mean Elder Rockwood. I didn't know you could call." He felt beset and bound by rules.

"Belinda," he said. "I forgot your voice. I needed a little refresher."

Dwight peered over the top of the newspaper. "I thought you missionaries aren't supposed to call women."

"Dwight, are you my mother? Do you think you can give me a little breathing room?"

"You want me to leave? Not a chance. I want to hear how you pious missionaries talk to women." Howard glared at him, and he snapped the newspaper back up, covering his face.

They talked about the weather. She laughed when he used the word y'all. "Please laugh again," he said. She did, but it was forced. Neither of them spoke.

"Still September first?" she said. "I'll be at the airport."

"Ah—." But she was already discussing her plans for the wedding. He couldn't open his mouth to slow her down.

Peterson wandered into the laundry and put his clothing in the washer. He stuck his head in the door. "Hey, Elder, let's hit the pavement."

Dwight grinned at Peterson. "Shhh, he's talking to that wildass Houston woman you told me about. It's been better than the soaps."

"Who's that?" Belinda asked Howard.

"My companion. Want to talk to him?"

"We're going to be late for our appointment. Who are you talking to really?"

"I've got to go," said Howard. "I can't say how I feel."

"I understand," said Belinda. "With your companion standing there and all."

Howard said good-by and hung up.

"It's about time, dammit," said Dwight. "You're a rod stuck in the wheels of progress. Can't phone, can't work on papers, can't do nothing. From now on my office is off limits to you."

"Sure, Dwight," said Howard. He laid a dime on the desk. "This's for your time."

"Disrespectful shit."

"You called Allison," Peterson said. "I know you did. I think you're crazy."

Howard climbed on his bike and rode ahead. Allison? He breathed deeply, putting her out of his mind—and smelled exhaust and the fumes from the oil refineries thirty miles away in Texas City. The smell of money, the Texans said. Belinda's voice still sang in his ear; the buildings still echoed the sound of her laughter.

Four

Allison's mother paced the boundary between lawn and garden, gesturing, her hands chopping the air as if she practiced karate. Allison's father bent over a row of chives. Inside, Allison lounged in the bay window of her parents' library. Eliot sat across the room in her father's chair, for once not reading. Her mother was tall—only an inch shorter than Allison—big-boned, with a face that was angular, like Allison's. Her father was short and quiet, his fingers full of vegetables.

Her mother had raged all afternoon since coming home from the university. That morning a group of younger professors, mobilized by Eliot, who was not even in their department, had tried to vote in her mother as chair, but the older professors had risen in force and put down the coup. The Department of Social Anthropology boasted only three women. The other two appeared composed and seamless, unlike her mother, who became hysterical over any injustice. Her mother's political passion would one day make her chair, but the men, careful in speech, were Texans or adopted Texans, never frivolous with power. A few in the department weren't even polite on the surface. One required his female teaching assistants to wear dresses and be ready to instruct any of his classes with five minutes' notice. "Are you intimate with the material or not?" he said to them. Women students were always in her mother's office complaining or asking advice. When Allison was grown, her mother told her what the boys in the department said about these cloistered conferences.

These same men had, when Allison was ten or eleven, patted her hand and called her darlin' even though they didn't dare call her mother anything but Dr. Franklin-Warren. When Allison turned thirteen, she called them darlin' back, venom in her voice.

Eliot's eyes twitched behind his lids. Outside, Allison's father handed her mother crowns of broccoli. "I have a bedtime story," Eliot said. He stood and walked half way to the window. "The mountain woman and her man live alone in a cabin in the Yukon, the last frontier."

"Anchorage is not on the Yukon River," she said. "And there is no more frontier."

He ignored her. "Each evening they shut and bar the door. The woman is tired from her day of trapping, hunting, and writing computer programs which make the work of big oil companies more efficient, and she falls into the arms of her man, who ministers to *her* needs, cooks for her, cleans house, pampers her. He's so convenient, so adaptable that she finds him tedious." She sat up and stared at him. "The windows are covered with oiled paper, and are narrow, so the bears and wolves which prowl around her cabin every night can't get more than a claw inside. Every morning when she strides out, she sees the grizzly's prints, long as two hands laid end to end. She has a recurring dream, very erotic, that she unbars the door and the bear shuffles inside to clamber onto her bed."

"I'm going because I want the job. The fantasy was not some back-to-the-primordial crap. The fantasy was thinking you'd follow me."

"The fantasy was thinking you could get me to give up my life to be with you." Eliot gestured—tight, spastic motions. "As much as it hurts, I won't do it." He opened the door.

"Toads who never breathe air outside their offices showed up!" she heard her mother shout, waving her arms and filling the air with words.

"Next time," Eliot called to her, "they'd better watch their butts!" Allison's mother and father both turned toward the house; neither smiled.

"Lois," Allison's father said, "you and Eliot did those old boys a genuine service. None of them have stood up on their hind legs and roared for three decades."

"Go to hell, Frank," her mother said. "I'm not in the mood for it."

"Just a minute," said Eliot to Allison. He smiled broadly as he walked across the lawn.

At last it had happened; Eliot had put words to what she had known all along. She walked across the room and opened the cabinet, poured more whiskey into a glass. His claim that he would exist only as a pale houseman was a smoke screen. If the nature of their relationship was equal here, it wouldn't change in Anchorage.

In the garden, Eliot stood over her father, who was rapidly picking okra and filling Eliot's cupped hands with pods. Her mother shouted at Eliot. He presented to Allison's mother his Charlie Chaplin face, wide-eyed, a sliver of a foolish grin. Soon her mother bent over, hands on knees, laughing. The three of them walked back across the lawn. Eliot carried the okra, his cupped hands high, as if lifting a chalice. Allison's mother walked with her hand on Eliot's shoulder. She leaned over and said something close to his ear. Their voices sounded from the kitchen. Allison tried to remember when she had first stolen a drink from the cabinet. Sixth grade? Fourth? She walked into the kitchen.

"I was beside myself," said her mother. "Now I'm calmer. Frank's got me chopping garlic and onions. Very therapeutic."

"Just don't cut off the end of your finger," her father said. He poured wine.

Eliot lifted his drink: "To Frank, the farmer, and Lois, the berserker."

During dinner Eliot engaged her mother, talking about the mechanics of their next stage of STIV. They had hired a pimple-faced boy, an undergraduate in computer science, to take her place, and she found that more offensive than Eliot's lack of commitment. Her mother smiled and leaned toward him as she had in the garden. Eliot had always liked Dr. Franklin-Warren as much or more than he did Allison. Her mother was possessed by vital, intellectual passions. Talking with her was like being swept away in a whirlwind. What person could resist?

At fourteen, Allison discovered that her mother regularly took outside lovers. She had gone to borrow her mother's faculty card to buy a book and had overheard a conversation between some graduate students. When she told her father, he said, "Your mother and I have an understanding."

When she was seventeen, her father moved out. It was her parents' first open break. Before he left, Allison had listened to him and her mother arguing for days in their bedroom, in the garden, the kitchen, so it was no surprise. He had been gone three days when a man showed up, one of her mother's friends from their years in Charlottesville, where her mother had taught and her father finished his Ph.D.

As soon as the man from Charlottesville came, Allison moved into the building in back of her mother's house, which her father had used as a study. She lived there through most of the fall, avoiding the strange man, who was taller than her mother but who had an offensively round boy-face. She couldn't remember his name.

The day before Thanksgiving, her father called. Allison was in the kitchen finding something to eat when her mother answered the phone. That afternoon the man was packed again, waiting in the living room. Before the taxi could arrive, Allison's father walked into the house, circling her mother's lover like a predator. He had walked out to the small house, and the man soon left, trying to say something to her mother, who held the door open for him, her face empty of emotion. Her husband had walked in, her lover out, and she stood in the doorway, as isolated and introspective as if she had closed her eyes and was savoring an exotic wine. Allison had gone out to sit with her father. He said, "Your mother and I are the apex of civilization." His face said that he had no more illusions. Their marriage was simply open to whatever draft chose to blow between them. Allison had decided two things: sleeping around was not for her and marriage made it easier to take advantage of someone.

Allison considered the flow of her life with Eliot. Success had been a function of companionship without constraint; now that there was constraint, they would break up. She watched the back of Eliot's neck, and something stirred low inside, as if once again she turned her hips up to receive him. Lovely, thick-bodied Eliot, only five years younger than her mother. He lifted his glass to her from across the table.

When she was four or five, her father had occasionally taken her to his mathematics lectures. She would sit in the balcony of the auditorium, her books and drawing paper spread around her, while he filled the hall with his voice. He once said to her, "It's a great help to me that you sit patiently for hours." She knew now his compliment was inaccurate; being left to herself had never required patience.

Eliot dozed against her shoulder, his hand inside her shirt, flat on her belly. She moved his hand away. Suddenly he pushed his face against her neck. "You know I have immense affection for you and your family," he said, his voice muffled by her flesh. She heard her mother moving in the kitchen. Allison had supposed at dinner that Eliot's interest in her mother might still be sexual. She knew they'd slept together before he met Allison. Now there was another story which explained his habit of doting on her mother: he'd wanted to be a son-in-law.

"If I stayed, what would we be like twenty years from now?" she said. "Would I go wild in a garden while you filled my lap with okra?"

"Who knows what could happen in twenty years?"

"I have a story for you. The professor nudges thirty-five. Every day he struts around the class, gesturing, so full of his material that he's invigorated, enraptured."

"So full of what?"

"Himself, his own fragrant bullshit. After class, co-eds crowd around him. 'What did you mean, Dr. Stone, when you said that the wallet has become a fatter phallus? Does this mean that women in business suffer from penis envy?'"

Eliot turned to the window. She couldn't see his face in the dark.

"With the eyes of these women on him, he feels young again. Among them he sees the daughter of one of the full professors. He realizes that, in addition to being ten years younger, she could move him closer to the seats of power. He reaches his hand toward her as if she were a plum. He thinks, 'What would it be like to have mother and daughter both?'"

He turned back from the window. "I've loved you as well as I could, Allison, but I still won't leave Houston. You don't have to make our parting unpleasant." He moved his hand across the back of her neck, rubbing there and on her shoulders, and her eyes misted. Get a grip, she said to herself.

Several months after she first met Eliot, she began to believe that he was someone she could spend her life with. They were compatible sexually, intellectually; they enjoyed many of the same things: the same bluesy rock, Italian and oriental food, the same kind of contemporary novel about relationships. Their differences had seemed superficial. She liked beer, he preferred wine. He was fastidious, she careless with appearance and schedules. She had hoped they might avoid the mistakes her parents had made. Marrying, for one thing, making love into a prison house. She'd been right about the quality of their love, just not the duration.

Her mind went to Howard. He would stick with the woman he chose. The only problem was his Mormonism. It had educated him—giving him consistency and sensitivity—for which she felt an odd gratitude, even if it made him unstable intellectually—but sooner or later, everyone graduated from school.

The fourth Saturday Peterson refused to play soccer. Howard begged and then fell silent, deciding on an experiment—forgetting Allison. But she still rose in his mind and tipped the ball backward over the net. She still sat on the grass in the lotus position, head hanging, supple, speaking with her strong, clear voice. Her words fell through his mind like inextinguishable sparks. "I'm playing soccer tomorrow," he said to Peterson the next Friday. "With or without you." That night, a downpour started, a full day of rain, then another, a deluge so strong and steady that Howard wondered if the Flood had returned despite God's promise. Peterson looked at the sky, and said, "It's God's hand." Howard said he was being egocentric.

Water ran down every street, pooled in Hermann Park. Even Peterson wasn't going to propose that they tract on their bikes when the weather was like standing under a shower, so the two missionaries and Dwight sat on the top step, back under the awning, watching the rain fill the bayou with roiling water that threatened to overflow into the lower apartments. Peterson read while Dwight and Howard played cribbage, but Howard couldn't keep his mind on the game. "This ain't no fun," said Dwight. "You're playing like a six-year-old." He took his cards and the peg board and went back inside.

Keeping one eye on Peterson, Howard wrote a letter to Allison. "What I've believed all my life, I no longer know to be true." He wrote about his struggle concerning whether to believe before his mission, but left Belinda out of the story. He described his parents, the desert surrounding Rockwood, his high school experience, but especially his mission, his gradual disillusionment. Then when the mail carrier arrived, he ran down in the rain and handed the letter to her through the window.

That night, with the rain a rhythm on the roof and the flood still rising in the bayou, he imagined sex with Allison. He played for himself every slow detail of the story of their mutual seduction. Then in the shower, with cold water pouring across his chest and legs, he said a prayer. "Father," he said, "give me a sign that you exist. Provide a way out. Give me the strength to remove this hook from my flesh."

Early the next morning, Howard's mother phoned to say that his father had suffered a heart attack. "Makes no sense," she said. "How could he have an attack and not even know it?"

"A heart attack," said Howard. "I'm coming home." He thought of God, grinning and sending the requested sign. His hands shook with anger.

"A heart attack?" said Dwight, who was standing in the doorway. "Who?"

"Dad's had a heart attack and you've gone apostate, blessing other women. Who gave you the priesthood?"

The phone was silent. Then she said, "Don't come home. He has some medicine which should keep him from having another attack. The doctor says he'll live to be a hundred like all the other Rockwoods. How can I get along with him for thirty-five more years?"

"I'll be on the plane tomorrow."

"Fiddlesticks. I knew I shouldn't have called you. Walter, he thinks you're nearly dead. Try to convince him otherwise." He heard her hand his father the phone.

"Howard," his father said, "what happened was just a ripple in the stream. Stay on your mission. People who come home early aren't worth a damn."

"He didn't mean you," said his mother, back on the phone. "He meant it's important for you to see it through. For your self-respect. I won't bless another woman until you get back."

"What?" said his father in the background. "What are you talking about?"

"Good-bye, Howard," his mother said. "Pay attention to the Lord's work. Don't let yourself get distracted. He's getting old, Howard. Your coming home won't stop that."

She hung up; Peterson and Dwight stood in the doorway.

"I should be home, not in this swampy, evil hole." The receiver dangled from Howard's hand. In the physical world, if you plowed a field and planted it, alfalfa or wheat came up, whichever you had put in the ground. If you cut off a finger, it would lie in the dust. In the spiritual world if you asked for a temptation to be removed, two more rose in its place. "Dwight, never pray. It's like the monkey giving three wishes: you always get something you don't want."

He marched out the door and sat on the edge of the festering bayou. He felt as dazed as a stunned steer—knocked on the head first by a woman who had no place in his universe, then by his mother who had quietly become an apostate, and finally by his father's failing body.

He imagined God as an ancient patriarch, so hassled by all his heavenly wives and children that he turned anarchic, actively culturing chaos on earth. God should not leave his children in doubt. The universe should be sure and safe. If he could just stop believing, he thought, his confusion would disappear. It was ridiculous being angry at God, when his father's heart attack could only be blamed on chaos and coincidence, the fallible human body.

After another night of rain ("The flippin' seventh," said Peterson), the clouds dissipated and the aggressive Houston sun turned the atmosphere hot and vaporous. Around lunch time, Howard followed Peterson as they rode their bikes between the University of Texas medical complex and the back side of the zoo. Peterson's legs pumped like the driving shafts of a steam engine, and he perspired like one. Howard's back itched from the sweat—dozens of needle pricks—as if he had just been tested for allergies.

They passed an olive-skinned man in a white suit walking with a small girl in a daisy-print sun dress, and then two women—spiked hair and black leather. That morning Peterson had insisted that since they didn't have anything better to do they had to tract—contacting blindly, following their spiritual sense. Howard refused to exercise his authority as senior companion to overrule Peterson, so they had uselessly knocked on doors, never getting beyond the introduction. They had pedaled down the tree-lined streets near Rice University. As long as they could keep a man or woman engaged on the doorstep, the air-conditioned breeze breathed into their faces. But the relief never lasted long. "No thanks, not interested" or less euphemistic.

Howard pulled his bike even with Peterson's. "This is a waste of time," he said.

"We're just paying our dues," said Peterson. "God blesses us for our industry in ways we can't know. I have a premonition we'll find someone golden today."

They turned under the arch into Rice campus, which wasn't far from Allison's address. Because of the over-reaching branches of live oaks and the high wall surrounding the university, it was quieter inside. Entering the campus, Howard always felt an edge of expectancy, as if essential arguments and problems were debated in the buildings. The students walking between classes had the attitude of being initiated into secrets—aloof, possessing a competent rationality. All confusion seemed to be prohibited.

Eliot, predictably obsessed with himself and his projects, asked her to at least outline the next section of STIV for the novice programmer. Why she had agreed, she didn't know. As she typed, she thought about Howard, wanting to see him again. He had mailed her a letter which described his whole life, as if it were a résumé. Her one reservation about him had been his religion, and remarkable coincidence, he was giving it up. She couldn't understand why he stayed with Elder Peterson, having no faith in the church they represented.

Answering the door, she said, "Speak of the devil."

"We only have a minute," said Peterson, but Howard walked in anyway.

She offered them drinks, but they wouldn't take beer or tea or even Coke. Finally she made frozen lemonade. They sat on her couch drinking glass after glass, as Peterson scowled at her and Howard talked about when his British ancestors came to Utah and the valleys were filled with grass, belly high to a horse. Their cows, sheep, and horses grazed everything down to stubble; those pioneers thought it would grow back as it had in England, but it never did. Instead sagebrush and weeds filled the valleys. And then he talked about the long rain storm and the difficulty of finding something called Postum in the stores in Houston. "It's hard to think," he said, "when the air is so sultry." Then he fell into silence. He stared at her computer, her poster of Denali, anything to keep from looking full at her. She wanted to slap him awake. Look at me or don't, she wanted to say. None of this weaselly glancing.

"Imagine yourself believing," he said suddenly. "Follow your instincts."

"Follow yours," she said. "You know what you want." Then she frowned. What did she want? She imagined Howard after sex. He might turn bitter and call her "slut." He might follow her to Anchorage. He might be damaged or feel himself damaged.

"Elder," said Peterson. "We need to get back to work."

"I have a story," Howard said.

She stared at him. "A story?"

"Before this earth, God's children had no spine, no separate will."

"One obstacle for me," said Allison, "is that your gospel has a male god."

"No," said Howard. "Mother and Father God."

"Elder," said Peterson, sitting on the edge of the couch. "Preach from the lessons." His face was tight and angry.

"You don't even believe this junk," said Allison. "Your letter—"

He interrupted her. "Together they created children, who hung around heaven, having nowhere to go. Lucifer offered to organize a world, send the kids there but allow no mistakes. The gods thought his plan left no room for growth. He got angry and they kicked him out."

Allison said, "I read somewhere that it was really the Mother God who was kicked out and then renamed by the Father as Lucifer."

Peterson set his glass on the table and stood.

Howard shook his head. "But Jesus had another plan. God's children could make mistakes, sin a little, exercise independent judgment, and then he would atone for their mistakes—a doorway back into the presence of their parents."

"What's your point?" she said.

"Just what I was thinking," said Peterson.

"Let me finish," said Howard, his voice sharp. "In the Garden of Eden, Adam and Eve still walked and talked with God, just as they had in heaven. Nothing had changed. No independence. Adam and Eve looked up with reverent child eyes, driving their parents crazy with obedience. So God, Mother and Father, tricked them, commanded them to multiply and replenish the earth and at the same time said don't eat from the Tree of Knowledge of Good and Evil. A paradox. Without knowledge, no multiplication. The problem was that Adam didn't dare disobey and didn't dare obey, like a mule caught between two haystacks."

"So back comes the devil, hero of your story."

"No. Eve is the hero. She was tired of holding hands, looking moon-eyed. If she could just clear her mind, she knew she could figure out how this multiplying business worked, but there was some fog there, some mist of innocence that kept her from making the connection."

"She had an itch," said Allison, "that wasn't satisfied no matter how she and Adam rubbed against each other."

Peterson walked toward the door. One hand on the knob, he pleaded, "Elder."

Howard swallowed. "So, when Lucifer told her that if she would eat of the fruit of the Tree of Knowledge of Good and Evil her eyes would be opened and that she would become like God, knowing good and evil, she jumped at the chance. She ate the fruit and became the Earthly Mother, the one who gave us the gift of life at the expense of disobeying her Father."

"I still don't get your point," she said. "Sometimes you must trust evil?"

"No," said Howard, "that's not the point at all. You're like Eve. Ready to move. To repudiate all previous knowledge and become your true self. To embrace what seems contradictory to you."

Was that the point of every story told by a man—control over a woman? "No," she said. She tried to figure why he was preaching to her. What was the advantage to him if she converted, when he doubted? It made no sense at all. It was as if religion had warped his mind permanently. "I'm done with revolutions. *You're* Eve. *You're* the one on the brink."

"No," he said. "I'm more frightened of change than you can imagine."

Elder Peterson walked back across the room, "We have a set of formal lessons we'd like to give you. They teach about the restoration of Christ's gospel through the prophet Joseph Smith, beginning with a visit by God the Father and his son Jesus Christ. If you listen carefully, the spirit will bear record that it's true."

She stood and gathered the lemonade glasses. "Elder Peterson," she said, "you are such a bastard." She gripped a glass in each hand. "Why don't you give up on me?" Then she was reminded that he had given up on her from the beginning. He crammed rhetoric down her throat to drive her away. His face was smug, as if he'd made a shot she couldn't block.

"Like most people, you don't believe in something you can't see," he continued. "That's perfectly normal. We live in a society that's so rationalistic that we've forgotten how to feel in our bones the movement of the Holy Ghost. But I bear testimony that your spirit, the spirit which can sense what your eyes can't see, the same essence that lived before this life, will live after this life. Intelligence or spirit is eternal. Your loved one, whoever he is, still lives."

She was furious. "Dammit. This has never been more than a wet dream for you two. I'll never convert. Now get the hell out of my apartment."

That evening while Peterson cooked, Howard walked downstairs. "No cribbage," he said to Dwight. He had been surprised by the Eve story that had tumbled out of his mouth. Talking, he had adopted someone else's voice, some woman's story of the Fall. Not his own. Telling the story, he hadn't felt that he was declaring knowledge or even, hypocritically, the truth for someone else. He had felt, for the first time in nearly two years, that as he struggled to interpret Eve, his soul was expanding again. Like the seed that sprouted or the man who had prayed, "I believe; help thou mine unbelief."

He said to Dwight, "I've got to talk to someone wiser than me."

"That's just about anybody." Howard ignored the joke and told Dwight that he couldn't tell if his feelings for Allison were based on love or a desire to rebel.

"You can't ever know something like that," said Dwight. "You just mess yourself up thinking about it. My rule is never allow no woman or church or anybody to have so much sway over me I can't think clear. But I do know what you should do."

Peterson thundered down the stairs. "What?"

"Nothing quick. Every time I've done something quick, it blew up in my face."

"Elder," said Peterson from the door. "Get upstairs *now*." Howard had never before heard panic in Peterson's voice. By the time he reached the outdoor stairs, he saw President Wister getting out of his car in front of their apartment.

"Thought I'd stop by for lunch," he said. "What are you having?" In the kitchen Peterson slid a slab of fried, processed meat onto a plate and laid the plate in front of President Wister.

"This is our staple," said Peterson. "We pour the grease out on the bread instead of butter. Saves money."

"I was thinking about my garden in Wyoming." President Wister stared at the falsely pink meat. "We grew tomatoes and peas and lettuce. Butter crunch." Still without taking a bite, he asked about their work. Then he said, "A wife and children are incomparable treasures."

After dinner the president interviewed Peterson. Howard sat on his bed, waiting his turn. It was like the last minutes before a test he hadn't studied for. Finally Peterson came out of the kitchen and he went in. Stocky, half a head shorter than Howard, the president reminded Howard of a bulldog. He trusted him because he was a rancher.

"I don't want to be transferred," Howard said.

The president sighed, looking out on the bayou. "Elder, you're sure that's how you want to start this interview—planting ideas in my head?"

"Should I have said I want to be transferred?" Howard smiled.

"Tell me about this woman you're teaching. When Elder Peterson gets anxious, I get anxious too."

"I think she's the woman I want to marry." Like the Eve story, it felt true for him as he said it, as if he was approaching something essential. Then he shook his head. When each random thought bore the mark of truth, he knew he was a wave tossed by every wind.

President Wister was quiet for a moment. "She's married and you want to marry her?"

"She's not married."

"This is the woman you think God has reserved for you? You think you're in a position to make a clear judgment?"

Howard said nothing.

"You haven't said anything to this woman, led her on in any way?"

"No. Well, I told her the Eve story."

"The Eve story?" The president watched Howard's face. "You were raised on a ranch. You seen a cow mire herself trying to get a drink?"

"Sure."

"I'll arrange a transfer for you. Up north, out of Houston. Country like you've wanted your whole mission."

"Transfer? I have only a month left."

The president laid his hands on Howard's arms. "I think it's best. Be careful, Elder," he said. "Be like Joseph—flee temptation. Keep your eyes on the Lord's work. He'll reward you later if you do. He has a wonderful woman in reserve for you, not some faithless atheist. Perhaps the one writing you from home."

"You're treating me like a child," said Howard. "As if I can't control myself."

"I don't think you're a child. You are a grown man, and your future is bright with possibility. I just don't want to lose you."

Watching the president's face, Howard's anger dissipated. It was clear that the man cared for him. In zone conferences, the president's talks were always carefully prepared and practical.

"Wait until you're released before you make any decisions. You'll have a month away from this woman to think carefully about what you want. Think about what you'd be giving up by deciding on impulse."

Howard knew he had filled his mind with images, not of an eternal family, but of Allison's thighs and face and voice. He thought about Belinda, and about their plans. Still she was a soft, sweet child compared to Allison, who didn't mince and sway. When she walked, she swung her legs like a pirate.

Allison bought a fifth of whiskey. It would be a purgatory drunk. Rid herself of affection for two men at once. She tried to remember how it had felt to love Eliot and decided that she had deceived herself. Sex was compulsion, not solace. Out of the cradle endlessly rocking. She numbered the loves of her life:

—Her father, from the beginning;
—Dante, a dog she had received as a gift from her mother's brother, border collie/black lab mixture;
—Sammy, a boy who had a tree hut next to their house in Virginia;
—Three boys in turn in the sixth grade, unrequited;
—Her seventh-grade health teacher—she had been mortified when he demonstrated the Heimlich maneuver on her;
—Herbert Phillipson, with whom she had experimented;
—Sting and, to her shame, Axl Rose;
—Bobby Stupeck, the wrestler, who knew when to stop;
—Mike Stock, a love of two years, ninth and tenth grades, who had prompted her study of contraceptives;
—the college student wearing a Mao hat in the UV library, who in his small office taught her fifteen ways to use a chair;
—the preacher's son from Cut and Shoot—she'd forgotten his name;
—Virgil Fortunado, captain of the high school soccer team;
—Walt Cottle, the mathematician, friendship and sex, not love (but then what was love?);
—Eliot, bearded, so self-contained he didn't need her;
—Howard, blocked erotic, mistaken mystic.

Allison took another drink from the bottle, trying to imagine someone with all power and no obligations. She tried to think of herself as a lord, making love to many women. She didn't know how much license medieval ladies had—certainly not much. Too much dress. Or was that an effort to contain the uncontainable? Precious maidenhead, covered by hoop skirts. Whoops, wrong era. How did women at that time get and use power? Men had greater latitude working their way up and down the social hierarchy. Limberness in social structures. Women probably managed limber sex too.

When Allison opened her eyes, the light in the room made the window opaque. She held her arms around her legs and rocked back and forth on her buttocks, a comforting rhythm.

Howard's voice was the oddest mixture of logic and mysticism. She stood unsteadily and coiled her hair on top of her head. She found the business card Peterson had given her. Walking unsteadily down the stairs into the dusk, she started her car and drove slowly toward the missionaries' apartment. Tonight she would just talk, but if sometime later she got him in bed and bound him to her, perhaps he would feel enough commitment to give up his former life and follow her to Anchorage. "Eliot," she said, "you were right to leave me."

With the moon, her one true friend, steady to the east, she drove the Loop. She felt like the last day before graduation from M.I.T.: everything was over but the words. More like dying and still walking, remembering the pleasures of life. Because the freeway was raised on pillars, she had the illusion that the car floated past the dark city. The buildings tower like buttes, Howard said when she first met him. The streets are deep as canyons.

Everything was dead, except for two or three restaurants lit below the freeway at street level, a few white floors high above them where cleaning people worked. Blade-skaters slipped like coyotes down one dark street; two homeless people stood under a light. Even the underground tunnels would be bright but empty—safe routes from building to building for the business types who paid her money for having fun with equations. Only on the edges was the city alive at night.

Howard, Peterson, and President Wister sat at the kitchen table and argued about the hidden sanctuary of the Lost Ten Tribes. "They'll emerge in power during the Millennium from under the North Pole," said Peterson. "They live in a giant cavern under the ice."

"Or they'll fly back from outer space," said Howard.

"They're not lost, like lost in a forest," said President Wister. "They're just scattered through Russia."

If Allison converted, thought Howard, not only to Mormonism but also to wifeliness, to marriageability, what was interesting about her would disappear. Another paradox. He realized that it wasn't a paradox to someone, like Peterson, who wanted a wifely wife. What Howard admired about her was her rebelliousness, unconventionality, and wildness. Even though his talk with the president had made him want to be sensible, Allison's qualities were antidotes to the lukewarm way he had felt about his life.

Someone knocked on the door. "Boys," Dwight called from outside. "Elder Boys. That Texas woman's here to see you. Told her you don't like to be woke up but she won't go away. I need my beauty rest, so you deal with her."

"Elder boys?" said President Wister.

"Tell her we can't go out at night," said Peterson.

"I can't tell her anything," said Dwight, already descending the steps. "She's drunk as hell."

Howard sat for a moment, then stood and walked toward the door. Peterson stood and followed. Allison was on the steps, leaning back against the iron railing. "I thought I'd come over and surprise you."

"I'm surprised," said Howard.

"I've been a shi—a schickhead."

President Wister appeared in the doorway. "Good heavens," he whispered.

"I decided if I dressed like a medium I might be able to get in touch with the spirits of you primitive missionaries." She finally saw President Wister. "Oh. An older elder."

"President Wister, this is Allison Warren," said Howard. "Allison, President Wister."

"This is your contact?" said President Wister.

"Contact?" said Allison. "What the hell's a contact?"

"Was our contact," said Peterson.

"Listen," she said to Peterson. "I may be a little drunk, but you don't have to cut me off hopeless—hopelessly—with no hope or compassion." Leaning farther back to look up at him, she nearly lost her balance.

"Don't you boys have curfew?" said Dwight from his office, which was next to the stairs. He emerged and saw President Wister. "Oh, I didn't know you had a chaperon."

"Dwight worries," said Peterson to President Wister. "Thinks he's our mother."

"I ain't got the figure," said Dwight.

"I don't want to sever relations," said Allison, speaking slowly and carefully.

"But they're severed," said Howard to Allison. "You should go home."

"I imagine us living in a cabin on the edge of a forest. You and I are biologists together. There's a little pond and every day I go out and collect plants, which I stuff into my bra."

"When you're sober, you don't want to have anything to do with us," said Peterson.

"How do you know what I want? Why don't you keep your mouth shut, Peterson."

"Elder Peterson," said Dwight to her. "These boys are ministers of their gospel and you need to keep up certain taboos with them."

President Wister looked from Dwight to Allison, dumbfounded.

Allison tried to walk toward her car; she stumbled and fell to her hands and knees. Howard and Peterson lifted her up. Howard looked into her slack face. She reeked of whiskey. "You can't even get yourself home." He was embarrassed by her drunkenness.

"We'll need to drive her," said Peterson.

"It's against the rules," said President Wister. "But we have no choice."

"I don't need your help," she said, waving her arms. She sat down on the sidewalk.

"I hope she's going to be all right," said Peterson.

"First time you've worried about that," said Howard.

"I'll call the police," said Dwight. "They'll haul her off."

"No," said Peterson. "We'll manage it."

Howard and Peterson each took an elbow and lifted her to her feet. Dwight backed her car closer to the steps and they helped her inside.

Peterson said, "Dwight, you'll take over as our leader when President Wister retires, if you don't watch out."

"I'd crack the whip, all right enough, for you Elder Boys. There'd be some real action in this city. You'd have to set up an assembly line to process all the converts."

"You'd need to be baptized yourself first," said Peterson.

"Told you I've already been baptized. By malaria once in the army, by scalding once when a boiler blew up on my back." He had a wrinkled area along his neck and one cheek. "By marriage twice, and that's the baptism of fire. And by the government every April. I don't need no more baptizing. But now it's time for bed."

"Another inspired transfer," said President Wister. "I just had the timing wrong. You'll be in Navasota tomorrow."

Peterson sat in the driver's seat; Howard helped Allison into the passenger seat and climbed in back. President Wister followed in his car. The air, even at midnight, was unbearably hot. Howard tried to remember what he had felt earlier, the communion of souls, the electric tension. He examined the dark mass of Allison's hair; she was another woman now. The president had helped him see more clearly. For the first time in months he thought with pleasure about going home. Maybe he would marry Belinda after all. Whatever else happened, he knew now that he wouldn't make a foolish decision.

Peterson was snoring, one paw flung up over his head. Despite the air conditioning, it was stifling inside. President Wister had driven home nearly two hours before. Howard pulled on his clothing and walked out onto the stairway. The air was thick, tinted purple; it smelled like a swamp. The moon was a pale disk. He heard the faint roar of a large cat in the zoo, nearly a mile away. Dwight's light was out, so Howard unlocked his bike and wobbled along the edge of the cement bayou. He had nothing in his mind but a desire to get away from the apartment where Peterson lay snoring.

Two shadows, a man and a woman, sat in the moonlight on the low wall of an overpass. Howard stopped, one foot down, then rode the angle of the bayou down to the floor. A drain pipe had spread a puddle across the bayou; the water sheeted up from his wheels. He lifted his feet up and away from the pedals but his ankles were sprayed.

"Evil night for a ride," the woman called, her voice thick, the words slurred.

Howard didn't look back. The tires might slip if he tried to climb the bank, so he dismounted and walked up. Riding again, he passed under great, dark trees; from someone's yard he smelled the aroma of tomato plants and excrement. His tires crunched across broken glass but didn't go flat. He floated behind dead houses and apartment buildings. He dropped to the floor of the bayou to pass under streets. A branch bayou came in from the other side.

Soon he passed two men or women going through a dumpster. Four shadows stood on the upper edge of the bayou. When he passed, they ran, spreading out across the cement, but he stood on his pedals and sprinted away. This is stupid, he thought. Rockwood, you must have a death wish. He pulled up out of the bayou and pedaled along a street, passing signs offering the services of clairvoyants, nude dancing girls, and bail bondsmen. The humid air, probably still 80 degrees, was thick enough to choke him, and he couldn't think, couldn't focus, could only pedal.

He rode into the parking lot of Allison's apartment. He dismounted and stood under her window, but her lights were out. Suddenly something hit him from behind heavy as a truck. He was on his face in the grass; he thought he might pass out.

"Peterson!" he rasped. "You don't understand!"

"I understand enough," said Elder Peterson.

"What were you thinking?" President Wister said.

"Let's get out of here," said Peterson.

Howard was lifted off the ground. His head, neck, and back hurt. He felt sick to his stomach. Peterson carried him like a child.

Back at the apartment, his legs still felt weak, so Peterson helped him walk up the stairs.

"I'll stay here tonight," said the president.

"I'm sleeping in front of the door," said Peterson. "He won't sneak out again."

Howard didn't think he could sleep, but some time later he woke from the falling dream; he had slipped wordlessly through darkness. Night filled his throat; he could hardly breathe.

F i v e

On the 25th of August, Howard rode
back to Houston from Navasota with his zone leaders. Elder Simone,
a black man, was from Pittsburgh, and Elder Salsbury from Salt Lake
City. Simone argued that one day, possibly in the Millennium,
women could receive the priesthood. "Just agree that, potentially, it's
possible."

"No," said Salsbury. "Women are universally, significantly different than men. Even as intelligences in the preexistence, they were different. It isn't in God's plan."

Howard said nothing, but their conversation brought back the
sound of Allison's voice. He remembered her saying once, "At what
cost do women enter the shelter of your church?"

He missed talking with her—missed feeling that time was alive
and his senses were amplified. At least at first, talking to her had been a
sharp-edged experience, like a long drink of cold water after a parched
day. Toward the end it had all become miserable and muddled.

During the weeks of walking the streets of Navasota and driving
through the countryside, he had alternated between the calm knowledge that the universe was only naturalistic and the fear that God might
punish him for disbelief. At various times, generally at night, he panicked at the thought that time was speeding faster and faster but he was

frozen motionless. He knew he had sacrificed vital experiences to be on his mission. If Belinda had agreed to marry him, they would have had two years of love. He worried that the requirements for graduating in range management had changed during his two-year absence. He could hardly imagine telling his parents and Belinda that he had lost his faith. Worse would be to live a lie, never sharing his doubt with anyone he loved. He had pondered various dramatic acts that might shock him out of his paralysis—seizing the microphone in a radio station to declare the gospel to thousands, swimming across the Brazos River in his suit, or hitchhiking south to Houston to see Allison.

The two elders took Howard to the mission home just off F.M. 1960. At the door he shook hands with President and Sister Wister and each of their children. During dinner, their daughter Susy talked about BYU. "Every building is dedicated to God. It doesn't matter if I'm in the library or the bookstore or the fine arts building, everywhere I go I can feel the Spirit." She asked about Howard's plans. He said he would either work his father's ranch or go to the University of Utah in Salt Lake City, where he'd study history, botany, and range management. "First thing, though," he said, "I'm going on a week-long horse ride. Get myself reconditioned to the desert." After dinner he sat on their couch, watching television, something he hadn't done for two years. He wasn't released yet, President Wister reminded him, but this small infraction was probably all right.

In Navasota he had examined his experience with Allison from every conceivable perspective. What would she have done if he had made it into her apartment that night? Despite his initial anger, Howard was grateful to Peterson. Still he wished he'd had one more chance, accompanied by Peterson of course, to talk with her, to clarify what he thought of the general moral and ethical structure of the church and why it would be good even for a natural rebel like her.

Howard had written to Belinda that he wanted to wait a while before they married. He implied that he wanted to experience courtship but wrote nothing about his loss of faith and his concern with their long-range plans. In a few hours his plane would leave for Salt Lake City, his sacrifice completed.

President Wister and Howard sat together in the terminal lobby. "You made it," the president said. "You're going home with an honorable mission behind you. I was worried for a while." Howard thought about the small choices which made big differences later. His brothers had returned from their missions and settled into their lives; he would do the same. The call to board sounded. Howard handed his ticket to the woman and walked down the tunnel. He found his seat and looked out the window. Suddenly, he was overwhelmed with despair—the same feeling as when Belinda said good-bye through the screen door. The plane would carry him back to his old life, and he would never find the impetus to return for Allison. He stood and walked to the front of the plane.

"Something has come up," he said to the stewardess. "I can't leave now."

"You're already boarded," she said. She put out her hand to stop him, but he pulled away. He passed the ticket taker, who glared at him.

"The plane will leave without you," she called.

President Wister was nowhere in sight. He imagined his parents and Belinda waiting at the airport in Salt Lake, so he rushed to the bank of pay phones to call his mother before she left home. "I missed my plane," he said, "but my luggage is on board. I'll call you when I get another flight." She tried to ask questions, but he just said "goodbye" and hung up. In front of the terminal, he boarded a taxi and gave the driver Allison's address. He wasn't sure what he would say to her, but he knew he couldn't just leave. He might propose. He might tell her that he hoped she would fry in hell. He'd claim her any way he could.

Thirty minutes later he pulled up in front of her apartment. The driver wanted forty-five bucks. Howard thrust the bills at him and ran up the stairs to her door. She might be inside with Eliot; then what would he say?

No one answered. He ran back down and tried to look through the window, but the angle was wrong and he could determine only that the drapes were open. She could have left for Alaska already; her red Mustang was gone. Someone watched him through the neighboring window, so he walked back down to the street. He felt lonelier, more disoriented, more foolish than he had felt since first coming to Texas. He was in no man's land between mission and home. He had ached to be free, but even though he had no companion and no serious obligations, he still felt bound about by restrictions. He stood in the street, looked once more at the apartment, and started jogging toward Dwight's.

He arrived, dripping with sweat. Dwight came out of one of the downstairs units dressed in hip boots and rubber gloves. Through the open doors of the downstairs units, Howard saw standing water. The stench was terrible.

"Well, I'll be shit and lie in it," Dwight said when he drove up. "If it isn't Elder Howard."

"You sure that isn't what you've done?" Howard said, holding his nose.

"Plumbing problems up the kazoo, Elder."

"Don't call me Elder. I'm on my way home. I'm nearly a free man."

Dwight took off one glove and shook Howard's hand with a flourish.

"Where're Peterson and Thompson?" Howard asked.

"They moved out when the toilets started backing up," said Dwight. "No loyalty whatsoever. I told them I'd get the place fixed up in no time, but they wouldn't wait." He looked at Howard. "You supposed to be alone?"

"I'm supposed to be at the airport, but I thought I'd say good-bye to my friends." He slapped Dwight on the shoulder. "You ought to move to the desert. You'd fit right in."

"Can't leave my place." He looked across the bayou. "She wasn't home, eh?"

"What are you talking about?" asked Howard.

"Can't fool me," said Dwight. "You got all the marks of a whupped man. But I don't think she's the type to move to the desert either."

"I wanted to say good-bye."

"Or maybe hello. You know, she came here the day after you left. That Elder Thompson's near-sighted as a mole. He stood on these steps and testified to her. Then she testified back to him, only she used more colorful words. Never saw her again." Dwight turned back to the apartment. "Well, thanks for coming. But I got work to do, bad plumbing problems. Business shot to hell."

"Dwight," he said. "Let me use your truck. I promise not to wreck it." He looked at the battered three-quarter-ton Chevy with a towing winch on the back.

"Lord, Elder, you don't want much." He shook his head. "Keys are on the engine block."

Howard drove to the University of Houston where they'd once tried to talk to Eliot in his office. Finally he found visitor parking and walked across campus. He felt exposed, as if he stood naked on the top of a cliff. Eliot answered Howard's knock.

"I'm on my way home," said Howard. "Thought I'd stop and say good-bye to Allison."

"I haven't seen her for several weeks."

"Has she left for Alaska?"

"She could have."

Howard turned to leave.

"Wait a minute," said Eliot. "Her mother just called and canceled a lunch appointment. She said she was headed home to work in the yard." Eliot gave him the address. "Just go over. If she's outside, she wouldn't hear the phone." He examined Howard. "So you're going to Anchorage?"

"No," said Howard. "I'm not."

"She is. That's why we split up. She wouldn't stay here."

Without answering, he left Eliot's office. He felt like a fool, missing his plane when he didn't even know if she was in town. The thought that he had missed her was unbearable. He wanted to talk, not just for an hour, but for fifty years. He wanted her in Rockwood with him, wanted her as his wife. She was so strong, he knew she'd adapt to ranch life. What arguments could he use to show her that their love was more important than going to Anchorage? Words might not do it. He had heard that women use sex to get love, maybe the reverse was true—that having sex with her would bind her to him. Others in

Rockwood had slipped; people gossiped for a while and then forgot the sin.

Finding the right street and number, he hesitated. What could he say to her, driving up in a wrecking truck spewing blue smoke? The house was red brick, in the middle of the block on one of the streets just north of Rice University. He knocked on the door; no one answered. Peering around the corner of the house, he saw a woman watering some flowers. "Mrs. Warren?" he asked. "I'm Howard Rockwood."

She studied Howard's name tag. He took it off with shaking hands and stuck it in his pocket.

"I'm trying to find your daughter."

"A Mormon missionary. Lord, help us," she said, turning back to her flowers. "I don't know where she is now. I'm not even sure she hasn't left without saying good-bye to me."

"Thank you," Howard said and walked toward Dwight's truck. Looking back, he saw Allison's mother frown. Howard felt his face and neck burn. Everyone made judgments; he was sick of judgments.

Allison was almost finished packing, but the air-conditioning had broken down. Earlier she had hauled a load of her things to a storage unit; she would ship the rest to Anchorage. Driving up the United States and Canada would make the move a genuine rite of passage, marking her rebirth as a new creature, one separate from Eliot. Her father couldn't come with his pickup until evening, so she lounged—sweaty, tight, bored. She ate candy bars and tried to imagine the cool air of Anchorage. A big truck pulled up outside, then someone banged on her door. "Not locked," she called. Howard stood in front of her, his tie awry, face white as an angel's. Her lethargy evaporated like mist. "Elder H.," she said. "I thought you'd flown back to Zion."

"I was on the plane," he said, "but a perverse spirit possessed me." He grimaced, as if regretting the words.

"Ha!" she said. "Not perverse. I'm glad to see you." She dumped her newspaper on the floor to make room for him on the couch. "You don't have to stand."

He chose a chair across the room. "I couldn't find you. I was worried you'd left already."

"Tomorrow," she said. "I won't give up my car, so I'm driving."

"Aren't you nervous? Heading off to Alaska?"

"Ready for it. Want it now."

"Long drive," he said. "It'll take you at least a week. Dangerous."

"You volunteering to spell me?" She smiled. Then, "Come with me to Alaska."

He said nothing.

"Funny. I've never seen you without Peterson. Where is he?"

"Still here," he said.

"Still pushing the word of God. Do you want something to drink?" He watched her, as if she were a snake or tiger, as she walked toward the kitchen. She barked at him, and he stepped back. She grinned. "Damn, you're jumpy. Soda or water?"

"Water," he said, his voice cracking.

She opened a cardboard box on the table and took out a glass. She filled it and returned. Their fingers touched as he took the drink. "Ice," she said. "I forgot ice."

"It's just fine," he said. But she was already back in the kitchen with the freezer door open, her hand on the plastic tray. He followed her, lifting his empty glass.

"Oh," she said. "Was it warm enough for you?" The tray slipped out of her hand. She laughed again. He picked it up and handed it to her. "I haven't been this clumsy since junior high." She twisted the tray and popped out a cube of ice, which she dropped into his empty glass.

He placed the glass on the counter and returned to his chair. She stood behind him; he didn't look back. Low behind each ear his mahogany hair became curly. The collar of his white shirt was crooked. She wanted to straighten it but knew he would flinch away. She sat on the couch.

"So," she said, "how was Navasota?"

"Nice," he said. "Beautiful country."

"You have good luck?"

"We baptized a prostitute," he said.

"You what?"

"It's a long story."

"How will she make her living?"

"The bishop is helping her find new work."

A drop of sweat ran down her side. "Damned hot. This is how I'll remember Houston."

He stared at his hands.

She frowned. "Well what *is* your plan?"

"I came to say goodbye." He slid to the edge of his chair. "And to talk about how I can see you again."

"You're seeing me now," she said. "I'll bet my Mustang to that old truck that you've missed your plane."

"Yes," he said. "No. I don't have a plan. I just couldn't go without first getting straight with you. Things were a little confused the last time." His face was weary, his shoulders slumped; she wanted him to smile again.

"I was wasted last time."

"I missed you," he said.

"I'm happy to see you, too, Howard." Then she laughed. "Why do I feel so awkward?"

"What if I flew up to visit before winter comes?" he said. "I'd like to see Alaska. I could try to find a place to stay for a few days."

"I have a better plan," she said. "I was thinking about driving through Denver, but it would be just as easy to go through Salt Lake. Rockwood can't be far from Salt Lake. You can keep me from running off the road."

"No," he said. "I'll just get another flight. My parents would worry."

"I've been thinking about your Eve story. Maybe we can figure a way to meet halfway."

"Utah is halfway," he said.

"Wasn't what *I* had in mind." She shifted her weight, ready to stand. "I was thinking more of some kind of experiment. Like you coming all the way to Alaska with me now. We see if we're suited for each other."

"No!" he said, too loudly. "I couldn't do that." He stood and moved closer to the door. "Maybe toward the end of September before school starts at the U. Maybe I'll fly up after I'm released from my mission." He was standing next to the door.

"Wait!" But he *was* leaving. His face was set, his hand on the doorknob. She knew if she kept her mouth shut, he'd be gone. She had never been one to ignore the sudden and surprising gifts of fate. She said, "I'll feel like hell if you open that door, Howard."

"Will you please marry me?" he said.

She stared at him. "Marry you!" She shook her head. "You turn everything so damned heavy. What makes you think I'd marry a Mormon patriarch?"

"I'm not a patriarch."

"Just give you time," she said.

"I love you," he said, his hand still on the door. "Do you love me?"

She didn't move, didn't look away from him. He seemed even more beautiful than when she first saw him. "You've been so ardent, I don't know what I feel. But I know I don't want you to go. I want you to be with me."

He turned away from the door.

"Howard," she said. She wanted to kiss the tip of his hawk nose; she wanted her arms around him.

He crossed the room and stood in front of her. Something inside her lifted and hummed like a jubilant song. She reached up and massaged his palm with her thumb. She found herself weepy. "What do you mean 'love'? What do you mean?"

He took both her wrists. "I don't know," he said. "But I want to know." He laid his hand on her shoulder. She hooked her hand around his knee, leaned forward, and hugged his legs. He cradled her head, one hand behind each ear; she felt his hands shaking. He kissed the crown of her head, forehead, eyelids, lips. "You taste like chocolate," he said.

She thought, Now we can begin.

II. Rockwood, Utah

*"And ye shall dwell in the land that I gave to your fathers;
and ye shall be my people, and I will be your God."*

—Ezekiel 36:28

Six

From the front, Howard's house was
symmetrical. Two stories high, a chimney at each end (the right-hand
one crumbling at the top), two white front doors, four balanced windows in front with glass so old and uneven that the dark Victorian furniture inside rippled as Allison approached the left-hand door. Two
halves for his ancestor's first two wives, Howard had told her; now his
parents lived in the northern end; the other side was used for storage. A
brass plate above the door read 1865. The brick was manila-colored,
sandy to the touch. Allison turned and discovered that Howard had
not followed her from the car. "You coming?" She walked back,
opened the door, and lay her hand on his shoulder. He flinched; she
tugged his hand until he followed.

Three days, he'd said to her, then had given her the kind of grin
that implied she'd quickly be converted to him and the desert both. She
agreed to his terms, but told him that the morning of the third day
she'd hove for Alaska, with or without him. She still felt the odd certi-
tude that she might be able to live with him for decades. But not in
Utah. And not with him as patriarch.

He pushed open the front door to the house. She followed him
into a musty entryway. She knew this was unfamiliar ground, and she
had determined before setting foot out of the car that she would not
react with anger, no matter what happened.

"Who's there?" a woman called. "That you, Howard?" Her voice rose in pitch until it broke at his name. To the left was a living room; to the right, stairs rose. The room had a high ceiling; a gilded chain supported a six-armed chandelier in which only three bulbs burned. The wallpaper was faded, printed with patterns of tiny flowers. Howard's mother rushed down the stairs toward them, carrying a notebook and several shirts on hangers. At the bottom she dropped everything, and the notebook popped open, scattering papers. "Howard," she said, hugging him, nearly knocking him down. His chin rested on the top of her head. Her hair was in tight curls, salt and pepper. Allison had imagined someone larger, more outwardly confident.

"I was so worried when you missed your plane." Then she turned and saw Allison. Her mouth and eyes widened, but quick as an eye-blink she smiled. "So this is your friend. It was kind of you to give him a ride." She spoke slowly, with a non-Texas country drawl; her voice sounded like a tenor saxophone, rich and deep. Allison bent and the three of them gathered the shirts and pages together. Allison picked up a package of letters. The return address said, "Elder Howard Rockwood." She picked up a sheaf of papers—in bold letters, "Minutes of the Rockwood Ward Relief Society Presidency Meeting."

"I'm trying to get myself organized," she said to Allison. "You know how it is in Relief Society, everything ordered perfectly. Well I'm the worst possible president. I've always had a talent for talking, but I'm trying to discover a talent for administration." She shouted, "Walter, he's made it." She spoke with Howard's inflection; Howard had her mouth, full upper lip, tucked-in lower one.

Howard's father came slowly through a swinging door which led toward the back of the house. He was white-haired, too old to be Howard's father. He looked like Henry Fonda in one of his last movies. "I heard him when he came in." He threw his arms around Howard. "How in hell did you miss your plane? I was scared to death you'd have an accident driving up—" He saw Allison and raised his hand slightly in an ambiguous motion. "—because God wasn't protecting you as a missionary anymore."

Protecting him from what? Allison wanted to ask. She focused on breathing, on controlling her temper, on giving them all a chance with each other before walls were flung up.

"This is Allison Warren," Howard said. Allison took Howard's hand, released it again. "These are my parents, Walter and Emily Rockwood." No one else spoke, no one smiled.

Howard's mother patted his side. "I can see that those Houston Saints invited you for dinner a few times."

"He looks fine to me," said his father.

"I meant it as a compliment," she said. "You were so skinny, there wasn't much to get a hold of before." She hugged him again. "Please sit down," she said to Allison. They all moved into the living room and sat with hands on knees, not speaking. As Allison watched, tears beaded at the corners of his mother's eyes, ran down her cheeks. "I don't know why I'm crying now." Nor do I, thought Allison, I've not harmed him.

Across the room hung the picture of a patriarch and his four wives, two to each side: the first had a face like a queen, wise and kind; one was thin-cheeked and black-haired; the third possessed a round, smiling face and light curls; the last was pale-haired, with gray eyes, and a thin and angular face—obviously Howard's and his father's ancestor. Allison stood and walked toward the painting. The patriarch looked straight out, stern as the Ten Commandments.

"When did you leave?" asked his father.

"Yesterday morning."

"Hell of a drive," his father said.

"We stopped at a motel," said Howard.

"A motel?" said his mother.

"I know I'm just an old Jack Mormon," said his father, "but isn't this damn irregular?"

"Walter," said his mother, "give him time to explain."

"We're together," said Howard.

"Together?" his father said. "What the hell does that mean?"

"Allison and I are together."

"You're engaged," his mother said. "You've brought a fiancee home from your mission. Why, you're as level-headed as your father's Grandpa Isaac."

"No," said Howard, "I'm not that level-headed."

"You're married," his mother said. "My Lord, you've gotten married."

"You're not hearing what I'm saying," said Howard.

"I've got a job in Anchorage," said Allison. "Howard's thinking of joining me there."

"We've only talked about it," said Howard.

I've caught a squirming Mormon rabbit, Allison thought. Caught but not held, no more than Eliot had held her.

"You're not married?"

"We're not getting married right away," Howard said.

Allison cleared her throat.

"Good," his mother said. "Then you can have time to think things through." Frowning again, his mother studied his face; then she shrugged, turning to examine Allison, who knew she had not adequately imagined how foreign Howard's parents would be. Howard looked at the floor and rubbed himself behind one ear. His mouth worked like that of a small boy. "Oh, Howard, you've put your foot in it this time."

Howard's face turned an even deeper scarlet. Certainly not his foot. Allison moved closer to him on the couch, reached for his hand. No one is dead, she thought.

His father got up suddenly and left the room. "Dad," said Howard, and went after him. Howard's mother sat staring at the floor. Allison pushed the door, still swinging, and walked through a short hallway, into a kitchen with a stove straight out of *Little House on the Prairie,* and across a large screened-in porch. It would almost be better if they called her the names they were thinking; that would cause a clear break. She could pull away again, the yellow-eyed wolf, moving easily north alone. But dammit all, she wanted a chance with him.

Howard's father marched down a lane through the field, his shovel over his shoulder. Howard waited in the barnyard. "Did you see him? He had a heart attack while I was in Houston. He looks as old as my grandfather did before he died." Howard climbed through the fence. "I'll be right back. I need to talk to him." Obviously he didn't want her along. She felt as if she'd walked onto a set of a Western melodrama. Next, she figured, the slighted woman would show up. On the way to Utah, Howard had told her about a girl he once planned to marry.

The end of the haystack went up like stairs. She climbed, slightly worried that a bale would come loose and throw her to the ground. From the top she looked across the narrow valley, made, as Howard had explained, by the centuries' long meandering of a small creek. The fields were variegated, light and dark green, with a swath in each field silvered with spray from sprinklers. She looked farther east at the gray, nearly barren hillside, the eastern bank of the valley. Above the dry hillside showed the peaks of the blue mountains they had driven through two hours earlier. The view westward was the same—gray hillside, sparsely covered with dry grass, blue peaks in the distance. The next town was forty miles back across white alkali desert. Nothing was green but the fields and the line of trees along the creek. Color had been fried out of the ground and sky. She took a tube of Chapstick from her pocket and coated her lips. Trees in the valley were either as massive as three-story buildings or thin, a hundred feet tall, standing like soldiers along the ditches and fence lines. To her right lay the houses of Rockwood—Howard's tight-assed Mormon town—and above that a mountain range black with trees and shaped like a knife blade.

Howard stood with his father on the bank of a ditch; Walter leaned on a shovel. Howard pointed back toward the barnyard and then down at something in the ditch. He laid his arm across his father's shoulders. His mother, the same woman whose letter had entranced Allison, came out the back door with three paper grocery bags; she dumped them into a rusty barrel. She looked up at Allison and then returned inside.

Howard finally walked back and climbed the stack to join her. "I told him he shouldn't have walked out on us. I told him he needs to accept us."

"He does?" said Allison. "Have we accepted us?"

"Yes," said Howard. "We're just negotiating the details."

Allison laughed but suddenly realized nothing was funny. Details eventually separated her from all she wanted to keep.

"He asked me about my plans. I said to stay here and marry you or go to Anchorage and marry." Howard climbed down the stack and headed toward the barn. She climbed down and joined him. "I can't believe how run-down he's let it get. It looks like someone else's property."

"I haven't changed my mind, Howard. My parents' marriage—"

"Kept them together."

"When it shouldn't have."

He stopped and turned toward her. "I thought that when we—"

"It did," she said. "I don't think of you as a one-night stand, two-night stand, but you're not so great in bed that I've forgotten about my job."

"What's that supposed to mean?"

"Nothing. I'm frustrated you won't come with me."

He trailed his hand across a plow, red with rust. "This should be protected with grease." They entered the barn, where two muck-filled pens connected to outside corrals. A cow and a horse stood inside. The milk cow had manure across her rump and sides. Howard pointed toward her udder, which had large scabs on it. "Look at that. And did you see the haystack? Both the cow and horse have been pushing over the fence and eating. They'll soon smash the fence flat and ruin the hay. He's let everything go."

"Any fool can see he needs your help." She wanted to be angry with him, but she was too embarrassed. Like him, she had believed sex would bind them—would make him follow her to Alaska. "We've both been fools." He finally looked at her. "Tonight. Let's go tonight."

He tried to untangle the wires of the gate, then walked into a small building for pliers and a hammer. "You promised me three days."

"Don't rub my face in it." Three days, she thought, and he'll work himself back so deep into this damned valley that he'll never leave.

Although she was nervous, Allison liked the feeling of moving with the massive horse. She and Howard rode through the orchard near the house. Her horse stretched its neck to crop the tall grass and pulled the reins out of her hands. She hooked the dangling reins with her foot, pulled the horse's head up, and kicked it forward. Howard opened the gate without dismounting. They rode through the front yard and north away from Rockwood. Soon a car passed them, then slid to a stop on the shoulder; a young woman flung the door open and ran toward them.

"Belinda," Howard said, his voice as somber as the toll of a bell. Her curly black hair bounced as she ran. She's beautiful, Allison thought. Full in breast and hip, not thin, not tall.

"Howard," Belinda screeched. His horse danced in place, and Belinda slowed, stroking the horse's neck until it calmed. Then she stood with her hands up on Howard's leg. "You didn't come, so I came after you." She lifted her foot, thrust it into the stirrup with Howard's, and stood, throwing her arms around him in the saddle. Then she kissed his mouth. The horse pranced sideways; Howard leaned back in the saddle, trying to keep his balance. The leather stretched and groaned. Belinda still held him, but they both leaned at a dangerous angle.

"Belinda, I'd like you to meet Allison Franklin-Warren. Allison, Belinda Jakeman."

"Allison?" said Belinda. She was nose to nose with Howard.

"I met her in Houston," he said, straining his neck back to get some distance between them. "It's been kind of a sudden thing or I would have written you."

"You would have written me?" she said. "Written me what?" She coughed a short laugh. "I suppose you're telling me you brought back a wife from Texas."

Howard said nothing; he tried to hold the horse still.

"That's right, isn't it?"

"Close enough," he said.

"I have your last letter in my car. It came Friday. You didn't say anything about this."

"*This* happened yesterday," said Howard. "Day before yesterday."

For a long minute, Belinda's face was blank. Then it turned hard. "You bastard!" she shouted. "You've done it again. I should have known." She turned toward Allison. "And you—!" Her voice lowered. "I don't know whether to curse you or thank you. He's not reliable."

Belinda slid off the horse, flinging the reins at Howard, and the horse jerked back. She grabbed Howard's foot and lifted. Already off balance, he fell, landing on his back, his foot tangled in the stirrup. Belinda marched toward her car. His horse pranced sideways, dragging Howard a few feet before he was able to kick loose. The horse bucked toward the fence and stood there quivering. Howard rolled over.

The door of Belinda's car slammed, and Allison heard the engine start. "You'd better get up," she said. "She's going to run you over." He pulled his legs under him. Belinda swung her car around, and he jumped out of the way. She spun gravel as she left.

"I thought she'd cry," said Howard.

"No," said Allison. "Anger is much better." She kicked her horse back through the orchard and into the barnyard. She got off and tied it to the fence.

"Allison," he said, standing next to her horse. "It happened so fast, I couldn't think."

She looked at his face. "It's over for you. You've finished with her."

"Yes," he said. "That should make you happy."

"Are you an idiot?" she said. "You just flushed a big chunk of her life down the toilet." He looked puzzled. Why *was* she angry with him? She hadn't known he was capable of such cruel neglect. Even a telephone call would have been better. Still her own reaction alarmed her; she was trapped in a soap opera, where every emotion was exaggerated.

The four of them sat for a late dinner—roast beef and potatoes, fresh corn, small carrots, with ice cream and sugared peaches for dessert.

"The feds can keep the hell out," said Walter, not looking at Allison even though she'd raised the subject. "We managed before—they had no right to take it over."

"Did all right ruining it," said Howard. "The Forest Service is bringing it back from the damage inflicted by J. D. Rockwood and the other pioneers."

"Walter," said Allison, her mouth full of corn, "you one of those ranchers who'd shoot a forest ranger?"

"Damn right," said Walter. Through the evening his talk had been jerky—stops and starts. She wondered if it was his natural manner or just Rockwood male nervousness about women.

"All bark," said Emily. "Bunch of old desert rats."

"Some are all bite," said Walter.

"Think they're John Wayne," Emily said. Her elbows on the table, she stared at Howard, her chin resting on her hands.

"What?" Howard said. "Did I forget to comb my hair?"

"I heard a ruckus," she said. "I guess you broke it to Belinda gently."

Howard opened his mouth and shut it again.

Emily turned to Allison. "I remember when Walter returned from his mission. He thought he was a hero or a god—the center of the universe."

"Well, I'll be damned," said Walter.

"Guess it's in their genes," Emily said. "I don't mean that. In the air. Returning missionaries, males anyway, think that they're like sheiks visiting the harvest, culling the herd, separating the sheep from the goats, the wheat from the tares. Picking the best mate for the great forever. Most of us, fools that we are, believe it too."

"I wasn't careful with her," Howard said.

"Understatement of the century. Seems to me you need to make some decisions."

"Yes," said Allison, trying to keep from grinning. "You need to make up your mind."

Emily turned to her. "This is a lighter thing to you than it is to Howard. We hadn't imagined that he would come home just to leave again. In fact, I can't say I wouldn't be satisfied to see you head for Alaska and leave him with us. But I want you to know also that you'd be welcome to stay here, as long as you plan to marry. You could set up in the other half of the house. It would take work, but we could get it cleaned up. We could have Bishop Hansen over tonight to marry you." She paused. "No we can't. I don't suppose you had a blood test."

"I'm on my way to Anchorage," said Allison. "He can come if he wants."

"Monday you could get a blood test. We could get a few rooms cleaned by then."

"It's just dusty," said Walter. "Nothing else wrong. Only leaks a little, a couple windows broken, pipes might be rusty, but hell, we'd have it livable inside a week or two. Maybe three."

"Walter," said Emily. "They can stay there if they want."

"I'm not staying," said Allison. She ate carrot after sweet carrot. She should be angry at Emily for inviting her to leave. But she had said it so earnestly. Emily, unlike Howard, seemed to have no deceit in her.

After dinner the four of them walked down through the fields. Allison tried to smell the alfalfa blossoms Howard had told her about, but all she could discern was dust.

"I design software." Crickets made waves of sound in the pauses between their talk.

"Oh, Lord," said Walter. He snorted.

"What?" said Allison.

Walter laughed, scratched his head, and laughed again. "I thought at first that you made women's underclothing."

"Yes," said Emily, "that's just what you'd think."

Allison laughed, glancing sideways at Walter. He was like Howard would be in forty years. How long would she have with him—two more days, twenty years? While Allison's mother harangued in the garden, her father filled her hands with tomatoes and snow peas.

"So how did you meet?" Emily said. "Start at the beginning."

"We were teaching Allison about the gospel," said Howard.

Walter said, "When did you get to the lesson on chas—"

Emily started moving before he half-finished the sentence; she nearly knocked him over. "Walter, just keep it to yourself." She took Allison's arm. "I don't know if that part of it needs much explanation. I meant, tell us about you. Where you grew up, all that sort of thing."

She told about her school in Houston, Charlottesville, and at

M.I.T., that her parents were professors, and what she knew about her job in Anchorage. "I feel like I'm being interviewed."

"Well, I guess you might feel that way," said Emily. "But I hope you can see that we'd be a little curious." She smiled at Allison, and Allison smiled back.

She wanted to say that coupling with Howard had been accidental, experimental, rather comical, something to take without anguish. But she knew, tasting the words that almost came to her tongue, that they would not work. "Right. How could you know my intentions?"

"What *are* your intentions?" said Howard.

"To steal you away to Anchorage."

"To be stubborn," he said. He turned away from them and walked along an empty ditch toward the lights of Rockwood. She started to follow, but then didn't, not wanting to avoid his mother's questions. She didn't want to be with him against his parents. She told them about how she and Howard had met, how she had become first curious, then affectionate of his bright and intense talk, his spiritual integrity.

"Spiritual integrity, hell," said Walter. "What do you know about spiritual integrity?"

"He is becoming true to himself," Allison said. "I sure don't mean commerce with God."

"True to himself. By throwing morality out the window?" He turned and walked up the lane; Emily and Allison followed, two women with peevish, childish men. She felt invisible in the night. Ahead across the field, two windows in the house were lit.

Emily cleared her throat. "Plenty of farmers in Rockwood don't know diddly-squat about how to manage their taxes. Walter sure doesn't."

Surprised, Allison couldn't think what to say.

When they crossed the barnyard, Howard joined them. She took Howard's hand, partly because she was glad to see him back, partly to establish domain. Walter was waiting on the back porch, and they all sat on two ancient sofas. Allison worried that they were full of rodents.

There was an awkward silence.

"One of us needs to make some money," Emily said.

"You think I won't take care of you?" said Walter.

"We have no retirement savings, no savings of any kind. We've only got the farm, which requires the kind of labor we can't give when we're old."

"We just talk Howard and Allison into getting married and staying here," said Walter. "Howard can help me get this place back into shape."

Allison opened her mouth, shut it again.

"You can't take two gallons of water out of a quart bottle," said Emily. "This farm can't support two families. You know that windmill property?"

Howard nodded.

"Here we go again," said Walter. "I guess I've got to get to bed." But it was a vain threat.

"We have a buyer, but Walter here thinks cheat grass is worth more than twenty thousand dollars."

"When people start selling off their land," said Walter, "they're finished as ranchers."

"It *is* worth more than twenty thousand, isn't it?" said Howard. "We shouldn't sell."

"We!" said Emily. "*We* can't sell land that James Darren claimed. That would be sacrilege. Walter, you have withdrawal shakes when you see a cheat grass patch which doesn't have a herd of cattle starving on it." She laughed suddenly. "We've done nothing but work since we were married, but we're no farther along than when we started."

Keep talking, Allison thought. You'll talk him away from the farm and right to me.

"What would you do with all that money?" asked Howard. Allison chewed her lip. Howard, apparently like his father, didn't have an ear for good sense.

"All that money?" She tapped one finger on the arm of her chair. "It would give me enough to go to school for a while."

"You don't need to go to school," said Walter. He looked away.

"Walter, do you realize that I have run our house on two hundred dollars a month for the past year? You want me to live that way the rest of my life."

"I didn't know that," Howard said. "I spent more than that every month on my mission."

"I want to do some things before I die—learn tax accounting and sail up a fjord, see a play in London or New York."

"You'll have it from me when I die," said Walter. "But for now I'm not chopping my ranch into pieces so you can fly around the world. That's the silliest idea I've ever heard."

"Stubborn," Emily said.

"It's testosterone," said Allison. "You don't know any stubborn women, do you?"

Walter glared at Allison.

"It was a joke," Allison said uselessly.

"A two-edged joke," said Emily. "Karl called while you two were riding. Everyone plans on coming next Sunday for your homecoming, not the far ones of course. I told him not to make any plans until you had a chance to talk to the bishop. He thought I was talking about *when* your homecoming speech will be."

"Mom, you're going to have to figure a way to tell people."

"No. *You're* going to have to figure a way to tell people."

"I can't face them yet," said Howard. "And we might be gone by then."

"I could call and tell them to come tomorrow," said Emily, watching Howard's face.

"Yes," said Allison. "We'll have a party to celebrate Howard and me getting together."

Walter snorted and turned away. Emily looked at her. "Might not be a bad idea."

"I don't know," said Howard. "How can I face them?"

"You're just going to have to go through it," said Allison.

"Don't you mother me too," said Howard.

"Seems to me that five mothers wouldn't be enough," said Emily. "Ten might have been able to teach you that you can't swim a river without getting wet."

Despite Walter's angry looks, Emily put them in a bedroom upstairs. "You both won't fit in Howard's old bed." Allison followed her into the attic room. Through the one window, she could see the corner of the barn behind the house and the lights of Rockwood. A brass bed stood against one wall. "This was my grandfather's room," said Howard. "Just before he died."

Emily stood in the bedroom door with fresh sheets in her hands, a half smile on her lips.

"I can make it," said Howard.

"No, let me," she said, pushing past him and stretching a fitted sheet across the bed. "I want to have it nice for you after fending for yourself for two years." She whipped out the top sheet and tucked it under, spread a blanket. "There," she said, holding a pillow with her chin, pulling the cover up, "you two should be comfortable here."

"I thought you didn't want us here unmarried," Allison said.

"I don't," she said. "But putting you in different bedrooms now is like shutting the gate after the horse is loose." She sighed and turned away.

Howard closed the door behind her. Allison laughed. "You should see your face."

Below them they heard Walter's shouted words, which echoed through the heat vent. "There's twenty rooms in this damn house and they've got to sleep in the same one. It's a damn pollution to my ancestral home."

"Stop swearing, Walter," Emily said, "It isn't as if your ancestors were models of chastity. Every one of them was a polygamist."

"What's impure about polygamy?" he said. "It was a divine institution."

There was silence downstairs. "I feel like I should be offended," said Allison. "Am I the pollution to the ancestral home or are you?"

"We both are."

"You don't believe that's what he thinks. He thinks I'm the slut."

"He thinks we've both failed." Howard sat on the edge of the bed. "You need to try to understand."

"Not after I leave here for Anchorage, I don't."

"I have him inside my head. Him and his father and his father's father."

"What happened to the mothers?"

He tapped his forehead.

"You should listen to them."

"I'm trying to. But they're hard to hear because the men are always bellowing. The men think you seduced me."

"What do you think?"

"It was a mutual seduction," he said. "We each out-flanked the other."

"Okay, Howard. You pass." She kissed him lightly. "If this kind of out-flanking happened in battles, fewer people would die." They heard faint voices again below them. She took his shoulders and pushed him back on the bed, which squeaked like a rusty Ferris wheel. She bounced and the bed shrieked.

He said, "Let me up." She threw her leg across him; he wrestled free. The voices were silent below. They heard a door slam. Allison bounced again.

"It's a chastity bed," she said. "That's why your mother put us in here."

"We could be in the other side of the house and they'd still listen for us. When we made love last night, it was as if God and all my ancestors were standing just above us in the air, watching in their robes and white beards."

"Damn," she said. "I'm surprised you could get it up."

"Not a joke."

"Not a joke for you. I've never met anyone so conflicted by sex."

"This is easy for you. I thought that doing this—with you—I would move beyond fearing God. Prove to myself that there is no divine moral law, only human and naturalistic laws."

"So?"

"It didn't happen. My ancestors are still whispering, 'Thou hast made thyself unclean with a woman.'"

"Sheesh, Howie. How do you think that makes me feel?" She lay back on the bed, staring at the ceiling.

"But then I see that they're smiling. I know they were all ranchers and polygamists. Virile. And it's like they're cheering me on."

"Now that's much better." She turned and looked into his twitching eyes. "You're not pretending. They're not a metaphor for you." She rested her hand flat against his face. "This is real. We are real. Stop talking like a crazy person."

A door opened and then closed below them. Mormons, according to Howard, believed in sex in heaven, only he wouldn't call it sex. Procreation. She wondered how long they'd last together. He was so odd—sometimes talking sense, sometimes babbling out of mystic insanity.

She listened to him breathing, felt his chest move slightly under her hand as they waited—for what? The attic shifted and creaked. The low-ceilinged room was musty as a tomb—a visionary patriarchal tomb. She had trouble breathing the dust-dry air. Because he was back in this house, back in his timeless valley, where the air hadn't moved for a century, patriarchs walked again in his head. If she could get him away to Alaska, she might save him.

She unbuttoned his shirt and ran her hand across his chest. "You're not wearing your Mormon underwear."

"Can't. I've violated my covenants." He pulled away, one hand holding his shirt together.

"Covenants?"

"Chastity, giving all my goods to God."

"You have goods? Why didn't you tell me you have goods?"

"Not funny. I took those covenants seriously."

"Not all that seriously." He glared at her. "So how will a covenant breaker fare in Rockwood?"

"I'll fit right in." He got out of bed and began undressing, morose again, as he had been at times during the trip up.

"Your parents want us living permanently in the other side of this mausoleum. But where would we go dancing? Where would I go when I need a rousing drunk?" She walked to the window, the floorboards creaking under her feet. She cupped her hands against the glass, looking out on the moonlit valley, Howard's dream valley. The willows were a dark line. Turning back, she took off her clothes and threw them in the corner where he had dropped his.

"That's one hell of a bruise," she said. "Let me see." She gently put her hand on his injured butt. He winced and moved away. She followed. She blew on the back of his neck and touched her hand to the back of his thigh, watching goose bumps spread.

"How does time work?" he said. He moved from under her hand and turned off the light. The bed creaked. "People think time is like a row of dominoes. Each one falling pushes the next instant into being. I think it's more like my father's pool of mineral water: the past is shifting under the surface."

"The past is set. It's the future that's shifting."

She sat down on the bed and studied his moonlit face. "No," he said. "The past is mobile."

She crawled on her hands and knees toward him. "Time is the squeaky bed on which the universe makes love." She settled beside him.

"This isn't the house I left. Not the parents I left. It's different because of you."

"I've just changed your perception."

"No. The past is different. Our being here has changed the nails and floorboards—and the ghosts. The ghosts are not the same ghosts. James Darren Rockwood—the one whose picture is downstairs—is here, different than he was. Mary, here. Josephine, Amy, Lucy, Isaac, Heavenly Father and Heavenly Mother. All different."

"You're talking like a lunatic again." She remembered Michael—his white, bloated face. "Death means there's nothing left. Especially no family chatting in Heaven afterward. Now is all we have. You started to realize this in Houston."

"But I didn't understand something essential. My ancestors, God himself, I don't hear them like I hear you. They're felt. Imagined so strongly that they have presence. No, I mean they have presence without my imagination, but I have no other way to get at them than imagination."

"You're just confused," she said. "So much has changed in the past couple of days."

"Don't condescend," he said. "Driving toward Utah, I felt again what I haven't felt for years—a comfort, tangible as a hand stroking me. Felt as if it was *beyond* imagination."

"It's called going home."

"No," he said.

"It's called having sex. Woke you up to yourself."

He shook his head. "It was a free gift."

"Same way I thought when I was thirteen," she said. "Egotistical. Every impulse was true because I felt it. Like a kid thinking other people can't see her when she shuts her eyes."

"No," he said. "I can tell when it's storytelling, when it's metaphor or imagination, and when it comes from outside my body. My cells vibrate with intelligence."

"That's your *impression*," she said. "It's also the impression of schizophrenics."

"I'm not schizophrenic. But sometimes I wish I could ask God what he wants from me." He spoke in a loud voice, then listened.

"Oh, lordy. You are nuts."

"Good night, James Darren. Good night, Abigail, Josephine, Amy, and Lucy."

"If only my mother could see me now," she said. "In bed with a certifiable lunatic." She whacked him with a pillow.

"Think of it, that lusty rancher James Darren has no body, unless of course he's been resurrected already, which I doubt because of his sins against the earth. None of his wives have bodies. Jeopardy. What is sublimation?"

She hit him again and he lunged for the pillow, falling partly across her. The bed shrieked. "We've got to be quieter," he said.

Grinning, she shoved the pillow up at him, and he pushed it back down, covering her face. Her breath caught in her throat. She flung the pillow up and shoved her hands in his face.

"What?" he said.

"Don't ever—" She couldn't speak.

"What? I was just playing around."

"The pillow. I couldn't breathe." She had once been to a sleepover with some friends. A girl had forced a folded blanket over her face until her lungs burned and the instinct for air had become a dry retching. And this even before she lay on top of the car in the flood and imagined Michael below her with water covering his face, filling his mouth and nostrils.

"Desdemona," he said, half-smiling. "Choking on darkness."

"It's not a joke," she said.

"Right. It's like my falling dream. Now you know."

She waited in the darkness for her pulse to slow. Finally she turned to touch him. He held her hand. So they had this in common. What holds you and your new lover together? her mother might ask her. Fear of death. Everybody's fear, just as love is everybody's consolation.

"Tomorrow is church," he said.

Not so similar after all. She was sure she had no impulse toward self-flagellation. "Why go?"

"I'm not a coward. It's still my church. The only way I can keep from leaving my church is to face the bishop. But what will I say?"

"Tell him, 'I kept trying to run away but she just—well, she just out-flanked me.'"

He flung his head back and laughed like a donkey braying.

After making love on the floor, they climbed into bed, but Howard couldn't sleep. He slipped out, trying to keep the springs from squeaking. He brushed his fingers across her cheek, then walked to the window. The haystack was hulking and dark, the barn a larger dark shape. The moonlight was white on the sprinklers. His body felt ripe with animal sin. He sat on the floor between the window and the bed where Allison slept. He imagined God stomping back and forth, as if just above in the attic. "The young fool's squandered his chances," he said, "polluted his temple."

Jesus held his hand out in a calming motion. "But, Father." The Holy Ghost fluttered around the room.

Grandmother God—who reminded Howard of Grace Montoya, arms thin as bones, face translucent, hair like a burning halo—leaned back on a dusty couch, "Settle down, all of you," she said. "Give him space to think."

Tangle-haired, Allison turned in her sleep, one arm flung above her head. Howard smelled her musky odor on his own flesh.

"Grandmother God," he prayed, "I'm in a bad way."

"You are a foolish mouse," she said. "But you cooked your own *frijoles*. Now eat them."

Seven

The next morning Allison dropped Howard at the Mormon church, which had walls made from boulders cemented in place. Cleared from the fields, Howard told her. Though he had asked, she refused to go inside with him. For all she knew, he might stand and confess his sin with her sitting there; the women might sew a red A onto the front of his white shirt.

Main street was wide for such a small town. She could see only three businesses—a feed store, a gas station, and a grocery. Houses along the side streets were mostly wooden, painted white or green. The newer houses were of red brick or aluminum siding; the oldest were Victorian in style, with walls made from manila-colored brick. Some lawns were bright green, others had been burned yellow-brown. Two dry years in a row and the town would blow away.

When she came to the main highway, she turned westward. Out of the valley, the ground was even drier—tumbleweeds, gray brush, sparse yellow grass, wire fences with gray posts, dusty air. A giant black raven sat on the crossbar of a power pole, waiting for a car to hit a jackrabbit. Allison drove a few miles and suddenly received a gift from heaven—a bar, Willy's Wet One. Neon signs, unlit, were in each window.

Inside she found half a dozen round wooden tables, grease stains on the top, and a bar along one wall, with red, padded stools. The five men seated inside turned their faces toward her, frowning, and every beer disappeared.

"Hello," she said. She felt like a character in a movie—Sigourney Weaver as Clint Eastwood. "Can I have a whiskey?" What else could she say? Four of the men were middle-aged; one looked to be Howard's age. She didn't know how to read them: were they desert bums drinking away their Sunday or profitable ranchers stopping off for a nip before a hard day at it?

They continued to stare. "No whiskey here," the man behind the bar said. "We only sell beer. And we don't sell that on Sunday." Every man had his hands under his table. "You have to wait until tomorrow and drive to the state liquor store in Hamblin to get whiskey."

"I should have just stopped at the grocery store," she said.

"No whiskey there. No beer anywhere in the state on Sunday." He looked out the window at her car. "This is Utah."

"You lost?" another man said—Levis, cowboy boots, and a toothpick. He grinned at her, an old flirty guy. "Or just passing through?"

"Passing through to where?" she said. Their laughter came sudden and loud as if the joke had been told before. "I'm visiting Howard Rockwood. He went to church, but my nose led me here." She sniffed and looked under Cowboy's table. "Well, what do you know, a beer in Utah on Sunday."

He lifted his bottle, taking a swig and grinning. "Walter's Howard?"

"Are there two Howards in this town?" she asked.

"I thought he was on a mission."

"He just finished," she said. "I gave him a ride back."

"I thought he had to come home and get released before he went anywhere with a woman," said a man who wore suspenders, a white shirt, and had a pot belly.

"You're one to talk, Vern, about obeying the finer points of the law," said a man in overalls. "That isn't a bottle of milk you have clutched between your knees." Everybody laughed again.

The door opened and Walter walked in. He started when he saw Allison but recovered and sat on the stool next to her. The bartender put a coffee in front of him. "Thanks, Willy," said Walter. He turned to Allison. "Mormons don't drink coffee. So Emily won't let me have it in the house. I have to come out here to get a cup."

"Howard better not try something like that on me," she said.

Willy took a beer from under the counter and put it in front of her. "We just left Utah," he said. The other men put their beers back on the tables.

"Unless the mission president released him before he left," said Vern.

"That's Vernon Todd," said Willy. "He's got only one train of thought and that one's generally late." Everyone laughed except Walter and Vern.

"So how's life at home?" said Cowboy. He grinned at Walter.

"Don't ask. It's like my wife has become a different woman."

"She woke up to herself," said Allison.

"That's right," said Walter. "I'm just having trouble getting used to it."

"Howard was in Texas, wasn't he?" said Vern. "He was writing steady to my niece, Belinda. According to her, they was about ready to send out wedding announcements."

This town is so small it's nearly incestuous, Allison thought. "Texas is where I met him."

"You're a Texan," said Vern. "You met Howard down there?"

"You're a curious man," she said.

"Howard's a good kid," said Willy; he was watching Walter, who slowly drank his coffee. "You're lucky to have met him."

"Yes, I am." She took a drink. "I'm on my way to Alaska."

Willy looked from her to Walter.

"She's got Howard thinking he wants to go with her," said Walter.

"And the sons of Israel wanted to take away Benjamin, the light of Israel's eye."

"I'm not constraining him," said Allison softly.

"Not hardly," said Walter. "It isn't your will or words that's constraining him."

One, she thought, two, three, four, five. And she kept her mouth shut.

"Willy's a frustrated preacher," said Overalls. "He came here twenty years ago to save all us Mormon heathens. Couldn't find any takers so he opened up a bar. Been thriving ever since."

"This is thriving?" said Willy.

"Wet Willy's Desert Chapel," said Cowboy. "Last chance at salvation."

"I was in Alaska one summer," said the young man. "Beautiful country."

"You're going to have to offer Howard a higher salary," said Willy to Walter. "Give him an incentive to stay and help you run your place."

"Can't even pay myself what I'm worth," said Walter.

"And that's only two bits a year." There was more laughter.

"Offer them the honeymoon cottage," said Cowboy. "Let them move into Max's old cabin. How can she refuse an offer like that?"

"I have a job in Anchorage," said Allison. "Writing software."

"Writing software," said Willy. "I need to buy a computer to track my finances."

"Willy, you don't need a damn computer," said Overalls. "You could figure your finances on the toes of a one-legged man."

"Can I get a computer that flashes a red light above the door when a deadbeat comes in?"

"That red light would be flashing all the time," said Cowboy. "People would think you've turned this place into a bawdy house."

"So two bits and the honeymoon cottage won't cut it?" Willy asked her.

"Does this cottage open onto the beach?" she said. "Does it have cable TV?"

"Mice and an outhouse," said Cowboy. "A bucket for drinking water. But it has a beach. Down the valley is a murky hot springs with dead Goshutes floating in it."

"Just Howard's style," she said.

The young man lifted his bottle. "To your success."

"Whose success?" said Walter.

"Her success, Howard's. He was in my graduating class. May you have a damn good time together in Anchorage."

"When's the wedding?" asked Vernon.

Walter looked at his coffee cup. "No wedding," said Allison.

"But—"

"Vernon Todd," said Willy, "put a fist in it."

"Your train was just derailed," said Overalls.

"To pleasure, prosperity, and long life," said Cowboy, lifting a can.

"Some of my sons are scoundrels," said Walter, staring at his coffee cup. "But Howard has a pure heart."

Allison raised her beer. "To Howard, the pure of heart. May it always lead him to someone who will care for him."

Walter lifted his cup high. "To Howard." Then he turned his stool toward the men sitting at the table. Allison drank another beer, listening to their talk about the drought, the Hunsaker woman whose husband had left her a month before she bore twin boys, the threat that the Forest Service might raise range fees, and the fact that Gerald L. Hansen should never have been called as bishop because his kids were not proper examples.

Howard walked alone into the crowded chapel and saw Belinda across the room. He was surprised by the rush of affection for her. If he hadn't left the plane, he might now be sitting next to her, planning their wedding in a couple of months. A hundred years earlier, he could have married both women. But he couldn't imagine Allison and Belinda lasting five minutes in one house: *Jeopardy*, he thought: What is the definition of critical mass?

His last time inside the church, he had given his farewell talk. His eyes brimming with tears, he had gripped the pulpit and looked down into the faces of the ward members, people who had been as constant as trees to him: old farmers in suits, their wives in dresses, his friends, including Belinda, who had come to wish him well.

"All things are possible to them who believe," that younger self had said. "If I have enough faith, I can baptize hundreds, like Paul or Wilford Woodruff." He had left town swathed in glory, a soldier in God's army. Then as now, he smelled the varnish on the oak floor and benches, trailed his fingers across the white plaster walls. Had his testimony, the swelling of emotion which he had felt early in his mission and not again until recently, been only the memory of home? Allison had suggested that was what he'd felt, driving back to Utah.

Brother Harker waved. "Howard," he called. "I mean, Elder Rockwood. It's still Elder Rockwood." People surrounded Howard: Sister Stukey, Brother Anderson, the Petersons. "Good to have you back. You look great. Nothing like seeing a strong returning missionary to give my own testimony a boost. I missed you." He felt odd that they couldn't see the change in his face. How would their smiles fade when word of Allison began to spread?

Belinda sat across the room between her parents. She turned when he entered but jerked her head forward again. Brother and Sister Jenkins, his parents' neighbors to the north, entered from the foyer. They scanned the congregation and hurried to greet him. Brother Jenkins gripped his shoulder. "It's good to have you home. Talk to you later." He walked to the stand and sat next to Brian Samuelson, who had returned from his mission as Howard was leaving. Sister Jenkins, who had taught him Sunday school when he was in high school, took his hand in both of hers. "I can hardly wait to hear all about it," she said. He still felt her touch on his hand as she sat next to him on the bench. Allison said he had come to church out of a desire for self-flagellation. She was partly right, but he realized that another motive was rebellion—the desire to shock the pious. He supposed he should pray for a spirit of contrition, but that would require him to leave Allison, who wouldn't marry him. He was terrified at the thought of her driving to Alaska without him.

His mother moved through those who stood waiting for the meeting to begin; she saw him, nodded, and turned away again. Women walked across the chapel to talk with her. She laid her hands on their arms, smiling. She glanced at him again, frowning. Then her face became animated, laughing at something one of the women said.

Bishop Hansen rushed in and stood behind the pulpit. "I'm pleased to welcome you to sacrament meeting." He pointed toward the back. "As you can see, Elder Rockwood has returned from his mission." The people in the congregation turned again and looked at Howard and Sister Jenkins sitting together. The bishop smiled at him then read the announcements.

Howard said, "He's going to ask me to come up and talk. I can't do it."

"You'll do fine," Sister Jenkins whispered. "All that practice in the mission field."

The bishop turned the time over to the chorister who led the congregation in singing "Zion Stands with Hills Surrounded." Barney Thompson stood to say the invocation. While Barney prayed, Howard watched Belinda from partly closed eyes. She didn't bow her head; she bit her lip, seeming—what?—frightened, angry, hurt? He wished he had been smart enough to avoid hurting her or anyone else. Was such a pure and insular sin even possible?

After the prayer came the sacrament song, "Behold the Great Redeemer Die." The deacons, one of them Belinda's little brother, moved down the rows with trays of broken bread, which was for the members the emblem of Christ's broken body. The room was quiet except for a few fussing babies. They said that a person ate damnation when he took the sacrament unworthily, but the thought didn't move Howard to shame. Despite what Allison said about his guilty demeanor, he felt no burning coals, only a dead calm, nothing moving.

A deacon stood in front of him, the tray of bread extended. He passed it on to Sister Jenkins, who stared at him before taking a small piece. On his mission he had told people that Christ could take their sins away if they repented. The second priest flipped his hair back out of his eyes and said the blessing on the sacramental water. After the prayer, before the tray of cups could come to Howard, he left his seat, aware that everyone was watching, and went into the hallway. He paced back and forth. He leaned against the door jamb, just out of sight, until the sacrament was over and the bishop stood again behind the podium. Having been a missionary and having received the Melchizedek priesthood, he would be excommunicated for his fornication with a woman who might leave him at any time. Around the edge of the door, he saw his mother frown and look back at the bench where Sister Jenkins sat alone. He could walk out through the foyer and across the lawn, never seeing anyone in Rockwood again.

Why had he coupled himself to Allison? The answer, unlike his futile efforts to feel shame, was clear. She rose two-handed before the net and caught the soccer ball. She undressed him in the motel room, quiet hands moving across his skin. She sat on the couch in her apartment, face intent, body inclined forward. She boiled the air with her swearing. She was as sudden as lightning, as crisp as a crack of thunder. He walked back to his seat and the members of the ward turned their faces toward him.

Bishop Hansen was still talking. An excommunication court used to be called a court of love. Now they called it disciplinary action, but the function of both was to flush sin into the open. If he refused to go to Alaska with Allison, if he stayed to help his father, she would leave. He would confess his sin to the stake high council. After a year they might let him rejoin the church. Such a repudiation of sin might allow him to reconnect to his former self.

In 1930 Solomon Rockwood, James Darren's son, had been excommunicated for taking a fourth wife, a woman twenty years his junior. By then members of the church had adopted the nation's revulsion to polygamy; he could keep his three legitimate wives, but taking a new one had been an act of apostasy. Kids who went to the cemetery for a thrill said they could still hear him moaning. He was warning others against his mistake, they said. Once Howard had read part of Solomon's diary. "August 15, 1934. It has been over three years since anyone in Rockwood has spoken to me in friendship." Death was not the ultimate isolation.

At the pulpit the bishop finally finished his testimony. "We're going to hear from Elder Rockwood later, I know." Howard's mother shook her head slightly. "But I thought he could bear his testimony now."

I spent two years trying to serve God, thought Howard. Two

years minus one day. He stood and prepared to speak from his seat. One of the counselors, a man Howard didn't know, was whispering something in the bishop's ear. The bishop shook his head vigorously.

"In Navasota, Texas, lives a widow and her three children, the Valdez family. We passed her apartment many times on our bicycles; the kids were always dirty and running wild. We knew later from talking to her neighbors that she saw men in the evening for money." He looked across the ward. Sister Sorenson, Brothers Jenkins, Hurst, and Wilkins, Belinda, her parents, Sister Jenkins—all the people he had wanted to see again. Not even the babies were making noise. "One day we passed her house and had the feeling we should knock. No one seemed to be home. Then a small child answered." He took a deep breath and went on. "She was sitting inside on the couch with her boy, bathing his forehead with a damp rag because he had a high fever. We told her who we were, and she didn't want to talk to us. 'Go away,' she said. 'Can't you see I have a trouble today?' We—my companion told her about the power the priesthood has for healing the sick. Then she let us lay our hands on her child's head. When we passed again the next day, she was waiting in the street. 'My son is well,' she said."

Howard looked over the people, remembering the weeks they had taught Sister Valdez. Her eyes had grown brighter and more clear as she believed. He had been jealous. "She began surprising us. When we came to teach, she would give us the gifts of her sacrifices. 'I told the men to stay away. They are no longer welcome here,' she said one night. 'Today I took my wine and poured it out in the garden. I smashed the bottle.' One day she said nothing, but her place had been scrubbed, the children bathed." One by one she had packaged the sins of her life and laid them aside, an arduous labor. Watching from the outside, he knew her steps were firm, steady, as she moved toward her own salvation. She had been a simple and sure woman, believing everything they said. Gripping the back of the bench, Howard let her clear spirit fill him and he spoke to the people of Rockwood from that feeling. "Jesus took her sins away. He can take away my sins and all of yours. Jesus takes away our sins." As soon as he sat down, the clarity left. Had he lied to them, his friends and neighbors?

Sister Jenkins reached to touch his arm. "Very nice," she said. "Exactly right."

He breathed the smell of wood varnish. Out the open back window, the cottonwood leaves rustled. All his life he had been taught that the universe was simple and unitary; now he knew it was not. Opposites were true, paradoxes were as commonplace as stars. As an act of faith, he chose the church and Allison both, both light and desire, and finally, impossible sweetness, he felt himself moving toward his true self before God.

Bishop Hansen stared down at one spotted hand laid on his desk. He appeared the same as two years earlier, still a man almost as large as Peterson but with a huge pot belly. He sat so motionless that he seemed only a shell, like the husk of an insect. If Howard jostled him, he'd crumble to dust on his chair. His white, bristled hair was thick as a carpet. He had been Howard's scoutmaster; they had talked and told stories before dozens of campfires.

"Howard," he said without looking up, "can you help me understand your misfortune?"

"I fell in love."

"We send you young men out on missions. We send you out knowing you'll face discouragement, hardship, and rejection. All soldiers conscripted to the army."

"I *was* ready early on. Then I lost faith in what I was doing."

"You should have come home." For the first time the bishop's face was angry. "Your mother said it happened the last day. Couldn't you wait? Couldn't you hold yourself back?"

Howard had once seen a jackass go after a mare, so frenzied that it paid no attention to a man beating its head with a shovel. Was he like that? He shook his head, but could say nothing. He knew that Allison thought this picture of their love was insulting.

The bishop looked up. "I hope this woman stands with you. She won't marry you, your mother says." Howard nodded. "You know we'll have to act." They sat in silence for a moment. "I wish you hadn't borne your testimony."

Tears came up in Howard's eyes. He had embarrassed his mother and this man, whom he counted as a friend. "You asked me to speak."

"I didn't know. You should have told me."

"How could I do that?"

"You couldn't have. By then you couldn't have. You said you lost faith?"

"I lived the form of it for about a year."

"What a tremendous waste."

"At the end I got fed up. A thousand tiny rules."

"Why didn't you break one of the tiny ones? Break all thousand of them." He shook his head. "You bore such a powerful testimony, but you say you don't believe. Now all the kids in Rockwood will find out what you've done. Will confuse them. Confuses me."

Howard could think of nothing to say.

Bishop Hansen leaned across his desk. "Marry her. You obviously care for her. Don't throw everything away. Marry her."

Howard started toward the door. "I was frightened to talk to you." He didn't say, because I didn't know how to tell you that I feel nothing.

"Of course, you were."

Standing near the door together, Howard patted the bishop's stomach, which bulged out just above his belt. "You need to go on a few hikes and backpacking trips."

"Used to be that every summer I'd lose weight. This is the price of a bale wagon."

"I doubt that the God I feared as a child is really God," said Howard.

"God hasn't changed. You have." The bishop was already returning to his desk. Shutting the door behind him, Howard heard the bishop dial and then speak.

Counting children, nineteen people circled the dinner table. Allison had never eaten with such a clamorous crowd. Two boys snickered over a joke that turned on the similarity between "fat" and "fart." The small girls were singing a song. "Jesus wants me for a sunbeam." They exploded the word "beam" and then shrieked with laughter.

"If you're not going to stop having kids, then we're going to have to buy more leaves for the table," Walter said before the blessing. Howard's two brothers were somber, as if they were at a funeral. Allison sat between Howard and Nancy, his sister. Nancy's husband was next, with their baby behind them in a high chair. The child was dark haired, with the Rockwood eyes, his grandmother's mouth. Allison wanted to close her hand around the tiny hand. Nancy and Sam were younger than Howard's brothers and hadn't yet settled into the apathy which marked the older couples. They continually touched fingertips and eyes over their new child as they took turns feeding him. Howard's two brothers didn't look at their wives. They interrupted the women to ask for butter or potatoes. One of Karl's kids shouted that he couldn't cut his meat. "Help him," said Karl to Sherrie, his wife. He was just as close to the child as she was.

Allison wondered again what was keeping her in Utah when she could be driving through Montana and British Columbia. Besides wanting Howard, who needed space to decide what to do, she was curious to discover the web of relationships that had created him. Everyone spoke at once—a babble of noise—and Howard glanced at her, embarrassed.

After dinner Sam said he would take the children to play in the orchard and on the haystack. "Have fun," he said as he left. Everyone watched the children push the swinging door. Then they sat in silence in the ancient living room.

"Sam has a new job," Nancy said finally. She told them about the private school in Salt Lake where he now taught music. "He's teaching one less class than before but he's also making a hundred dollars a month less."

"Mom said she's found a buyer for that bench property," said Karl.

Howard's father said nothing.

Simon filled the silence: "My son Steven's gotten surly. He won't talk to me anymore."

"He's a teenager," said Emily. "What do you expect?"

"This is drastic, though. Won't do his homework. Won't do jobs. Won't tell us where he's going. Won't come home on time."

"Sounds like Howard," said Karl.

Allison laughed; everyone turned to look at her. She said, "Have him tested for drugs."

"I don't think he'd take drugs," said Karen, Simon's wife. "I don't think he'd do that."

"I don't know," said Simon. "I wouldn't even know where to go to have him tested."

"Try your doctor," said Emily. "He'd know."

Then the room fell back into silence. Karl scratched the back of his neck; Simon stared at the floor. Say it, you pompous prudes, Allison thought. Get it over with. "I think I'll go outside for a walk," she said, standing.

"Don't leave," said Karl. "We'd like to get to know you."

She gave in and sat down, angry because she didn't know how to change the mood in the room. Howard stretched, his hands behind his head. "Those kids were sure noisy at dinnertime."

"They're just rambunctious," said Emily.

"They are that," said Walter.

Simon turned toward Howard. "Don't worry, Howie. Your time will come."

"My time for what—deafness?"

"Children."

"So you're going to Alaska?" asked Nancy, leaning forward.

"Yes," said Allison. "You know, mining computers for gold." She felt foolish, but Nancy smiled.

"I'll bet you're good at it," she said. "You seem like the type who could do anything."

"We thought you were going to stay and help Dad," said Simon. "He could use you." Oh, Allison thought, not morality at all, economics. Why weren't his brothers like Nancy?

"He should feel no obligation," said Walter.

"We come out when we can," said Karl. "But you can't long-distance farm."

"You think I don't know that?" said Howard.

"Why are you trying to make him feel obligated?" Allison said.

"You don't understand," said Howard. "Every letter I wrote said I could hardly wait to come home to work with Dad. And he does need the help."

Wrong move, she thought. Blood is thicker than sex.

"Karl, you haven't been out for nearly a year," said Emily. "Except to dig potatoes and cut your Christmas tree."

"That's the point," said Simon.

"Why not get married?" said Sherrie. "Why not? If a young couple is going to be together they need to get married."

"Married?" said Allison. "Hell, no. We're still just passing acquaintances. We've got a ways to go before we're a 'young couple.'"

Karl looked at Simon and they both laughed. Simon leaned toward Howard. "Passing acquaintances. When did you pass?" He turned his head and smirked at her; when she didn't look away, he flushed slightly. Watch out, you bastard, she thought, I'll eat you alive.

"Without marriage," said Sherrie, "society falls apart. Look at what's happening today. Look at the divorce rate."

"You have to be married to get a divorce," said Nancy.

"When someone gets married," said Emily, "it's a bond between them and God and the world. I commit to this man. It's what makes families secure."

"I agree," said Simon. "I agree that it would be best if they wait to have kids until they're married. That way their kids won't be illegitimate."

"Simon," said Emily. "You could learn a little tact. It never has been your strong suit."

"She's right, Simon," said Karen. "You aren't careful with your words."

"I'm just calling a spade a spade. They need to consider the effect on potential children."

Walter spread his arms out. "I'm glad all of you could come," his father said, the emotion breaking his voice. "I love all of you." He struggled to his feet. "Guess I'd better go move that pipeline back to the beginning of the field." He pressed his lips onto Emily's cheek, and she touched her hand to the spot.

"Howard," he said. "Would you like to help me?"

"Me, too," said Allison. "You're not leaving me here."

Escaping the room felt like coming up from under water. She walked to the truck and stood with her hand on the door handle. "Damn them," she said. "Howard, I'm not good at holding back like this. The sons of bitches."

"They've expended their moral fervor," said Walter. "They'll be docile now."

She and Howard dragged the pipe trailer over and hooked it to the truck. Walter drove to the field where the sprinkler pipes lay. He said to Allison, "Drive slow along the edge." She slid over into the driver's seat and he joined Howard at the back of the truck. He placed his hands on Howard's shoulders. "You've found a woman," he said loud enough that he apparently wanted Allison to hear. "Now love her. That's the best thing a man can do, the hardest thing a man can do." His manner had been so abrasive at first. How could she have known he had a tender heart?

When they returned an hour later, Simon and Nancy and their families had gone. Karl waited on the back porch. "Oh, hell," said Walter, "here it comes."

"Dad," said Karl. "We've got to hit the road, but I want to talk to you about something. Mom wants to sell the windmill piece; you want to keep it. There's a way for you to sell it and keep it." Sherrie and Emily came out of the house and stood together on the edge of the porch.

"Something for everybody," said Walter. "Sounds like the devil's plan."

"Hear him out," said Emily.

"Over in Sanpete everybody's buying cabins. Mountain land which used to go for two hundred dollars an acre is worth five or ten thousand now. People pay silly amounts for a useless piece of ground and then more to have someone put up a shack like a chicken coop for them to camp in one week during the summer."

"People would vacation here?" Allison said.

"She's right," said Walter. "People want pines and a mountain stream near their cabin. Anyway, I need it for grazing."

"Sell ten lots—at least fifty thousand. If we pipe the water up ourselves, we can sell the lots for ten thousand. We bulldoze a flat place and the lots are worth fifteen thousand. It's like picking money off a tree."

"If only there was a tree," said Allison. Howard glared at her, and she thought, Damn, I'd better keep it shut.

"All these improvements will cost money."

"I'll pay for them," Karl said.

"He's made of money," said Walter.

"You're thinking of spending our down-payment savings," said Sherrie.

"It's a way you could keep the land and get money off it. Those small lots wouldn't cut down the grazing at all."

"People don't want cow manure all over their lot," said Walter. "Anyway, this is primarily a hay and livestock operation. I start having too many different projects, and I'll end up broke."

"Too late," said Emily.

"You won't have to do anything," said Karl. "I'll take care of it all."

"Dammit, no. I won't sell any of it. Don't talk to me about it again."

"Right," said Karl. "Shut your eyes to something which could make me and Mom a little money. When there's a resource that could benefit someone else, and you sit on it, even though it does you almost no good, then that's selfishness, pure unadulterated selfishness." Walter walked out the back door; Karl followed, gesturing. "You'll end up like Grandpa, sitting alone on it. No good to anybody." His father shut the door in his face. Karl turned back, surprised. Then he saw the others watching him. "Right," he said. "We're going to go home now." He started out after his kids, who played in the barnyard on the haystack. "Go pack," he snapped to Sherrie.

"I'll just help Emily finish."

"Right, but let's not take all day."

"We can clean up," Emily said. "There are plenty of us."

"Great," said Sherrie. "I'll get everything together."

Soon Karl came up to the porch with his kids, harping at them. The last one, the oldest, stuck his tongue out at Allison. She stuck her fingers in the corners of her mouth and nostrils, distorting her face. Karl turned and looked at her. She smiled at him. "Good bye," she said.

Karl was surprised, but then he grinned. "Oh, damn," he said. "That was a disappointment."

"Don't swear, Karl," Emily said. "You knew he wouldn't go for it."

"I don't really care about the land. I just hate seeing you and him angry with each other."

"So you made Walter mad at you, too," said Emily. "It's a step forward."

He looked at his mother and then grinned. "Pretty dumb, eh? Well, I'll probably be stupid again. I'm not giving up on a good idea just because he's too set in his ways to see it."

Sherrie emerged from the house. "All ready now," she said, her voice too cheerful.

"Sorry, Sherrie," Karl said. "I had no reason."

"Right," she said. "You had no reason." Karl followed her out to their car.

After dark, Howard and Allison walked along the edge of the canal.

"A pack of piranhas," she said. Utah was not for her, and not because it dried her lips.

"Look!" He pointed toward the closest mountain, which was a moonlit shadow on the other side of Rockwood. The fields were bright from the moon. "We could have all this."

The fields were black below the horizon, the Milky Way a bright swath above.

"I'm cold," she said. She trotted ahead of him up the lane. She decided to cut through the alfalfa, even though the long stems tangled her feet. Then she stepped on something soft. She bent down and suddenly her face was wet, her eyes and face burned as if she'd been sprayed with acid.

"Howard," she said, but the liquid—acrid as urine, hot as acid—was in her mouth and down her throat. She coughed and sucked for air, knowing she was pulling the acid into her lungs but unable to stop coughing and sucking for air. "Howard!" she rasped. "Help me!"

"Skunk," Howard said. "Shut your eyes and try not to breathe." Then his hand was on her hand, pulling her. She jerked away, bending forward, hands on knees, and vomited. She coughed again, choking on the liquid still in her lungs. She couldn't breathe, as if she were drowning in urine and vomit. Her eyes and lips were on fire. Then she was lifted off her feet and carried, bouncing, across the field. His shoulder was in her stomach and she couldn't stop coughing, couldn't get air, couldn't get her hands up to wipe the acid from her face.

He threw her to the ground; her eyes, mouth, and throat had dissolved, eaten away by the burning acid. Icy water splashed across her face and body, kept coming until it filled her mouth. Coughing and sputtering, she turned to her stomach, trying to get up, but fell back to the ground. A small dog barked in her head, wind roared in her ears. Her body jerked in spasms trying to get air. She knew she would suffocate. The air was thick as water, and she felt light-headed.

"Lie still," said Howard. "Wait until you can breathe."

"What's wrong?" someone called as if from the other end of a pipe. Emily. "Oh, no," she said, closer. "What's wrong?"

"Skunk spray," Howard shouted. "It hit her eyes and she's breathed it in."

She felt Emily lift her shoulders; she felt Emily's legs under her shoulders, Emily's hands on her face. "Heavenly Father," Emily said, "let her breathe. In the name of Jesus, let her stop choking." Then Allison felt her head tipped far back; she allowed herself to become still. With her head far back, she sucked a small breath, one that didn't burn, then another, and another breath. Opening her eyes, she saw only a blurry film with one bright light.

"Let's carry her inside," said Howard.

"Not yet," said Emily. She pushed down Allison's hands. "Don't rub your eyes."

Allison lay still, focusing on breathing. Something touched her face, a warm cloth. "I'm washing your face," Howard said. Warm soapy water ran across her face dripped into her eyes. Her face and throat burned. She couldn't quite get enough air.

"She's breathing better now," said Emily. "What were you doing down in the field? Why didn't you stay in bed?" Allison felt Emily's hand on her forehead. "Let's move her inside. I think she's breathing all right now." Allison felt herself jostled and then lifted. They laid her on the floor on something soft. "Can you see at all?"

"A little," whispered Allison. "It's blurry, like underwater, stings like hell."

"What's going on?" said another voice. Walter.

"She's been skunk sprayed," said Howard. "She seems all right now."

"My damn throat's burned off," she croaked. "Not all right."

"Don't talk. I'm cutting your clothing off," Emily said. "Hold perfectly still." A door shut. Allison felt the motions of Emily's hands, then the cloth fell away, and cool air passed across her body. "Let's lift her into the tub," said Emily. "Can you feel the edge of the bathtub?" Allison heard the running of water. Someone thrust something against her hands, a bucket. "Pour water across your face," she said. "I'll be right back."

Allison ran some water and, tipping her head back, poured it into her face. Her eyes still stung, but she could see. Her throat still burned, but she could breathe. She was not going to die in Rockwood, Utah. She opened her eyes under the water to flush the spray out. She blinked and blinked. "I can see better now," she called. The bathtub was white and the bright ceiling light hurt her eyes. Soon Emily returned with an armful of bottles filled with something red.

"What's that?" said Allison.

Emily set them on the counter, five quart canning bottles in a row. "Tomato juice," she said, "Counteracts the smell." Then she shook a bottle and, using the edge of a spoon, opened and handed it to Allison, who poured the juice on her head.

"Damn!" she said. "That's too cold."

Emily handed her a rag. "Rub it in." She shook another bottle and poured it down Allison's back. Allison arched at the cold thick liquid running down her spine. "I should have warmed it." Emily rubbed her back with a cloth, dipping it in the puddles of red juice at the bottom of the white tub. Allison sat in the tomato juice, swabbing the heavy cloth across her legs. "I stepped right on it. I hope I broke the little bastard's back."

"Pour some on your face," Emily said. "You need to wash your hair with it."

Allison drank some into her mouth, swallowed. It burned as bad as the skunk acid. "Damn!" she said. Her eyes still watered. "Tear gas," she said. "Natural tear gas. I'll smell like skunk for the rest of my life."

She felt cold air from the opening door. "Go find her some clothes," Emily said, pouring another bottle over Allison's head. She felt Emily's fingers in her hair, massaging her scalp, rubbing her back with the rag. Allison shivered from the cold juice, but Emily's hands soothed her, moving in a pleasant motion. "This won't take all the stink away." Emily turned on the tap until all the tomato juice ran down the drain. Then Allison showered and sat again while Emily poured three more bottles of juice across her. The door opened and Howard threw in some clothing. Emily shut the door again. Allison showered again and stepped out. Emily lifted a pair of polyester slacks and an old red hunting shirt. "Some of Howard's old clothes."

The pant legs were too short and the shirt too big, but Allison dressed and followed Emily out to the porch. "Go change," Emily said to Howard. "I'm sure some of it got on you, too."

He went inside, and Emily turned to follow. "Don't leave me," Allison said. She sat on the back porch, and Emily sat next to her.

"Don't talk. Your throat's had enough damage."

"When I first met Howard, he saved me from walking in front of a car." She felt herself shivering. "Now I owe two lives."

"Fiddle," said Emily. "I don't know anybody who's died of skunk." She went inside.

Howard returned and together they climbed the stack to where Howard said he had spread a pair of sleeping bags. "I don't want a second night on that squeaky bed."

The air felt icy and she burrowed into the bag. Soon Howard was inside, his arms around her. "I thought I was dying," she whispered. She had seemed to float in a pool of fire.

"It just enhanced your natural aroma."

"Shut up." She held him tight. Emily's hands and voice had come to her out of pain and darkness.

Eight

The next morning Walter drove them out to view the western part of his ranch, forty miles away into even deeper desert. Allison sat between father and son, trapped; both were eager to describe their operation. They wintered the cattle out west and drove them back to Rockwood each Easter.

Walter also told her that the summer before, he had decided to make a little money by building a bath house over the hot mineral pool on his property, to make a place for sheep herders and tourists to soak their tired bones. Allison looked out the windows at the stretch of white and gray desert, marked by gray desert bluffs, barren as west Texas. Tourists? When he started to dig the foundation, up came a grinning Goshute skull, hardly decomposed. He had called the University of Utah and soon a team of anthropologists were working the dig.

When they arrived, Allison saw that the edge of the pool was covered by a blue canopy. A mummified, doubled corpse lay on a table—a large figure with a small one bound across her belly with inch-wide bands of leather. "We've named her Marilyn Monroe," said Walter.

Allison stepped forward. "Don't touch," said a woman—one of the university anthropologists. "They're very fragile. We're hurrying to get them back into a brine solution."

"She died in childbirth," Allison said. The mummy woman's

hands were at her sides, not curled around the child bound across her belly.

"Probably," the man said. He looked up. "Have we got skunks in our tent again?"

"It's me," Allison said. He looked askance at her and then went back to his work—using a thick-bristled brush to remove salt crystals and particles of black clay from the woman's face. The woman's mouth and eyes were three flat lines. Stoic in death. There, Allison wanted to say to Howard, that's the condition of your ubiquitous ancestors. The face chilled her. She imagined the woman grimacing in childbirth. "The valley of the shadow of death," her religious Aunt Jenny called it. That valley had nearly killed Jenny, nearly killed Allison's own mother; one inheritance of the Franklins was a narrow pelvis.

Next to the table lay a fiberglass box, coffin shaped; in its cover were set humidity and temperature gauges. Allison bent face to face with the corpse. The skin had no pores, taut as stretched leather. Her face was thick and dark, stolid beyond suffering. Allison had never before seen anything like the face of this woman, hundreds of years dead. Her features—sharp nose, high cheekbones, wisps of hair—were familiar as a dream. Everyone who lives dies, Allison thought. Howard, toward the end of his mission, had flirted with that truth but had reverted to his belief that the universe was populated by dead ancestors. She thought of Michael breathing water, of this woman lowered dead into the heavy water. Her chest tightened, and she jerked herself away.

"We've found three so far," said the man.

"Yes," said Walter. "One in July and two this past week. We hope to find more."

"Two?" rasped Allison. Walter pointed. From the mud below the tables grinned another face, shrunken but hardly decomposed, skin white with crystals of salt, leathery eyes closed. They had only cleared the mud away as far as the top of the corpse's shoulders; it looked like someone buried in sand at the beach.

"The pond shifted and buried them in mud," Walter said.

The man pointed to thongs tied around the woman's ankles. "They must have tied boulders to weigh them down."

"We first thought they were sacrifices," the woman said.

"Maybe it was the Goshute Mafia," said Howard.

"That was another theory," said the man. "Some kind of revenge."

"Now we just think that it was for burial preservation," said the woman. Allison stood on the bank of the pool; the water was deep, as black as the volcanic ridge. "We can't find a bottom to this pond, the roots go so deep. They may have thought of the pool as a passageway to the next life. Reborn in this heavy mineral water, salty as the ocean." Allison looked down into the water; the gray banks made the water look milky. The woman's people had hoped to bind her and her child through that difficult passage. Perhaps they had stood on the shore where Allison now stood, conducting some paltry, insufficient ceremony as they laced the dead child to its dead mother. Allison had no confidence. The only sure binding was that which the child had accomplished, dragging its mother after it into death.

She had seen enough. Behind the dig rose a black volcanic ridge, three or four hundred yards high, rounded like a grave mound. It extended south out of sight. Across the white and gray alkali flat were scattered dry bluffs, blue in the distance, misshapen like the grotesque bodies of prehistoric reptiles mired in mud. Stark and dry as a moonscape, except for the impossible sunflowers, seven feet tall, which grew in the margin of the road. Rockwood town was forty dust-choked miles away across the desert.

She opened both doors and sat in the truck, hoping Howard and his father would catch her hint. Covering her face with a map from the glove compartment, she tried to sleep. She still saw the face of the woman as if it hung suspended above her. Much darker, more composed—no, indifferent—than Michael's face when they pulled him from the water. Howard and Walter remained at the dig for what seemed hours, actually only forty minutes by her watch.

"It's been three days," she said, when Howard finally came back to the pickup. "I'm going to Anchorage in the morning. I want to get back to your house and get some rest."

He frowned. "Three days is tomorrow *evening*. How about a short detour before we go home?" He drove up the small valley toward a ramshackle cabin. The cabin was covered with black tar paper on the walls and roof; a huge flat boulder served as the doorstep. Following him inside, she smelled dust and mice and heard the ticking of feet behind the refrigerator. In the middle of the room was a wooden table, covered with stacks of books; against the walls were a bed piled high with worn-out blankets, a large black cook stove and a refrigerator. "This is it."

"Is what?" she said.

"I thought we might sleep here tonight. The anthropologists are driving to Hamblin for groceries. They'll give Dad a ride." He pointed to the chair behind the table. "My grandfather used to sit here. He had a white bristly beard. He'd bring out the cribbage board and then dish up metal bowls of stew while I shuffled."

She looked around the cabin, hardly knowing what to say. She knew from what Emily had told her that morning that Howard's grandfather had sat behind the table for twenty years before he died. Alone. One day he had gone crazy and, folding his clothing on his bed, had climbed naked in January up the side of the black ridge. "His joints were bad by then," Emily had said, "so he couldn't walk without crutches. I've never understood how he made it up there." The family had a private theory about what was in his head. Before his death, he had been saying that he heard Marilyn Monroe wailing from the rocks above his cabin. He asked Walter once, "Do you think she'd be kind to a decrepit old man?" He had been dead for several days before Walter drove out from town. He had followed the tracks in the snow and found his father, blue, his fingers, nose, and privates gnawed by coyotes.

She said, "I will *not* sleep in this son-of-a-bitching cabin." In Anchorage the first thing she would do was drink until she forgot this man who was determined to become his father and grandfather. "This old coot in Willy's said this should be our honeymoon cottage. Now you get me out here and you tell me you want to spend the night. Feels like the Twilight Zone. In the morning I'd wake up looking like that corpse."

Howard touched her. "She died in childbirth," he said. "We can go back to Rockwood."

"Damn right we can." She turned and found herself nearly running to the truck.

Allison strode into the brightly lit kitchen, still warm from the heat of the day. Emily sat at the table, her head down. "What's wrong?" said Allison, walking forward to touch her arm.

"I don't know how to think about it. Bishop released me as Relief Society president."

"Released?" said Allison.

"It was important to me." Walter sat next to her, placing his hand on her forearm.

"Did he call you to something else?" asked Howard.

"You just went too far," said Walter.

"Thomas Feldsen told him."

Howard frowned. "Who?"

"New in town," said Emily. "I wrote you. The man who told his wife that the only thing that kept him with her was the children. Well, he told the bishop to keep me away from his wife."

"Keep the Relief Society president away from a woman in the ward?" said Howard.

Allison watched their faces for clues.

"He was kind. Let me talk about the ward, me and Walter, you and Allison. Then instead of giving me stupid advice like get a makeover or repent or whatever, he talked to me about Walter's father, how he went off in the desert because he could get along with cattle better than he could with people. He said that Walter is his father's son. Howard, are you your father's son? Then he gave me a blessing. He told me I'd be comforted through trials that are coming."

"How could he release you?" said Howard.

Emily twisted her hands in her lap. "I knew it was coming. I gave priesthood blessings when I don't have the priesthood. What do I do now?"

"Keep talking to women," said Allison. "From what I can see, you're good at it."

"My father's house is a house of order," Emily quoted. "I can't act without authority." Her lips and hands fiddled. "I didn't know I'd enjoy being in charge. All my callings before have been teaching or organizing dinners. I like speaking in front of large groups. I give women solid, careful advice." She wiped her eyes with the fingers of each hand. "They want to unload all their problems onto me, as if I were Bishop Hansen or their therapist. I'm not a therapist, and I'm certainly not a bishop. Maybe an angel of the devil inspired me to give those blessings."

"There's another way to tell this story," said Allison.

Emily folded her hands in front of her. "I just needed to be more patient."

Allison sat down at the table. "Being submissive will eat your guts out."

"It didn't *feel* evil. I told them, 'Stand up to your husbands. You are daughters of God.' But that's another reason he released me. A few weeks ago I gave a fireside in Hamblin."

Walter said, "That the one where you told all the young women they didn't need men?"

"How do you know anything about what I said?" said Emily. "It was a young women's meeting and you don't even go to your own meetings."

"I go to Willy's," said Walter. "Vernon tells me."

"Well, Vernon has it wrong. I told them that—" She shook her head with frustration. "The bishop wasn't at that meeting either."

"What *did* you say?" asked Howard.

"I talked about morality." She looked from Allison to Howard. "Last summer one of the leaders gave the girls a lesson on chastity. She offered them gum, and then when they tried to take it, she chewed it and stuck the wad against their palms. 'Who would want chewed gum?' she asked them. And then she held up a rose, plucked the petals off. Same message—you're not worth anything if you've made a mistake. A couple of the girls' mothers complained to me, so when this young women's fireside came up, I decided to give them another view. I told them that they should stay chaste not to please a man—they all have this belief that men are like princes, I don't know why—but because they are powerful daughters of God."

"So just tell the bishop what you told them," said Allison.

"I did. He understands that whoever reported to him has it wrong, but he believes that the young women need the kind of warning their leader gave them. So many young people are unchaste, he says, that anything that can keep them pure is good." She faced Howard. "I told him that there was another way to keep them chaste: tell them that their destiny does not depend on pleasing men. That kind of thinking makes girls confused, timid, or false." She took a breath. "I compared sex to roast beef and potatoes. If you eat them early the meat is raw and the potatoes are crunchy." She glanced at Allison but continued speaking to Howard. "Then I told them that even if they had sex, their petals were not plucked, their gum not chewed, virtue not destroyed, and that they could still find a man to love them. Then I told them that once a man, Jesus, stopped by a well and asked a woman for a drink of water." As Emily remembered the talk, her motions and voice became animated, as if she gripped a pulpit in front of a crowd. "He spoke to her in a kind and open way. He saw into her inner soul and he taught her. When he left, her life was transformed. There were three reasons he shouldn't have even talked to her. One, she was a woman, second class. Two, she was a Samaritan, hated by the Jews, and Christ was a Jew. Three, she was a sinner, and why should a holy man talk to a sinner? 'After the water I give you,' he said, 'you won't thirst anymore.' What is that water? The gospel. What is the gospel? Forgiveness and remission of sins. He forgave that woman. Can't he forgive you, Howard?"

Howard's face, usually mobile and expressive, was unreadable. "I don't know that," he said. "I want to know it, but I don't."

Walter stood and walked to the stove. He turned the burner up under the frying pan. He cut a pat of butter with the spatula. "Let's have some dinner. We'll all feel better." He looked in the fridge for something to fry.

"I'm not hungry," Emily said. "I'm going to make new plans. Maybe go back to school. I'll have time now."

Allison woke to Howard leaning over her on the bed. "Marry me," he said. "Marry me." She started to respond, but he put his mouth against hers and then bounced off the bed. He was already dressed. The room was still dark, but outside the barnyard had turned gray. Pulling on her pants and shirt, she followed him down to the kitchen, where he handed her a pair of rubber boots. "Daylight's wasting. Come help me move the pipes." The boots flopped around her feet.

Outside he pointed eastward toward the steaming meadow and creek. Long rows of silver sprinklers turned above the black fields. She shivered in the cold air. "I'm freezing."

"Want to drive?" he asked, as if the dilapidated truck were a Mercedes. She climbed in and ground the reluctant starter. He directed her down the lane where the skunk had sprayed her. Though most of the sky was filled with dark clouds, a clear band showed above the mountains where the sun would rise. She drove south along the canal and parked next to the first line of sprinklers. Howard climbed out quickly, walking ahead of her toward the top of the line. Damn, she thought. After all I've invested in him, he's made a decision. Either/or: slut or wife. No room in his head for lover.

The nozzles tapped, turning slowly. The spray showed white across the hayfield. She passed him, grabbing the handle of the valve that would turn off the water. "Men call women wife when they're married. They start thinking they have rights. They start presuming."

"That happens when men aren't married."

"I like the idea of two people running together like wolves," she said. "Nothing constraining them to be together except their free and natural attraction for each other." She looked down at the crank, which would shut off the water. "How does this work?"

"You're so idealistic," he said. "That arrangement would last maybe two years."

"Then it should last two years." She turned the crank one way and then the other. It sprayed cold water in her face, but the level of the sprinklers remained unchanged. "It's not working," she said. "Okay, what's the secret?" She flinched as the spray from the first sprinkler splattered cold across her back.

"Exhilarating, isn't it?" he said.

"That's not quite the word I had in mind. It's six-thirty in the morning, I'm standing in half a foot of freezing water, getting sprayed and—" She flinched as the water hit her again.

"Push the handle down while you're turning."

"Oh." She turned the crank and watched the water die from the first nozzle, then the next and the next, down the field.

"See, that wasn't so hard. Now you've shut the water off." He patted her on the shoulder.

"You're acting like a husband. I'm not a spaghetti-head."

"Sorry." He unhooked the valve. "We wait for it to drain now."

She looked into the next field where a short stocky man was moving pipes. "Brother Jenkins," Howard said. He pointed around the valley. "Brothers Sorenson, Olson, Stringham."

"Such a brotherly valley." She tapped a dry, long-stemmed weed on the disconnected valve. "It's going to choke your mother."

He said, "I have no say in your decision?"

"Eliot's words exactly. He meant that he couldn't control me." She shook her head. "Can you understand why I don't want to be a wife?"

"Barely. Personality seems more important than marital status. Men who aren't married are authoritarian with women. I don't understand the difference."

"So?"

Finally he smiled. "So it's down to our moral compunctions. Whose have priority?"

"Mine," she said.

"You're asking too much of me. How can I be happy if you insist I give up everything to be with you? You want me, but on your terms."

She tapped him on the head with the weed. "Whatever you do, don't turn into a whiner." Beyond him, toward the horizon, the coming light turned the undersides of the clouds luminous. Brother Jenkins was lifting the pipes quickly, walking as water drained out of each end. He had a fourth of his line moved already. "I would give you room. Come with me."

He shook his head. "You're already forcing me. Please don't *persuade*. Just shut up." He unscrewed the first pipe and carried it quickly to the valve, plugging it in.

She twisted a pipe and lifted it, unable to get one end off the ground. She moved to the center of the pipe and wrestled it across the field. "Damn. Your neighbor makes it look easy." She set down the pipe and scooped a handful of water off the ground, flinging it across Howard.

He chased her and tried to make her sit in the water, but she twisted, leveraging him down with her hip. He sat looking up at her. "That's cold," he said.

"Give me a year," she said. "Stay with me a year and I'll marry you if you still want me."

"A year in Anchorage?"

She nodded.

"Married?"

"No," she said. "If we marry now and go to Anchorage and you don't like it and want to come back, we're stuck. I want you free to do what you want."

He looked around at the green and silver field. "A year?"

"I can't wait on this job. You can wait on the ranch another year. Even if your father is slowing down, he's still managing." She looked at him, waiting. "It's the best compromise I can offer. I vowed I'd never marry, never put myself under anyone's control that way."

"I'm giving up the ranch and my conscience. You're giving up nothing."

"How are you giving them up? It's just delayed gratification."

"You will be open to persuasion?" His voice was sarcastic.

"I am a stubborn woman," she said. "But we've been together only five days total. Who knows what will happen? We need to test ourselves."

"We need to declare ourselves before society and God. Commit first, then test." But she could see that the fire had gone out of his voice. "A month."

"Nine," she said, grinning.

"Three months."

"Six. End of bargaining." She breathed deeply, a slow breath in, a sigh out. "Do you know that after you left for Navasota, I thought about you all the time? You're like a disease."

He caught his breath; tears ran down his face. "I'd give up life to be with you."

Rain fell around them. "Dammit!" she said. "I'm going to Alaska, coldest state in the Union. I'll never be warm again." She grabbed the front of his jacket. "Howard, you simple man, you want everything perfect." She pressed her lips against his ear. Moving forward, he pushed her off balance, and she slipped, pulling him down on top of her into the water. She shrieked at the cold. "You bastard!"

"Are you all right?" he asked.

She locked her arms around his neck. "Damn you, Howard. Why did you come to Texas? I wish you'd stayed in your desert." The rain splattered as they untangled and stood. Howard waved to Brother Jenkins, who stood in his field, hands on his hips, watching. "Nothing constrained," she said. "It feels so good to have agreed." She grinned at him, and he returned an unsteady smile, weak like Utah beer.

After finishing with the pipes, she ran through the rain, feeling it wash cold across her face.

"See what I'm giving up," he said.

"You haven't given up shit yet." Leaping into the truck, she started it, revving the engine.

"I'm starving," he said. He kissed her throat, her neck, her soft mouth. "Allison," he said. "Allison, Allison, Allison for breakfast, lunch, and dinner."

"Nothing for me, thanks," she said. "Let's hit the road. I want to get you out of Rockwood before you change your mind."

Allison stood on the walk as Howard held his mother on the front step. She was crying. "Why couldn't you just wait and get married? Why can't you get married now?"

Howard didn't answer, he just stared at the green field to the south of the house.

Emily laid her hand on Allison's arm. "Please take care of him."

Allison watched her face. "Good luck with your bishop."

Emily finally smiled. "I don't need luck with that kind man."

Then Walter surprised her by touching her shoulder in what she thought was a friendly gesture. "Ride herd on him," he said. "He's flighty like a yearling colt."

"I will," she said. Howard grimaced.

"The honeymoon shack will be waiting, if you decide to come back," said Walter.

"I'll keep that dire warning in mind," she said.

"What?" said Walter. "It's a fine cabin."

Emily wiped her eyes. Allison said, "I don't want to be your enemy."

"I know you want to see if Howard is the kind to stand or bolt under the halter," said Emily. "I just wish you'd unbend a little. It would be so easy." She pushed the swinging gate, pushed it again when it swung back.

"Did you know there was a Rockwood who went prospecting in Alaska," said Walter to Howard. "I believe it was near Anchorage."

"Damn," said Allison. "I thought we'd be getting away from them."

"A woman," he said. "Hardly any of the family know about her. There's records of my grandfather marrying three women. When my father was about a year old, his mother was killed in a conflict over irrigation water. Shortly after that the other wife left town. One of your cousins has a letter from her, written to J. D. from Anchorage, where she had dressed like a man and was prospecting. Somewhere near Anchorage."

"I might find her grave," said Howard.

"I told you so you won't feel so lonely," Walter said. "Our people have been there."

Allison rolled her eyes. Suddenly she hugged Walter and Emily, hustled Howard into the car, and drove up out of Rockwood Valley as the deep, beautiful thunder sounded. Ahead, across the desert, black clouds roiled toward them. Wild lightning danced on the horizon.

Howard watched her in glances as they sped north across the desert, a hundred, sometimes 110 miles per hour. The car seemed like a Viking ship or a space capsule. She seemed a steady enough pilot as they raced toward the top of the world and a new life. His ancestors came across the plains parallel to the Oregon trail, leaving it at Utah; he would take up the journey again, following a Rockwood woman to Alaska. After a year, maybe two, short like a mission, they would come back to the ranch. As she drove him farther away, the trees of town—green, then black, then no more than a dot—finally sank into the white desert.

III. Anchorage, Alaska

*"But, the Lord liveth, that brought
up the children of Israel from the land of the north,
and from all the lands whither he had driven them:
and I will bring them again into their land
that I gave unto their fathers."*

—JEREMIAH 16:15

Nine

To get his bearings, Howard ran the coastal trail in Earthquake Park. The mountains were high and bare-topped, their flanks and foothills covered with evergreen mixed with deciduous trees. Next to him a dirt cliff fell to acres of mud flats. His travel book said that the flats were created when the 1964 earthquake dropped a subdivision into the inlet. Behind him Anchorage spread across a wider ledge between inlet and mountain. Across the inlet to the north stretched a jagged line of peaks, white tipped. The book had a picture of McKinley/Denali, but from this angle he couldn't be sure which it was. To his left lay Turnagain Arm. Somewhere nearby, the Rockwood outcast, his great-grandmother's sister, had settled alone to prospect. He imagined her working the streams, dressed as a man, panning for gold. Out of sight to the west lay Siberia; south stretched the long and jagged coast, the mass of North America.

He squatted on the edge of the dirt bluff. Below, the waves came in cross directions, making the gray water churn. The next question—after the heretical questions of how to have faith when the universe felt like unstable fluid and how to be a Rockwood without a ranch—was simply how to live with Allison. The only pattern he knew, his parents' marriage, wouldn't work. Her philosophy was to gulp life like beer, to be open to caprice. His own habit of thought had been trying to be invisible to an authoritarian God. That had been the lie for much longer than the past two years.

Allison woke and dozed, languid as a reptile in her sleeping bag laid on the green shag carpet. The night before (was it Saturday?) she had ridden her Mustang like a descending rocket down the Matanuska valley. Howard had slept as they flashed through Palmer at one in the morning. Soon after Palmer they crossed a narrow flat where the mountains came almost down to the inlet. Her lights had flashed on cliffs to their left and, to their right, on misted bogs and dwarf evergreens with black, clumped branches. She drove through a tunnel of trees, and then they were on the outskirts of the city. Suddenly the freeway disappeared and she drove a street as rambling and haphazard as any trunk street in Houston—strip joints, travel agencies, a small-craft airport, tourist shops. She cut left, driving toward Northern Lights Boulevard along Spenard. They passed a ten-story building, a block-long strip mall. Few people wandered the cold sidewalks, but every fifth business was a bar—yuppie, strip joint, Alaskan rustic, or neon punk. The windows and doors pulsed with colored light and muted sound. She was so weary that her vision twitched, but she still wanted to roll Howard out of the car into the carnival of faces, smells, tastes, and sounds. She postponed that pleasure—they would have at least six months of running the Alaskan night together. She finally found the apartment. She and Howard had flung out their sleeping bags before sinking into unconscious sleep.

When Howard returned from his run, he slipped in next to her. She wrapped her arms and legs around him, feeling like the snake that had tempted Adam out of Eden—no, like Eve, who, according to Howard, had led Adam to a new world. She decided that Western culture had grafted together the figure of snake and Eve—creating a rapacious, tempting woman. Then she wondered how a Freudian would misread her impulse toward snakiness.

"Have you figured where you are?"

"Inside a dog-ugly apartment," he said.

The apartment complex was stained wood—a deep russet with

black streaks. A black shingled roof fringed the flat top, looking like the toupee on the mean Stooge, Moe. Inside were dark walnut wall paneling, green shag carpet, and startling orange kitchen counters and sinks. It smelled like a bear's den. She regretted trusting an agent.

Suddenly the building shook and thunder sounded. Her first thought was another earthquake, but then she remembered seeing the airport on a map. "Must have been designed in the seventies," she said. "That agent ripped me off."

Soon he was up again, dressing in his missionary suit. "I'm going to look for a church."

"There's a Mormon church up *here?*" she said. "Are they *everywhere?*"

The closest chapel was a red brick building, ten blocks south of the apartment. Inside, Howard found a mix of people. One tall Asian man walked up to him and shook his hand. "Welcome, Brother, are you visit or to stay?"

"Visiting. I'm from Utah."

"That is *no* problem. We forgive even state of origin." He grinned. "Brother Yamamoto."

They sat together on the bench. The passing of the sacrament was such an odd combination of familiar and new that tears formed. He passed the tray of bread on quickly when it came to him. The first speaker was a deacon-aged boy, who read a story about a woman who found the Book of Mormon in a locker room. The woman stole and read the book, transforming her life. "I know that God lives," the boy said. "I prayed to him this week and he spoke that truth to my heart."

Howard felt like a foreigner, seeing the meeting with new eyes. He wondered at the simple faith. His own was so tangled that it hardly existed. Instead of a stern and unforgiving patriarchal father, he tried to imagine a distant and pure god, one who didn't traffic in any kind of power. Could such a dispassionate god understand his greedy children?

The second speaker, a woman in her mid-twenties, stood behind the podium. "As many of you know, my trailer burned this week. But I am grateful me and my two children are alive. The trailer burned in five minutes and started at the furnace near the doorway. How is it that we lived? I know only that I woke. `Get out,' a voice shouted inside my head. So I got out. I grabbed my baby and my little girl and I ran. The door exploded behind me. I'm grateful to God and to the Parkers for taking me in. I know that God loves me because I am alive." Howard thought, In some other city a family burned in their trailer because no voice woke the mother. Who can penetrate the mysteries of God?

A dusky-skinned girl across the aisle held a sleeping baby, while a toddler whined and clutched at her knees. She glared at the stand where the bishopric sat. He imagined that the young man who stared at the ceiling and smiled vaguely was her husband. Howard considered holding the crying child, but both mother and child would certainly misunderstand his action. A woman excused herself past Howard and lifted the sleeper out of the mother's arms and returned to her seat. The younger woman pulled her unhappy child onto her lap.

Howard had quashed the impulse to help, the impulse that his mission president's wife preached was native to all daughters of Eve. She said that women's birthright was compassion; motherhood was commensurate with the priesthood. Was it also in Allison's nature, just buried so deep he couldn't discover it? He was more the mothering type than she was. What was Eve like? Grandmother God, whose voice Howard had imagined, seemed unlike any of these women.

He smiled at the coincidence of the closing hymn—"Oh, My Father":

When I leave this frail existence,
When I lay this mortal by,
Father, Mother, may I meet you
In your royal courts on high?

Eve's other quality, one shared by his mother, was adaptability. Eyes closed, Howard pictured again the geographical masses around him, tried to feel Anchorage as home, this city he would wander like the Rockwood prospector. She had left behind her woman's clothing, her polygamous husband. He had left behind the subtlety of the desert; Alaska was starkly green, dramatic mountains and water. He had also temporarily left the work of ranching, which he would have left anyway to go to school. He imagined his father out west clearing third crop hay, then standing on the wagon and facing north, the direction of Alaska, one hand on his sore back. Howard shook his head. Behind him in their apartment lay the woman he had followed; he would leave her for no father or field in earth or heaven.

Monday Allison drove to work in the dark. She had believed that workday Anchorage would bustle, a city on the edge, unlike post-boom Houston, where the program for oil people was to retreat, retrench, and slip their money underneath a different shell. But here traffic seemed light, and not many people walked the sidewalks.

She found the small square building, a defunct bank, which housed Allied Word, the tech-writing and software company that would contract out her services. Lisa Orden—Allison's supervisor—marched across her office, with the height and bearing of Napoleon, but with a coiled braid on her crown.

"We're scavengers," she said. "We feed on the carcass. The North Slope is dying. Oh, there's still oil up there, but the major players are moving to Vietnam or Indonesia, where they can pay nothing for wages and have no environmental laws to work around. So we scavenge and take the place of company employees. We take their jobs because we're quicker and better than they are. And because the companies don't have to marry us—we're just a one-night stand."

Lisa walked past the cubicles of her "team," introducing Allison to Mary, Nick, Ben, Francine, and Yoko, from Georgia, Oregon, Mexico, Nebraska, and Japan. They glanced at her briefly, measuring her as if *she* were the competition, then turned back to their work. The team had a secretary, Mark from Alberta, large as Howard's former companion Peterson, but with sculpted features, graceful and handsome as Cary Grant. "We're a diverse group," said Lisa.

"So I filled the Texas slot," said Allison.

"Mark," said Lisa. "Take her to her battle station."

"Right," said Mark. "Follow me." He showed Allison her cubicle which was about the size of a large closet. "No view," he said.

"Bummer." Allison saw that Mark's was the other cube in the middle. On her monitor was a yellow sticky note with two filenames on it. Mark said, "Lead Dog asked me to copy these to your hard drive. They need to be debugged."

"Lead Dog?"

"Never to her face," he said.

She sat at the monitor. "What are these for?"

"Read them and find out," he said.

"Is this a test?" said Allison. "I've already been to school."

Mark smiled as he left. Allison brought up the first program and read it once. It was an accounting and inventory program and one section contained category names such as Seldovia Princess, Anne Marie, Northern Lite, and Aleutian Maid—names of either boats or whores. The program included none of the complex simulation programs that Lisa had told her she'd be working with. The second received input from an unnamed source and sent reject or accept messages forward. She finally figured that it was designed to check specifications for some kind of pipe. She quickly fixed several simple problems in the two routines and almost pressed the return key to send them back to Mark's terminal. She jerked her finger away from the key. Was this the role she wanted to create for herself, editor of other programmers' mistakes?

Allison walked to the bathroom and then went back to her little box to eat the sandwich she'd brought. She wanted to call Howard, but there was no phone in the apartment yet. Chewing, she stared at her screen and wondered who had written the programs in the first place. They were a mess. And their execution times were laughably slow. Allison didn't know how open Lisa would be to advice. Anyone who was into power games—trying to make a newcomer crumble—probably wouldn't listen. She shrugged and spent the next six hours, minus another bathroom break, pounding the keyboard and talking to herself. There was occasional traffic outside her cubicle, but she didn't look up. When she was finished, the only original elements left in the programs were the names of the mystery women.

She sent the programs directly to Lisa's computer. Two minutes later, Lisa appeared and said, "That's some pretty good stuff. I give all my software hires those stupid programs—then I give the debuggers three weeks' pay and show them the door. Nothing in the contract says I can't do that. Now we've got to figure out what to do with you. The great little project I was going to give you was canceled last week."

Allison stood.

"So I'm going to have to offer you something that's pretty damned ugly," Lisa said. "It's ruined two or three careers, already. So if you take it, don't say I didn't warn you."

"Well?" said Allison.

"It's called CES—Corrosion and Erosion System. Most people just call it the cesspool. It's had more hands on it than a New York hooker, but we've never been able to get it to work right. The users are always mad."

Mark, dressed to leave the office, walked past, shaking his head. "On her first day."

"Go home," said Allison.

"Anyway," said Lisa, "the client is out of patience. We've got to fix CES or we'll probably lose all their business. And that would mean *a lot* less work around here."

"I'll do it," Allison said. Three hours later she realized that Lisa had manipulated her, had made her *want* to give a twelve-hour day. She shook her head and went back to work. On her first day, she couldn't afford nostalgia for her free-lance ways.

By Friday night it was time to howl. She pulled Howard out of the apartment. On Spenard Street she saw a sign, Chilkoot Charlie's, and she coasted into the parking lot. The building was covered with split logs, the bark still on, and looked like the movie set of a western fort. She turned off the key and felt the thrum of bass guitar, the thump of drum and dancers. For a moment she felt odd, as if the earth had twisted suddenly on its axis and she sat outside the Cajun Queen in Houston—a tremor of perspective. Then she knelt on the seat and kissed him, her arms around his neck. "I'm going to love this city. Everything I could want is here."

Inside was a smoke-filled hallway leading to a confusion of rooms, crowded with people. Howard held back at the doorway, but she pulled him into the smoky maze—split log and black vinyl, bartenders flinging down foaming glasses, sawdust on the floor, a tangle of hallways, three or four bars, people sitting at tables or dancing in every space and corner. No one person had designed the building, she was sure. Whoever was in charge at the time had just flung up another wall every time business got better. Like the city itself, the joint was tumbled-together, raucous, and diverse—probably something like hell for a Mormon. She watched Howard's bewildered face. "You're frightened." He seemed not to see or hear her. A band played country near the entrance, but as she led Howard farther into the tangle of walls and rooms, she heard a cross-jangle of straight-up rock and roll.

She laid down money, grabbed a glass, guzzled it, and then she and Howard danced. She rubbed her chin against his goatee of tan stubble. He looked unhappy, bumping against the other dancers. So she kissed him, slipped her tongue between his teeth. She danced away from him, whooping and straight-stepping, shaking her shoulders. She had stolen him away from Utah, her Mormon boy: bright like a comet but as unstable as a black hole.

Later she drove the margin between dark mountain and gray inlet. Moving southward through the curves, she felt that she and Howard were like Captain Cook floating up the inlet on the brink of new discoveries. She sang old Beatles songs into the chill wind coming through her open window. The heater was on full blast. "You say you want a revolution, well, you know, we don't want to change the world." They were children of Aquarius, decades too late.

She stopped next to a mud flat, which glistened in the moonlight. She stood on the front bumper of her car; he sat in the passenger seat. Her fine light high made the starry night seem like black velvet. Tacky and unreal. Gauche like a Mormon missionary. She shouted through the glass. "I'll try to translate my feelings into terms you can understand." She tipped forward like a pushup, nose against the glass. "I feel like we are the first man and first woman."

He opened the door and looked up at the mountains. "Trapped in the garden."

She couldn't think of an answer but knew he had it wrong—Utah was the trap. She swung her feet to the ground. The brighter glint of water lay farther out. She walked down onto the muddy shore—canyons, crags, and flats of mud—unlike anything she had seen before. It was plastic, like putty. Suddenly she dropped thigh-deep into a hole. The mud gripped her feet and legs; she couldn't pull herself out. "Howard," she called. She rolled, finally wrenching her legs free. Her shoes were two feet down. She crawled quickly to higher ground.

Howard wiped her off with newspapers he found in the trunk. "Damn shoes cost me a hundred bucks." Howard laid newspapers across the seat. Shivering, she turned the heat on high. As they pulled away, a silver curve of tide swept slowly up the inlet.

Wrapped in their sleeping bag on the floor of their apartment, she said. "If I had died, swallowed up by that mud, what would you do?"

"Is this a trick question? I guess I'd go back to Utah."

"Whatever else you do," she said, "don't do those Mormon things to me."

"What are you talking about? Work for the dead?"

"Yes," she said.

"In the temple?"

"I don't even want to hear about it."

"What's the big deal?" He stared at her. "No bodies involved. Just names on slips of paper."

"I knew that."

"Vicarious ordinance work. First is baptism and the gift of the Holy Ghost," he said. "Then endowment and sealing. It's all so they can progress—" he showed his teeth, "—change out of themselves, like Eve."

"None of it," she said. "Swear to me. I want none of it done to me. It's a lie. You shouldn't give hope to *anybody* when there is no hope. Especially not to yourself."

Lying in their new bed while Allison slept, he thought about her repugnance and anger at work for the dead. Seen from her eyes it did seem peculiar—baptizing a child dead for a century or joining a man and woman whose bodies lay decomposing in the ground. He had never considered the idea that someone might see it as a dishonest manipulation of hope. What *would* he do if she died? He doubted that her vicarious baptism would make him feel he would see her again. If he found a way of getting his temple privileges back, it was unlikely that he, an unrepentant sinner, could be bound to a woman who would probably be a heretic in the afterlife. He had been so frightened of losing her that he had followed her to Alaska, but what if the recent motions of spirit were just his fearful imagination? If there was no following, life here was a lonely terror. He wrapped his arms around Allison; she moaned and shifted slightly away. "I would despair," he whispered. "That's what I'd do." Then he wondered if she was right, that his fresh desire for faith was merely a retreat from a fear he could not endure.

The next morning they drove south along the inlet. "Boor tide," said a service station attendant after they described the curve of water sweeping over the mud. "You were lucky to see it." The summer before, he said, a couple had gone three-wheeling out onto the mud at low tide. Their vehicle became mired, and when they climbed off, the mud fastened around the woman's ankles like a vice. After trying uselessly to free her, the man finally went for help, but the tide rose eight feet during the hour and a half he was gone. Allison imagined her own feet bound, like the Goshute woman, her arms and hair floating free. When they were back on the road, she told Howard what she had pictured, and he laughed. "Cosmic. Another sister in death."

Allison shivered, "It reminded me of my brother, when I climbed out to the roof, and he was trapped inside. I get paranoid when I think about it."

"I'm sorry," he said. "I didn't remember."

"How could you have remembered?"

"I thought there was nothing irrational about you. What you just described is like my dream of falling through darkness."

"Fearing death is not irrational. It's a biological reaction. Every organism fears its own end. Hearing the voices of God and dead ancestors—that's another story."

"I don't physically hear voices. But I do fear death." The highway left the inlet and entered tangled forest. "I do fear death." Then off to their right emerged a massive snow-covered peak with a river of white glacier flowing down its side toward them. Suddenly something swelled inside, the crest of an emotional wave which had no apparent origin or cause. He opened his mouth to tell her but no words came.

They stopped the car and jogged together up a trail. To her, Howard seemed perpetually wide-eyed—at the moose they jumped, at the expanse of mountain above them, the white-topped peaks distant across the inlet, but especially he appeared to be surprised at her. She constantly found him watching her, his mouth working.

They found a mossy bank, where the branches of a pine curved around, and she kissed him and removed his clothing.

"I'm a biological mechanism," he said. "You touch me and drugs flow into my veins."

"You want to be unaffected? You worried it's not *spiritual*? Not spiritual sex? Isn't that a contradiction even for you? My crazy religious aunt said the flesh is an enemy to God."

"Spirit and body are one thing. Not separate. No hormones without spirit. The reach of electricity across synapses is spiritual."

"Not for me," she said. "This kind of talk is a real downer for me." She looked down. "For you too," she said. "Your flight of abstraction distracted you."

"No," he said, "it's those hikers coming up the trail." She wrestled into her clothing, but, for no reason she could figure, he bolted, bounding through the bushes like a buck deer. "The spirit is not an abstraction," he called back to her, his white butt flashing.

Making love against the shower wall, water running warm down his back and thighs, Howard imagined someone in the next apartment with his ear against a water glass. As if Howard was the person listening, he heard the fast breathing, the soft thumping, the animal noises which fell from both their mouths. "She is mine," Howard said to the committee of gods and ancestors eavesdropping, the clamor of voices he knew was just imagination. "I will not give her up." His skin slipped across her skin, one flesh, infinitely precious. Then came the uncertain voice of Grandmother God, "Who wants you to give her up? Why do you cling to sin, when you can embrace joy?"

Afterward they ate supper together, smiling at each other across the small table. He felt pleasantly spent and believed that they might stay together, building toward marriage, creating a unity of flesh and spirit, one being, out of such moments. He could feel it happening, the construction of something out of touch and talk. He wondered if he could do the same with his faith, reconstruct faith out of the flashes of light he had felt since meeting Allison. Could he embrace hope by choice, giving it priority over fear? Because they weren't married, he would be cast out of the Community of Saints. His healing required a paradox, that he view Allison as a foreigner, or there would be no converting, *and* as a fellow citizen with the Saints, or there could be no true marriage. No shaking of his head could clear the confusion. The City of God must be like no city on earth. On earth obedience and love constantly battle.

Ten

During Allison's first week of work, Howard took the bus to the University of Alaska in Anchorage—smaller than the University of Utah, where he had planned to go before the water of his life overflowed its ditch. He found himself full of hope at the possibilities before him: school in a new place, a woman to love who loved him, and a culture outside of missionary and Utah culture. It would be a time of freedom to re-create himself in an image closer to his nature than what others had imagined for him.

He found the administration building and walked up to a window with a young woman behind it; her hair was a startling green. Even the late deadline for adding classes had passed, she told him. It would take another week to get admitted, the best he could hope for was starting classes after Christmas. "I can catch up," he said, but she simply called, "Next!"

He ate lunch in the cafeteria and strolled down the glass-enclosed walkway that led from building to building. When Alaskan blizzards came, students would walk to their classes encased in glass. The experience would be extraordinary, as if the classes were open to the caprice and beauty of the spruce forest which surrounded each building. But for now he was only a tourist. Another problem: even after he was admitted, he could only take classes in general biology, nothing more specialized. They didn't have range management. He thought about sitting in the apartment all fall and then trying to get excited about material he'd already covered at the University of Utah. A year of life wasted.

He walked the mile to Alaska Pacific University, and found the same situation, with a degree less suited to his needs—Environmental Science—and tuition twice as high as that at the nearby UAA.

Frustrated, he decided to explore his new city. He took a bus downtown toward the Alaskan Museum of Natural History. Inside, he found small models of the people who had lived in Anchorage anciently—miniature Eskimos dragging a tiny whale onto an icy shore, small fishermen with a wooden salmon trap shaped like a funnel, Aleuts who lived in houses which were mostly underground. He wondered about the origin of those ancient peoples. Scientists believed that they had traveled from Siberia across the Bering Strait. Mormons taught that Eden had been in what is now Missouri and that Noah's Ark had moved humanity to the Old World.

In the next room he found life-sized dwellings of more modern peoples—the Eskimo, the Aleutian Islander, the modern prospector. The designers of the display had modeled large figures with Athapaskan features, but with skin, eyes, and hair uniformly gray, the same dead gray as the water in the inlet. The native dwellings were rounded, not the square walls of modern peoples. Inside each were a man and a woman, various children. He imagined surviving through the howling winter with Allison in a round underground home, far from the city.

Inside the prospector's cabin, a gray-faced man weighed gold. Had Howard's ancestor returned daily to such a cabin with her gold dust and nuggets? Like Howard, she must have felt excited, but also lonely and displaced. Perhaps she had married or found a companion. She must have thought about Utah and her family, two thousand miles away.

Outside, he wandered closer to the inlet, the edge of the city— houses, streets and yards—suddenly dropped fifteen feet, marking the edge of the earthquake fault. Grass had grown over the long wound in the landscape; roads were re-paved. Out in the inlet, a freighter moved toward open sea. He jogged along the coastal trail, running for an hour before he came to the bluff above the inlet where he had stood on his first morning in Anchorage. From this new vantage, the whole city seemed to be sliding, certainly not a place brimming with possibility. He turned and ran along Northern Lights Boulevard until he saw the black brow of their apartment building.

He was bone tired, but after his shower he walked east until he found a convenience store where he bought a newspaper. He spent the rest of the afternoon looking through the want ads. Most of the tourists had fled, and the prime salmon run was finished in Bristol Bay. Work is nearly impossible to find here in winter, they said, when he called the employment office.

Mid-week he found a job, which he kept for ten hours. He had borrowed Allison's car and driven past the Portage Glacier and across to Seward, nearly a two-hour drive. At the pier he saw a sign for crew to clean oil from the shore of an island ten miles out. Back in Anchorage he phoned the number and discovered that the boat left daily at six.

When Howard rose at three-thirty, he knew he had been a fool to take the job. Arriving at the dock, he was the ninth man to crowd into the boat, which was hardly larger than his father's truck. While the craft was moving out of the bay and onto the ocean, Howard was queasy but able to control his nausea by looking out at the water. Then, so that one of the men could take water samples, the boat slowed, crawling up one side of a mountain of water, sliding down the other, rising and sliding. Howard clung to the edge of the cabin, his eyes on the distant coast. Then he smelled the stench of fish and looked down, where a dead salmon floated. Even after his stomach was empty, he continued dry retching. He found a bucket and cleaned the side of the boat. Crossing back to the mainland that evening, the whole world rocked and heaved. Howard lay down in the sleeping compartment under the bow, but that didn't help. He had to get up several times to vomit, bent over the side of the boat.

"I quit," he said as soon as they touched shore.

"Why didn't you tell me you'd never been on the ocean before?" said the foreman.

He phoned the city soccer association, but the leagues were over for the year. On several evenings he and Allison jogged to a park and kicked her ball around, but the pleasure for both of them was the dynamics of running with a team. He hiked the foothills and mountains, wary of bears and moose. Once he nearly jogged into the side of a bull, antlered, tough, and rangy. The bull stared at him with the gaze of the wild-eyed cow his father called "the Sunday School Bitch." She had regularly put them both on the fence. Howard turned and raced down the trail; he climbed a tree, waiting for the beast to come thundering after him. The bull never came.

One day, while Allison was at work, he used the last of his money to rent a seat on a small plane which took him on a half-day tour of Denali. Peering through the windows at the gigantic mountain, he imagined himself in the middle of a movie. Every second he expected to hear the engine sputter, the first sign of another great adventure.

The next day he borrowed three hundred dollars from Allison and bought a backpack, a pair of boots, a prospector's pan, and a guide to prospecting. Dropping Allison at work, he drove toward Palmer on the Old Glenn Highway. The streams that fed the inlet were ice-rimmed and broad like most rivers in Utah. He smelled spruce, fresh water, and a musky plant that didn't grow in Utah. Even under the growing snowpack up high, the mountains were verdant, unlike the desert where all life is marginal. He squatted until he couldn't feel his frozen fingers or his cramped legs. After three days of work he had about half a teaspoon of color. He had no idea whether it was really gold. He put the gold pan in a closet in their apartment.

He had mixed emotions about his first week. Given the time and space to wander the city and surrounding mountains, he could step out of the definitions of his previous life. He had always driven himself toward goals created for him by others. His teachers and mother had expected him to become a biologist, and he had thought that his goal as he pushed himself through high school and the first two years of college. Then his whole culture from the prophet to Belinda had expected him to go on a mission. That experience had not been the unfolding of his true self before God. Even now, he occasionally felt like a kept man, living on Allison's wages in her apartment, captured to service her needs, when really any man would do.

Howard's mother sent them ironic postcards from Utah. "Having a great time," said the caption, "wish you were here." Howard stared at the picture—a man in woolly chaps riding a giant, antlered jackrabbit. Allison grinned, wondering how the image could make him homesick.

Emily wrote a letter too, which Howard read out loud. "Walter drove the cattle out west. Most nights, he stays in Max's cabin. To be closer to the cows, he says. Beware Allison, I think the longing to be a hermit is genetic. He comes back for Sunday dinner. We talk some, usually ending up arguing. You'd think land is land, money is money, but we view them so differently."

"She'd go to school if she had money," said Allison.

"They're changing too fast," said Howard.

"Good for them," she said. "Stirs up the murky waters."

"You preach change for others, but not for yourself."

"What? I left Houston. I'm living with a visionary fanatic. Huge changes."

Howard read on. "The new Relief Society president, Sister Nebekar, is very timid and by-the-book. The bishop said in church that righteous women submit to their husbands. I think righteous men submit to their wives. Women still visit me with their troubles. I tell them, God loves you. Sin is not the cause of your unhappiness. God loves you. I say it until it's a chant. We pray when we're finished talking, but I don't lay my hands on their heads. I hope I can get my calling back or get a new one. Love, Mom."

Allison stood behind Howard and rubbed his shoulders. "We could send her a check."

"We couldn't. I would like to give my mother money to go to school, but I can't. Why don't you ever call your own parents?"

She shrugged. "I don't want to be your mother's daughter. I just like her. I'd like to help her out." Then she realized that she didn't call her parents because they didn't need her.

"Patronage is not dead. The grease of money solves all problems."

"Matronage," she said. "It doesn't condescend or demand repayment."

"Pffft. You bought me, now you want her. How's your job going? Are you happy?" His voice was harsh.

"Yes," she said. "It's very satisfying."

After the first snow, Allison bought them both cross-country skis. Howard spent his mornings falling down, scraping the skis across rocks because the snow wasn't deep enough. One Saturday they drove above Anchorage to where the snow was deeper. A trail led along the timberline toward a bare ridge. He watched the other skiers thrusting forward with their arms and legs, and he tried to imitate. Allison caught on fairly quickly, but Howard still felt awkward.

"I thought everybody skied in Utah," said Allison.

"Ranchers don't ski," he said.

"You're not a rancher now," she said.

"How could I not know that?" he said, and heard the bitterness in his own voice. "Scares me I'll never get back home. Skiing my life away. My grandfather's uncle was an old bachelor rancher, had a place just west of Rockwood, up against the mountains. He went to Salt Lake City for church conference one weekend."

"Cowboy loose in town on a Saturday night."

"He met a woman. Monday he met her family and Tuesday he married her. They moved into her mother's house, he thought for a short honeymoon. But the old woman was sick; his wife didn't want to leave her alone. He never came home again. His cattle mixed with his brother's herds. Finally someone filed on the water and the land was useless."

"You talk about him as if he lost his soul."

"He lost his land," Howard said.

"Howard, you can never slide back inside your old skin."

"How can you say that? How can you keep saying that I haven't changed enough?" He knew that she thought his losses superficial—home and land and church. Even if he still hoped to return to all three, she refused to try to understand his longing. He pushed off on his skis. As he topped the ridge, his arms and legs were shaking from the effort, but she was only twenty-five yards behind him. When she came up, she didn't try to talk. The forest sloped toward the water. Anchorage sprawled below them on the margin between mountain and inlet. Then he swooped down off the ridge toward the car, falling only twice.

That night she said, "I'm sorry." Then: "But—" She frowned and turned away, for which he was grateful. He couldn't think what to say to her that hadn't already been said.

The next week he found work at Salmon, Inc. But the ticket to Naknek on Bristol Bay was six hundred dollars, as much as a ticket to Utah. He would get his money back if he stayed to the end of the contract.

"You don't need to do this," Allison said when he asked her for a loan.

He told her about the job, showed her the pamphlets of fishing boats and beautiful shoreline. "Pay is low at first, but there's overtime."

"You'd fly back on the weekends?"

He told her it would be too expensive but that the job would only last another month or so, until the season was over.

"Why not just fly to Utah then, work there for a month?"

He stared. "I hadn't thought of that. I hadn't thought of just going home for a month."

"You won't come back if you go home." She took his face in her hands. "You're holding your breath till you get back to Utah? Like your mission?"

Naknek was a harbor and rows of wooden, ramshackle barracks, mostly empty. During the winter it shrank to about the size of Rockwood, two or three hundred people in a small village near the barracks—a grocery, a trading post/hardware store, and six bars. Howard's job title was slimer; for twelve hours a day he stood at a long, wooden table, ankle deep in muck, blood and mud mingled, and lined up sub-grade salmon for the header—$5.90 an hour for the first eight hours, $7.90 after that. The slimer opposite was from Sand Point, Idaho, and talked constantly about the Nez Perce girls he'd had back home.

A hamburger was $9, a glass of milk two-and-a-half bucks. Howard slept in a bunk, on a mattress that seemed as old as his grandfather's in the cabin. He woke with red marks all over him—the descendants of the bugs that had plagued the original gold rushers. After a week he gave it up and flew back, losing his $600 because he reneged on his contract. His check for the week was $316, net.

He cashed his check, laid the money on Allison's laptop, and slept for a day. When he woke, he found a newspaper ad for a worker in a dairy, an hour by car from Anchorage on the far side of Palmer. Allison bought a bike to ride to work; he could use her Mustang.

Mornings and evenings, he attached the milkers to the cows' teats, the air heavy with the familiar effluvium of manure and milk. He named the cow that always shouldered her way to the front of the line Lead Dog, after Alison's tyrannical boss; the last cow he named Dwight, just so he could write and tell the old fart about it. The main drama was when a cow entered out of place, and the milkers, most of them natives, knew that a new order had been established. The cows' udders were so painfully tight that milk leaked on the ground in streams. Through the middle of the day he mixed feed, moved half-frozen manure with a front end loader, and cleaned the stainless steel equipment. He felt as though he were in heaven.

One day at the dairy he had heard on the radio that an aging bull moose, disoriented and enraged, wandered the streets of Anchorage. He imagined Allison trampled under his hooves and battered by his antlers. Because they had no phone, he nearly drove back to check on her. He knew his imaginings were unreasonable. But still he was anxious being away from her. After his fifteen-hour day, he generally drove too fast through the darkness, hardly looking at the snowy road, the dark mountains close above. Every night he was relieved to find her alive, warm in their bed or frowning down at her laptop.

Weekends he cooked for Allison and then after dinner they made love. Listening to the changes in her breathing as she drifted deeper toward sleep, he imagined her dead. If blood stopped in her veins, if electricity no longer enlivened her brain, she would be gone from him forever. He was frightened that she might lose interest in him and drift away, but imagining her death terrified him. They had never married, never pronounced covenants in the temple, never been sealed by the power of the priesthood. The bishop wrote him that he and Allison might remain separate throughout the eternities. What did God think? Howard knew he had proceeded foolishly, but still, it didn't feel like sin to love Allison. Sin, in this case, might be only disobedience, a principle he believed was evoked easily by his mission president, his teachers at church and school, and even his parents to force him to adopt their own vision for him. When he wrote his thoughts to his mother, she wrote back that it might be time for him to move beyond adolescent rebelliousness and join the adult world. If a man and a woman lived on an island with no other beings in the universe, they might not be sinning to join physically without a contract with God and other people. She wrote that the most frustrating and also most important part of her life had been negotiating with his father for four decades. If coupling were impulsive and temporary, that would be lost. That made sense to him, but didn't seem exactly positive. One night he told Allison that she was being naive to think that society was extraneous to a true marriage. "We have a contract," she told him. "We are in a testing period, a courtship for six months. After that, we'll see." Part of him liked the idea of a courtship with sex, but at the same time he was frightened that God would give him no concessions if one of them died. If their love was earthbound, they might never find each other in the next life.

One night he had his dream again; actually no one fell, but the feeling of terror was the same. He was sinking slowly into mud; then it was Allison going down into water and mud until darkness filled her mouth. He crouched on the side of the highway, clinging to her body. He tipped her head up; gray water ran from between her blue lips and she was lost forever.

After three weeks Allison decided that heaven was the wrong word for Anchorage. One day she stared at her computer screen while the compiler worked. Thirteen-hour days, as arduous as forced marches, had transformed her first impression, and she thought with longing of her free-lancing days when she'd had weeks of little work. Lisa Lead-Dog Orden had given Allison a glacier of programs to rewrite or debug. "I've never even had a boss before," she told Howard during one of their rare talks. Reality for her had become oil and code, code and oil.

Worse than that—Howard was unraveling. He'd become as clingy as a lost child. Her first week and a half of work, he had cooked for her every night, waiting inside their apartment, amorous as a new bride. At first it was sweet. Then he asked for money to outfit the kitchen, he tried cooking with unusual spices, he was sad when a dish didn't work out well. He was so odd—clutching at her, false and happy. Once he smiled across the table at her, a sappy, puppy dog-friendly smile. "More?" he said, holding out the plate of skewered shrimp and vegetables. Eliot's pale white houseman in the flesh, trite as a revelation.

She laid down her fork. "Dammit, Howard," she said. "What the hell is going on? What is this—some asinine scene from *Leave It to Beaver?*"

He still held the plate. She thought he'd turn and dump it in the sink. "I don't know who I am," he finally said. That night in bed he had turned his back to her, face to the wall. The next morning he decided to go to work at Naknek, the job that had lasted half a week. Even after getting the job at the dairy, he was an emotional black hole. She stared at her computer screen and chewed the sandwich she'd bought from a machine. Throughout history women had abandoned their former identities and gone with their men. Men were not so resilient.

Anchorage perched on a ledge between the Chugach Mountains and Cook Inlet. She and Howard had walked at the north end of the city where the streets dead-ended, starting up again ten feet below, more evidence of the big earthquake, when a section of the city had slid toward the ocean. Howard had asked her, "Has it ever stopped sliding?"

Now the snow became permanent; night seemed to stretch longer every time she went home. During the days Houstonians moved indoors, out of the heat, but at night the edges of the city became alive with bright motion. She used to roll down Westheimer toward the Cadillac Bar, driving with the top of her Mustang down—the warm and humid wind blowing into her face. Streams of cars passed her, mostly kids ranging the night, hanging out the windows of cars, faces flashing past. One night high school boys driving a white Mercedes called to her, "Nice car. Take us for a ride." From a jet once she had seen the streets and freeways of Houston as a huge wheel of white and amber light. The jet had banked and the wheel had turned, spinning her off to Chicago, where she had lived with Eliot through a bitter cold winter. She felt ready to jump again.

The next week she convinced Lisa that long-distance troubleshooting was silly; on-site work would be more efficient. With software managing interaction between a computer and something else, a massive drill rig for instance, anything could be wrong—software, hardware, the equipment itself. "Fly me to the people who are having the problem. It will save days. Send me up to Prudhoe Bay." Early in October Allison flew to the North Slope. She'd be there for two weeks, then she'd have two weeks off. She solved the problems quickly; the operators on the job looked at her afterward as if to say, "That was simple. Why didn't I think of it?"

She didn't like the North Slope, a thousand miles of howling wasteland, flat as Houston, barren as Howard's desert. But she liked flying back and forth, floating above the jagged mountains, the lakes and forests. It seemed to her to be an imaginary land. Once, when the jet banked to descend into Fairbanks, she saw a small pack of wolves sunning themselves on a hillside. She pointed them out to the grizzled well rigger who sat next to her. "Wolves mate for life," Allison said to the rigger. "Mormons for eternity."

"I wouldn't mate with neither one," said the rigger.

On Allison's first week back from the North Slope, clouds blew in from the northwest, across the gray water of the inlet. The city was swathed in snow. That night Allison answered the phone—Emily. "I start school after Christmas. I can have a degree in accounting in three years." She paused. "He still won't sell. It has me beside myself. Some day I'll pay you back."

"Don't think about paying me back," said Allison.

"I've thought about getting Walter declared mentally incompetent."

"Is he?"

"Has been for years. Now what's left of his mind has gone west. He's taken up prospecting."

She lifted the receiver from her mouth. "Howard, your mother thinks that prospecting is grounds for getting someone committed."

"It is in Utah," said Howard.

"Not committed," said Emily. "Declared. Being declared wouldn't affect him at all. And when he's in town he skulks about."

"She says your father skulks about. Another sign. Your average skulker is mentally unstable and can't hold property. That means you, Howard." She talked into the receiver. "Your son already shows an inclination to skulk. I suppose it's genetic on the Y chromosome."

"But unfortunately prospecting and skulking aren't enough to keep someone from owning property. What gripes me is that I've found another buyer who will pay even more for that bench property. She's a rich masseuse from Salt Lake."

"Masseuse?"

"She wants to build a big lodge up in the pines on the ridge."

"Where she would give tired ranchers a rubdown? That'd go over big in Rockwood."

"I don't think ranchers are her clientele or she wouldn't be rich. Anyway the money was right: $40,000."

"$40,000," said Allison to Howard. "She wants to sell the bench land to a masseuse."

"Might be worth selling. Let me talk to her." Allison held the phone away from him.

"He and a partner," said Emily, "have been poking around in the desert buttes. This guy wants half share in the ranch before he'll tell Walter where the mother lode is."

"That'll thrill Howard," said Allison, grinning. "The farm slipping away to a stranger."

"What in hell is happening down there?" said Howard. Suddenly his voice had no good humor in it. He grabbed the phone, and she dropped it, her hands held wide to show her displeasure. He talked to his mother for half an hour—gesturing, pacing, pleading. The rest of the evening he was in a black funk, once again counting his losses.

The next Sunday Howard bolted awake. His body was clenched so tight that he was sure veins in his neck and the backs of his hands would burst. He lay on the bed and waited for the hand of God to slap him from life in an instant. Finally the panic left, and he found himself hungry. Without waking Allison, he ate four eggs and eight pieces of toast. He was bewildered because he thought he had worked past his terror of God.

That day he walked from street to street. He decided that his own fear of God was unreliable, but that he needed to discover a basis for trust. Near the ocean was a Catholic church, which was empty. He walked to the front and examined the stylized statue of Christ, smelled the perfume of candles and incense. He imagined the chant of the priest in Latin. The Catholic God was abstract, perfect, distant; sitting on his throne, he calculated the mathematics of symphonies, sunsets, repentance, and the food chain of the Alaskan tundra. Certainly this God was unlike either the malevolent Old Testament patriarch of his felt experience or the kindly grandfather described in Mormon Sunday school. On his mission Howard had gone to a Pentecostal revival. People sang and shouted and danced around; God was like a fever in the believers' veins.

Perhaps God was androgynous. Not like the cruel Old Testament God, not like the grandfather of his childhood, or the businessman of his mission, a God who delegated to men first. When Howard prayed to any of these patriarchal images, he had no feeling for himself or what he had done, nothing but guilt and fear. Even the Grandmother God had given him scant comfort; she smiled and he felt that everything would work out. But she seemed to lie; it wasn't working out.

Allison's claim that they needed time to test each other and that the only true bond was directly between the man and the woman made sense, but at the same time he felt that in his life sin and love mingled. He couldn't separate them. If God was neither male nor female, God might not be embroiled in sexuality, confused and debilitated by conflict and division. But he also knew that this picture of God made no sense biologically. The Mormon idea of God as a complex family of beings made more sense.

From the Catholic church, he walked to a Christian Scientist reading room, where he talked to the attendant. "Suppose a man commits a terrible sin, but committing it he finds that it was also the most beautiful thing in his life. What should he do?"

The woman stared at him. "Rephrase the question," she said. Then she turned back to her reading, shutting him out. Walking home, he decided she wasn't just putting him off, but still it didn't help to know he was asking the wrong questions. He wanted answers, not more questions. Grandmother God giggled, one hand to her mouth as she rocked. "Silly lamb," she said. "You think this world is full of magic?"

Toward the end of October, Howard received notice by certified letter that the high council in Hamblin was taking disciplinary action against him.

"You wanted this," Allison said, feeling sudden panic. "I can see the relief in your face. You want men who know nothing about your situation to pass judgment on your morality."

"I'll take three days off at the dairy."

"I should tie you up and lock you in the closet."

"This could put me right with God," he said.

"Shut up! How does getting kicked out of a church make you right with God?"

He shrugged, unable to explain. Submitting himself to the charity of God's representatives might help him requite his image of God as cruel and vindictive.

"I'll loan you the money for the ticket," she said. "I'll give you the money."

"I owe you too much already," he said.

"What? You don't want to be dependent? You don't want to use my money?" After she wrote out the check, he drove to the agency to pick up his ticket. She flicked on her computer and stared at the screen, figuring what she'd do when he didn't come back from the desert.

So before he left, she married him. He said, "If I were a foreigner who needed asylum, would you give me a technical marriage, make it possible for me to stay in the States?" She recognized it as a Howardish ploy. "If I'm married, they may not excommunicate me."

"Will this make your virtuous? Will your piety return? Can you understand how offensive this is to me—to be lusted after and then married out of religious scruples, not love?"

He opened his mouth and shut it. She stomped out and drove her Mustang up past Chickaloon. His motives were distasteful to her. She thought wryly that most of her anger had to do with his refusal to abandon his religion, which had been her plan for him. Driving nearly eighty and watching for policemen, she thought that if all religion were cut out of his being, he would no longer be Howard, no longer be the man she was choosing to have with her.

When she returned, he said, "It terrifies me that you might leave me. It makes me so I can't speak rationally. But I want *you*. I want to be bound to you."

"But I want to be have free commitment, not marriage, which distorts the relationship."

"I know you want that," he said. "I just don't understand the difference."

"Our one month of trial has not been an overwhelming success. I wanted two years." She turned to him. "Being married will help you with them? Help you stay in your church?"

"I think it will."

She considered. While she could see nothing positive in his church, it was something essential to him. "No common property."

"What if we buy a house?"

"We don't want a house," she said. "No joint management of money. You work until you pay back what you owe me. Then we each pay our own bills."

"I can't pay half of this apartment and half of food."

"One fourth. Until you get your degree."

"Fine," he said.

"No one has assumed priority in terms of where we live."

"You mean we stay in Anchorage," he said. "You mean *you* have priority."

"I'm saying you're not dragging me away from a good job back to Utah when your father can't run the ranch anymore." She looked at him, waiting. "It's the best compromise I can give."

"Very vague." he said.

"You want it definite?"

When he shook his head, she said, "No children."

"No children! Why get married?"

"Good question."

He deliberated. "No children until you're ready."

"Yes. No damn sneaky rhetoric about procreation and bringing little spirits to earth."

"Okay," he said.

"And," she said, grabbing his shirt-front, "never, never, never call me wife. I'm not wife. Not possession, servant, breeder of children, not any of that." Her face was alive with anger.

He nodded.

"All this in writing."

"You don't trust me."

"You got that right."

"I can't believe you changed your mind. Gave up your one moral principle."

"My one moral principle! Hell, you're blind to my morality. Anyway, I'm already married to you. I've been prayed over by your mother and insulted by your brothers. That's marriage, isn't it?"

The next day they stood before a justice of the peace with two street people he dragged in as witnesses. After the brief ceremony, they went out to dinner, Texas style ribs and baked potato. Then they found a bar with a country band, and Allison taught Howard the Texas two-step. She bought a bottle of champagne, guzzled some without a glass, poured a little on his head. He smiled and went into the men's room to wash. When it was half gone, she dragged him out to the parking lot and broke the bottle against the front bumper of the Mustang. "I christen you Howard II, the Alaska Rover." Howard picked up the pieces of glass and threw them in a dumpster.

"You what?" Allison's mother said on the phone. "I saw it in his eyes. Like a pit bull. Now he'll get you pregnant. Are you ready for that?"

"I'm on the pill."

"His determined semen will find a way. He'll call it a miracle. Why did you do it?"

Allison explained about the disciplinary action.

"I want to talk to him."

She motioned Howard over, and he placed his cheek next to her cheek, so they could both hear and talk. He explained why, even though he was married, he would still have to go to Utah. "It's a matter of timing," he said. "I'll either be excommunicated or disfellowshipped."

"Disfellowshipped," said Allison's mother. "What an ungodly term. Sounds like some kind of castration."

"It means I'm kicked out but not kicked out," said Howard.

"I don't understand that kind of thinking," said Allison's father.

"Every religious group discriminates," said her mother. "If someone breaks the rules, they are a pollutant to the group. It's a particularly *Christian* tradition. Mormons aren't unusual. By the way, a month ago two Mormons came to see us. A huge one and a small nervous one. I told them that instead of flying home, you rode up with Allison. They were impressed."

"Impressed?" said Allison's father. "They were damned excited."

"It's against the rules for a missionary to be alone with a woman," Howard said. "You've made me a legend in the mission."

"I was worried that's what I'd done," said Allison's mother.

Eleven

"Keep your mouth shut," his mother said as they started across the flat toward Rockwood, "and they won't excommunicate you. Try to defend yourself, and they'll think you're rebellious and unrepentant. Tell them that you're married and then keep quiet. Let them talk themselves into forgiving you."

"So you know all about high council courts?"

"I know how it goes in meetings with the priesthood. You plant a seed, it grows, and the brethren claim it as their own. Works every time. And it's not called court now. It's a disciplinary council. No assumption of innocence. It's downright un-American."

"It's still a court of love," said Howard. "And it will put all this behind me."

"Oh, Howard, you've always been so worldly and yet so innocent." She laid her hand on his arm. "Even if they do the worst and excommunicate you, you can work your way back in. They'll let you be re-baptized in a year."

"I've started thinking of God as a grandmother and a grandfather, patriarch and matriarch of a clan, all of them working out the affairs of the earth, sometimes playing tricks, sometimes blessing, sometimes cruel. Maybe I don't belong."

"I recommend you start with that," she said sarcastically. "Howard, they're disciplining you for fornication, not apostasy. If you get close enough to people, so they open up, you find that they believe a wide range of things about God."

He felt space opening around him—the wide bowl of the desert, the violet peaks. The knife-blade shape of the Goshute range rose toward them, as familiar as his mother's voice, both stroking him calm. Still, after Alaska, the colors seemed washed-out—dusty green cedars, gray sagebrush, yellow cheat grass. The highway led straight as a ruler-edge toward the black-green trees of Rockwood. The sky was deeper blue than in Alaska, the air drier, less misty.

His mother frowned. "How does it happen that a man has no more use for human companionship?"

"You mean Dad? It's just the work. He tells himself that being with the cattle is a sacrifice he has to make."

"Why not come home?"

"Long drive when he's tired. He starts a game of cribbage with his partner and then it's too late. Some of my best memories are playing cribbage with Grandpa and him. Maybe it's a male thing—a male community."

"His partner's quit." She gave him a half grin. "Male bonding. Over cribbage? If it could be a coyote or a rattler sitting across the table from him, or a computer, your grandfather would have been just as happy. You, his own grandson. Did he tell you any stories? Talk to you at all about what was going on in your head?"

"He told me stories. He told about Marilyn Monroe living on top of the ridge."

"I should have guessed he'd tell you that one. Did sharing that fantasy make the two of you closer? That man was completely sunk into himself. I'm frightened that Walter will soon be lost to me."

At the house Howard quickly changed his clothing, hoping to get to the cabin before nightfall. When he came down, his mother was in the kitchen making up a food box. "I'm going out with you. About time I delivered another load of food." She dropped in four cans of tuna. "While he seems to no longer need people, I need even more to be in the middle of them."

"Has the bishop given you a new calling?"

"No," she said. "So I bear my testimony on Fast Sunday." She sat in the driver's seat; he climbed in the other side. "A few women still come to me for advice. They're filled with guilt for the most petty things—can't get the washing done, husband doesn't like the food they cook, can't handle their children. I don't mean that their problems are really petty, but they have a load of guilt big enough to encompass adultery, murder, and treason and all they've done is make mistakes with their children or refuse their husband sex."

They topped the pass and westward spread the even drier desert of Goshute Hell. He looked past the oddly shaped bluffs, at Haystack Peak crouched pale against the sky, a hundred miles away on the border of Nevada.

"I tell them to set some limits with their husbands, something I wished I'd done. Their husbands say, 'I thought you liked being with the children all the time' or 'I didn't know you wanted to take an evening class.' Then they talk, these women say. Their lives aren't changed dramatically but their husbands respond differently to them. They stay home with the kids while their wives go out places or they help with the housework when their wives work. I wish I'd had more than six months as their leader." She paused, furrowing her brow. "I guess I've seemed too much a feminist, angry with men. Plenty of non-feminist women are angrier than I am. Mary Fieldsen believes that God invented polygamy because so few men make it to the celestial kingdom. Cynthia Peterson believes that the only chance men have is that at the judgment seat Christ weighs every married man and woman as if they are one creature. Augusta Jensen believes that God gave men the priesthood to temper their incarnate evil natures. I think there's nothing incarnate about it. Allison told me that any delicate spirit watered and fertilized with testosterone for nine months is going to turn aggressive."

"I hardly know you anymore," he said.

"You sound like Simon." Her face became tired. "He doesn't want me to change either."

They topped the last low hill before the ranch. "Look," Howard said, pointing toward a dark mass around the haystack—cattle. Closer he saw them shoving each other against the fence, stretching their long necks to scratch on the top wire. They found Howard's father sitting in the cabin. The fire had gone out and he had a blanket wrapped around his shoulders; he hadn't lit a lamp. The cabin smelled of old wood smoke, propane, and unwashed Rockwood male, the exact aroma of memory. He could have been walking in on his grandfather. Howard's father had a geological survey map laid out on the table in front of him. It was marked with red lines and yellow circles. He looked up, disoriented.

"Howard," he said. "Last week Albert told me they'd convened a court for you." Howard had never seen him so forlorn and old. "I sent a letter back with him, telling President Robinson what I know about your character. Did it help?"

Howard looked at him. "The court is tonight. Who is Albert?"

"A crooked snake," said Emily. "His former partner. Still slithering around."

"He's no crookeder than I am," said Walter. He faced Howard. "I wondered if you'd even bother to come. I thought it might be a good idea to stay away."

"Dad," Howard said, "Allison and I are married."

Walter stood and clasped him on the arms. "I'll write another letter. They should certainly take that into account. I mean, isn't marriage a form of repentance?"

"Some might say it's embracing your sin," said Emily—a slow smile.

"The cattle are about to break into the stack," said Howard.

"I was just going out. Look at this. These circles mark formations which could have gold or silver in them. You know that this whole area was booming early in this century. There's still a lot of ore left."

Howard moved the maps to one side; his father looked up. "We haven't fed the cattle together since the winter before my mission."

While his father pulled on his overshoes and coat, Howard cut some pitchy pinion kindling and lit a fire in the cook stove. The inside of the stove was thick with black, shiny creosote, which could burst into flames if the stove became too hot. Stuart Eastman's deer hunting cabin had burned five or six years earlier because, year by year, the creosote had built up. Howard's mother lit the lantern and started peeling potatoes. He walked to the gate of the stackyard. His father started the tractor and pulled it up to the gate. Howard climbed through the fence, threw one bale back over, and carried it a hundred yards away from the stack into the field. Most of the cattle followed, enough that he could open the gate while his father pulled the tractor inside. Three animals went in on the opposite side, but he and his father drove them back out. Howard shut the gate against the rest of the herd.

He climbed to the top of the stack and kicked a bale from the edge down onto the wagon. At his next kick, the corner of the stack fell, a tangle of bales tumbling down. "Are you all right?" he shouted, scooting himself back to a more secure place.

"I wasn't on the wagon," said his father from below. "Don't *you* fall. You might injure your dignity." Howard threw bales down while his father stacked them. From the stack he saw that the blue tarp was gone from the pool where the Goshutes had been buried; the only evidence of a dig was the disturbed mud at one edge of the pool. Low, soft clouds appeared overhead and then floated across the flat. He examined the faint lines of fences, borders of the Rockwood land.

When Howard was small, his grandfather had homesteaded the farm. It was not a part of the land which came to the family from James Darren; Howard had always felt that it was more like wilderness than the settled Rockwood fields and pastures. He loved the low gray shadscale brush, tall rugged greasewood, even the white alkali flat. The tall black ridge, standing like a wall behind them, was a form from myth, a pattern for his dreams.

Howard and his father loaded fifty bales. Then his father drove slowly out of the stack yard toward the cattle, while Howard kicked the bales off the back. He tried to imagine Allison with him, driving the wagon. It would be a frosty August in Houston before that happened. The first cows ran behind, extending their noses high, reaching toward the hay with their long, thick tongues. Together he and his father walked back through the herd, cutting the wires and spreading out the sections. It felt good to be working with his father.

They ate and Howard got ready to go back to Rockwood. His mother said she was staying the night with Walter. "My presence won't help you at the court."

His father didn't want to be there either. "I couldn't stand it," he said. "I'd sooner watch you strapped to a table and cut open by half-wit surgeons." As Howard drove away, the two of them stood together in the doorway of the cabin, framed in light from the lantern.

Sixteen men dressed in dark suits sat around the oval table: Brothers Sorenson, Allen, Jacobs, Richards, Dakin; his father's uncle, Edgar Rockwood; others he only recognized; three people he didn't know at all. President Robinson smiled from the head of the table. Howard had played soccer with his son and knew him as a fair and compassionate man. "You've never been formally released from your mission, so you needed to come before this body to report. Do you have anything to say?"

Howard let his breath out—a long sigh. "I had a good mission. I was happy with the people I converted." He told them about Sister Valdez and Sister Montoya. Brother Allen frowned deeper as Howard talked.

"Bishop Hansen informed me that something irregular happened at the end. Could you share what that was?"

"You know already," said Howard.

President Robinson looked down at his hands. No one spoke.

Howard said, "I had sex with my wife before we were married." He remembered his mother's advice and said nothing else.

"You said wife?" said Brother Jacobs, whose hair had thinned since Howard last saw him. "You've since married the woman?" Several of the men smiled and nodded.

"Yes," said Howard. "We're married now."

"They live in Anchorage," said Uncle Edgar. "His—wife—has a job up there."

"Down there," said Howard.

The men all stared at him.

"It's at sea level." Damn, he thought, keep it shut.

"When did you marry?" said one of the men Howard didn't know. His head was bald, rimmed with white hair.

"How is that relevant?" asked Brother Jacobs.

"The timing might indicate how repentant he is."

They all looked at Howard. "Last week," he said. "Actually, the beginning of this week."

The bald man frowned, considering.

"Repentance is repentance in my mind," said Brother Jacobs.

"Or was it an act of desperation?"

"Desperation?" said Brother Jacobs. "She wasn't pregnant, was she?"

"No," said Howard.

"So there was nothing constraining him to marry her. How is it an act of desperation?"

"What do you think about the covenants you made as a missionary?" said Brother Allen.

"I thought of them as important, but obviously—" He shut his mouth and waited.

One of the other strangers leaned forward; he wore a bright red tie and a cream-colored suit. "Has this woman converted?"

"No. She was never converted to marriage either. She thinks it causes hypocrisy and entraps women. I finally talked her into it. That's the only reason she married me."

"How many times did you sin?" asked Brother Small.

"Again," said Brother Jacobs. "What possible difference does that make?"

"The difference between a stumble and a head-long fall," said the president.

"They've lived together in Anchorage since the beginning of September," said Uncle Edgar. "They were married last week. It's not as if it's a mystery what was happening."

Three of the men folded their hands in front of them. When they realized the simultaneity of motion, they all pulled their hands back.

"But she was the woman you wanted to marry," said the man with the red tie. "The woman you love."

"Yes," said Howard. "I love her."

"You said you talked her into marriage. How did you persuade her?"

Howard considered how to answer. "I told her it was important to me that we have a legal and moral commitment."

"Do you think you could have used that logic before you sinned?" asked Brother Allen.

"I knew it wouldn't work then," Howard said. "I knew she'd just leave me."

Brother Allen nodded.

"We're here to help you get on with your life," said the man in the red tie.

"Have you done anything to reconcile yourself to God?"

Howard thought about his prayer-like conversations with the roomful of gods. "After it happened I felt cut off from everything I was. I have prayed. I've been attending church in Anchorage." He wanted to say more, but he shut his mouth.

"Have you thought of the effect on other missionaries?" asked Brother Allen.

"I've thought that I've made my parents unhappy, God unhappy, my companion Peterson unhappy, the people in Rockwood." He nearly opened his mouth to say that like Joseph Smith he would, if necessary, go to hell to retrieve the woman he loved. "My mission president unhappy."

"Do you have anything else to say?" asked President Robinson.

"This may not make sense to you," Howard said. "I started wrestling with my faith in God. I'm still wrestling. I feel like I'm finding myself. I didn't expect—I mean, the church has become very important to me."

"Thank you," said the stake president. "Please wait outside."

"Disfellowshipped," Allison said on the phone. "That's like limbo." After the high council informed him, Howard had driven too fast to Rockwood, grinning the whole distance; he had not been kicked out and the way was clear back to full fellowship. He was to keep attending church, and report to the stake president in Anchorage once a month.

"They said they didn't want to lose me," he said. "I didn't know I'd care so much."

The stake president had put his arm around Howard, saying, "We cannot allow this kind of behavior in the church. We have obligations to God to keep pure the community of the faithful. You have married and show sorrow for your act, now bury yourself in the gospel. Put yourself in the middle of the Saints in Anchorage." Howard had wept.

"I care because you care," she said. "When will you come home?"

"Day after tomorrow."

"I'll believe it when I see your wandering face." She hung up.

Smiling, Howard switched on lights as he moved through the house toward the kitchen. His soul still brimmed with light—married and now straight with the church. He felt vital, self-connected, new. He filled a frypan with his mother's scanty leftovers. The attic creaked in the wind. Every time he was alone in the old house it seemed that the ancient Rockwoods stirred and shifted, but on this night, joy not melancholy rose from the creaking boards. As he used a fork to shift the piece of chicken, the cold potato, and bottled beans around the frypan, he imagined Allison there with him, requiting the ghosts with vigor and hard-headedness.

After rinsing his plate and scrubbing the frying pan, he moved up to his old bedroom and looked out the window. The yard lights were burning at the Hansen and Jenkins houses. Brigham's Peak was a dark mass above town. Navajos, he had read, believe that the gods required them to live between four sacred peaks. When he was in the shadow of his own mountain, his soul settled into itself. Anchorage might never feel like home. In this house five generations of Rockwoods had talked, eaten, slept, and made love.

He dreamed that he struggled upward through a conduit, inching toward the visible sky. A rope dragged from his leg; he was to pull it through to the other side. The pipe was so narrow that he could only crawl with his arms above his head. His muscles ached from pushing himself forward on his toes and elbows. The heavy earth pressed on the flimsy pipe. Toads croaked in front of him; the faint light reflected off their eyes. The thud of their leaping bodies echoed.

Waking, he looked at the moon reflecting off the snowy field, at the dark line of willows along the old canal. Forty miles westward, his mother and father slept in the old cabin. Would she reclaim the old man from vagueness and solitude? Could she reclaim herself from apostasy? Howard turned on lights as he walked back through the house, where his father and his father's father, and that son's father had rubbed sweaty fingers across every wallboard, tracked barn and field dirt across every inch of floorboard for so long that no number of mothers and sisters could wash out the marks. Part of what he wrestled with was his belief that God's family was only an extension of his earthly ancestors, that the same culture existed on heaven and earth. Living with Allison, he had started speculating on the differences between God's way and man's.

Rockwood men were native princes; women merely transplants. Howard's mother grew up in Bountiful, daughter of a banker there. Howard's grandmother was the daughter of a Salt Lake orchard grower, who became rich selling bench land to developers. As a girl, Howard's grandmother had played where rich people now lived in their mansions on the eastern foothills. His great-grandmother was from Virginia; his great-great-grandmothers were from southern England and Wales, lush as a dream. They must have been mystified by their husbands' need to possess barren desert and wear themselves out making it blossom.

He walked down to the room where his mother kept her sewing machine, her scraps of material, her books, journal, the file containing articles about household and garden. The small room had been her only private space; after living with Allison, he knew that kitchen and bedroom were communal. He sat where his mother had sat. A ghost hand lay on his shoulder, and he had the illusion for a moment that he was two people, boy and mother. He closed his eyes and remembered her guiding the cloth under the rapid, nearly invisible needle. She reached for her thimble, bit the thread off, rewound a bobbin. She had hunched over the stitches, glancing sideways at him, smiling, her foot on the treadle of the clattering machine.

Often, late at night, his mother had read in her sewing room. "Aren't you coming to bed?" Howard remembered his father calling. "In a minute, Walter, I'm just at the end of a chapter." For thirty years she had held her own in her husband's house and town. His father's voice calling her to bed must have seemed light years away.

Once she had complained to his father, "You leave me here sixteen hours a day, tending the babies, but as soon as they're old enough to work you take them from me. I'm left waiting for you all to come home. Always waiting." Howard said to her, "I won't leave you, Mother. I'll stay with you." She had smiled and hugged him; later he proved her right by following his father across the fields and mountain pastures—imbibing patriarchy and the romance of land.

When he was eleven or twelve, his mother decided to remodel the front room. Someone at a lumber store in Salt Lake advised her to strip off all the old paint and wall paper, strip it to the old lath, and then use screws to attach sheet rock. She had picked a spot behind the bookcase to begin, using chisels and drywall tools to clear a patch a foot square, digging through yellow, blue, and orange paint; through violet, flowered, and velvet wallpaper. Finally she uncovered some rusty chicken wire and dry lath, the spaces packed with crumbly plaster. She said she was tempted to use dynamite, start over from scratch. Instead she gave up, spread putty in the hole and put up yet another layer of wallpaper. Sitting in the old house alone, Howard found it impossible not to turn symbolic about his spiritual inheritance; you never did get to the bottom, no matter how much you scraped away.

He imagined his mother leaving to attend the university. "I'm finished with house and garden," she would say. "I'm finished with wife." Allison rejected all wifeliness; her pills, which he wanted to flush down the toilet, kept her from motherhood. He thought of holding their unlikely child in his arms, as his brother-in-law Sam held *his* child, smiling down. The longing passed through his arms into his body, a physical ache. He tried to imagine Allison cradling a baby, cooing at it, but he couldn't. He had nearly left the church for this aggressive, careless, independent, powerful woman. He shook his head, bewildered. For her he had clambered early out of Eden, had followed to Anchorage, where the air was thick and cold, the horizon foreign, where he had not even a sewing room for his own space.

What brought men and women together besides sex? He'd read that after long marriages people found it difficult to imagine being with anyone else. His mother and father had struggled against each other for decades, an absolutely transforming experience. His father had once said, "I didn't need to go to the university, I had your mother." Howard had thought he meant that Emily was better educated; now he wondered.

He walked down to his parents' bedroom and sat on the brass bed where they had probably conceived him. His grandparents' first summer bed had been a quilt spread across wheat in the granary just outside the window, a building his father now used as a tack room. The old double house was so full of wives and younger children that they had slept in the shed until Max could build a newlywed house, the adobe down the road where Bishop Hansen now lived.

Howard lifted from the shelf above his parents' bed his father's memory box. On top was a bound genealogical record. His father's aunt had traced the Rockwood line back to England, back to a royal family, through record, legend, and wishful thinking, to a biblical family, to Adam. Temple ordinances bound son and wife and daughter to father, a phalanx of Rockwoods marching into the Millennium. "That which you seal on earth will be sealed in heaven." When he told Allison about it, she'd said, "You want to be connected to *all* your relatives?" Underneath the genealogy was a copy of J. D.'s diary—a record of his stewardship over pastures and range, holdings that extended synchronously through the landscapes of earth and heaven.

James Darren had grown up the son of a peasant farmer on a rocky estate on the border of Wales and England. Once he was accused of poaching a rabbit. Rather than face his own father, who was stern and unforgiving, he ran away to Liverpool, where he met the Mormon missionaries. He came to America and settled in Nauvoo, Illinois. When the Saints were driven westward, he selected land to the west of the River Jordan, where he began building his sheep and cattle herds. When his animals depleted the grazing, he explored southwest. In 1864 he wrote about leaving the Salt Lake Valley and coming to the desert: "We drov acros a gravel bar & down into the valley near the creek the grass was shoulder high to a man on a horse." Spreading his herds across this new land, J. D. established an inheritance—becoming greater than any British lord, a king in this life and the next. "My children grow up strong & are better than the children around them the best bodied and best minded children on the face of this earth I found good land & married good women & set about building the Lords kingdom on earth." The lesser wives of James Darren had claimed land for him, surviving alone in isolated valleys, helping to colonize nearly seven sections of land. The patriarch traveled the circuit between his farms, houses, and wives, plowing each field in turn.

Howard came through the second wife, Eliza—a dark-haired, solemn-faced woman. She had been a servant first; J. D. had paid her way from Liverpool in return for a year of work; then later she became wife. How had the transition felt, under his heaving body? Was she quickened to pleasure or fear as through her he claimed dominion in earth and heaven?

Howard could describe to Allison or his mother his father's desperation at the thought of selling land, the bishop's fear of losing control in the ward, Howard's own lust to return, to raise up cattle and children in the desert, but it would be like describing color to the blind, or sickness to the healthy. Strange ideas about women, men, land, sex, power, and God intermingled in every Rockwood male.

He dug in his father's box for pictures, some garish in color, his smiling family standing before a photographer's backdrop—an impossibly green landscape with a water wheel on a river, a scene as unlike Rockwood as could be found. Simon had shoulder-length hair; Nancy a dress hardly longer than a shirt. Karl, Stuart, Stuart's wife Ellen, and Howard's older sister Darlene—all smiled out of bliss and innocence; he was a baby on his mother's lap. He found a picture of his parents, newly married, posed on the stairway, the only background the jointed wood boards of the wall. His mother and father looked up into the camera as his mother served him their first breakfast in the old polygamous house. Howard had always wondered who held the camera, how it would be to begin marriage in a house already filled with relatives, alive and dead, all focused on building the kingdom through having children and gathering land. From deeper in the box, he pulled up a dark picture, faded around the edges. It could have been Howard or his father because of the hawk nose and lean face but was labeled his grandfather as a boy. He leaned against the stone porch which was ten steps from where Howard looked into the past through the frame of the picture. He wondered if the waves of light still oscillated, faint as the molecules of a scent, where Max had stood six decades earlier. In the box were worn copies of faded pictures of James Darren wearing his striped prison uniform, another of Mary, the first wife, posing in the front room, twenty feet from him in space, eighty years in time. All his ancestors' spirits on death had simply slipped into another dimension, parallel to this one. Other images might still quiver on the air in the dark and musty house, which was a Book of Life, recording every motion, every secret act of submission or domination.

Great-grandfather Solomon, who lived with his children when he was old, died on the toilet down the hall. Howard's father, Walter, had found the body when he got up in the night to relieve himself. Walter was seven; maybe that's what made him so distant, the shock of that early morning vision. When Howard was small, at night he had turned corners slowly, fearful of meeting his great-great-grandmother, the stern patriarch, or his pale great-grandfather, shuffling with his drawers around his ankles.

Howard's grandfather, Max, who had frozen to death and had been gnawed on by coyotes, wore a plaster nose in the coffin. Howard and Karl, nine and eleven, had wanted to lift the temple robe and determine whether the mortician had reconstructed the old man's privates. Howard had wondered how Christ would restore these parts to his grandfather when the molecules and cells had been digested, transmuted into bestial cells and molecules. Those particles would be as hard to gather as waves of reflected light, both dispersed by the passage of time.

During the funeral Howard's aunt had started forward. "He's here, I can feel his presence. The old man is here." She meant the spirit of James Darren, but when Howard looked around the room, he saw nothing. His flesh crawled with the thought of the savage pioneer still walking the earth. Who could bear his scrutiny? Maybe the female prospector had felt the same way, had dressed like a man and ridden north, a renegade. Inside the dark house Howard felt a kinship with that nameless woman. She must have been like Allison, respecter of no person.

Allison had disturbed the ghosts with her open, confident, and expansive motions—laughing in their faces. In the room just above his head, she had ridden his shuddering, unconsecrated body. Suddenly the Rockwood house seemed to him a mausoleum, where princes and queens were buried, where stiff and obscene ghosts still twitched.

He stuffed one sleeping bag inside another. It had started snowing so he wrapped the doubled bag in canvas and laid it on the haystack where he and Allison had slept. Snow powdered the canvas, swirled above him. "Let the old coots go," Grandmother God said to him. "Make your own way." The flakes fell and melted on his face. Forgetting the past was impossible; he could only continue to transform it by his changed perspective.

While he was eating breakfast, his mother telephoned. "Where are you?" he asked. He pictured her standing next to an impossible pay phone in the middle of the desert.

"I'm in Hamblin," she said, "at the hospital. I drove through before dawn and couldn't find you. Your father had another heart attack."

"I'll be there in a half an hour."

"They've given him more medicine to thin his blood out. Soon it will be like water. I was so frightened when I couldn't find you. I thought they'd excommunicated you and you'd done something to yourself."

When Howard arrived, the nurse said his mother was downtown shopping for groceries; his father would be released when she came back. Howard found him asleep with the blinds drawn. He sat next to the bed. His father's face was in shadow. He was old and pale, worn out. Howard had never watched him sleeping before, had hardly seen him lying down. Always his father balanced a sprinkler pipe, wrestled a calf down with a knife between his teeth, tamped the dirt around a post with a shovel handle.

Soon his father's eyes opened. "Howard," he said. "Your mother said you were coming."

"How did it happen?" said Howard.

"Too much ranch food, I guess. I'm all clogged up with roast beef and gravy."

"Feeling all right?"

"Damn tired. Not worth a nickel."

"You need a long rest. I'll stay in Utah as long as I need to."

"Stay here forever. Get that woman down here. We've got no other options."

"She loves her job, flies all around Alaska, tells all those oil drillers how to run their computers. And she makes more money than you can imagine."

"I can imagine a lot of money."

"Just double what you're imagining," said Howard. He would lose his job in the dairy.

"Maybe if you had a baby you could convince her."

When Howard's mother returned, the nurse wheeled him downstairs and they crowded into the small truck. Neither his father nor his mother spoke until they were half way home.

"So sell it," his father said. "Just don't talk to me anymore about it."

"That's gracious of you, Walter."

Neither one showed any indication of opening their mouths again, so Howard finally started talking. As they crossed the gray flat, he told them about the fishing boats fanning out as they left the Naknek harbor, about snow swirling above the Cook Inlet, about a yearling grizzly which had walked through their neighborhood, staring in the windows, disturbing the residents.

He phoned Allison with the news. "He's all right, but I need to help him a week or two."

"Call me a prophet," said Allison. She hung up without saying good-bye.

He drove west, an hour-long trip, to feed the cattle. Sitting on the tractor, he pushed the button to warm the engine and looked over the fields, spread below the long black volcanic ridge. Steam rose from the mineral pool and from the breaths of cows walking toward him, lured by the sound of the starting tractor. After loading the wagon, he tied the steering wheel so that tractor and wagon followed a great arc while he stood on the back and threw down the bales. Then he walked the same path carrying pliers, scattering the hay. That evening he sat in the cabin, with canned stew heating on the wood stove, and thought about his grandfather, father, and about Allison, who had said that she never wanted to live in Utah.

When he returned to Rockwood at the end of the week, he found that his father was well enough to ride out with him. "You need me to drive," his father said. Before they left, Howard tried to call Allison. After the phone rang seven times, he remembered her schedule. He and his father drove the snowy gravel road over the western mountains into deep desert. Allison, raised in semi-tropical Houston, couldn't see that Rockwood was a garden compared to the west desert.

On the ranch, Howard climbed to the top of the stack. He inched forward and lifted bales off the edge. The hundred-pound bales fell without turning; they shook the wagon when they hit. After he had a pile of bales, he climbed down and laid them in compact rows on the wagon. Just as he finished, his father returned from chopping ice on the watering pond.

Howard stood behind the tractor on the tongue, while his father drove down toward the cattle. Walter shouted, "Come, co-o-ome and get it, come and get it." Howard walked the tongue back to the wagon and climbed up the stack, kicking the bales off one at a time. After the last bale hit the ground, he jumped from the wagon and began pulling the wires and spreading out the hay. His father tried to lift a bale, dropped it, and sat. "I can't even open a single damn bale," he said. "I don't know what I'm going to do." Howard held a tangle of wire in his left hand, pliers in his right. He pushed his way through the hungry, fat cattle.

On Sunday, Howard built a fire in the old cabin and made sure his father had enough wood. He was worried about leaving him alone, but what was life worth if you couldn't do what you want? It's life, Howard thought. I can't live here with Allison.

He waited in the house in Rockwood all evening for Allison to call. His mother was out visiting women. Finally the phone rang. Allison complained about the cold, about being alone. "I'm thinking of taking up serious drinking again. All I do is work and sleep."

"Soon," he said to her. "Soon as I can."

"I want to see the flash of your bright eyes now that you're right with your church. They've gotten dimmer and dimmer since we played soccer in Houston. I should sue you for false advertising."

"Go ahead," he said. "We'll settle out of court. It'll take years to work out the details."

"Empty threat," she said. "Come home, you wandering fool. I really miss you, Howard."

"I love you," he said, and realized it was the first time since Houston he'd said it.

"Thank you," she said.

Next to the barn was a low building with a caved-in roof. The walls had been made from two-by-fours nailed flat against each other. Howard spent the evening and the next morning tearing it down. That afternoon he hauled most of the boards west in the pickup. He began work on a manger with wide uprights, between which the cattle could feed. He lined bales of straw to create a trough. His father was not strong enough to load and unload the wagon, but he could roll bales off the stack into the trough. Two days later Howard finished.

Walter complained. "It spreads diseases when they always eat in the same place. That whole fence row will turn to muck."

"Saves hay leaves," said Howard. "They won't tromp on what they eat."

"You watch. They'll pull their heads out to chew and all the leaves will fall in the muck."

"I have to go home," Howard said. "This way you can feed them."

"This is your home."

"I talked to Brother Jenkins," said Howard. "He can help you too."

"Damn," said Walter. "I want you here with me. I need you."

When Howard slept in the cabin, the cold breathed through the walls; he felt it even under a pile of greasy quilts. The wind whined in the rocks, almost a human sound. "Hear that?" said his father. "That's what drove your grandfather over the edge."

Everybody is on the edge, he thought. That's why we shore ourselves against impulses that seem irrational. He pondered the being (imagined whisper, impulse, psychological force?) which he had named Grandmother God. Nothing like the destructive voice his grandfather had followed up the ridge. "You're in charge," he had felt the silent Grandmother saying. "You can create good out of the bad in your life." Her voice was nothing like the voice of guilt which he could only name patriarchal, after his stern male ancestors. But both were imagined voices, he knew. He hoped that the sporadic gifts of spirit which had swept uninvited through him would some day add up to a truer voice. But whether imagined or somehow connected to God, this feminine voice (his own neurons sending messages of healing?) again and again had calmed him. He recognized it as the voice of his mother made larger. Whatever the origin of the imagined being, Grandmother God had taught him that church was not a room of answers, but a pathway of questions. Answers fell like sloughed-off skin behind him. He hoped that he could next learn that Grandfather God was not an impossible mix of modern businessman and Old Testament patriarch. Howard knew that prayer was a form of eternal calculus, a way of making closer and closer estimates of God's person-ness. But for the first time since he was a child, he had faith in the process. The wind blew against the cabin, his father snored. He couldn't see the stars, but he knew that limitless universe opened above him, an incomprehensible mystery.

He helped his father feed for three more days. Each morning they finished earlier. His father seemed more energetic, didn't talk about prospecting as much. On the third morning, Howard drove to Rockwood for Sunday and found that Allison had called, saying she would fly down that afternoon. He felt his heart soar with hope. He would have another chance at convincing her that Utah was beautiful, Edenic, or at least habitable.

Twelve

The frigid wind blew through the wall, and Allison drew the blankets around her face like the hood of a coat. That bastard Howard had played her like a victim in a New York shell game and had gotten her into his grandfather's cabin: "My father's just not healthy. Only four days." Now he was cooking a hot breakfast for her, some kind of canned meat fried in a pan and bread toasted directly on top of the black stove. The smells of grease, mice, dust, and the gas that fired the refrigerator lay heavy on the air—to say nothing of Walter's effluvium. His last bath had probably been in the hospital. Out the window the desert was snow and light.

"Sleep well?" asked Walter. Both men were so cheerful it was nauseating.

"We're all going to freeze our butts off today," she said. "They'll find us stiff as fish."

"Is this the Alaskan pioneer talking?" said Howard.

"That's a good name for you," said Walter.

She made a face. "Even the North Slope is warmer than this. Damn, that grease stinks."

"I'd better go see if that heifer is close," said Walter.

"Alaska," said Howard. "I like it." He handed her toast, black on one side, white on the other.

"Why would it matter if a heifer is close?"

"Close to calving. She was bred too young."

Allison stared at the burnt toast, and he finally took it from her and carried it outside. "See, Alaska," he said when he came back in, "good as new." He had scraped it on one side. She laid the thinner slice on her plate. He poured her a cup of his father's coffee. Standing at the stove, Howard shoveled the mess of egg and falsely pink meat into his mouth.

"I wish I wasn't so hungry," she said. He filled another plate and shoved it toward her. She ate without looking down. "Tell me a story about love. Something to warm me up."

"Once upon a time a woman and a man and the man's father lived in a cabin. Love was a rare bird. Then the father went to town for Sunday dinner."

"Isn't today Sunday?" said Allison grinning. "That's a good story."

Slipping on his parka, Howard raised his eyebrows at her as he left. All the warm air in the cabin rushed out with him. Soon he opened the door again. "I thought you wanted to drive."

"I'll be right out." She hated being grumpy, out of control. She put on her snowsuit, her parka, gloves, and ski mask, but still felt as though she had stepped out onto the North Pole. The north sky was as black as the volcanic ridge which ran along the western boundary of the ranch. She went back inside and wrapped a blanket around herself before returning to the bitter cold.

The temperature had risen slightly the day before, melting the surface of the snow, which had refrozen during the night as a crust. Wisps of snow blew out of the holes left by her feet. The desert was gray. A wreath of steam rose from the slate gray pool, and the ridge hovered like a huge welt behind the cabin. "Let's get this over with," she shouted.

Howard, up on the haystack, couldn't hear. Walter walked toward the burial pool, calling for the cattle. "Come and get it. Coooome and get it." Howard was only half-finished loading the wagon, so she stood as close as she could to the hot engine of the tractor as he threw bales down, five or six at a time. Moving to the north end of the haystack, she looked down on the cattle, which huddled on the south side of a board fence down on the flat.

Walter stood on the bank of the pool like a diver measuring his steps. If he stepped in, it would be death by baptism; she remembered from talking to the anthropologists that the Goshutes believed the deep pool was a birth canal into the new world. The three mummies were gone; the Goshute woman with the stark face and the child bound across her belly now lay in a special morgue at the University of Utah. Walter didn't want them in the pool, he'd told her, and the university lawyers were wrestling with whether the current Goshute tribe, across the desert on the edge of Nevada, could demand that the corpses be returned to their proper burial.

Rimmed by gray alkali, containing water hot enough to melt the snow, the pool looked like an evil egg, an eye. Babe, she said to herself, don't get superstitious on me. Death was no channel to anywhere. The heart stopped beating. Consciousness and identity were illusions of evolution. The wind whined through the rocks as if it were a woman wailing, the illusion that had proved deadly to Howard's grandfather. Allison shook herself and turned back toward the wagon. The bitter landscape was as foreign to her as Pluto. The North Slope was only slightly less congenial. At least she was a visitor there, able to go home after a short stint.

With Howard perched behind, she drove out on the flat. The cold wind penetrated her blanket and coat. The cattle had turned toward the sound of the tractor. She drove in a wide circle through the fields while Howard threw bales off the back. The cattle followed, some running up to the wagon and twisting their heads sideways, long tongues extended, to chew the corners of the moving stack. The lane below the cabin had turned white, outlined by gray-white and gray-green brush. Near the pool it joined the main road, which also showed white, a bank of gravel bisecting the valley. She saw the yellow of a snowplow crawling past.

After Howard had cleared the wagon, she stopped the tractor. Walter and Howard began to cut the bale wires and kick the hay out. "Do you want help?" she shouted.

He shook his head so she turned the tractor and drove along the black ridge toward the cabin. The volcanic rock, partially veiled by the first wisps of falling snow, was beautiful but so stark and cold it terrified her. She felt emotionally unsteady and wondered if she could hold herself together for two more days. Along the base of the ridge, a smelly stream flowed from the pool. The stream was so laden with salt and other minerals that nothing grew near it. The exhaust pipe from the tractor rose above her head, but the fumes still choked her. When she arrived at the pool, she shoved her foot down on the clutch, flicked the gear shift to neutral, and climbed down from the tractor. The ground was disturbed where they had taken the three corpses from the salty mud. She bent to touch the surface of the pool—warm as a bath. She'd like to walk down into the pool, be warm all over for the first time since Houston.

The next morning after feeding, she again drove the tractor to the pond. Under cover of her blanket, she removed her coat, shirt, pants, and underwear, and put them in a plastic sack. She dropped the blanket and walked down into the water. Her feet, calves, thighs, belly, chest, and finally shoulders turned warm. After a few minutes the cold air felt good on her face. She kicked back, buoyant in the heavy water. The wind blew snow horizontally over her head.

Howard stood on the bank. She smiled up at him. "What the hell?" he said.

"I've been cold forever. Come on in."

"You look like a mermaid."

"You look like a big chicken. It's nice in here."

"There are more bodies below you, you know."

"No," she said. "My being here changes it. I'm renaming it the pool of life. The only baptism I'll ever agree to." He grimaced. She tried to make chicken noises, but they came out like the barking of a dog. "I'm no good at imitating animals."

"The woman who imitates animals." He laid his clothing on the wagon seat and slid into the pool. They touched fingertips in the water. She swam behind him, skin on skin, but as soon as she stopped treading, she slowly sank in the salty water. The snow whirled down from the immense white above her.

Out of the pool, she wrapped the blanket around herself and started the tractor. Howard put on his shoes and sprinted naked toward the cabin. "You'll get frostbite," she called. He beat his fingers against his thighs. "I'm not worried about your hands." She reached the cabin first—hot as an oven inside. Walter poured soup into bowls. Howard leaped across the doorstep, buck naked.

"I had to add water to it three times," Walter said. Still holding the pot, he turned to stare at them. "You're all red," he said to Howard. Howard took the teakettle which always stood on the stove and poured hot water into the washbasin. "I'll go check that heifer again."

At the washbasin Allison cleaned the mud off her knees and hands. "Wasn't that great?" he said.

"We can bathe naked in a lot of places." She wrapped her arms around his chest. "You can freeze your whacker off anywhere."

"Not in our own pool. Not run naked across our own land."

"Yeah, and your father can always be there to record the moment," she said. "Freeze in poverty. I'm scared spitless that it's your fate. Just over that ridge are three old hags weaving time, making sure that you'll end up blue and chewed up like your grandfather."

After dressing, Howard went out to help his father finish. Allison lay on the bed and drew up the filthy quilts. She imagined the Goshute woman walking the valley. She squatted on top of the black ridge and gave birth to a child under the tent of her skirts. She cuddled the small blue child to her breast and keened, her neck back like a wolf or coyote.

When Allison opened her eyes, Walter had the stove open, putting another log in. His face reflected the red light of the fire. "You don't like it here," he said. "Not many women do. I couldn't ever get Emily to stay with me out here. Not more than a day trip. Oh, once or twice she's spent the night."

"What do you see in it?"

"Beyond its natural beauty—possibility. Range for cattle. Nobody crowding me."

She shrugged. The phrase colder than hell no longer seemed paradoxical.

"You'd have to look through my eyes." He peeled potatoes and opened another can of the pink meat. "I won't call you Alaska if you don't like it."

"I don't mind."

Later she swallowed the scalding stew, watching the two men whose faces looked more and more similar.

Mid-afternoon, the wind had died down, the fire was roaring, and the cabin was warm inside. She had her arms wrapped around Howard, wanted to have him in her arms for a month. "I know it makes no sense to you," he was saying, "but the court did make a difference to me. They treated me with respect. It strengthened my confidence that God won't abandon me." They had the afternoon, evening, and all night alone. It wasn't enough.

"I can show you fifteen ways to use a chair," she said.

"A myth. I can only think of one or two." He paused. "Maybe three."

She said, "What's the end of this court business?"

"In a year, they'll let——."

"No," she said. "What's the end of it for you? Will you become pious? Will you decide you're not happy until I'm baptized?"

Howard traced a finger down her spine.

"Two weeks without you is too long," she said.

"You're two weeks on the North Slope."

"But *you* know I'm coming back," she said.

He turned away from her. "I built a new fence around the stack yard so Dad could feed alone. I was ready to fly to Anchorage when you said you were flying here."

She pulled him close again, and he turned to her. He kissed the tip of her nose, took her upper lip between his lips, kissed her long and deep.

"Oh," she said finally. "I've missed that. When I'd wake in the morning, I'd find myself hugging your pillow."

He kissed her again and then lay back. She touched his face, moved her hand across his chest and belly. "Anchorage isn't easy for me," he said. "I went there to be with you and you're gone half the time." Their legs crossed over and under between them.

"I don't think Lisa will change the schedule." She pushed the hair back out of his eyes. "Roll over. I'll rub your shoulders."

"Maybe I could fly up with you."

"We'll ask her," she said. "She'll say that I'm up there to work and that you'd be a distraction. She'd be right."

He touched his left shoulder. "Here," he said. "That's where I'm always tight."

With her fingertips, she tried to find the knot.

"I can't tell what the end will be," he said. "I don't have a goal about it. After the court I slept, or didn't sleep, alone in the house."

"Ghosts were walking." She moved her palm across his butt and down his hairless leg.

"That night I rebuked the stern patriarch god. I drove a stake through his heart."

"Not really."

"Right," he said. "Not really. I just left the house and slept in the snow. But since then, since seeing that the God I had imagined had flaws of my own making, of my culture's making, I started to feel that God might be more like my mother's father, a wise and kind man. My mother says that he never raised his voice to her. He had a round Danish face and he grew apples."

"How could I have known?" she said.

"What?" He turned onto his back.

"That you're a sensitive man. I wanted you because I thought you were malleable."

"Should I be insulted?"

"I was a fool," she said. "But part of me was smart. Part of me sensed that I'd want to spend my life with you."

"We're married," he said. "You're stuck with me."

"Your grandfather sat right there behind that table, dreaming about Marilyn Monroe. That's such a sad story, such a lonely man.

He's dead, but I feel so sorry for him." She wrapped her arms around Howard again, her breast to his breast, hips to his hips, unspeakable consolation, unfathomable communion.

That evening the heifer tried to calve. Allison didn't want to help, but Howard insisted. After they drove the heifer into the corral next to the haystack, Howard rummaged in a shed, a flashlight held between his teeth. He said something that sounded like "Cheese goink coo kai." He pulled out an apparatus—a five-foot pole with a flat brace at one end. He handed her the flashlight. Chains and a cable with a winch on it dangled from the pole. The heifer stood in the mucky corral with her head down and her tail out. Howard slipped a lariat around her neck and cinched her against the bars of the corral. "Point the light where I need it."

"Where do you need it?"

"Where my hands are." The calf's hooves protruded from the heifer's vulva. He took the chain off the apparatus and slid it along the hooves up into the vagina. With the chain secure, he shoved the brace up against the heifer's butt, just under the protruding hooves, and reattached the other end of the chain to the winch. He wound the crank until cable and chain were tight, then he bore down on the pole. The heifer bellowed, a long low sound which turned to a groan and trailed off. He turned the crank and bore down again.

"Stop it!" said Allison. "You're going to kill her."

"The head's stuck." He thrust his hands up into her vagina, his right arm up to the elbow. "Give me some slack." He pointed with his chin. Allison pushed a lever, and the cable hung loose. "Now," he shouted, his hands inside the cow again. "Let's pull this calf." The light between her teeth, Allison cranked and bore down on the pole, cranked and bore down again. She shivered and the light shook on the cow's butt; the icy wind blew snow around them all. "I see tongue. Tongue and nose." The cow bellowed again and toppled over on her side. He kept his hands inside, moved down on one knee. "Turn it, Allison, dammit, turn it." She pushed down with all her weight on the calf-puller, cranked and pushed again. Suddenly the pole came loose, and Allison slipped, sitting hard in the snow and mud. She held the light and saw that the calf lay in a pool of liquid, shrouded in the afterbirth.

"It's dead," she said, but then one leg shifted.

Howard knelt in the snow, hooking away the membrane with his fingers. He lifted the calf and staggered toward the cabin. The heifer lay in the mud with her legs extended horizontally. Allison watched, anxious for the animal, but not wanting to touch her. Soon Howard came out of the cabin, went over to the haystack and lugged back a bale. He broke it immediately behind the heifer. "Kick it under her while I roll her." He flung hay under the heifer's legs. Using the rope, he pulled her neck and shoulders vertical until she gathered her legs beneath her and lay more normally. Taking the light, he brought from the shed something large as a tent—a canvas tarp—and spread it across the heifer.

Inside, the calf lay on a blanket in front of the stove. It had its head up, nosing at him. He grabbed a towel from near the wash basin and wiped the yellow slime from its body.

"We just made four hundred bucks," he said, his voice gruff. Then she saw him wipe his eyes with the sleeve of his shirt.

"It's alive," she said. "I thought sure as hell it was dead."

"This is what it's all about," he said, and the feeling changed for her; the two of them, bent over the calf, seemed a damned sentimental tableau. One more argument in a campaign. When his father returned the next afternoon, he and Howard slapped each other on the back as if something marvelous had happened. It had been wonderful to see the calf butting against her mother's flank that morning, but their emotion seemed excessive.

The morning before Thanksgiving, she packed her suitcase early, but Howard and his father puttered around all day. Finally after feeding that afternoon, Howard tried to start the truck. Soon he was back inside. "Battery's dead."

"You planned this!" she shouted, furious. He turned and left the cabin.

"Damn," Walter said. "I took the jumper cables back to Rock-wood." He lifted a long chain from the corner of the room and shuffled out the door. Allison put on her coat and followed. Walter started the tractor and backed it up to the truck. Howard hooked the chain and then climbed into the truck, cranking down the window. He waved his arm for Walter to go. Walter started forward slowly, then shifted gears and pulled down on the throttle. The truck tires stopped turning and the chain popped loose.

Walter backed the tractor again; Howard bent under the bumper of the truck and reattached the chain. They started across the field. The truck slid at an angle behind the tractor but didn't start. Walter pointed across to the main road, which was graveled, and the caravan pulled across the fields. Allison stamped in the cold, but the thought of reentering the smelly cabin kept her outside. Finally both vehicles stopped, Howard unhooked the chain, and the truck came back up the valley toward her. She loaded her suitcase and Howard's into the truck bed. She sat between father and son in the cab of the truck, and Walter drove.

"Old battery," said Walter.

"Can you get a new one in Rockwood?" she asked.

"This one still has some life in it."

She opened her mouth, shut it again, and they drove up the long narrow valley. Rockwood would seem like heaven after this barren place. Howard claimed they needed the land in the desert as well as in Rockwood in order to make the ranch work. She thought it just another way of excluding women from their lives. It was clear why Emily and before her Max's wife had refused to follow their husbands west into a frightening and isolated wasteland. At dusk the truck passed a flat-topped butte with huge boulders lined along its crown, sentinels which seemed as tall and rectangular as those at Stonehenge. Out on the flat they passed through patches of surreal fog, so thick that she couldn't see the road.

"Sometimes sheep bed down on this flat," said Walter. She imagined the truck rolling over bloody, white sheep bodies. She knew that part of her fear was not just of injury or death, but of the strangeness of the desert and the eerie fog. The defroster was broken, and the windows misted over. The fog grew thicker, filling every low place and spreading across the flat. On the other side of Lookout Pass, the fog became even more dense. Walter stopped the truck, and Howard lay flat on the hood on his stomach, raising his arms to either side like a swimmer to point the direction his father should turn. An hour later they were at the edge of town. A gleaming spot of light approached—someone's yard lamp. Suddenly a white horse crossed in front of them and ran into a field next to the road. Howard leaped off the truck and shut the gate. They crept down the street; fences and parked cars were transformed. Two months earlier she had driven that same road with a new and hesitant lover. Now she had a husband—disorienting. The other road felt as if it were in another universe—the bright road on which she pulled up to his parents' house. She didn't feel different: as Howard said, it was the past that had changed.

Walter stopped the truck. "We made it," Howard said. "What an adventure!"

She stared at him. He had translated even the surreal and deadly fog into fun. She shook her head in wonder. The desert was a condition of his mind, an aspect of his faith; for her, it was strange and foreign. Eventually it might divide them, despite their growing love for each other. "I thought I was going to die," she said.

"Not even sheep are stupid enough to be out," said Walter. "That's why we were safe."

Emily had built a fire in the old cook stove and the kitchen was wood-fire warm. The windows, with fog against them, were white and opaque. Howard opened the oven door, laid a towel inside, and moved a chair close. "Put your feet inside," he said.

Allison sat and lifted her feet carefully onto the towel in the hot space.

"I can't believe you dragged her out there," said Emily. She sat at the table crimping the edges of uncooked pie crusts. "What's even more bewildering, Allison, is why you let them."

"As if you've never been out," said Walter. "You had your days of foolishness with me."

"When I was young and naive."

"We weren't young a decade ago. And we sure as hell weren't young a couple of weeks ago when we spent the night out there."

"No, we weren't young," said Emily. She turned to Allison. "You warm yet?"

"Not yet. I've been thinking of crawling in the oven and shutting the door."

"Baked Alaska," said Walter. Allison grinned. "Remember when we were snowed in, Emily? You was eight months pregnant with Stuart. I finally used the tractor to break trail out to the main road. We caught a ride with the county snowplow."

"I didn't think you would even remember I was pregnant. Let alone which child."

"I remember." He looked at his hands. "We've changed since then. We've changed away from each other."

"You going to cook them in the old oven?" Howard asked his mother. She poured a hot cherry mixture into two of the ten shells she had laid out across the table.

"No," she said. "The temperature's too hard to regulate."

"It's done fine for you plenty of times," his father said.

"Yes, and every time I cooked I was anxious that something wouldn't turn out." She handed the two men each a bucket of apples and a peeler.

"I can't use that contraption," Walter said. He pulled his pocket knife out.

"A knife wastes too much apple," she said. He peeled an apple with his knife, one continuous coil. Allison nodded in the warmth; the desert was just a bad dream.

"You've changed too," Emily said.

"I said *we've* changed. I was sitting out there in my father's cabin, angry as I could be about how different you'd become, and then I realized where I was sitting."

"We've done it to each other. I feel like I've had to beg for too much."

"You did have to beg. I'm sorry about that." He held an apple in one hand, his knife in the other. "I didn't pay for that land. My father gave it to me. His father gave it to him. It didn't feel like it was mine to sell."

"A buyer's already signed an earnest money agreement. It's already done."

"I'm not going back on my promise. I'm just explaining why I put it off so long." He halved an apple and cut the core out. "That's not all of it. For thirty years I thought of the ranch as mine. It seemed like selling a child. But then I sat out in my father's cabin, looking across that barren alkali land that I've tried to farm for decades and I thought what's the use of it?" His voice turned tremulous. Allison looked up at him. "Just don't sell the house, too."

"I have no plans to sell this house. After I start school, we'll need it here for both of us to come back to."

"Your halfway house," Allison said.

They both turned and stared, as if they were surprised to discover someone else in the room. Allison slipped an apple slice, tart, into her mouth.

Walter leaned toward Emily. "I wish Gerald had never released you. There's no woman in the ward who could match you. Him releasing you so soon was an embarrassment to you."

"I didn't know you thought anything about it."

"Of course, I thought about it. Gerald's too damn heavy-handed. He's driven you farther out than you wanted to be. He's driven you to do crazy things. If he had helped you with the women from the beginning, none of this would have happened."

"Whatever he is, Gerald's not heavy handed. He's talked and talked and talked to me. He's seen it my way and seen it his way, and made a careful decision. I'm grateful—he's helped me understand my own mind better through all our talking."

Thanksgiving morning Allison and Walter slipped out to Willy's for a cup of coffee. "We'll be right back to help," said Walter.

"I've heard that before," said Emily.

The same men were still sitting at the stained wooden tables—

Willy, Vernon, the man in cowboy boots, she couldn't remember his name. The only one missing was the young one, Howard's friend.

"Good morning," said Willy to Allison as she sat. "So you're back to stay?"

She frowned at Walter. He lifted his hands.

"If you say something enough," he said, "maybe it'll come true."

"So you're not pregnant either," said Vernon.

"Walter," she said, "you've got to stop this bullshit. No matter how much you wish it, wishing's not going to get you a grandson. That takes Howard's sperm."

Cowboy Boots laughed and slapped his leg. "Pull in your loop, Walt," he said. "You ain't goin' to rope this one."

"We're eating at one o'clock," said Walter to Willy. "Emily says you're welcome."

"Vern's invited me already."

"I told her we should have asked you two weeks ago."

"That's all right," said Willy. "How's Emily?"

"The stake president told Gerald Hansen to discipline her," said Vernon. "He told the bishop that she's like the serpent in Eden."

"Now how would you know all that, Vern," said Cowboy. "Are you privy to the conversations of them with power and authority?"

"I know what I know," said Vernon. "He told Gerald to stop being undecided. He told him to nip apostasy in the bud. If he had any—" he glanced at Allison.

"Balls?" she said.

"—he'd have acted a long time ago."

"Let's go," said Walter. "I don't have to sit here listening to this dimwit."

"My own wife asked me why she shouldn't have the priesthood if I'm good enough to have it," said Vernon.

"It's a reasonable question," said Willy. Walter stood and moved to the door.

"Then she said a few things about my character that I won't repeat," said Vernon.

"Ain't the truth a painful thing," said Cowboy.

Vernon glared at Walter's back, as Walter let the door swing shut behind him. "Anything that comes between a man and his wife ain't of God."

Allison finished her coffee and followed, nodding at Willy. She opened the passenger door and climbed in. Walter said, "That man doesn't have the sense God gave a pissant."

Howard went down to the cellar, transported back in time by the musty smell, and hauled up a cardboard box of butternut squash. "It's too damp down there," said his mother. "They're all going moldy." They sat on the screened back porch; he cut the squash and scooped out the seeds while his mother laid the halves on cookie sheets. The porch table had become the storage shelf for old bottles, boxes of seeds, odd tools, and Louis L'Amour novels.

"I read ten or twelve of these in Anchorage," said Howard.

"I could never see the point of reading more than one," she said. "Your father read them all the time, but they all seemed the same to me."

"They make me homesick."

"It's a made-up world," she said. "How can you be homesick for a story?"

Emily placed a bucket of carrots and one of potatoes in front of him. He picked up the peeler and started on the carrots. Through the screen he saw Bishop Hansen walking down the road toward their house.

"I dreamed I entered into a room where Walter leaned against the wall," said Emily. The bishop came around the corner of the house. "He looked bigger than he is. Big and slow. He didn't look at me. And I can't remember anything else."

"Who was big and slow?" said Bishop Hansen, and Howard's mother jerked and dropped a potato. "Sorry I startled you."

"So nice of you to visit, Gerald."

"All those women chased me out of the house. They don't want me around. I had two choices: working on my shed or walking down to chat." He extended his hand toward her and then toward Howard. "How's Walter?"

"Stronger every day," said Howard.

"He's happy to have you back. He told me so." He turned to Howard's mother. "Can we talk a moment?"

"Of course," she said.

Howard stood and walked into the house. He stood just inside the door.

"Belinda said you gave her a blessing," the bishop said. "She said you did it in the name of Christ and by the power of Walter's priesthood. Then she said you told her not to talk about it. But she was anxious, rightly so, and wanted to talk to me about it."

She finished peeling her apple. She said, "How long have you known me? Have you ever known me to be careless about the gospel?"

"That's why I don't understand what you're doing. Do you believe I've been called of God?"

"You know I do," she said.

Then Howard felt self-conscious, eavesdropping, and entered the kitchen. Allison had rolled out a circle of dough. She tried to lift it from the cloth to cover an apple pie, but the pastry tore. "Dammit to hell," she said. "My mother could do this, why can't I?"

"I think it has to do with respect. The dough curls up when it hears that kind of language."

Allison nodded toward the porch. "Who's that?"

"Bishop Hansen. Mom gave a blessing to Belinda."

Allison started toward the door, but Howard caught her arm. "She can handle it."

They heard the bishop's voice. He said, "—like setting out on a trip through the wilderness with Satan as your pathfinder. You're like a stranger to me. Sometimes I've wondered if you have an evil spirit that I should cast out. Or that you're one of those split personalities." Then their voices were softer.

After a time Emily reentered the kitchen. "Well," she said. "He's made up his mind."

During Thanksgiving dinner, Allison watched Walter, who had

sunk into himself, taciturn as an old bull. Howard often moped, but Walter had it down to an art. Allison told Emily about her work, flying above the Alaskan wilderness to the North Slope.

"You're like James Darren Rockwood, first settler of this valley," Howard said to her. "He writes about how beautiful the grass is, but at the same time he's calculating how his herds of cattle and sheep will double. His herds ruined the grass here."

"That's environmentalist talk," said Walter. "No true rancher would talk like this."

"I don't ruin anything," Allison said.

"You just make it possible for others to ruin it," said Howard. "The pipeline, the Valdez spill, all those oil rigs."

"I've never been an idealist," said Allison. "I just work."

"Remember that trip we took to Denver?" said Emily.

"Damned fine bulls," said Walter. "Best thing we ever did for the herd."

"Maybe we could take another trip. Maybe we could fly up to see Allison and Howard."

"Who'd take care of the cows?"

"Brother Jenkins could for a week."

"I'll think about it."

"Well, whether you join me or not," she said, "I'm going one of these days."

"Whether we can afford it or not?"

"I want money of my own," she said, "so I can decide for myself without asking your permission. How can I be sixty years old and not have my own money?"

Walter looked as though he'd been hit with a rock. "It is your money," he said.

She slumped into a chair. "I'm sorry, Walter," she said. "Something's-a-pulling at me. Like a hunger. I can hardly stop myself from doing what I know is evil or harmful."

"Oh, Emily," Allison said. She put her arms around Howard's mother and held her. Over Emily's shoulder she saw Walter, whose face showed wonder and bewilderment.

After dinner she and Emily washed dishes while Howard and his father stood outside in front of the truck. Allison watched them from the kitchen window, the yard light shining down on their heads. They had the hood up and Howard was pointing to the battery and saying something while his father stroked his grizzled beard.

"Howard is not the Howard I sent off on his mission," said Emily.

"Right."

"When I first met you, I thought you had ruined him, but I was wrong."

"He's changed me, too."

"What was wrong-headed in him. Feeling like the prince of the family because he was the youngest. That's gone. Some of his bossiness. You're more relaxed. More yourself."

"More myself."

"At first you were so desperate to get him away from here that you were unpleasant."

"Those would be fighting words from anybody else." Allison thought about her future with Howard—learning from their differences for forty years. "What's it like having a baby?"

Emily froze. "Are you pregnant?"

"No, I've just been thinking about it."

Emily slid a plate into the steamy water. She lifted her hands out and shook them once.

"Evan, my first child, came early. I kept telling Walter I wasn't ready for it, despite the clear signals, that I needed just two more weeks before I could have the baby. He didn't say anything, just kept driving toward Hamblin, getting more and more angry. Finally he said that it was coming whether I wanted it or not. The baby came before we got into the delivery room."

"I'm going to make Howard do it," said Allison. "He's the one who wants it."

"He's been hinting?"

"Hinting like a bulldog."

"Do you want me to talk you into it?"

"No," said Allison. "I just wanted to let you know I was thinking about it. Some day it'll happen. I want something that Howard and I have made ourselves."

"I won't tell him we've talked," said Emily.

"Not a word," said Allison.

In the middle of the night, Allison got up to get a drink. She looked out the window onto the moonlit orchard. The branches cast stark shadows on the snow. Then a shadow moved under the trees, someone bundled in a big coat walking under the trees. Peering closer, she recognized Emily's coat. By the time Allison dressed and followed out into the orchard, Emily was gone. Back inside, Allison brushed her fingers through Howard's hair, laid her hand on his neck. She felt that she could fly with her own arms to Anchorage.

Thirteen

Allison knew Howard would pine for Utah, but at first he seemed satisfied to be with her again. He had lost his job at the dairy, so he spent a couple of days asking for work at every business within walking distance of their apartment. He was hired at a Chinese restaurant, where he washed dishes and swept.

His first Sunday back, he came home from church and told her that the bishop had asked him to work in the church library, a job which involved handing out pictures, chalk, pencils, and paper to the teachers. He told the bishop he couldn't because he had been disfellowshipped. "He knew already," Howard said to Allison. "The stake president had talked to him. He told me that he wants to fellowship the disfellowshipped. He wants to meet you."

At home he prepared exotic dishes, abstracted from what he saw the cooks make at the restaurant—water chestnuts and sliced avocado on rye toast; rice, tomatoes, and ground pork stuffed in the shells of onions; salmon fillets wrapped in spinach leaves and steamed; potatoes and sliced zucchini boiled with canned meat. He read books about people who crashed their planes in remote wilderness and survived through ingenuity and cannibalism. He read romances about the imaginary West when the roles of men and women were clearly defined. Cowboys herded cattle, robbed banks, and out-fought bears, Indians, and sheep-herders, while protecting their soft and voluptuous women. She told him that his longing for the ranch made reading these books like viewing pornography.

One day he bought a fluorescent plant light and hung it in a corner of the main room of their apartment. He bought black potting soil, which he smelled and rolled in his fingers as he filled brown, decomposable cups. He planted tomatoes, squash, and green peppers.

"What are you going to do when they get too big?" Allison asked.

"I'll find a place," he said. "If we plant them in five-gallon buckets, we'll eat ripe tomatoes all winter. Imagine it, we're making dinner and we want a salad. We just walk across the room and pick them off the plant. It'll smell like a garden in here."

"This takes the place of the ranch?" she said. He turned his back to her and she knew that she'd somehow offended him. She put her hand on his shoulder.

"I'm trying to make Anchorage my home, at least for now," he said. "I get desperate when you won't even talk about moving."

She left for work without speaking. I get desperate too, she thought. She pictured herself as Emily, waving as Howard drove to the west ranch. She'd sit inside that enormous decaying house and stare at the walls, wait for the sisters to drop by and try to convert her. Howard thought of the town as Mr. Rogers' Neighborhood—orderly, productive, congenial. Most of what she knew about Rockwood was interpolated from watching Emily. It was as if Emily wore one of those animal collars that kept her inside an electronic fence.

"He's treading water," Allison said to Mark, who was taller than she but wide as a barn, kind as her father. "He thinks if he thrashes hard enough he can walk on it. But I'm not going to give up my job for him."

Mark nodded and smiled.

"Even when he's not talking about going back, he's thinking it, willing me to want to be in Utah, to be a Mormon woman. Maybe he talks to me in my sleep, hypnotizes me. Tell me I'm crazy, but I saw this baby at the grocery store the other day. My insides melted. I wanted one bad. Dammit, can you imagine me as a mother?"

"You should tell Howard," Mark said—the hint of a smile.

"His vision for me is barefoot and pregnant on that ranch."

"Silliest thing I've ever heard," said Mark. "Why would he want that?" Then she remembered that Mark had been raised on a farm on the plains of Canada.

She grimaced. "I dreamed the wolf dream again." Mark knew she dreamed about running down caribou, slashing at their hindquarters, howling into the night wind. "This time there was a den of pups. I felt a pull down my whole body, as if there were a hook in my belly."

"Biological clock," he said. "Happened to my sister. She found a man and then broke up with him as soon as she was pregnant. She and her kid live in Calgary." He smiled. "I can imagine you as a she-wolf, you have the spirit of a wild thing. I—you—" He leaned toward her. "Are you happy with this Howard?"

She watched his face, seeing an affection for her she hadn't noticed before. "What's in your head, Mark?" she said. "Are you treading water?"

"His whine will become unbearable. I'm giving you room to reconsider your error."

"A small room," she said, "a closet. You're breathing down my neck."

Later she remembered her words, and her skin woke to the possibility.

"Math is hell," Emily wrote. "I wish you two were here to translate this gibberish. Besides math I'm taking two women's studies classes— Women and Christianity and Feminist History. The women here are wonderful. All of them are younger than I am but familiar to me, like recognizing someone's voice and face I'd forgotten I knew. Even those classes are *hard*. I've forgotten how to study and write. What a gift you've given me, Allison. Some of the Mormon women in my classes have started a reading group. We read and talk, read and talk. We each have our pet peeves: the power structure of the church or the ways men think they own women's bodies. Other women's peeve is authority. Mine is patriarchal attitudes toward land and work. Who'd have thought I'd love talking politics. I feel so strange. The earth's never seen a less political animal than I am. I meet with the bishop weekly. So far I've kept my mouth shut, referred women with problems to him, and given up excessive speculation. But I sit in church and someone's droning on about genealogy or staying home with your children, and I know I could wake the audience up. Then I am swallowed up by the injustice of my punishment. I know that kind of thinking is my enemy. Soon Gerald will give me another calling. I'm not going to leave this life with what I have to say unsaid, with the blessings dammed up that could flow through me. I'm meeting with him and swallowing my anger. You say it's unhealthy, Allison, but I'm doing it."

Allison said, "It's sad. Your mother's made to be a preacher, a healer, and she's born into one of the only churches in the country that won't let her do either. You're born to be a rancher and you've set yourself up with a woman who won't live on a damned ranch."

She saw him set his face to argue and held up her hand.

"Not now," she said. "I don't have the energy to start into it right now."

After Christmas Howard started school. None of the classes would help him graduate, even if the U accepted them, so he registered for whatever seemed interesting: Taxonomy of Animals Native to the Alaskan Tidewater, Botany of the Tundra, History of the Northwest Territories, and Arctic Wildlife. He enjoyed exploring the herbarium, examining the plants laid between sheets of thick paper. The smell of the dried plants reminded him of haying, he said. One Saturday he went ice fishing with one of the graduate assistants, a Tlingit. They drove to a small lake on the Kenai Peninsula and augered a hole in the ice. He caught ten trout in one hour.

The wind blew white clouds, heavy with snow, across the inlet and over Anchorage; usually these clouds dumped on the city before lifting over the mountains behind. Ahead was the hope of spring, when it would be light for more than a few hours every day and the spirits of everyone in Anchorage would rise. Howard planned to take a tidewater field class.

He loved his work at the restaurant, cutting up exotic vegetables and small sea animals. Even cleaning the stoves and floor gave him satisfaction. "Too clean," said the cook. "Food tastes different now. You drive all my customer away." The aromas from the cooking food pleased him, as did the knock and whistle of the old steam heater, the taste of the various dishes, the voice of the cook and the waitress arguing in Chinese. The restaurant closed at eleven, so he came home about midnight, after cleaning up. Each night when he came in, Allison rose from her computer and they fell into bed, holding each other until they fell asleep. "If it weren't for the ranch and Rockwood," he said to her. "I could live here forever."

Then in mid-April when Anchorage began to accelerate toward summer, Allison watched his soul settle into a dead calm. He was apathetic about school, church, cooking, or even her, when she was home. She gave him the present of a night away from Anchorage. They drove down Turnagain Arm of the inlet to Alyeska and ate dinner at the resort. They took a late night tram to the top of Mount Alyeska and watched the northern lights, sheets of curling, whipping light, and the white mountain and dark water of the inlet below.

Back in their room, she drank a little wine while she took a long bath, just enough to give herself a pleasant glow, like sunrise at midnight. When she came out of the bedroom, his face stopped her, mournful as the face of a hound dog. "What?" she said.

"I'm stuck in that crappy apartment alone every night," he said. "All winter it was dark."

"Not now, Howard. I've been planning this for weeks." His words seemed adolescent, melodramatic, rehearsed. She had read one of his western romances; the woman in a cabin on the frontier had said almost the same words to her cowboy husband when he came back from building a fence one day. Allison laughed out loud and his face turned angry. "Sorry," she said. "Right now you're trapped in an expensive resort hotel. Ruins some of the effect." She wrapped the towel more tightly around herself and sat on the couch. He joined her there and lay his head on her shoulder. The cowboy had told his woman that she had garden and children to divert her. You have everything you could want, the cowboy had told her. Then she ran off with a gambler. Howard wanted to run off with a cow. She felt moisture trickle down her back.

"I thought you'd be compensation for any loss." Another rehearsed line. His voice had a liquid quality, uncontrolled. "Maybe we need to change something."

She snorted a laugh, and he moved away from her on the couch. "Listen to you," she said, tipping her face up to look at the underside of his chin. "I thought you were making it okay."

"So did I," he said.

She thought, You're a junkie kicking a fatal habit. A snake splitting a five-generation skin. Eve—but that was cliché now.

"You turn hard as stone whenever we talk about going back," he said.

"Back? Scares me. Scares me that somehow you'll brainwash me, drug me, or hit me on the head and drag me comatose out there." To that sagging house and barren desert.

"Right," he said, sarcastic. "People who are married—"

"Don't give me that people who are married crap. I've never wanted it." She watched his face. "So tell me straight, convince me. None of this whining."

He stood and walked to the window and looked out on the side of the snow-packed mountain. She lay back on the couch, wishing they were tuned to each other enough for love-making without all his talk. Soon he turned to face her. "You've been there," he said. "Everything is dry and you bring water out of the ground or out of the mountain and grow a crop that needs twenty-four inches of water to grow. Like magic." He sat on the arm of the couch. She lifted herself and he slid over, cradling her head on his lap. "Then the cattle—their long heavy bodies, bulls with good thick loins and hindquarters. Right now, fields are greening, farmers plowing."

Thrusting their plows into the furrows with all their might. Or was it sickles? Some metaphor which coupled farming and sex. Despite herself, she grinned, pushing her face into his stomach. His language was ardent, excessive even for him. She suspected a trick.

He said, "Alfalfa coming up smooth as cloth in the fields in the spring." He touched her head, worked his fingers through her hair, and massaged the base of her neck.

"Yes," she said. "Oh, yes. That feels so good. Just stop talking for a minute." With his hands working her neck, she felt her body become languid. Fifteen minutes later she was relaxed enough for sex. She turned and lifted her lips to his.

"I want a child," he said against her mouth.

She sat back from him, bewildered. "A child?" Could fertility of woman and land be identical in his weasel brain? Or was he using the ranch as a bartering chip? She twisted from under him and left the bedroom. "Damn you," she said. "Damn your twisted brain."

"What? What did I do? I want the ranch and I want a child. I can't have both."

But she knew that they were connected for him. He wanted to shackle her with child, bind her down, make her a real woman. He'd say, Somebody has to provide for you while you're with the baby; ranching's all I know.

She forced her voice level. "I don't think that's a good solution to your isolation here. Your mind is as tangled as a thorny hedge," she continued. "A woman is not a field."

"You're drunk," he said. "You're not making sense."

"Not drunk enough. You want to become the new hero patriarch of the Rockwood clan. You want to do to me what every Rockwood, what every *Mormon* male, does to his woman. I'll have none of this conniving. Talk to me straight about having the ranch or talk to me straight about having a child, but none of this whining, conniving manipulation."

"My desire for a child is biological," he said. "You've taught me that. I want a child."

"It isn't biological in a man," she said. "Sex is biological in a man."

"It's replenishing the race. Pure biological impulse."

"You have a filthy heart," she said.

"What?" he said.

"You want that old Rockwood house filled with babies and a

woman there producing them. He pumps them in, she pumps them out. It's your idea of dynasty."

"Simon made his wife commit to a dozen children before he'd marry her."

"You're *proud* of it. Mormons must have an extra gene, keeps you focused on reproduction. Babies raining from heaven. Splat, splat. What do you want from me—thirteen babies, so you can strut in front of Simon? Why stop there? Twenty-one, so your great-great grandfather can look out of the fourteenth dimension, or wherever you think he is, and shower blessings on you?"

"One," he said. "I want one."

"One for *now*. You'll try to wear me down, I know it."

"Maybe two," he said. "Three. No more than three."

Never, she thought, never tell him you think about it too. "I bought wine to put us in the mood," she said. "I guess you won't take a little to relax you."

He lay in bed, eyes on the ceiling, working himself farther into lethargy. She proceeded to seduce him. But that was the wrong word, she decided; seduction implied some resistance, some play. Howard simply didn't care. She felt whirled back to her last days with Eliot—drunk and straining to love. Finally Howard gripped her, his eyes closed. She was hopeful, believing that he allowed his body to carry him to a territory deeper than manipulation and loss. She composed a mental letter to Emily. "Not math, but Howard is hell."

Then his father died.

Hearing the news, Howard slumped forward against the table. They had been eating and Allison looked up at him from her plate of food, seeing only the phone dangling from his hand.

"Walter or Emily?" she asked. "Tell me what's happened."

"Heart attack?" Howard lifted the receiver and asked his mother.

"He's back in the hospital?" asked Allison.

"No," said Emily. "Not a heart attack. He fell off the top of the stack."

"Fell?"

"He was feeding the cows and slipped."

"Tell me what happened," said Allison.

"The sheriff said he fell twenty-five feet," said Emily. "He landed on an old oil barrel and broke a rib. It punctured a lung. Brother Jenkins found him the next day." Howard stood without speaking. He saw a bale tip outward; his father clawed the side of the stack as he fell.

"Howard?" Emily said.

"Howard?" Allison said.

"He fell off the stack. He's dead." He spoke to his mother again. "When? When did he die?"

"Sheriff said it was certainly the fall that killed him."

"He felt no pain," Howard said to Allison. He swallowed. "His body was out all night?"

"Oh, no," said Allison.

"Yes," said Emily, "but the cows were all around the stack through the night trying to get in. It was a miracle they didn't break the fence down. They were milling around him all night."

Howard looked at Allison. "Cows kept the coyotes away."

"They did what?" asked Allison.

"The funeral's day after tomorrow," said Emily.

"I'll get the first flight I can," he said.

"I'm coming, too," said Allison.

"We'll be there tomorrow," said Howard.

"Everybody else will be here," said Emily.

"We can go tonight," said Allison. "I can take my work with me."

"Evan and June are coming," said Emily. "Darlene and Roger. Everybody."

"How are you holding up?" asked Howard.

"Another attack would have put him in the hospital or a rest home," said Emily. "He died feeding his cattle. I can't imagine how he'd rather have gone."

"Did the cattle step on him?" asked Allison.

"I heard that," said Emily. "Tell her, Howard. Don't leave her in suspense. Somehow the cows didn't break in."

"Maybe he had a heart attack," said Howard. "Maybe that caused him to fall."

"I don't want to know about it," said Emily.

"What did she say?" said Allison.

"He was in the stack yard," said Howard. "Cows couldn't get in to step on him."

"He's gone," said Emily. "He was gone from me before he died. But all spring I've imagined him out there working, walking through his herd like a king." She made a noise as if someone hit her in the stomach. "We both did what we wanted."

"Can Brother Jenkins feed the cattle?"

"He's been helping every day anyway," Emily said. "Now you'll want to take it over. You know, sometimes you can see something coming but you can't put your hand out to stop it?"

"I did see it coming," said Howard. "I imagined him climbing the stack and falling off."

"That isn't what I meant. I meant that this will make trouble for you and Allison. I didn't want that to happen."

"But it's happened."

"What's she saying?" asked Allison. "I want to talk to her." Howard handed her the phone. "Emily. I'm sorry it happened this way."

"He died happy," said Emily. "More than will happen to you or me or Howard."

"You know I'm flying with Howard?"

"I'll be glad to see you," said Emily. "It's been too many months."

After she hung up, Allison found Howard in the bedroom, stuffing clothing into his suitcase. He had cleaned out his drawer. "How long should I pack for?" she asked.

"What?" he said. He seemed dazed. "Three or four days."

"You're not coming back."

"I could have stopped him. If I'd stayed with him, this wouldn't have happened."

She folded sweat shirt and Levis into her duffel. "He could have slipped with you right below him, watching."

"I could have done something." He looked at her. "What if he was alive for a while? I could have taken him to town, to the hospital."

"Your mother said he died happy."

"Yes," said Howard. "He died happy. Would that console you?"

"No," she said. "It was a stupid thing to say." She put her arms around his head and hugged it to her chest. "Howard, my love, I don't know what to say."

"He's with the others. Max and Ellen, Solomon and Sophia, James Darren and Mary, Eliza, Amy, and Lucy."

She listened to Howard recite the names. He seemed comforted by the crowd of men and women. She pictured Walter lying on his back in the middle of an icy flat. Cattle, their heads held low, marched in a circle around the body as it grew stiff and cold.

"If he's with them," Howard said, "why does it hurt so much?" He laid his head against Allison's shoulder and closed his eyes. She stood and pulled him to the couch where she sat with him draped across her lap.

Staring out the jet window at the jagged coast, Howard thought, about the shock of his father's passing. They said that knowledge of the afterlife takes away the sting of death. Without closing his eyes or bowing his head, Howard tried to pray. Father in Heaven, he thought Grandfather, Grandmother, Jesus, I can't bear this loss. Allison got up to go to the bathroom, and he closed his eyes and tried to sleep; he and his brothers and sisters would probably stay up all night talking. He imagined himself walking down through the herd, breaking bales for the cattle that crowded around. The snow was ankle deep and a bitter wind blew. His father walked on his left, scattering hay; his grandfather Max was on his right. He didn't have gloves or chaps; wires cut into his fingers and sharp stems of hay lacerated his knee as he lifted each bale. He felt something like a hand on the back of his head, light as air.

Fourteen

After the funeral and the prayer at the grave,
Allison stood with Howard at the cemetery. She watched him climb
over the fence and pick some lupine which he placed on his father's
grave. "He would've wanted real flowers," Howard said. "He wouldn't
have liked all these greenhouse plants." Howard placed the lupine in
water in a tin can, and they stood next to the mound of dirt and looked
out over the valley. A tractor crawled across a field below them. The
fields stretched west from where they stood; the soil was muddy and
green, every field verdant. A sheen of grass covered the foothills. A
plume of smoke rose from the edge of someone's field.

"He's in heaven dragging burning rags soaked in diesel along a
weedy ditch."

"Diesel in heaven?" said Allison. "He's probably burning whiskey
and champagne. They'd have no other use for it in Mormon heaven."

"I guess in heaven there might not be weeds."

"Spirit weeds."

"That fits him. He was a spiritual weed." He looked at her.
"They're going to ask me to take over the ranch. No one else can do it.
I'm going to have to do it."

She grabbed him by the throat. "What am I going to do with
you?" Time like a spiral bringing her back to the same dilemma. "I'm

216

becoming more a pagan, but it isn't three old women, it's a bunch of hag-like old men weaving my life. They've decided to force me through the same experience again and again until I'm broken." She felt suddenly dizzy; she wished another skunk would spray her across the face to distract her.

About all she remembered from the funeral was how weary Emily looked, standing with her seven children and their spouses around her greeting Walter's friends. "What will I do without him to push against?" Emily had said. "I'll hurtle off into space." So Allison and Nancy held their arms around her from opposite sides until she seemed steadier. The funeral was long, speakers and singers, more speakers and singers. Some old ladies warbled a sweet song which began, "The West, a nest, and you, Dear, Oh, what a dream 'twould be," and ended with "A cradle and a baby, The west, a nest, and you." They announced that it was Walter's favorite song, but Allison decided it must be Howard's manifesto. Then Walter's cousin, a man everyone called Uncle Edgar, told an interminable story about a time when he and Walter had gathered pine nuts which they, out of the goodness of their boyish hearts, gave to a widow. Howard whispered to Allison that the two boys had actually stolen the nuts, but Walter's mother, Ellen, made them give them back. Uncle Edgar ended with a warning to the living about improper use of the priesthood, which, because of the way Emily frowned as he said it, must have been directed at her. When the procession arrived at the cemetery, Allison saw Bishop Hansen talking to Uncle Edgar under a tree, shaking a finger in his face. "He's my guardian angel," Emily had said. "He's making sure I have today to mourn my husband."

So now they stood in the cemetery, while Howard worked toward telling her that he would never leave Utah again. Damn, she thought, he's lost in spite of all my care.

"On the plane I watched you work on your laptop," he said. "You could do that here."

"Not without clients. How could I keep a freelance operation going out here?"

"Drive to Salt Lake or Provo. Computers are booming in Utah. Second Silicon Valley."

"Yes," she said. "I've thought of that. But I like mingling with people, banging against them. Even Lisa. I like watching the faces of people when I fix easily something they've struggled with for weeks. I know it's the worst kind of vanity and aggression, but I love it. Sitting in front of the computer in Rockwood? Horrible isolation."

"This is what they call being at an impasse."

"Compromise," she said. "You spend the winter in Alaska, when you can't farm. I'll spend spring and summer down here."

"Would Lisa agree to that?"

"She'll agree to whatever I ask," she said. "She needs me."

"Won't work. The cattle have to be fed. A million things to do on a farm in the winter. A farm is all or nothing."

"I'm going to miss you," she said. "We should never have married." She turned and walked down toward the house.

Watching her back, Howard thought of twelve hundred acres of land and three hundred cattle with no Rockwood to manage them. Why couldn't she understand?

That evening Bishop Hansen asked a sister to answer the phone and tend to the door, so that the family could be alone. The older grandchildren played with the little ones in the backyard.

Crowded into the living room, the fifteen adults avoided looking at each other. Nancy turned the pages of a photograph album—the only sound other than the whisper of Karl's hands rubbing together. Their mother shifted her gaze from one to another of her children. Howard sat on the floor, his back against the brown coal-burning heater. He looked up at the chandelier, installed by Great-grandpa Solomon when he had the house wired for electricity. He traced his finger in the dust under the stove, feeling that they were all in a coffin, trapped with the dead air.

Allison leaned back on the couch, her eyes closed, but Howard knew she wasn't asleep.

"Remember our trip to Denver?" said Nancy suddenly, her voice too loud. She held up a page of pictures—their trip to buy five new bulls from a Colorado ranch.

"Dad thought it would make our fortune, if we got those good bulls," Karl said.

Nancy turned to their mother. "I remember that you had a doubled piece of cardboard which you unfolded to make sandwiches."

"It's funny we didn't think to stop," his mother said. "All that beautiful country and we drove straight through it."

Nancy passed around the photograph book. One picture was of the guest house at the Angus ranch, where they had stayed overnight. Howard remembered walking with his father and brothers to the pens filled with square black bulls—shiny, vigorous purebreds. His father had climbed the fence, striding through them. Proud animals, unafraid, they had barely moved to let him pass as he examined them, carefully choosing five heavy yearling bulls. Nancy lifted the album to show more pictures, holding them toward the family and talking about each one, as if she were the teacher of a children's Sunday school class— Walter, Karl, Nancy, and Howard starting toward the mountain on their horses; the Pioneer Day picnic at the stone church; their father, Evan, and Stuart laying shingles on the roof of the church.

Howard looked at the others, who smiled with nostalgia. The pictures were like vortexes, swirling them back. He wanted to distance himself from the memories, to clarify his vision of what had actually happened in order to gain a non-eulogizing sight. Suddenly he imagined his father, a sinner, falling through the limitless void of space, clawing the vacuum as he fell.

Everyone jumped as the phone rang, and then Sister Delbert's voice, low, explained.

"Remember when we went to that family reunion in Salt Lake?" said Emily.

"Dad had a fight with Uncle Edgar about whether Solomon drank coffee or not."

"Uncle Edgar said that it wasn't in Solomon's character to break the Word of Wisdom."

"He was an apostate polygamist," said Howard, "rationalizing how he cheated on his wives, and Uncle Ed was worried about whether he tipped a cup at the sheep camp."

"Now that puts a harsh light on it," said his mother.

Simon laughed and shook his head. Nancy looked at Karl and gave a snort of laughter.

Emily said, "I couldn't believe it today when he told the story of the pine nuts. 'Poor Widow Stukey doesn't have any.'" She started giggling, and Howard didn't want to look at her. The tears rolled out of their mother's eyes. She sobbed with laughter. Howard sat back, holding his mouth stiff, then he burst out, bleating like a goat.

Sherrie laughed with them, but Allison and the other in-laws glanced at each other, their faces worried. To Howard, that was even funnier; he wrapped his arms around his sides and tried to stop. He could only think of Uncle Edgar, so self-possessed, worrying about the purity of Solomon Rockwood's eating habits and missing the most obvious facts.

Finally he wiped his eyes: "What will Sister Dilbert think of us?" That sent them into another fit. Then his mother stopped, but the tears continued to run down her face. Suddenly Howard couldn't remember what was funny either. Nancy shut the picture album.

"We shouldn't have left him alone," Karl said. "I should have come out more."

"I shouldn't have left at all," Howard said.

"When he was in the hospital," said Karl, "you know, when you and Allison were here last November, I drove over and blessed him to recover. I felt inspired. Now he's dead."

"He couldn't bear not to be active," said Evan.

"Mom and I have been talking," said Karl.

"Karl," said Emily.

"Let me have my say," said Karl. Emily folded her arms, pressed her lips together. "Mom sold the windmill property, but I've talked to her about developing the piece south of there, up in the foothills. It's a better piece anyway. I thought she was in favor of it, but now she's changed her mind. I wanted to find out what you thought."

"Whatever she wants," said Evan. "It's hers to do whatever she wants."

"I want to run it for a year," said Howard. "I want to try it. At the end of the year I promise it will be worth more than it is now. Then we can either sell it or I'll buy it myself."

"Well," said Allison. "Who wanted to be bound by marriage?"

"Let me know when you're finished discussing what you want to do with Walter's and my property," said Emily. Evan nodded his head but kept his mouth shut.

"None of us wants a cut," said Nancy. "It was meant to be ranched by Rockwoods."

"A year?" said Stuart. "We can wait that long. I'm sure all of us can. I know that Dad hoped one of us would work it."

"I'm going to develop the foothill property," said Karl. "I'm going to pay myself a commission and then each of us will get part of the profit above that."

"Do any of you have any problems with me taking it over for a year?" asked Howard. They all looked at each other and shook their heads.

"It's sold already," said Emily. "I sold *all* of it to Brother Jenkins."

The room was silent.

"Thank God," said Nancy.

"Thank Emily," said Allison.

"How much?" asked Simon.

"Three hundred and seventy-five thousand," said Emily.

"We can give it back to him, can't we?" asked Howard.

"I don't want to get into a fight with any of you," said Emily, "but as soon as you could every one of you left this ranch and Rockwood."

"Not me," said Howard. "I've longed to come back."

"Howard, longing and doing are two different things," said Emily. "You could have come home and worked it with your father, but before that could happen you aligned yourself with a woman who will *never* live here."

Allison opened her mouth and shut it. Howard looked from her to his mother. He shook his head to try to clear it.

His mother turned to Karl. "I've sold *all* of it, including the foot-hill property. Frank wanted that piece as part of the whole. I had nothing against you playing around with it, Karl, but he wouldn't go for it."

"We could have all paid off our mortgages," said Karl.

"We still can pay off our mortgages, you idiot," said Simon. "Leave her alone."

"The money will be for women," said Emily. "I've decided to establish a house for battered women."

"You'd give it to someone else before you'd give it to us?" said Simon.

Emily looked at her son. "Every one of you left as soon as you could. If I could give it to you and to them both, I'd do it in a second."

"Mother," said Stuart. "You didn't trust us enough to talk it over with us."

"What would you have said? Imagine what would happen if we tried to discuss it. We're half a minute from shouting at each other right now. Can any of you imagine us talking civilly about it? Walter and his brother came to blows over it and they're as Christian-minded as you are. The money goes to me. You may feel you have a right to an inheritance, but you all left. Be mad at me forever if you want. You can twist your lives into bitterness or you can accept it and go on with your lives. I decided it was better to do it and talk later than to argue forever about whether it should be done."

"You're going to keep it all?" said Simon.

"Without being cruel to you, I need to say something. Your father didn't think about dying. He left no will; he set nothing up to protect the ranch. As soon as I try to transfer it to you, the government takes thirty-three percent, a hundred and twenty-five thousand. Two hundred and fifty thousand is left. That would be just over thirty thousand for each of us—not enough to pay off your mortgages." She held her hand out toward Evan and Simon. "Of course, there would be enough to do you some good. I think it would completely pay off Evan's mortgage because it's so small, but it would hardly help spread out over everyone's mortgages. And it would be gone."

"You could give it to us a little each year," said Karl. "You can give a two thousand-dollar gift and nobody pays taxes."

"But I'm not going to do that. None of you are so destitute that you can't survive without the money. Walter taught you how to work, and *that's* your best inheritance. I don't know yet everything I'm going to do with the money. Maybe I'll travel around the world ten times. Maybe I'll change it to gold and sit on it. Maybe I'll have enough to do some good for people who can't take care of themselves. I'm just glad to finally have some options."

"You can't do this," said Simon.

"It's already done," said Emily.

Howard dragged Allison west, "to feed the cattle one last time," he said. Over the pass they dropped onto the flat, where green short grass covered the hills. The flat dropped away from them in all directions but the south, where a gray craggy mountain lay. From far away she saw the same black ridge, then, at length, the cabin set back in its shadow.

"Here's where he fell," said Howard, stopping at the stack. Allison heard a cow bellow; that raucous siren would have enticed Howard away from her. She had always found getting men easy, had never loved a man she didn't get. But she would have been unable, except for Emily, mother-in-law and friend, to bind this one.

"Brother Jenkins told me to feed them away from the stack," Howard said. "I guess some broke in the other day." Howard started the tractor and drove it into the stack yard. He threw the bales down. "Don't fall," said Allison. "You're standing too close to the edge."

He lifted the bales outward and dropped them. They shook the wagon as they hit. She stood to one side. Finally he climbed down and showed her how to drag them into place on the wagon. "You'll drop one on my head," she said.

"I'm aiming," he said. "Not at your head."

Yes, she thought, like your father aimed.

Standing on the wagon, she looked toward the haystack. She imagined Walter lying crumpled on the frozen ground, Max lying on the black ridge with coyotes chewing on his available parts. "Your mother is an angel," she said. "She's saved you."

His face turned angry. "Don't say she saved me. I didn't want to be saved."

Then Allison drove the tractor out of the stack yard and down toward the cattle. Howard stood behind her on the wagon tongue. "Cooome and get it," he shouted. "Cooome, coome, come and get it."

"They're still trained." Allison watched the cattle trail toward them across the flat.

Howard looked at her. "They come for the sound of the tractor. The voice is superfluous. I thought you'd notice that."

"Not superfluous," she said. "It's like singing. The tractor is the rhythm, you the melody." She felt like Perky Polly, cheerful in the face of his doubled sorrow. She didn't know what else to say, so she kept her mouth shut.

When they came to the cattle, he climbed onto the wagon and threw the bales off while she drove in a huge circle. The tractor roared and stank, but driving across the greening desert was pleasant. Afterward they walked up through the herd. Howard pulled the wires off the bales, making a croissant of hay; she lifted the thick sections away from the mouths of the cattle and tossed them in a larger semi-circle.

When they finished and the tractor was parked, he led her to the top of the volcanic ridge. Black rocks lay in a jagged fall down the hillside. Sitting on a sharp-edged boulder, Howard pointed to a flat rock as large as a bed. "They found Grandpa Max there," he said. "My father down there." He pointed to the stack. "They found my great-grandfather Solomon dead on the toilet in the Rockwood house."

"The best part of you is *not* underground." She stood on the rock, paced the place where his grandfather died. "You'd have frozen too in the winter, except for your mother. Shameless man—you'd have run up here after an imaginary woman."

Then finally his face softened. He said, "I would have fried my face in the summer. My ears would be tipped with melanoma by the time I was sixty."

"Starved in the spring," she said. "Frozen in the winter."

"No one to talk to. No stores, movie theaters, libraries, museums, restaurants."

"No bars," she said.

"None of the pleasures of civilized life. Just a pool where dead Indians once floated."

Allison looked down at the pit of water. "When you put it that way, it sounds almost appealing." She put her hand on his leg. "So how will our story end? He slowly grew bitter and left the woman he loved?"

"The woman gave up and lived with him in a cabin on the shore of the ocean."

"In stories," she said, "you're stuck with win and loss. In life you're not."

"The man rode off into the west to ranch with his woman. Win, win."

"Win for him, not for her. Translates into loss, loss, because they'd both be unhappy."

"But isn't it beautiful here?" he asked.

"I have to admit that it is. Marginally. But I still wouldn't want to live here. The woman, cooped up in a cabin, turned real bitchy. She took to taxidermy for recreation. One day she mistook her husband for a coyote."

"Outside of stories, it's lose, lose."

"No," she said. "We're not leaving this country forever. It's not exclusively this or that."

"But it's not mine."

"That's right," she said. "That's what you lose. You lose mine, mine, mine."

"You're as bad a capitalist as they come and you accuse me of being possessive."

"No. Money falls like dust through my fingers."

"I'd like to leave quickly," he said.

"Right now," she said. "I can get the tickets changed."

"You're made of money," he said. "I'm being bought off."

"The man started feeling kept. That fantasy ruined his life."

"Right," he said. "Money is irrelevant, all this is irrelevant." He flung his arm out as if he were trying to hit a bothersome fly. The good feeling was gone.

You better pull out of this, you son of a bitch, she thought. I'll not live with a morose and whining man.

Back in Rockwood, they threw their things into a suitcase and slung them into the rental car. They each hugged Emily twice and then drove north toward the airport. What now, Howard? she thought. What will you dream of now?

Fifteen

Stranded overnight on the North Slope by
a late spring snowstorm, Allison lay in her rented room, ate sugared
donuts, and drank whiskey. The bitter wind drove the snow horizontally against her window. At least this building, tighter than the cabin
in the desert, kept the cold outside. Six weeks had passed since she and
Howard had last had sex. It was, as her mother or Eliot would say,
symptomatic.

The day after returning from Utah, she had flown to the North
Slope for a two-week stint. Howard had been reserved, even morose,
when she left, but she had believed that two weeks would be time
enough to become reconciled to what his mother had done. But when
she returned to Anchorage, he was still brooding, and they had never
reconnected: he turned to the wall and snored; she worked late at her
computer; he read a western novel until three in the morning or put on
his coat and walked the streets. Their talk turned quickly to peevish-
ness or snappish sarcasm over trivial aggravations. *Not* making love was
their habit, as if they had forgotten how it was done.

In the night the storm blew away southeast, and the next morning
she called Howard (his voice showed that he was still in a funk) and
flew home. Looking down from the airplane, she knew that her plane
flew along the margin between the frigid vacuum of space and the rock

and water of earth. If the plane did not bank at a precise angle, she would be caught in limbo forever. Finally they landed in Anchorage and she relaxed.

Her worn-out Mustang was at the mechanic's, so she phoned Mark to pick her up. "Howard's being a jerk," she said after swinging her duffel into his back seat.

"Kick him out," said Mark. "Buy him a one-way ticket."

"No," she said. "I have an investment in him."

"Investment? Then stop payments. Take on somebody else. Me, for example."

"You're so subtle, Mark. If you weren't my friend, I'd slug you. I'll slug you anyway." She hit him hard on the arm with the point of her knuckle.

"Wear this." He handed her a necklace, three long canine teeth on a silver chain. "Tell him, either he snaps out of it or these ghost teeth will crawl across and gnaw his neck in the night."

"Where did you get these?"

"Last summer I found a skeleton on a hillside. Eight feet long with the tail."

"Bear?"

"Wolf. The skull filled my day pack."

She sniffed the wolf fangs and curled them in her fingers. "Thank you." The teeth had once chunked flesh out of steaming caribou. They were cold, white bits of wolf soul, ferocious. She looped the strand around her neck.

Inside the apartment, she groped for the kitchen light. Some trick of shadow reminded her of entering her parents' apartment after playing in the streets of Atlanta, and she was calling for her father, who should have been working on his dissertation. But he wasn't home.

She found Howard asleep on the bed, a book open on his chest. He wore sweat pants, but was bare above the waist. She touched his chest; he flinched. He opened his eyes, blinked, shut them again. "Wake up," she said. "I've brought a friend for dinner." In a previous life she would have lain across him, spoken her love with her lips brushing his.

"It's not ready," he said. "I didn't want to see anybody tonight."

"She's a ghost friend. She lifted her chin, showing him the necklace.

He reached up to finger the teeth. "Did she put up a fight?"

She took his hand, but he pulled free. "Mark found them." The cover of Howard's book showed a big-breasted woman lying in the arms of a cowboy. She touched the book. "The real West," she said. "You're drugged on romance." The cowboy had wide, muscled shoulders, a rugged face—generic male beauty. The woman's breasts were bare nearly to her nipples and each was as large as her upturned face. Caricatures.

"I'm almost finished," Howard said. "It's the exciting part." He rolled back on the bed and flicked on the light. "The Indians have stolen her away and he's going to save her."

"Then he'll mount her and ride into the sunset," she said. Maybe that's part of it, she thought. After nearly a year together, we've lost our fantasies: she no longer thought of him as raw material in her hands, and apparently he no longer thought of life with her as an adventure. "I'll cook dinner."

"It's my turn," he said. "Thanks." He lifted the book again, blocking his face. She was irritated that they'd lost the rhythm of talk—which, all fall, most of the winter, had helped them through disagreements. They had easily modulated from words and eyes to hands and bodies. She turned away. Two weeks before it had done no good to shout. He had smiled at her fury and retreated into lethargy as thick as Utah fog. She should take Mark's advice.

She pulled a fat salmon out of the refrigerator, another gift from Mark. It had been defrosting for the dinner Howard hadn't cooked. The best salmon she had eaten was the first one, the one served to her at the Corsair, steaming on a tray. The first was always the best, then it grew tiresome. She would cook this limp and freezer-burned fish now, before it spoiled, but it threw her off. She had imagined coming into a warm house, meeting the aroma of cooking food, sharing a long talk during dinner, even longer play in bed—a slow, easy dance. "This is stupid," she said. As a teenager, she had fought with her mother, or worse, played passive-aggressive games with her, weeks of silence and stifled anger. "It's a waste and I won't have it."

"Won't have what?"

"The silence," she said.

He gave her silence.

She wanted something new—a mauling, teeth and claws. "You're pouting." Still nothing. The barren ranch still hung in his imagination like Atlantis, ever green and impossibly lost. Anger was a lump under her breast. She rubbed the inside of the fish with sage and salt and shoved it into the oven. She washed and walked back to the bedroom, drying her hands. "So what's your plan, bucko?"

Without looking up he said, "I feel invisible."

"What?" She grabbed the book out of his hands and threw it in the corner. "Say it," she shouted, "say you want to go back to your god-awful town." She wanted to slap him out of his lethargy.

"Not invisible, but like I can't see myself." He propped himself up on his elbows, his eyes wide, clearly thinking that she would hit him. "Once I wanted to go back, and it kept me motivated. Now, what's the use? I'm not asking a rhetorical question. I'm in a bind."

"You're bitter with loss and can't get through it," she said. "Maudlin." They would wait in this tense space until the machine of his mind finally shifted like her Mustang's transmission in winter. And then she might discover he was in reverse.

"Not just loss. It's being in a vacuum of ambition. It's me and God and money and the lost ranch and my dreams and—" He paused. "It's a multifaceted bind. Talking doesn't untangle it." He got up to retrieve the novel. He seemed as dramatic as a soap opera bitch.

In the bathroom she sat on the toilet lid, her feet up on the tub while she unlaced and removed her boots. Multifaceted bind. Multi-faceted bastard. Propping her boots over the heat vent to dry, she walked down to the kitchen and started some rice.

He said, "I'm past blaming you or my mother."

"The hell you are." That clammed him up again. She didn't know what to do. Her parents had either shouted problems out or had simply found someone else until the problem was buried. Never a solution. Much which was twisted and hidden grew in that supposedly open atmosphere. Neither parent had ever gone without sex. That would have been like trying to stop a faucet with your fingers. But this felt just as twisted. She peeled some wilted carrots and put them in a pot with some Dijon mustard and brown sugar. She turned the heat on low and then lay on the couch, holding the newspaper, quickly drowsy. Soon she woke enough to go to the bathroom. He was prone on the bed, barricaded behind his book. Reading these fictions didn't help, picturing men who rode off into the west, leaving their women pining after them. He peered from behind his book like a sniper. Sometimes she wondered if he could even see her face because of all the ghosts of dead relatives swirling between them. It must be hell having a transcendent imagination. Soon he stood and she heard him taking plates out of the cupboard and silverware out of the drawer.

She came up behind him and ran a nail down his spine, cutting across each knob and valley. He said, "My skin feels alive and dead when you touch it, like the flesh of a zombie."

She slumped into a chair at the table. "Let's eat the damn fish."

"I feel owned. Paid for."

"It's circumstantial," she said. "A condition of where we each are. Accidental. Not intrinsic to us. Can't you see it?"

"Bullshit!" he said, face to face with her. She felt the rush of adrenalin. "Bull*shit!*"

"Now!" she shouted in his face. "We finish this now!"

But then the anger disappeared, and he turned back to the cupboard. "I can't believe you said that money is circumstantial. I could run a two-hundred-and-fifty cow herd. I could manage a six-hundred acre ranch." He dumped the fish on a plate, flinging it onto the table. Allison looked down at the juice draining out of the broken skin. "I can't imagine how my mother adapted to living in the desert—adjunct to my father's plans. Somehow she survived. I can't." He clapped his hands, bouncing them apart.

She said, "Did she withhold sex to get her way?"

He stared at her. "How would I know?"

She felt her body shaking and thought it lucky they didn't own a gun or a baseball bat. "Can't you see what you're doing to us? We have something unusual. Do you remember the night in your grandfather's cabin? How that felt? Not the sex but the talking, the touching. Like—like a communion. I've never had anything like it. You want to throw that away?"

"Your old song—*my* fault," Howard said. "You blame me so hard that I can't *see* myself. You talk to me as if you're my mother or therapist or older sister. I finally decided not to push it. Not to push anything."

She stood. "So I have to wait until you figure it out?"

He played his game and she felt no loyalty. She thought about Mark—open, rough, Canadian Mark. Maybe it was time for another leap. A leap from this melancholy husband. Leave him shackled with the marriage he had arranged. But taking another lover and then coming back was her mother's solution, confusing and destructive. A way of giving no man power over her.

Allison didn't feel hungry, so she went into the living room, lying again on the couch and reconsidering Mark. She occasionally discovered him at the door of her cubicle, watching her. Mark, the secretary. Would you like to take some dictation? she'd say, her voice a Mae West. She grinned; he was large as a bear and took no crap from anybody, not even Lisa. That messed up the daydream of seducing someone with less power. She'd always been upset by the stories her mother told her about male professors with their hands on the knees of women students. Heavy Texas accent: "I'm sure, darlin', if we just put our heads together, we can discover a solution to this little problem concerning your grade." Everyone, Howard included, lived fantasies. And then she realized another source of her anger; Howard might be right saying that she acted like the big sister. She *had* always thought that she could somehow save him. She felt embarrassed and even angrier, not wanting him to reveal her flaws of character.

And then he was in the doorway. "Here it is," he said. "I'm striding across my land, tall as John Wayne. And my cattle are grazing the new grass, really going after it. And it's so real that I decide to supplement that watery, useless grass with cottonseed cake."

"Son-of-a-bitching TV mini-series about ranching."

"Yes," he said. "But only because there's no ranch. Except for that, I would be doing it, not dreaming of doing it."

"Where am I in this fantasy?" she said. "Striding shoulder to shoulder or knitting back in the kitchen? Holding down the hearth? Producing the children. The nest, the west, and you, dear. A cradle and a baby?" The worst part was that all his propaganda made it seem as though she was capitulating even to think about having a child. Woman and child fit into one narrative for him. The mother tied down. There was no room to talk about other ways of being parents, how to have a child that wasn't a stereotype of Mormon pioneer heritage.

"Striding shoulder to shoulder," he said. "But you won't. Wouldn't."

"Couldn't. Not my career. You think I'd be equal to you as a rancher? Why would I want that? All that would be available to me in Rockwood is sitting in the house. And then you'd want a baby to give me something to do. But this whole conversation is stupid because it's past."

"Yes," he said, the hiss of a snake. "All the decisions were made for me. You should have seen your face when Mom told us she'd given the ranch away."

"Sold the ranch. I'm sure I felt relief."

He smiled. "I've invented a woman."

She couldn't tell for sure if he was joking or not. She laughed, a deep, rasping cough. "Let me guess. She's seventeen."

"Sweet face."

"Belinda's face."

"No. Submissive. Belinda was never submissive. She took charge, told me what to do, just like you do. This woman is passive and clear-skinned as a baby. Body soft in all the right places, tight in all the right places. She knows only one word—'Yes.' She has the fingers of a Swedish masseuse."

"You impregnate her, assert your patriarchy. She waddles around the house smiling at you. 'Yes, yes, yes.'" She said it sweet and false.

He wrapped his arms around himself. "You think I'm serious about wanting this kind of woman? It's a release because I can't have what I really wanted. You won't even let me be sarcastic. You want to be the one with clear vision."

"And you won't let me participate in your sarcasm."

"Listen," he said, taking a step forward. "I feed the older cows in a sandy, brushy swale so they'll bed down there. The heifers are in the shed, lying on straw. Every day I walk through them. I can tell, just by looking, which cow is going to drop her calf that day. If she's not around, we go looking for her. Often we see one just born, slick with mucus, bobbing its head as she licks it off. Sometimes one's stiff as a board, dead on the ground, sometimes dead in the cow. Every calf that lives is four hundred dollars that fall. But not just that, it's life, organizing a life, breeding cows, being something like God. Every minute I can, I plow the fields row by row, I breathe for a hundred hours the stink of diesel. I'm up all night if I need to be. I'm deaf from the roaring tractor. But then it's regular and brown—beautiful. Then spears of barley or wheat come up, a sheen of green."

She knew this part of his dream was not ironic. He would ruin their union by lusting for what was no longer his. They lived in the middle of a verdant paradise, green exploding on the mountains and hillsides all around the city, and he was visioning desert, all the time watching her with his steel-gray eyes wide enough that she could fall into them. Her throat tightened and she felt she might suffocate. She lay back on the couch. Panic scrabbled in her brain—not even of losing him but being unable to leave him, the terror of being amorphous, losing her boundaries again, as she had when she was a drunk teenager. That had been a little death, a little decay of skin and flesh.

"Your hands are shaking," he said.

"Damn right," she said. "You're too stubborn to ever give this up." Never, unless she went to a place with him where he could become like his father, and require that she become like his mother, strong but repressed. She remembered Emily's face, her powerful desert face, despairing the night the bishop released her, the night she panicked that he would cut her off. Emily's soul curled up like a fetus. That would happen to her if he succeeded in getting her to Rockwood. Allison knew that they were both being stubborn, both terrified of what the other wanted, but Howard's face was miles away across a wide, black void, unreachable.

She headed for the door, and ran down the steps. "Allison," Howard called. "Allison, where are you going?" A voice from the depths of lethargy. Such a pathetic voice, black-hole sad. Delicious to leave. By the time she reached the service station at the corner, the attack of panic was gone and she felt the same electric freedom she'd felt leaving Eliot.

She called a taxi and had the driver take her to the Blue Moon where Mark often hung out. Wading into the smoke-filled room, she grinned, a she-wolf on a night run, and as if in answer to her howl, Mark was seated at a table in the back.

"You're here alone?" she said.

"Where's your appendage?"

"Reading cowboy stories about passive, voluptuous women."

He grinned.

"Dance?" she said.

"Sure," he said. "You know, as many times as we've talked about your mother's project, I've never understood the attraction in virtual romance."

The band covered a Rolling Stones tune, "Honky-tonk Woman," playing it with even more bump and grind than the original. She led him out, wanting some kind of violence. She swayed, and then let herself go, jerking her body wildly. She smiled when Mark looked at her oddly. He held his hands out to her, and she brushed his fingertips. Her breath came faster and she calmed down, strutting, shaking her shoulders and hair, on the edge of jumping on the small stage with the band and screeching out the words: "She was a ho-o-o-onki-tonk woman." Before three songs were over, she dripped sweat. Mark's dancing was more subdued, he participated as a watcher, licking his lips. She felt good, James Brown good. They danced until she was exhausted and drank until she felt happier than she had for months.

Finally, very early in the morning, he asked her to come home with him. "I could," she said. In the car she slid across the seat next to him, and he swung his bear-like arm around her, rubbed his cheek against her hair. He drove fast through the sparse traffic. "Where do you live?"

"Hillside," he said. "Not far from Lisa."

She knew he had slept with Lisa, an affair between boss and secretary, so cliché. Which put it in a dynamic of power for her. A game of win and loss. Like her parents' faces the day her mother's lover left. Whoever loves least has the most power. The car flashed under the dark trees, back into the moonlight. She thought about Eliot's story of the pale houseman and the seductive bear; she was trapped in the middle of a prophetic hallucination. She imagined herself standing at Mark's doorway while he fumbled with his key. Then inside? How would what was happening with Mark, her friend, help her deal with Howard, her love? "Damn," she said, sliding back across the seat. Who would have thought that Eliot's ghost would conspire with her superego?

"What?" Mark said.

"Howard," she said. "I'm still a one-man woman."

"No," he said. "You can't do this to me."

"My intentions were good," she said. "No, I was selfish and bitchy."

Glowering, he turned the car in the street, the tires screeching. He drove back along Old Seward and turned onto Northern Lights Boulevard. Allison thought back to her first night in Anchorage, about her excitement for the future. Nothing was as clean as it seemed beforehand, nothing so bright. Mark said nothing, and she wondered if she'd ruined their friendship. Still sullen, he dropped her at the front of her building and drove away.

The apartment was dark, the bedroom silent. She felt full of energy, wound up like a jack-in-the-box. She should wake him, seduce him, if possible. Was it rape when a woman forced a man to have sex? She waited, her nose to the door, but she couldn't hear movement.

She pictured him naked, cross-legged on the bed. She'd lay her palm flat against his chest, and he would flinch again. "Where is your head now?" she would say.

"Floating above the inlet. Free of all encumbrances."

Then she would lay him down. "Girl," she thought, "your hard drive has crashed." She realized that she wanted not sexual surrender but fresh growth, re-connection, and then sex. She pulled a sleeping bag from the closet and lay across it on the couch. Then she opened the door and stood inside the bedroom—still no sound of breathing. She flipped on the light and the bed was empty. The closet door was half open, every piece of his clothing was gone.

"Damn," she said to the door. "Damn, damn, damn." She considered letting him go. Then she pulled on her tennis shoes. Fool, she thought, never run after a man.

She called a taxi, but it would take nearly an hour to arrive, so she told them to go to hell and started jogging the mile to the airport. She found him sitting at the gate for the flights to Seattle. His denim bag sat on the floor next to his feet. "This is dramatic," she said. "Will you rush off the plane at the last minute?" He held a ticket stub in his hand. She took it from him and looked. His plane left at seven in the morning, five hours away. She gave him back his ticket.

"How did you pay for it?" she asked.

"Money left from my father's life insurance. Mom gave us each a thousand dollars."

"I would have given—"

"Right," he said. "You would've paid me off."

"What—" A mist had come into her head. Something like a hangover without the high before. All their lives focused onto this one moment. "What are you going to do?"

"Finish at the U."

"Range management?"

"Yes."

"And then?"

"I haven't thought that far ahead."

"Back to Rockwood?"

He shook his head.

She said, "I thought that's what you wanted."

"I waited until one," he said. "Where were you?"

"Dancing with Mark," she said.

He stared at her, frowning. "I'm not going to Rockwood," he said. "I can't live there now." His voice was unnatural, hard and bitter.

"You still blame me," she said. "It's impossible. Even if I wanted to, I couldn't give you back your ranch."

"No!" he shouted, his face twisted with anger. She heard the clatter of something dropping. Turning, she saw a custodian watching them; the lid of a trash can lay on the floor near him. Howard stepped forward to the window; he cupped his hands against the glass and looked through them out on the runway. "I left because you've been—"

"What?"

"I guessed right," he said. "You were with Mark. I knew because of the necklace."

"I couldn't do it."

"Do what?"

"We danced, and I made Mark take me home," she said. "But you weren't there."

"Danced until one."

"Yes. I was mad as hell with you, and I wanted to have sex with him, but I couldn't."

"Oh," he said, and looked down.

She saw that he believed her without question. Tears swelled in the corners of her eyes. "I couldn't leave you," she said. "I was frightened when I saw your things gone." She shivered. He sat back down in the airport seat, and she took the one across from him. He stretched his hand toward her, then pulled it back, tentative as a bird. "I didn't know your father would die. We both thought we had time to do everything."

The custodian worked on the trash can close to their chairs, so Howard lifted his bag and they moved over to the shops. He chewed his lip, still turned in. She remembered him working his mouth while he sat on the grass in Houston, the knees of his suit pants stained.

"You're smiling," he said. "What's funny?"

"You're not smiling," she said.

"I thought you wouldn't come back," he said. "I was more frightened than you were."

"No," she said. "On a scale from one to ten, I was a ten. You couldn't have been more frightened."

"Let's never scare each other," he said.

"It's got us talking again," she said. "Can I talk you out of leaving?"

"You probably can. But I want you to tell me a few things." They sat at a table, she with her coffee, he with cocoa. "Your aversion to Rockwood. Is it because it's country? Because it's Mormon?"

"It's past."

"Not past until you explain. We've only talked around it."

"My job. I've said it a hundred times. It was just my job."

"That's all of it?" he said. "That's why your body shakes with anger?"

She took a breath. "You imagined that you were John Wayne striding across your land."

"John Wayne doesn't stride."

"Shut up. Here's how it is with me. The guy in charge of the site swore when he first saw me. He said, 'I need solutions, not a damn woman.' I didn't react. I just went to work. They had a program which they'd had to override for months. It managed a drill's response to resistance. They finally had to shut down, because broken drill bits kept shredding the casing. I solved the problem in eleven hours. But he still won't speak to me because he's frightened that his bosses might wonder what's wrong with him if a woman could solve the problem that had stumped him for so long. A frightened man is dangerous. He makes me tight when I'm around him. But he doesn't dare fire me. And that's only the logical part of it. What about all the crap he can't even describe to himself. Boys are frightened of strong women. A strong, mean woman confuses them. Like a mother gone bad. Serious cognitive dissonance."

"Rockwood. I asked why you get the shakes about Rockwood. You're on a tangent."

"Rockwood is the center of Utah."

"Utah?"

"It's worse than Texas for—ah—a kind of deference toward women that is really contempt. They're diseased with it." She took a drink of the scalding, bitter liquid. "Some of it even in college in Massachusetts. 'Is your math background really that solid?' A slight hesitation, as if a strong woman freezes them. One bastard believed I solved computer problems by intuition. Before puberty I played soccer on boys' teams. And it was just fine. When I was their goalie, they won games if they were good enough to make a single goal. Nothing got past me. Well, when I was twelve, my breasts sprouted." His eyes flicked down. She batted her hand at him. "Okay, so I'm still blooming. Anyway the boys started hesitating. At first I used that second of hesitation to charge them. Knock them on their butts and lift the ball away. I thought I'd just gotten better. Then one guy started giving me this simpering grin. Not just physical attraction, but something like, 'What are you doing here? I can take you anytime.' I slammed the ball in his face. Broke his nose." She looked at him. "The coach asked me to leave the team. I still don't understand that kind of holding back. The hesitation that isn't courtesy, isn't some odd effort at respect. It's condescension, envy, fear. So when you talk about walking across your land like John Wayne, I want to either strangle you or run away."

"I was being sarcastic about myself."

"The hell you were."

"Utah," he said. "You've told me about Texas and Alaska and Massachusetts. Nearly every place in the world but Rockwood. In reality, ranchers are liberal. They accept any woman or child who can work. There are plenty of women ranchers."

"I can believe that," she said. "But Rockwood's different. The town is different. Think about what they've done to your mother. You can hardly see how strong and smart she is, because she's your mother. She could lead a company, if the company were smart enough to recognize that women's ways of managing work are relationship-oriented instead of task-oriented." She frowned into his face. "See, you don't even believe it. And your father and the bishop are such kind men, but they hold her back by their expectation of her."

"I can see it," he said. "I still think that there are different forms of patriarchy. My father and my mother's father were not authoritarian men. Some are much worse. My great-great-grandfather used his wives and children to build a kingdom. His granddaughter left twenty volumes of journals—a diatribe against him and his sons for making their children work, using them up for the kingdom. The night of my court, I was in the house alone, and I could feel how destructive patriarchy can be."

"Work isn't bad," Allison said. "What's bad is having the credit taken away."

"But I'm not my grandfather," he said.

"I still say that living in Rockwood you would have been. The west, a nest, and you, Dear."

"I would've liked the chance to be different there."

"So we've said the same things again."

"No," he said. "We've never said anything clearly before."

"It's still murky," she said. She looked out the plate glass window at a departing jet. "What can I do to get you to turn that ticket back in?"

"Keep talking," he said. "Like you have tonight. Don't just assume I understand you and am just being obstinate."

"Practical," she said. "What can I do that's practical?"

"I want to finish school."

"In Salt Lake?"

"Somewhere."

"Why not here?"

"Environmental studies? Even that would be all right, if the program wasn't watered down." He paused. She fiddled with her coffee cup, twisted the ends of her hair. "Will you give me the money to fly to Juneau?"

"Juneau?"

"They have an oceanography school there."

"Oceanography? You puke on a boat."

"I want to try studying tidewater. Shoreline zoology."

"You playing another game here? Not much similarity between range management and tidewater zoology."

"So I make decisions on impulse," he said. "I make repeated leaps of—of foolishness."

"No. Don't repent of that. It's your best quality. Let's get out of here."

He only lost seventy-five dollars on his ticket. There were a couple of taxis outside, but Allison suggested that they walk. They stuffed his duffle in a big locker and walked toward home. The cool air passed through her shirt, chilled her arms and stomach. She started jogging, Howard groaned and then moved up next to her. He passed her, she passed him. Soon they were running, full out. She finally pulled ahead, sprinting toward the entrance to the airport, where she stopped and waited for him.

He said, "You're trying to give me a heart attack. So you can be free again."

"You all right?"

"I didn't know you were in such good shape," he said.

"I run every day at lunch. We have a treadmill."

"A man can run a horse down. The horse has more speed but the man has stamina."

"You made it up."

"No," he said. "My grandfather made it up. By the third generation of telling, it's true."

Instead of going back to the apartment, redolent of lethargy, they turned toward Earthquake Park and the inlet. Howard stood with his toes hanging over the unstable dirt rim. The cross waves made the roiling water seem to churn.

"All my life I've had the Benjamin Syndrome," he said.

"I can tell when you're lying, but tell me, what is the Benjamin Syndrome?"

"The Old Testament Benjamin—the spoiled, chosen child. He was Israel's last child, one of two from the favorite wife. Israel lost Joseph because the brothers were jealous and sold him into slavery, but Israel still had Benjamin—the *special* child. If Karl wanted the ranch and I wanted it, who would Dad have arranged to get it? All my life I got what I went after. Including Belinda, including you. Shameless, spoiled child."

"Everybody wants," she said.

"I've decided that my mother was right. I had already chosen to leave the ranch when I chose you. My decision to go back was done in bad faith to myself."

"When did you realize this?"

"Saying it, I know it's true. No. I've really been coming to it since we returned." He paused. "So Anchorage is paradise for you?"

"No," said Allison. "Of course, not. Lisa's a stupid fascist. She hates me because I'm better than she is. And then I think, is she what I'll become because I like shoving it back in the face of anyone who has power over me? Will that be what destroys my love of writing code?"

They walked along the edge trail, where Howard had run when they first came to Anchorage. The inlet lay beneath them, and the lights of the city spread before them and to their right. They sat on a log at the edge of the trail. "I've always had the feeling," he said as he laid his arm across her shoulder, "of what I wanted—something unusual, intense—a vision from God. Something better and stronger than what I've ever had. Not a sexual experience, something beyond that. I always thought that if I could clear out everything that I've been and start over, it would be all right. I thought anything would be better than this fumbling and groping. But I know that there's nothing better than fumbling and groping." He smiled slow but bright as a child. "Speaking purely metaphorically."

"My romantic Howard, always stuck in the here-and-now. Isn't that the hell of it?" She turned into him, kissed his mouth.

"Remember when you first saw me?"

"Yes."

"Tell me what you thought then."

"I thought you were a gay IRS agent. If I'd known how weird you really are, I'd never have spoken to you."

She kissed him again, moving her lips harder against his. His hands were around her shoulders, soft across her back under her shirt. He touched his lips to her hair, brushed his fingers across her skin.

"I'm freezing," she said. "And ravenous."

"There's salmon left."

"Ice cream," she said. "Rum flavored ice cream. Is there a 31-Flavors anywhere?"

He laughed. "Let's go back to the apartment. I'll make some cinnamon toast and cocoa."

"Ice cream."

They jogged toward the lights of Anchorage. The storm which had held her on the North Slope, weaker now, had come south. Icy drops fell from the infinite space above them. They entered a subdivision and walked through it and miraculously found an all-night diner. He laughed, clear and vigorous again. "We want ice cream," he said to the woman behind the counter, "two big bowls."

"Closest I can come is whipped cream," she said. "I'm out of ice cream for the night."

"On chocolate pie," said Allison.

"Apple," said the woman.

"Done. And coffee."

"And root beer," said Howard.

They sat in a booth, eating their pies. Howard reached across the booth and pulled the necklace out of her shirt collar. He lifted the silver chain over her head and laid it on the table.

She drew around the necklace with her spoon, a thin circle of whipped cream. She drew another circle around that one, brown, of coffee, circling white and brown until she had five circles. "I'm laying a spell on you, Howard," she said. "The spell of the wolf. You can never leave me."

He rubbed both hands down across his face and smiled. "Just where I wanted you," he said. "But some day we might leave Anchorage. Some day I get to have a say."

"Of course," she said, watching his eyes, the speckles of gray across his irises. "But for now no more blue funks when talking solves them so easily."

"Summary statement," he said. "It means you're finished talking."

"No," she said. "I just want to move the conversation to a more tactile language." Her fingers and lips did have a memory of the texture of his hair. She knew that soon they would walk back to the apartment, where they would reverse the trend of the last six weeks. Yes. She imagined his hands holding tight to the back of her neck as they moved together, imagined her body straining toward comprehension of his.

IV. Eagle River, Alaska

"For we know that the whole creation
groaneth and travaileth in pain together until now.
And not only they, but ourselves also,
which have the first fruits of the Spirit,
even we ourselves groan within ourselves,
waiting for the adoption, to wit, the redemption of our body.
For we are saved by hope."

—ROMANS 8:22-24

Sixteen

According to the new détente, any subject was open for talk. They practiced on smaller decisions, such as whether or not he would actually fly to Juneau for marine biology courses. They weighed the cost, the time away from each other. He finally decided not. He could graduate with a degree in biology in one year at Anchorage and wait for graduate school to specialize. Meanwhile, when graduation approached, she would shop around for a job in a city which had a suitable graduate program.

"We'll talk about swearing next," he said.

"Hell no," she said. "Do you want me weighing my words when I talk to you?"

"Yes."

One day when she was just back from the North Slope, he drove her up above Eagle River, about half an hour from Anchorage, and showed her a wooded plot. He spread slick brochures across the hood of the Mustang—Lincoln Log structures in various stages of completion. "You buy the precut logs and just put them together." She stared at his excited face and laughed at the strange rhythm of her life, at Eliot's fables coming true. He presented her with a list of building materials that reminded her of Thoreau's list at the beginning of *Walden:*

precut logs—$12,000
foundation—$1,000
land—$15,000
wiring and plumbing—$2,000
"Is it insulated?" she asked.

"I'm sure it is," he said. "Why would someone sell non-insulated cabins in Alaska?"

"Have you ever built anything like this?"

"I built a hog farrowing house once," he said. "Really, it's easy. I built all kinds of sheds on the ranch. I know the basic principles. And I can read. No more $800-a-month rent for a one-bedroom apartment."

She saw that he was determined. "Write it down," she said. "List every expense and then double it." She decided that it would give him something else to do, occupy his nervous energy. She made him borrow $35,000.

"We won't use it," he said. "We'll be paying interest on money sitting in my checking account." For his first try at a loan, the bank rejected him, so she said she'd pay half, and then co-signed with him for his share. "We're breaking our post-connubial agreement."

"Things change."

After sales tax, the pre-cut logs cost nearly $13,000; then he discovered that the bathroom and the kitchen cupboards and counters, all shown in the photograph, were not part of the original package. He could buy the materials from them for $6,000 or he could buy the plans for $200 and go to a local lumber yard. He had to pay $1,000 for bulldozing the spot where the cabin would rest. He'd forgotten about wiring. An electrician estimated the job at $1,200. Allison worked hard at not even thinking, "I told you so," and he worked hard at not apologizing for his mistakes.

Allison knew what was coming next. It's my turn for compromise, she told herself; he's given up more than I have. She pictured him checking off his list: "The nest, the west, and you, dear. A cradle and a baby." She believed that two of the four, she and a nest, would not satisfy him for long.

One Friday he called her at work and asked if she would be on time coming home. "I have a surprise for you." When she stepped in the door, the house was full of the wonderful smell of broiling steak. Tonight, she said to herself, you'll make yourself talk about it.

Before he could get to whatever emotional arguments he had cooked up—maybe sitting on the couch, looking at pictures of his nieces and nephews when they were babies—she said flat out, "If I get pregnant, I could lose my job."

"Wait! We've got apple pie and ice cream." He was Mr. June Cleaver; Allison choked on a laugh. He grinned, too. Watching his face, though, she saw how close to the edge he was.

"Could you do some work at home?" he said.

"I wouldn't be able to go up to the North Shore for half a year, or more," she said. "They won't let me on the plane after I'm six months along."

"How do you know that?" he said.

"I asked." He leaned forward beaming and touched her on the arm. She swallowed once and bit back the dammit-to-hells. "But that doesn't mean we've decided. Part of being open is the guarantee that bringing up a subject doesn't mean that we've already decided."

"Don't you think you're important enough to Lead Dog that she'll keep you on?"

"Our income would go down."

"I could get another job."

"You should finish school."

"We could start saving."

"By not buying a house?"

"Does it come down to house or baby?"

"No," she said. "Nothing as absolute as that. We just can't save as much." She bit hard on her lip, then couldn't resist asking. "Why? This is a test question."

"It *is* biological," he said. "I want to make a child with you."

"And part of me wants to make one with you. I want a little Howard around."

"Howlison," he said.

"It's because every one of your damned ancestors had ten children and you can't stand not to have even one."

"Probably. Just because that's a dumb reason doesn't mean there aren't other reasons."

"Namely?"

"It's what we do. We make copies of ourselves. God sends spirits to inhabit the bodies. Then we carefully raise the children. It's what God made us to do."

"So for you it's biological and cultural and, dammit all, spiritual. Can you understand how that last one repulses me?"

"No."

"What happens when we have sex? Are there spermlike intelligences swimming in the air, waiting their chance to dive into my belly? I don't believe it. So it's like a lie for me. You say that spirit and matter are one, but you still believe that something exists when the body dies. It makes no sense." She found herself on the edge of tears and was angry with herself. "Michael's gone," she said. "It feels like courage to face that fact. It feels like cowardice to avoid facing the truth."

"I can't argue with you," he said. "Neither of us can convert the other."

"Will you take the child to church with you?"

"Do we have to decide this now?"

"Yes. I want to have a child. It makes no damn sense to me, not a particle of sense, but I want a child. I want to have a child in my arms who looks something like you, but without your cowlick. I want to raise it up carefully. I've started thinking that we can maybe help a child avoid the damage done to both our parents. Raise a child in a moral and ethical house."

"That's the best reason for a compromise between a Mormon and a heretic," he said.

"Atheist," she said. "We should give my belief its right name."

"We'll let her choose," he said. "We'll teach her both perspectives; she'll be bilingual."

"And confused." She frowned. "But it's as close as we can come. We'll talk and talk and talk to her, when she's old enough to understand. But if you want her religious, you'll have to teach her God when she's young. Otherwise she'll never believe."

"This can't be a contest," he said. "We'll have to invent a non-polarized way of talking."

"Nearly impossible. It would take a couple of geniuses to do it." She showed her teeth like a wolf, mostly because she believed their talk had been too idealistic, too impractical.

"So, we've decided," he said.

"Not yet. I haven't told you my reasons."

"Such as?"

"It's something you want, and I trust you in this, don't ask me why. It's something I can give you. Also I want a baby myself. I've wanted one for some time. Again don't ask me why, because it hardly makes sense to me. I don't want to wait until I'm thirty." She shrugged her shoulders. "You'll have to wear condoms for three months."

"All the time? We used to emasculate bull calves with little circles of rubber."

"You're so perverse," she said.

"Shake on it?"

"On your perversity?"

"No. On our agreement."

"The hell with shaking," she said. She moved past his arm and wrapped her arms around him. "I want more commitment than that."

Memorial Day they flew to visit Emily for a few days and help her paint the trim of the old house, tear down the barn, and plant tomatoes and squash in her garden. Raking the plowed garden, Emily was somber. They worked and then talked into the night, sitting in the old kitchen. "I'm going to rent an apartment in Salt Lake this fall," Emily said. "All my friends are in Rockwood, but I can't stand it here anymore."

Allison hoed small hills and pushed squash seeds into the dirt. "You'll love the city," she said, but Emily didn't appear to be hopeful.

"I can't look at Bishop Hansen, no matter how caring he seems, and think the same as I used to about him. I was dead wrong to do what

I did, borrowing priesthood I had no right to. I went through a fence I shouldn't have, and now it seems real good over there. How could it be unrighteous if I felt God's power flowing through my hands? Bishop Hansen said I was mistaken. That it couldn't happen that God would color out of the lines, so to speak."

"He said color out of the lines?" Allison stood from her planting.

"Of course, he didn't. Sitting here, I decided I was a fool to let a handful of men beat me. It's not just their church; it's my church, too. My ancestors sacrificed. I have years of service. But then I thought I'd be a bigger fool to fight them." With the hose, Emily filled holes with water for the tomato plants.

"Wouldn't work anyway," said Allison. "They're all the same. You get any three men together and they'd work you over the same way."

"I don't believe that. My bishop will never 'work me over.' What stopped me thinking about rebellion as a solution is I've never known any good to come from fighting. I'd just turn myself into a bitter woman, mourning like Howard for my lost dream."

"This is no world for idealism," said Allison.

"I'm learning that," said Emily.

"I knew it when I was two. And Howard's finding his way out of bitterness."

"I shouldn't have said it that way. I can see he's not bitter. What did you do to him?"

"Gave in on every point, other than living in Utah."

"So," said Emily, "you're going to have a baby?"

Allison stared at her. "We're working at it."

"It will be a beautiful child and you'll raise him well. Can you imagine how happy this makes me?"

"That was part of the decision. How could something you want be bad for me?"

"You trust me more than I trust myself. The bishop made me promise not to give any more blessings. I'm permitted to hold their hands and pray with them but not to even say the word priesthood."

"Oh, Emily," said Allison. She touched her on the arm.

"I gave him my word." She pulled a flat of tomato plants toward her and began laying the small plants into the muddy holes. "I imagine all us women sitting in heaven. We have our feet up, and we're drinking Cokes out of icy glasses. Below us are all the men in the world, all the husbands in hell. We're sipping our Cokes, and they're begging for some. But if we pour out a little, it just evaporates before it can reach their mouths. So we say, 'What's the use?' and go back to our talk." She pulled the flat behind her, crawling across the garden.

If Emily was somber, Howard was anything but. He was jubilant to be home in the spring. Calves were butting their mothers' udders across the valley and all that new life inspired him. Their trip to Utah marked the end of the three-month wait for the contraceptives to be gone from her body, and they made vigorous love in the upper room of the polygamous house. She made comments about bulls and bucks in spring, but he apparently found her wisecracks stimulating because the next night he was even more energetic.

Predictably, a month after their Utah visit, she missed her period. She was stuck up on the North Slope and couldn't be sure, but the morning of the summer solstice, when she returned to Anchorage, she peed on a strip of paper.

"My garden's been planted," she said to Howard, when she flew home.

"Hello and hallelujah!" he said, apparently missing her sarcasm. He was unbearably smug for several days, smirking around the apartment when he wasn't at school or work.

She called her mother. "I'm pregnant," she said. "We're keeping it."

"Well," said her mother. "Frank," she called. "It's Allison. She's having a baby."

Her father lifted the other phone. "A grandfather," he said. "Damn. My only consolation is that thirteen years from now I can observe your pain."

"I was a model child," said Allison.

"Aunt Jenny claimed you were possessed of seven devils. She wanted you exorcised."

"Will you stop drinking?" said her mother.

"Already have," she said. "I got pregnant in Utah. In an old polygamist house."

"You should have stayed out of Utah," her mother said.

After Allison hung up, she had an odd daydream: Walter and Howard's other ancestors peered through a microscope, which let them observe the horde of Howard's swimmers fanning out as they invaded her uterus. When one of the swimmers sank its head into her egg, they cheered and drank root beer to celebrate.

Howard's first use of the loan money was to buy a chain saw with a long blade, which he used to cut down the largest trees on their lot. Brother Yamamoto from Howard's church was a contractor. He showed Howard how to dynamite the larger stumps and cut around the roots of the others. Toward the end of June, they drove up to watch the bulldozer clear the brush and smaller trees, and flatten the area for the cabin. The smell of diesel reminded Allison of driving the tractor in the desert.

She discovered that Howard was a competent organizer. He rented forms for the foundation and bought spacers so that the floor wouldn't crack. Brother Yamamoto brought cement working tools and, most importantly, knowledge. Together the three of them connected the forms and tied the iron. That afternoon a truck poured the footings and the slab. Allison strapped on knee pads and helped, using a trowel and a rake to smooth the cement.

The Fourth of July fell on a Sunday, the first anniversary of their meeting in Hermann Park. Howard planned to make good use of the long weekend. He arranged for the logs to be delivered on Saturday. He talked to Todd, his friend from the botany lab, and Brother Yamamoto convinced four other men from Howard's priesthood group to help. Allison invited Mark. The semi loaded with the pre-cut logs was supposed to arrive at seven, but it was late. Howard handed out axes, shovels, and grubbing hoes, and everyone set to work on the tangle of wood and brush pushed up by the bulldozer.

"Let's play ball," one of the men said, standing spread-legged and swinging his axe. Howard pulled the cord and started his chain saw. The men pulled on their gloves and swaggered toward the work, watching each other with side glances. Mark wielded his axe as if it were a part of him. Allison tried her hand, imitating Mark's motions.

"Whooo," whooped one of the men. "Look at her go."

"Solid," said another.

Brother Yamamoto said, "We can do this. You sit." She smiled and kept chopping.

Mark cut with three strokes what it took the others six, but after half an hour he was resting more. "Too long in an office," she said, nudging him as he sat on a log. "Even the brothers are outdoing you."

"Brothers?"

"Brothers from the hood, you know. The white bread brothers."

He glared at her and attacked a thick tree, still attached by the roots. "Who's resting now?"

Allison leaned on her axe and watched Howard's face, which was vital and intent. For a moment she saw him as a rancher managing a spread, ordering his hired hands. She and Emily had saved him from that isolated and impoverished life but did so against his will. She moved close to where he used the chain saw on the last stubborn root of a five-inch fir tree. He turned off the machine.

"You all right?" he said. She was silent.

"You could have left me," she said quietly. He looked up, sweat dripping off his face. "Anytime in the past year you could have left me."

"But I didn't."

"Yes," she said. "I know that." She turned and went back to work.

They had almost leveled the pile of dirt the bulldozer had left when the semi arrived. The driver used a forklift, which she had hauled behind the truck, to set down the bundles of support bars, logs, and trusses, as well as the plywood, tar paper, and shake shingles for the roof.

The walls fit together like Lincoln Logs. The brothers and Allison carried the timbers, one by one, to the wall and handed them to Howard and Mark, who stood on step ladders. They lifted the logs high and slid them down the long bolts which had been set in cement. Brother Yamamoto supervised and made sure the logs didn't bind as they slid down the supports. By lunch time they were half done; by evening the walls of the house were up.

Monday they lifted and fastened the trusses into place and nailed down the pressed wood sub-roofing. Brother Yamamoto and the four others shook everyone's hands and walked toward their van, clapping each other on their shoulders.

"I thought I was stiff Sunday morning," said Mark, "but I'm really going to be suffering tomorrow. Still it sure felt good." He trudged toward his car.

"Thanks, Mark," she said.

"It was nice," he said. "Showed me how much I hate the office."

She and Howard walked inside the cabin; she looked up at the white wood of their own roof. "One day," she said. "I can hardly believe it."

"Now it slows down. Working after school and before work, it'll take me all week to get the shingles on. We won't finish until well into September." They sat on a pile of logs in front of the cabin as the forest darkened.

"Show me what to do," she said. "I have two weeks."

"That's good," he said. "Soon we'll be in our own place."

"I didn't think we could do it," she said.

"Thank you," he said.

"For what?"

"What you said earlier."

"I wasn't apologizing," she said. "I couldn't have lived there."

He shrugged. "I sure could have," he said. "But not without you."

Far away she could see the faint strip of the inlet, but hardly any of Anchorage. They might have been alone in the wilderness. She was no Eve, but he was like the best of Adam and Eve combined. He had adapted to her world, made it his own. She had never before heard of a man who had done that.

Still, sometimes he was so—what?—Howardish that she could hardly bear to talk to him. Coming home from work once, she found brochures of pregnant women spread across the kitchen table. He said, "I'll be there for you."

"What the hell are you talking about?"

"I'm your coach. I hand you chips of ice and help you breathe to manage the pain."

"Damn the pain. I just want to be put out."

"They don't put people out anymore. You need to be awake and alert so you can bond with the child. After you're already well into labor, they give an epidural to help with the pain."

"This is coming too fast. Ice chips?"

"For dehydration. You can't have liquid in your stomach because you might vomit and aspirate if you have an emergency C-section and they knock you out."

"You should have this kid. You're the one who's studied all about it."

His hand explored her stomach; she lifted it away. "What? You don't want me touching you?"

"Touching is different than an examination. You're weirder than hell about this."

A month and a half later, she found herself again on the North Slope, crouched over the toilet bowl. She felt as if she rode a small boat on a heaving sea. A foreign matter had inhabited her body, pumping its waste into her bloodstream, disrupting her hormonal balance. All day at work she had been unable to consume anything but saltine crackers and small sips of Coke. *I* wanted this, she said to herself. *I* wanted this.

She imagined another self who had stayed with Eliot. She could have had dancing in Houston bars, more howling at the night. But while Howard was repressed a dozen ways, he continually stretched his own boundaries. Even in the short time they'd been together, they had both changed dramatically. Life with him felt like an adventure of significant negotiation. Eliot never stepped outside himself. Even his dancing was careful. Too sensible in bed, too cerebral, like a controlled and elegant opera, more noise than dancing. After all, he was the inventor of STIV, which assumed that sex was not a mystery but a language. Especially since their marriage, when Howard had become more relaxed with her, sex was like jambalaya. Despite his tangled background, he possessed a slow courtesy. He took sex seriously, even reverently; procreation is like a sacrament for Mormons. Despite his Victorian morality, he had shucked off embarrassment. Probably because of his ranching background. He had once bragged to Allison about all the beasts he'd watched copulate: cows, horses, sheep, chickens, and hogs; also rattlesnakes once (writhing, coiled around each other), skunks, and porcupines, which he claimed did it in the high, thin branches of willows or pine trees. He said that the male emits a shriek of pleasure at climax and falls from the tree.

She said, "You're anthromorphizing."

"About falling from a tree?"

"No, that a porcupine feels pleasure."

"They all feel pleasure," he said. "All of them."

Despite his faults, or because of them, he was Howard, her remarkable, unpredictable Howard.

Through August he framed the inside of the cabin walls with two-by-sixes, making space for thick insulation. Then he framed the downstairs rooms. A common area took up half of the ground floor, a kitchen behind a bar and a bathroom, the other half. Above the kitchen and bathroom was an open loft, the bedroom.

"There's no privacy," she said.

"And there is in our apartment? We want to get away from other people, not each other."

He bought some used cabinets from a man in the ward who was remodeling. He hired someone to tile the kitchen floor, bar, and counter top. He bought interlocking, hardwood floorboards and knocked them into place with a rubber mallet. He rented a sanding machine and smoothed the floor, then laid down a polyurethane finish. He built a chair and a bed out of poles, bought mattress and cushions.

September 20, close to the anniversary of their first year in Anchorage, they moved out of their apartment. "Eliot read it in my face," said Allison, as they hauled in their meager furniture. "He knew I'd end up in a cabin in the wilderness."

"Hardly wilderness," said Howard, pointing to the outskirts of Eagle River a mile below. He hung his tomato plants from the balcony.

"I was going to plant them in our own soil," he said. "But I decided I want to take them inside in the winter."

She laughed. "Howard, you have permanent dirt under your fingernails. You'll never get it out." Something that felt like gas bubbles moved inside. "I keep thinking that I ate something to give me a bad stomach. But really it's that something has possessed my body. A snake with teeth is going to burst out of my belly."

"That's morbid," Howard said.

"Whatever happens now, I have to deliver it. Scares the hell out of me."

"Women have done it before," he said. "You'll be great."

"I wasn't worried about how I'll do. This is a more significant worry than that."

"Hey," he said. "Do you remember Peterson?"

"Of course, I remember Peterson," she said. "He made you seem like a liberal. He made you seem logical. He's what fooled me into loving you."

"He sent me a card. He married the mission president's daughter, and they're pregnant, just like us."

"*We're* not pregnant. *I'm* pregnant. *She's* pregnant. But you and Peterson sure as hell aren't."

"Anyway. I thought it was a remarkable coincidence."

Despite all the mental walls he'd broken down, Allison knew that he still thought of time as a straitened path, laid down by God at the dawn of creation. Foreordained. Perhaps the path changed behind and before him, transformed by the act of walking, but it was still a conveyor belt, moving toward heaven. You got on it or off of it; and God knew all the steps from the beginning. She thought of time as a coiling, whipping snake, sometimes swallowing its own tail.

Emily was not happy in Salt Lake. "I've started my major classes," she said on the phone. "I'm failing—literally failing. The accounting equations and the math just won't fit into my head. I'm older than everyone in my classes."

"Talk to your teachers," said Allison.

"I've tried, but it's as if we speak different languages. I think that my age and my Utah accent make me seem stupid to them. I've never failed a class in my life." She complained that her apartment was small and unfamiliar. The women in her Salt Lake ward had friendships already formed. They were friendly on the surface, but couldn't relax and spend an hour talking. "As if I had the time to spend talking with all my school work." She said she missed her friends in Rockwood; she also missed the women who came to her with their troubles.

Allison was surprised at her mournful tone; she had thought Emily would bear up under any challenge. She said, "Become a sociologist instead of an accountant."

"I don't know if I can manage college," said Emily. Then she told Allison that Bishop Hansen, her one faithful friend, called her every week. "We have an appointment. Five o'clock Tuesdays. He tells me what's going on in town. He talks to me and *listens*." The smell of the city bothered her, the inability to get away from people. "And all of them strangers. When I smile at them, they look at me as if I'm a fool. If they look at all."

Later Allison described the phone call to Howard. "She's really bummed," she said. "Have you ever seen her depressed?"

"No," he said. "She's always been the one to cheer up everyone else."

"Well she's depressed now. She's different. She's wondering if school was a good idea."

"Maybe it isn't, at least for her," said Howard.

She frowned.

"What?" he said. "You think that your self-absorbed definition of what is good for her has ethical superiority over my self-absorbed definition of what is good for her?"

"You are so bizarre," she said. "You think like a New Age redneck."

Toward the end of October, Allison drove him to the Mormon stake center in Anchorage. Except for the boulders which covered the Rockwood building, this one looked the same. Both were Mormon suburban in style. Howard's bishop had arranged a meeting with the high council to review Howard's spiritual condition, and possibly return him to full fellowship. His bishop had spoken on the phone several times with Howard's former stake president in Utah, and they both agreed that his repentance was nearly complete. Walking in, Howard asked her for the seventh time not to say anything, no matter what. The bishop, who had the most toothsome grin Allison had ever seen, greeted them. But she could forgive him his mouth and nervous manner because he was trying to help Howard become happier.

After half an hour of waiting in the hall, she saw Howard smile as he emerged. She followed him back in and shook the hands of sixteen grinning men in white shirts and ties.

To celebrate, they ate dinner at an Italian restaurant. They touched fingers across the table, feet underneath. "I want to know you when you're ninety," she said. "I want to see you now that you don't have anything to brood about."

"I'll always have something to brood about. I brood to gestate my life. To masticate my life."

She lifted her glass of wine. "To Howard, may his eyes always flash fire."

"Flashed fire?"

"Today you were your jubilant self. Your Houston self."

"I'm right with God. I no longer fear him." Then his body was seized with sobbing. She slid across on the bench and held him tight, rocking with him as if he was a child—a large handicapped child.

The next morning they skied up the valley near their cabin. The conditions were bad—a heavy sludge that stuck to their skis. But the sun glanced off the snow, tree shadows lay parallel across the snow. They flashed in and out of shadow. It was jogging on skis, jogging through country that was so green and white that it hurt to look at it. At the top of the ridge, they turned back, took off their gloves, and stamped in the stinging wind. The gray inlet spread below them. "This could convince me to become a country girl," said Allison.

"Funny. All fall and winter, all this passed in front of my eyes, invisible."

"You weren't up here," she said. "You were wandering Anchorage."

"I prospected in places like this," he said.

They swooped down through the trees like two falcons. He wove back and forth behind her, crossing and recrossing her tracks.

Then a girl ran away from Rockwood to be with Emily. "Another abused girl," Emily said on the phone. "Happened when she was small, about ten years ago. Back then, it was her Sunday school teacher. Took advantage of a monthly class party they had at his house. Last week he was made advisor to the horse riding club she's a member of. She's frightened he's going to start with her again, so she took her parents' car and drove to Salt Lake—too frightened to sleep another night in her house. At first she just sat on my couch, crying. Then she told me who had abused her. Someone who is a fine citizen of Rockwood. 'I dreamed he came into my bedroom,' she told me. She checked all the windows and locked the door, but she was petrified. She sat on her bed with a bat, waiting. When she went back to sleep, she had the dream again. She said that when it was happening, he threatened her, said that he'd start with her sister if she ever told. Said he'd hurt her parents. Ten years later she's still petrified. Even after telling me everything, she was still beside herself, but I had promised the bishop I wouldn't bless anyone, so I just prayed with her, I held her hands and prayed. She seemed calmer."

Allison was silent.

"Please don't tell me I should have gone ahead and blessed her."

"No," said Allison. "That wasn't what I was thinking. I was thinking that she drove two hours to be with someone she trusted. It's remarkable."

"I called the man and told him what she said."

"No," said Allison. "No, Emily."

"What?"

"You have to be smarter about it."

The phone was silent. "I need your encouragement, Allison. I know it wasn't smart. He just denied everything. He says she made it all up."

"I'm sorry, Emily. I just mean—my mother is good at this kind of confrontation. It takes a certain kind of ruthlessness. Your strength is not in being ruthless. I just hope he doesn't do anything to her."

"I've thought about that. Or what if he gets frightened and runs away from his family? Both would be bad. I helped her report it to Child Protective Services, which is the state organization my bishop in Salt Lake said to call."

"Good."

"He said he'd sue me and the girl for defamation of character."

"I don't think he can do that." But Allison wasn't sure. "Do you know a good lawyer?" Idealists wander this world like lambs, she thought, but she didn't want to see this one hurt.

"He's also talked to the stake president in Hamblin and turned him against me. I know both those men are pressuring Bishop Hansen to do something about me. The bishop was honest enough to tell me that much about what's going on. And that's frightening—the uncertainty. I'm sure the bishop thinks I've broken my promise."

"Talk to him."

"No. I have some pride. Bishop Hansen needs to trust me or not trust me. I won't go to him apologizing." She paused. "I'm sorry about what I said, Allison. I do need to be smarter."

"What'll the bishop do?"

"I don't know. It would be ironic if I have to face disciplinary action for something I've stopped doing." She paused. "That man told the family of the girl that I may have had improper relations with their daughter. They've considered bringing charges against me. I'm facing a suit, perhaps criminal charges, and perhaps a church court. I thought that moving away I'd be free of this kind of tangle. Now I'm in it to my neck."

After hanging up, Allison lay in her bed, her arms folded across her chest. "Dammit," she said to Howard. "I wish we were there right now. I'd go hunting, by damn. I'd show that man the wrath of a Texas woman." But Emily wouldn't want it, she wouldn't approve even verbal violence. Allison strained to understand her forbearance.

Seventeen

The Goshute woman, dressed in white deer-skin, stood next to Allison's bed. She panicked, rolling to her hands and knees, clutching at the blankets. Howard was downstairs dressed only in his long thermal underwear, standing in front of the stove. His face glowed red. "You couldn't sleep either?" he said, grinning like a devil.

"I just had a bad dream—one of your desert dreams."

"Tell me," he said.

"You know, I never remember dreams," she said. Then the image of this one slipped to the surface. "The angel of death came to me dressed like an Indian." Allison sat on the edge of the bed. "Or maybe I just saw you pacing the house in your ghost suit."

Howard looked at her over his shoulder. "Is anything wrong with—?"

"No," she said. She held her hands across her belly.

"You need to be careful," he said. He came up the stairs toward her.

"It was just a dream. I'm not superstitious." The Goshute's face had not been dusky. It had been pale like her brother's.

"Look at this bed," Howard said. "Bolts of fear can't be good for either of you." He unknotted the sheets and blankets, fluffed her pillow.

"Okay, so I won't be afraid next time I have this dream." She snapped her fingers. "Just like that."

"Just think round thoughts. Pleasant, rhythmic vibes."

"Oh, go to hell," she said. "Want to feel?" She took his fingers and held them against her belly. "She's awake and kicking." He moved his hand away. "Wimp," she said and got back in bed. "Before I got fat, you couldn't keep your hands off me. You always wanted to examine."

He went back downstairs to the couch. When he couldn't sleep, he twitched and twisted, keeping them both awake if he stayed in bed.

She woke again just before her alarm was set to go off. It was still dark. The window above the bed wasn't tight, and cold air breathed through. Clouds streamed across the gray inlet, and when they passed over the cabin, they seemed almost close enough to touch. The past week they had dumped three feet of snow.

Allison wrapped her arms around herself, pushed her mouth and nose into the crook of her arm. She could use another body in the bed. She thought of Emily alone in her apartment in Salt Lake. The city was Allison's element, but it was foreign to Emily, and she was away from her community, the women she loved. She and Allison were both made lonely by circumstance.

Howard climbed the stairs, bearing a bowl of Cream of Wheat, steaming, in his two hands. "My grandfather fixed me this in the desert." He had sprinkled it with brown sugar. When Allison stirred, she brought up lumps, some an inch across. She flapped the spoon against the mush.

"I don't understand how you achieved such large clods."

"Dumplings," he said. "I cooked it that way on purpose."

She pushed the bowl away. "It drives me crazy when you're so damned cheerful." Howard ran out to start the car.

She dressed and walked to the stove, swaying from side to side. "Quack, quack," she said, warming her hands. She heard the car engine roar and then idle. She felt the child kicking again—a daughter, she knew from the last ultrasound. "Kick, kick away. Some day you'll be Pelé woman and be able to kick a soccer ball." Howard and Emily both told her that spirits traveled from Mother and Father in Heaven to the bodies of women. A hazardous journey. Mark, who was currently into bee pollen and higher states of consciousness, told Allison to talk to the baby and to give her a prebirth name. Howard called her "Cletus the Fetus." Even though she sometimes felt foolish, Allison did talk to the child. For the past few weeks, without having any specific ailment she could point to, she had felt the baby's attachment to her become uncertain. Perhaps the act of naming could hold them together. You're getting as feeble-minded as Howard, she thought.

He came in the back door and she heard him rummaging in the storage room. He came out with the tire chains. "Just in case," he said, "Even though we've got studded tires." She pulled on her parka and waddled after him out to the car.

"Marian," she said. "Emily-Lois, Eve."

"No, Howardette," he said. "She shouldn't have a name less dignified than her father's."

"You don't have a dignified bone in your body." He had the hood back on his parka, and she examined his tangled swirl of hair. "You don't have a dignified follicle." Her belly was small for six months but the weight still threw her off, making her walk awkwardly. It bothered her that no name would stick.

"Have patience, hasty one," she whispered. "You have three more months." She shook her head. Talking to someone who couldn't hear. Like Howard praying. She was dreaming dreams. Next she'd hear the Franklins and Warrens proclaiming Texas pride in her head. "Follow your destiny. Return to the lands of your forebears." What she wouldn't give for a stiff drink to drive the fog away.

While Howard put the chains in the trunk, she slid behind the steering wheel and waited for him to climb in. "I'm dropping you," he said. "For once you'll be early."

"But I feel like driving. And slow is my new mode."

The clouds had moved away, leaving the spruce above Eagle River powdered with snow. She drove carefully down the road from their cabin, two ruts with berms of snow on either side. She reached Hiland Road and started the zigzag course down the mountain. The snow on the road was packed hard as rock.

They could see a hint of light from sunrise, still more than an hour away. Even so, they could make out the inlet in the distance, gray like the mud in the burial pool. She imagined all the water under the earth connected, heavy veins of liquid. Passageway to the next life. The Goshutes were no more superstitious than Mormons, she thought. Imagination weaves fairy tales to protect the weak, protect them from a good, strong, biological fear of death.

Suddenly she cramped, a severe low pain; she bent forward over the wheel. "Ohhhh, damn," she said. She stamped her foot down on the brake and felt the car slide. One wheel dropped into the ditch at the side of the road.

"What's wrong?" he asked. She couldn't answer. "Can you move?" She shook her head.

"Just let me sit for a minute," she whispered, finally. He tried to take her hand; she didn't move to let him. She heard him get out and open the trunk. Finally the cramp faded, leaving a dull ache. When he closed the trunk, she saw in the rear view mirror that he had found a shovel.

He opened his door again. "Is it false labor?" he said.

"Not this hard," she said. "It shouldn't have happened."

"We're going to the doctor," he said.

"I don't need to go to the doctor. I just need to lie back for a minute. I'll be all right."

The door closed and she heard the thud of the shovel against the front tire. She knew that her dream came from the memory of the Goshute mummy. It was as if the shrunken corpse had filled with life and walked or floated 2,000 miles north, as if her dreams warned her of something about to happen to her body. What was the connection between dream and life, mind and body? The anthropologists had laid the woman on the table. Her head was white with crystals of salt, shrunken but hardly decomposed; her teeth grinned, leathery eyes shut, the child bound across her belly. Childbirth, said her Aunt Jenny, is the valley of the shadow of death. A straitened valley for a child to pass down; every Warren had a small pelvis. Her aunt and mother both had difficult labors, culminating in Cesarean sections.

Howard walked to the front of the car. He stuck the shovel in the snow and braced his feet, ready to push. "Okay," he shouted. "Nice and easy."

Emily said that God answered prayers. "Emily's God," Allison said. "I don't know you, but I'm telling you I don't want to lose this child." She put the car back in gear. "We want to stay together." She nudged the gas, hearing the wheel turning against the snow.

"Stop," shouted Howard. "It's just spinning. If I can't get us out soon, I'll find somebody to help."

"I'll just call a taxi," she said.

He dug some more under the front wheel. "No, somebody will come along soon," he said. The smell of exhaust nauseated her, so she turned off the engine. She called on her cell phone to tell Lisa she was sick. She didn't understand why Howard didn't want a taxi.

She heard him rummaging again in the trunk. He took out one of the sand bags he'd put there for weight. That's my Howard, she thought, prepared for everything except life itself. With difficulty, she maneuvered into the passenger's seat, lay back, and waited.

"Damn," Howard said, as he poured sand behind the back wheels and kicked it under. "Damn, damn, damn." For some odd reason, he felt almost as if he was praying. He got in and backed slowly, then faster—and the car was on the road again. He braked and turned to her. She held out a hand, fingers tipped with red.

"Howard," she said, "I'm bleeding. This isn't supposed to happen."

"We're going to the hospital."

"I think I'm going to lose her." Her jaw clenched with the pain. The car was cold inside, but sweat stood on her forehead. She held her arms around her own shoulders, despite her heavy coat. "Ohh, ohh." She bit her lip. Her eyes closed and she reached across the seat to grip his hand. "They can't help me." A tear beaded at the lower corner of her eye, ran across her nose, and dropped to his jacket. Another tear beaded, then another. "I'm such a wimp." Soon she tightened with pain again, her breath catching, her knees drawing up. "I'm not supposed to bleed."

He put the car in gear and started down the winding road, driving too fast. He made himself slow down. She flinched again. "Oh, God. Oh, no." Howard rubbed the still-fogged window with a glove. Finally they were off the mountain. The road skirted the south end of Eagle River and then merged with the three southbound lanes of the Glenn Highway. He hated the Glenn Highway in the winter.

Allison didn't move, didn't talk. Behind them a white cloud of snow billowed. Her hand gripped the arm rest. Howard saw cars off the road, one or two every mile, pointed down in the ditch that divided the highway.

"I'm going to lose her," Allison said.

"Fatalism is the worst kind of superstition. We're not powerless, you know." But he saw her face white and frightened, and he drove even faster. Between cramps she lay sideways on the seat and rested her head on his lap. Turning onto her back, she reached upward between his arms to touch his face. For several miles they drove past the fence bordering Ft. Richardson and then, finally, went under the Muldoon Road overpass and into Anchorage. She clenched in pain, relaxed again.

Seven minutes later they slid to a stop outside the hospital's emergency room. Howard flung open his door and ran around the car to Allison's side. Nurses emerged and loaded her onto a wheelchair, pushed her inside. Howard parked the car and came back through the entrance way in time to follow the wheelchair into one of the examination rooms. "I'm her husband," Howard said, as he helped a nurse lift Allison onto the examination table.

The nurse took Allison's blood pressure and temperature and hooked a fetal heart monitor around her belly. Howard paced in the small room, wondering if he should have given her the blessing he'd hinted at. He could have simply dropped one hand from the steering wheel, but she wouldn't have liked it. Let her be all right, he prayed. I don't even care about the baby, just let her be well again. The door opened and a doctor entered, washed her hands and, as soon as she was gloved, began a careful examination. After a minute the doctor said, "I don't think she's lost the fetus. We need an ultrasound before we know what's happening. And I want to admit her."

"Thank you," said Howard.

Another nurse positioned a gurney next to the table and helped Allison slide onto to it before wheeling her through wide double doors. The nurse told him that the public elevator could be reached only from the front door. He walked outside, entered again, and finally found Allison's room. Her face was as white as alkali clay and she breathed unsteadily. She reached out her hand for him, and he sat next to the bed in a chair. Soon she was finally able to sleep.

Later a nurse brought lunch. There was another bed in the room and Howard lay on it, watching the gray sky. Allison turned on her bed, her hair pulling more and more out of the pony tail she had put it in, frizzing around her neck. She held the blanket between her arms, against her cheek, tucking her knees up toward her elbows. When she woke, Howard gave her soup and 7-Up from the tray. She ate even that liquid food slowly, laboriously.

"I could still miscarry," she said to Howard. "Happens a lot."

Mid-afternoon, a technician gave her an ultrasound. Allison watched the monitor as he directed the gray, flat-bottomed instrument across her belly, which had been smeared with an amber gel. The child was curled, floating in what showed on the screen as shadows of flesh and liquid. Howard bent and examined the image. Allison could see the small girl's arms and legs, the coil of the umbilical cord. The picture of the moving child had reassured her before, but now the tissues that were supposed to bind them seemed tenuous.

Back in her room, Allison's own obstetrician, Dr. Perry, told her, "Your placenta is beginning to detach." He pointed to a cloud on the image. His face was as broad and red as a Utah farmer's. "Some doctors would keep you here. But you might as well be home because if you're going to lose it you're going to lose it. But what you really need is total, horizontal rest."

"Lisa will fire me," Allison said.

"The longer you can keep her," said Dr. Perry, "the better her chance of being healthy."

"Let her fire you," said Howard. "We'll make it."

Allison called the office. "Stay in bed," said Lisa. "You think you're indispensable? Mark's the only one around here I can't let go."

"I'll be at home. I can work there."

"You should be in the hospital," said Lisa. "Not at home."

"For three months? No. Put stuff on my computer and I'll work it over."

"Stubborn," said Lisa.

"Stubbornest bitch you know," said Allison.

Moving like a great, dull animal, she walked to the bathroom in the corner of her room. When she returned to bed, Howard rubbed her back and neck, which felt good. He fell asleep on the chair next to her bed. She watched his pale, innocent-worldly, Howardish face, his delicate brown lashes. Tears fell from her eyes. Soon he sat up, trying to wake himself.

He said, "Is something wrong?"

"What if she dies?" He moved to the bed, held her two hands together in his. "I don't want to be here. I want to go home."

"Tomorrow," he said. "Maybe tomorrow."

She thought about the narrow Franklin pelvis, about the danger of losing the child. Howard told her that his fear of God had relapsed into a tentative trust. Despite her own beliefs, she recognized that he was happier, more stable, since he'd given up trying to be an unbeliever and reconciled himself to religion. It was in his blood. What would he do if they lost this child?

Allison's bed in the peak of the cabin filled with the greasy smell of Howard's cooking, but the view of the inlet comforted her. She ate sitting cross-legged on the bed—a bowl of potatoes and canned meat boiled in tomato sauce. "You've reverted to functional cooking."

"My grandfather made this all the time."

"And look what it did to him. I'm frightened you'll drag me out there, bury me there." She imagined she was in that cabin, a hundred miles from a doctor, and that she looked down not on an arm of the ocean, dark below her, but on a white plain.

"You know I've given up that dream," he said. "Why do you keep bringing it up?" He walked down the stairs without saying anything else, and she knew she had hurt his feelings.

The next morning she panicked and called Emily. "I'm on my back. Howard is taking care of me."

"You're not seriously ill?" asked Emily.

"I just have to be careful the doctor said. I bled. I was in the hospital for a day."

"Oh, Allison." Her voice wavered.

"I'm fine. But I'm going to puke my guts out. Howard's frying onions in butter. It smells real bad." She called down to Howard. "Your mother says for you to go buy me more celery."

"I bought two bunches yesterday," he said. "Those are gone already?"

"He won't make a celery run," said Allison. "Tell him." She held the phone over the balcony toward Howard.

He climbed the stairs and bent over the phone. "I'm taking care of her, Mom."

"Howard's a good boy," Emily said when Allison took the phone back. "A simple soul."

"How are you doing?"

"I'm lower than I've ever been before. Because I didn't fit in well at the ward in Salt Lake, I've tried driving out to Rockwood on weekends for church. It's very uncomfortable being in sacrament meeting with a man you've accused of abuse. His name is Samuel Fitch and he glares at me with tremendous hate whenever we meet. If nothing else, that proves to me that the girl was telling the truth. 'You are a woman who has sold her soul to the devil,' he said to me last week."

"So he still denies everything."

"The girl told me that some people from Protective Services came out and interviewed her. They want to build as good a case against him as they can, so they told the girl's parents that they would wait a month or two before they do anything in case another girl, hearing about the accusations, might build up the courage to come forward. They say it's highly unlikely she's the only one."

"How did word get out? You didn't tell anyone, I'm sure. If your bishop did, I think he could be in trouble."

"Samuel was the one. He told a few of his friends about the accusations. They're upset because any woman can accuse a man falsely and ruin his reputation."

"Shitheads," said Allison. "Sorry."

"The Protective Services people told the girl's parents to take her out of the riding club and to make sure at least one parent of the other girls is always with the club."

"Have you told the bishop exactly what happened when that girl came to your apartment? Have you told him you didn't break your promise?"

Emily was silent. "He has to trust me. So far he doesn't. When I'm in his office, it's as if he's lecturing a bad child. He's forgotten who I am."

"Delta has a direct flight from Salt Lake," said Allison. "Come up over Christmas and we'll take care of each other. Leave that beastly desert."

"Sometimes I'm tempted," she said. "I picked up the papers to get approval from the state to have a house for battered women here. They're sitting on my desk. I can't seem to work up the interest to even fill them out."

"When I have this baby, we'll fly down and slap you out of this Rockwood gloom and lethargy. That's supposed to be a male trait."

"I inherited it through marriage. It's possible that you will too. It will be nice to see you. Good-bye, Allison." Allison heard the crackle of something frying. The smell of burned butter rose to her bed. Howard came up the stairs with a plate of toast and greasy eggs.

"Throw that crap away," she said.

"This is for me. I've got orange juice for you."

"Eat it downstairs. Eat it outside."

"How is she?" he asked. "I wanted to talk some more before you hung up."

"She's low. She's depressed because the bishop won't tell her that she can respect herself." Still angry about what was happening to his mother, she glared at him. She couldn't resist the cut. "You would convert me to that kind of thinking?"

"No," said Howard. "Not to that kind of thinking."

"You can't see that it's all connected?" she said. "It's like a disease."

"We Rockwoods are adaptable," he said. "See, I can listen to you without getting angry."

"Dammit, Howard," she said. "No one is adaptable to all conditions. She's suffering."

He sat down on the edge of the bed and dialed the number. "No advice," said Allison. "Just listen to her." For once he did what she said.

The last part of November was like a tunnel of night; the sun rose in the south and stayed low until it set a few hours later. Allison woke and dozed, keeping her body quiet. The cabin felt like an underground prison, one that admitted no light. She believed that the placenta was coming loose and that her child would die. But surprisingly, she didn't bleed again.

Howard did his housework and hers, seldom talking to her, moving quietly up and down the stairs: cooking, bringing her food, loading the fire, scrubbing the floor. "You're too much of a slinker," she said to him one day. "Noise won't bother me. I'm bored out of my gourd." So he immediately made a symphony of banging pots with a wooden spoon. He sang U2 songs to the rhythm of the washing machine. "Maybe I was wrong to ever let you down, but I did what I did before Love came to town."

Later she dozed, willing the baby to stay. "Steady now. No need to be an early bird."

Several times she woke to the ticking of snow against the window. When it was more clear, she sat on the bed with the binoculars and watched the dirty ice and the dark gray water in the inlet, the gray sky.

Some days the clouds blew away and the bitter wind seemed to come through the wall to her bed.

After one of the storms, Howard, wearing his red parka, shoveled the driveway outside her window. When he came in, he stamped his feet and banged his hands together. "The car won't start." He brought the battery in and hooked it to the charger he had bought. He discovered that their electric dip stick had stopped working, so he drained the oil and heated it on the stove.

"You're going to burn us out," she said. But by noon he had the car going and drove to his classes.

Lisa moved Allison back to the boring work she had done when she first came to Anchorage. Her commissions were much lower. Lisa's words, "Only Mark is indispensable," came back to her with new meaning. Toward Christmas she had to draw from her savings. "I spend money too easily," she said. "I wish I'd saved more."

"We don't have to pay rent," Howard said.

"Just taxes and interest."

"We've still got my job."

"Yes, we have that," said Allison.

"Don't mock. Some day soon they're going to make me a cook and then I'll get a raise." She buried her face in the pillow, grinning and thinking about all the ways he ruined food.

Days Howard went to school and worked as an unpaid intern for the botanist, but nights he worked at the restaurant. Allison was alone most of the time. She relaxed into lassitude, floating on her bed toward lotus land. When Howard came home, she felt like baring her teeth and growling.

Then one morning mid-November Nancy called and told her that Emily had wrecked her little truck driving back to Rockwood from school. "She took a turn too fast. Slid on ice and rolled it all the way over onto its wheels again. She drove it on in to Rockwood, but she had to duck down because the roof was smashed in."

Allison called Emily at the hospital. "I was careless," Emily said. "Drove like it was summer."

Allison thought of her rattling inside the truck cab as it turned around her. "How bad were you hurt?"

"Not a scratch," said Emily. "Well a few scratches. How are you?"

"Can't work much, can't do anything but ride this damned bed. I'm living in a cocoon made of the smell of Howard's cooking."

"Two low women. Allison, what should we do? I can hardly find the energy to do my school work. I'm going to fail more classes than accounting."

"Move to an island in the Pacific. Start humankind over. Make sure it's done right this time."

When she told Howard what had happened, he called his mother and scolded her as if he was the parent. "Stay in Salt Lake when the roads are bad."

The child grew larger every week, and Allison sat on the bed with her legs apart, her arms and hands limp. Her stomach bulged until she thought her skin would split. She no longer had the energy to change her clothing or wash her face and hair. Howard slept on the couch, so he wouldn't disturb her. He usually ate breakfast quickly, then left the house. Daylight was a closing window, less than six hours.

Thanksgiving Day, two and a half months before the due date the doctor predicted, they celebrated with canned quail, sweetened carrots, and Coca-cola. "When it's winter, it's hard to believe that things will grow again," she said.

"You're real depressed," he said. She glared at him, and he went outside. When she looked in the mirror, she found that her face had become pale and luminous, like the skin of an old woman.

Belinda called Howard. Allison answered and handed him the phone. He moved across the bed, his back to her, murmuring into the phone. "Not ever?" he said. She heard the words "I'll call Nan." He spoke too softly for her to hear more. While waiting for Howard to finish, she imagined that his invention, Grandmother God, appeared to Emily, passing through the adobe walls as if the brick had become liquid—just as an angel had passed through walls to get at Joseph Smith in one of Howard's myths. "You are to form a church in my image." Better that the grandmother said something practical. "Sign and send those papers. Knock down some walls and make that house a house of women" or "Get out of Rockwood." Get to a place where the seagulls don't call "God, God, God" and the air doesn't reek of patriarchy.

After he hung up, Howard touched her. "Your face is tight and angry."

"What did she say?"

"Mom hasn't come out of the house for two weeks. Like a hunger strike."

"She's not eating?"

"She did fast for three days, but Belinda talked her into eating. She won't come out to go to school. Belinda makes sure she has food. Won't go to church. Won't let any visitors from the church in. Shuts the door in Bishop Hansen's face. Nan has finally talked her into moving in with her. Maybe they can get her to finish out her classes, get back some of her self-respect."

"She'll become like your father, your grandfather." She wanted to fly down but knew that no airline would let her on the plane. She thought Howard should fly down, but he wanted to wait until Emily had a try at living with Nan.

The next morning Allison found blood again. Howard rushed out to start the car. The wind blew against the log house, making a low sound like an oboe. A half hour later he came back in. "I can't figure out what's wrong," he said. "Maybe it's water in the gas. Maybe the timing chain has slipped. I'm calling the ambulance."

"Taxi," said Allison. "Just call a taxi."

She dozed, woke to a slight pain, dozed again. Finally she sat up on the bed and looked out the window. Howard leaned down to the window of a taxi; he turned and walked toward the house. Allison got up slowly and dressed herself.

"You should be lying down," he said.

She finished and walked out into the yard.

"*Qué pasa?*" said the driver of the taxi. "You need an ambulance?" Howard opened the door, and she lowered herself to the seat. The Goshute baby had been reattached to its mother with leather bands. You can't beat death that easily, thought Allison. The driver apparently thought she was going to have her baby any second; he drove too fast down the mountain and on to Anchorage until they reached the doctor's office.

Dr. Perry ordered another ultrasound, and found that the placenta was more detached than before; he showed her the dark curve of her uterus, the dark cloud of the fetus, the white line between them. "Nothing I can do," he said. "You *are* resting, aren't you?"

She and Howard looked at each other. "Yes," she said.

After Howard left for the restaurant, Allison called Emily and asked her to come for a couple of weeks. "I'm alone," she said. "I need you to care for me. Howard's gone all the time."

"I'm a sucker for people who need me," Emily said.

"I know. I figured that's the only way I could get you away from Rockwood. We can have a good time together. A women's time without Howard. I'm alone all day and half the night."

"You need a nurse," said Emily.

"I need you," she said.

"We're a pair of invalids," said Emily. "Both of us disasters waiting to happen."

"You've become a pagan?" said Allison. "No faith but in fate?"

"I don't need to believe in fate or be a pagan to know that disaster happens," said Emily. "It's just the nature of the world."

Howard drove to the airport to get his mother. She looked older than he'd ever seen her—limp and listless. "I'm glad you're here," he said. They drove up the winding road in the dark. Allison had turned up the gas logs and the room was warm.

Emily walked upstairs and hugged Allison. "I'm the walking wounded," she said, "and you're the lying wounded."

Allison stayed in bed night and day, allowing her body the space to heal itself. She lay in warm baths, talking to the child. She knew her words were useless, and she counted it as evidence of how unsteady she was emotionally. Emily rejected Cletus or Howardette and renamed the baby Nicodemus—Nicky for short—because she was a waverer.

Emily moved around the house on feet as quiet as a ghost's. Her eyes were dull, her hands slow; nothing about her was as vital as when Allison first knew her. She sat for long periods of time, looking at the floor or the wall, out a window.

Often, when the two women needed to talk, they instead found themselves issuing proclamations:

"You can will your body to heal itself," said Emily.

"Take your own advice," said Allison.

"Body and soul," said Emily. "We're subject to powers no one controls."

"You are a mind and a will, a strong woman."

"We are transients, here a minute, then dead and buried."

"The earth is just the earth. Only what you touch and see."

"The earth is a cross on which we are sacrificed," said Emily.

"Believe your own words from when I first met you. Your soul is eternal, indestructible."

One morning they found that the weather had turned warm. From her window Allison saw puddles melting in the roads. She watched but Howard didn't come until nearly midnight. Then the three of them sat on the bed, talking. He said that, walking between the giant pots in the steaming kitchen of the Chinese restaurant, he felt as though he had been consigned to hell. Allison dozed; the pleasant rhythm of their voices was a balm to her.

Although Allison was careful to keep herself still, control her fear, she knew that resting hadn't prevented her bleeding a second time. Once the unnatural process of detachment started, she felt it would continue to its end. Emily fussed over her, bringing dinner up and talking to her while she ate. Emily read positive things—Benjamin Franklin's *Autobiography* and the New Testament. They often circled back to the same arguments. Emily told Allison that depression could cause physical problems. Heal thyself, said Allison. She knew that her own sadness was the natural fear of death; she thought that Emily's problems came from not trusting herself enough.

A few days after the solstice, and contrary to expectations, Allison hadn't bled for two weeks, since before Emily came. The doctor told her she could get some exercise, so she went on short walks with Emily along the roads near their cabin, passing under the dark spruce and birch. On Christmas Eve they stood and watched a moose chewing willow. Allison didn't know what she'd do if a moose came after them. There had been a story in the newspaper about a moose stomping a man to death. When they climbed back to the house, they built up the fire inside, opened the door, and sat watching the flames. Howard walked in, red-faced because the car had slid off the road and he'd had to walk two miles in the cold. "It's the jolly elf himself," Allison said. He read the Nativity, and Allison's mind slipped again to the Goshute woman, pictured her squatting in a blue cave in the desert, dropping her child onto the frozen ground.

Early in January, when the days were growing subtly longer, Allison had another appointment with Dr. Perry. He examined her carefully. "Thirty-eight weeks," he said. "We've about made it."

"Good," said Allison. "I'll be glad when this is over."

"It's never over," said the doctor. "Don't relax your care for her," he said to Howard.

"Relax?" said Allison. "How could he relax more? His mother has been taking care of me."

The Goshute woman stood between the cook stove and the bed. She walked the house. Sometimes she had the withered face that Allison had seen, sometimes she had Emily's face. Allison woke and found Howard holding her.

"Another evil dream?" he asked. She heard Emily turning on the couch downstairs.

"I don't believe in dreams," said Allison. She discovered that she had been holding her breath. The baby was still—sleeping, the doctor had assured her—but Allison poked and massaged her stomach until the child moved again.

"She's going to be plagued with insomnia," Howard said.

"It will be genetic from her father," said Allison.

The next day Allison felt well enough to work; she kept at it steadily all morning. Emily cleaned or sat in the room below her, giving her space. At lunch Emily talked about flying home. "I'll come back to see the baby," she said. "I've missed the beginning of school."

"I didn't know you were missing school. Why didn't you say something?"

"I don't even know if college is the thing I need right now. But I do need to try to gather myself. I need to be in my home."

"Go then," said Allison. "I'm fine now. We'll be fine."

"I'll be glad to get back to more consistent daylight. I don't know how you make it through the winter."

After lunch Emily walked up the stairs. "I'll be back soon. I have hardly seen this place you live in."

Allison worked some, dozed some. Two hours later Emily still wasn't back. Allison stood in the yard and peered through the binoculars, but it was getting too dark to see. Howard would be in the library or class for another two hours, then she could call him at work. Emily's tracks—she had borrowed Allison's snowshoes—led south, upward through the trees. Allison thought of calling 911. She thought of Emily, a desert woman, who had braved winters nearly as cold for forty years. Emily had worn Howard's coat, warm as a down sleeping bag.

Allison pulled on her boots and coat. She stepped into her skis, then slipped them off and tightened the straps on Howard's snowshoes. She wrote Howard a note and stepped on the snowshoes, fastening the buckles.

The night was cold, probably ten below, and she pulled her scarf across her face. The tall, thin trees cast long shadows on the snow. She felt like she was waddling through a Jack London story: not a hard-as-nails frontier man, or a wolf-like dog, just a pregnant woman, following her mother-in-law—who might have lost her way.

The snow was powder on top of a two-inch crust. She walked in Emily's tracks. Clouds passed across the moon, the trees were black, fields of light and shadow moved across the snow. Bears had come this low before. Still Allison grinned into the frigid breeze, glad beyond rationality that she hadn't called for help. She shook her head, picturing Emily down, frozen stiff, gnawed, like Howard's grandfather, Emily's father-in-law. The night was so bright. She felt, not like a wolf, more like a brown bear moving heavily through the snow.

She wasn't used to walking, especially with snowshoes, and her feeling of exhilaration changed when she tired before she was out of sight of the cabin. She began to feel like a fool. Then she smelled smoke, saw a glimmer of light through the trees. Closer, she saw criss-crossed logs, a fire, a bulky-coated figure bent over the flame like a street person. Emily's adventure had only taken her ten minutes away from the cabin.

"Hey," she called. "Emily."

Emily whipped her head around. "Allison," she said. "You shouldn't be up here."

"I was just following a wild woman. I was afraid you'd fallen in a drift or broken a leg."

"I'm just fine." She held up each foot. "Only frostbite." She stood and came toward Allison.

"Are you serious?"

"No frostbite," she said. "I was on my way back and couldn't face another eighteen-hour night in that cabin. Only because it's not my cabin." She took Allison's arm. "I'm worried you've overextended yourself coming after me."

"It's beautiful," Allison said. "Let me rest for a minute and we'll head back."

Emily brushed the snow off a log and helped Allison sit.

Allison said, "Two weeks in this country and you're ready for home."

"Ready for something. I lie there in your cabin, and I think about Walter. Wish he wasn't gone. This is a hard time to be alone." She turned her gloves above the fire. "Sitting here, I've been thinking about the fires I sat over with Walter, our first year, before we had children. On the cow herd, deer hunting, or just camping together. Even after we had Evan, we went. Then after I had two babies, it was too hard to camp with them. He still counted on me for work. I drove tractor plowing, harrowing, or planting. I held the calves while he doctored them. It was all right. But it gradually changed." She looked at Allison. "Children change everything."

"Howard says he'll help mother the child."

"I give him four months. I think he'll be real good at it, but I give him four months. Most men would last a week."

"Damn," said Allison.

"Don't look so glum," said Emily. "You'll work something out."

"So what are *you* going to work out?"

"I had hopes of making a home for women. I pictured a healing place, women in both sides of the house, upstairs and down. Good food, sitting up late talking about our lives."

"You imagine people half healed before they get there."

"That's right," said Emily. "I imagined Eden or Paradise."

"You said 'had.'"

"I told you that Nan got me to send in the papers to the state. Well, I did it. But Bishop Hansen told me that most people in town are against the idea. Before he got mad at me, I asked him if he'd support me. Even then he said he'd have to think about it. He thought it was a good idea for me to have something like this, but he wanted to keep out of it. Now I'm sure he won't help me. He made me promise not to bless women with the priesthood, but he won't bless them the way they need to be blessed." Emily smiled. "Anyway, that's why I need to get home. To try to get courage to work through some of these tangles."

"You can do it, Emily. You have the money, a building; you're good with harmed souls. It's perfect."

"Another problem is the building. I thought we could break down a few walls, redo it completely. But the foundation's crumbling, the walls are rotting."

"Build a new house."

"In Rockwood?" she said. "I've lived there forty years. Now it's a hard place to be. But if I try to buy property closer to a city and then build a house, I don't have enough money."

"Get a contractor to evaluate it. Someone will be able to tell how to fix it up."

"I've been so tired of trying to swim upstream," she said. "But maybe I can try again." She put her hands on her knees and stood. "My feet are real cold. I think it's time to get back."

Allison's clothing and limbs were stiff from the cold, but she followed Emily as they clomped down through the trees. Clouds still skidded across the moon. Allison stopped next to a dead tree which had snow thick on every branch.

"You all right?" asked Emily, turning.

"We'll kick Howard out and live here forever," she said.

Emily tromped back and took her gloved hand. "You don't want that."

"Of course, I don't. I just want to keep you here."

A white light flashed through the trees, white light and dark body, Howard kick-stepping up on his skis. "What's wrong?" he called.

"Nothing," called back Allison. "We just went for a little stroll."

Emily laughed out loud, a laugh like Howard's own, the wheezing bray of a donkey. The sound echoed off the trees.

"You scared me," he said. Allison threw a crust of snow at him, and she and Emily stomped past him. He swooped below them, dark as a wolf slipping through the trees. Inside the cabin they shed their coats, pulled off their boots.

Allison lifted her sweater. "She's kicking again. You should feel." She took both their hands, thrusting their cold fingers against her warm, round belly. She looked into their faces as they felt a heel or fist knocking to get out.

Eighteen

Emily sat in the chair at the corner of the bishop's desk. He wore a plaid shirt and wool pants; he had just come in from feeding his cattle. His hair was white, cropped short; when she had first met him, it had been longer, brown. From his face she knew he'd be firm with her again.

"I'm glad you finally called me," he said. "This business about Sherryl's accusations has been a real hardship—for all of us."

"We're older now. Everything is a hardship." He leaned forward, but before he could speak she said, "Remember when I married Walter? They put you and him in the elders' quorum presidency." Brother Jenkins, who had bought Walter's farm, had been the other counselor. The three couples had met to make plans. They decided that the best thing they could do was to have a barbecue every month. "We had every single elder and prospective elder in Rockwood out to our parties. Weren't those good times?"

"What do you want to talk about specifically?" he said.

"I need to sneak up on it," she said.

"When you talk about what good friends we are," he said, "I feel like you're sneaking up on *me*." He didn't smile. "Like maybe you're giving priesthood blessings again?" He clasped his hands before him on his desk. "I don't know what to do with you, Emily."

"I have been so discouraged," she said. "In the beginning I didn't plan anything. It just seemed to happen."

"You know I've had several meetings with Sherryl. She told me she drove to Salt Lake, and you prayed with her in your apartment."

"What did she say to make you mistrust me?"

"Nothing specific," he said. "She was so worked up, she couldn't remember if you put your hands on her head. She just said your prayer made her feel calm." He rubbed his palm against the side of his face. "I wish I'd never been called to be bishop."

"Gerald," she said. "You're going to have to make up your mind to trust me or not." She felt that the office was as small as a coffin and she would suffocate if she didn't get out soon.

"You promised me," he said.

"Yes, I did. Once should be enough."

"Right," he said. He stood and walked to his window, which looked out across Ralph Stringham's fields. His hands were clasped behind his back. "I'll act on that trust," he said finally. He walked back to his seat.

"Thank you," she said. "I held her hands. I did everything you suggested. I made sure it was nothing like a priesthood blessing." She felt as if the room had suddenly opened outward, and she found tears standing in her eyes. "But I sure shouldn't have called Samuel Fitch, even if I'm convinced he did abuse Sherryl."

"That's probably right," he said. "It's stirred up a real hornet's nest. I don't know who to advise to do what."

"So Sherryl's parents and Samuel are both talking to you?"

He nodded.

She folded her arms across her chest. "What *are* you going to do?"

"It's odd that no other girls had any trouble from him. I'm sure I would have heard from Sherryl's parents if anyone had spoken up to the state people." He cleared his throat. "I've read about young women who imagine cruelty so clearly that it becomes real."

"But you've talked to her?"

"Yes."

"Can you still think she made it up?"

"No," he said. "You're right. I can't say with good conscience that she's made anything up." He shrugged. "You know one thing you've done to me?"

"What?"

"You've made it so I can't talk without second guessing myself. I was interviewing with Sherryl and most of what came to my mind to say to her either cast doubt on her story or was encouraging her to forgive and forget. So I just kept my mouth shut and listened."

"You are a wonderful man, Gerald. I've always thought that Susan would help you turn out all right."

Finally he smiled. "I've talked to a dozen people in this office who want me to stop you from going ahead with this home for women. They don't want that kind of women in town."

"Women whose husbands beat them? That kind of woman already lives here."

"Who knows that better than me?" he said. "You don't need to convince me. It makes no sense, but some of them connect this mess with Sherryl and Samuel with the home—as if abuse will happen more here if you establish this house. At the same time, they somehow don't see Sherryl as one of those women."

"Well, it's all so new to them," she said. "No wonder they're confused. After these women come to church a while, people will change their minds. They'll see them as people."

"Come to church?" he said.

"Yes, I intend to encourage them to come to attend our ward. It can be part of the healing."

"Oh, Emily," he said. "You're hopeless."

"Hopeful," she said. "You owe me something."

"Me owe *you*?" He grinned, then the smile flickered away. "What do you want now?"

"Let me explain," she said. "When I blessed those women, I was filled with warmth. Such a clear strong feeling." She looked at him. "It was no different than the feeling I've had when others have blessed me."

"I don't understand how that can be," he said.

"But I have promised you I would give it up," she said. "I'll never bless another woman by anyone's priesthood as long as I live. It was a mistake."

"Someone might say you gave up what you had no right to in the first place."

"Yes," she said. "I want you to do me two favors."

"I'm afraid to ask."

"I'll tell you, whether you ask or not. First, I want you to support me in this home."

"Can't I just stay out of it?"

"No," she said. "You don't need to say anything to anybody, in church or out of church. You just need to help me, paint or pour cement, anything. If people see you working on it with me, they'll gradually change their minds—without any of the confrontation that would happen if you try to convince them with words." She paused. "And you know it's a good thing."

"I'll do it," he said. He looked relieved at getting off so easy.

"Second. I want you to pray for women."

"I pray for women all the time."

"That we will one day receive the blessings," she said. "All of them."

"No," he said, shaking his head. She watched him and waited. He moved to the window and looked out again. "Maybe. Maybe I can do that."

"Thank you, Gerald." She stood. He offered his hand, but she gave him a quick hug instead. She left his office grinning; for months, maybe years, she hadn't felt so happy.

Nineteen

Howard told Allison that God must have a specific purpose in mind for the new woman soon to emerge from her belly. "Why else would she be preserved through all these crises?"

"We're not out of danger yet," said Allison.

The night before they went to the hospital, her pains waxed and waned, not the definite contractions she had anticipated. She rolled on the bed, unable either to sink fully into sleep or to rouse herself enough to read or take a bath. She felt her belly; the baby seemed to be sleeping. An undertow of terror pulled at her, and she wished Emily had stayed.

Late the next morning she called the hospital and told them to get a room ready, even though the pains weren't progressing to regular intervals.

"Finally," said Howard, "we're going to get this done." He knelt on the floor in front of her and prayed. "Bless child and mother to pass through this unscathed, whole and well." As he spoke to his invisible God, he looked so much like a little boy that she had to stroke his hair.

As they drove from Eagle River toward Anchorage, the sun rose a hand's breadth above the south horizon. Thinking about the prayer, she panicked, certain that her narrow pelvis would hinder her child's already difficult passage. "The valley of the shadow of death," she said.

"Don't think it," he said. "Don't talk about that possibility."

"So talking about it might change something—might tempt fate or God?"

"No," he said. "I succumbed, for a moment, to weak-headed superstition. Nothing will go wrong."

"Anyway, I was talking about my pelvis, narrow valley." Her voice rose and she felt panic as another contraction clenched her body with pain. "My mother and aunt both had trouble."

"Breathe," he said. "Don't lose control."

"Go to hell," she said. "I'm controlling by speaking my fear."

After Allison was admitted, the nurse, a heavy Innuit woman, examined her and took her pulse. She then lifted Allison's gown and spread gel across her belly. With an instrument shaped like a cordless hair clipper, she took the pulse of the baby. Howard heard a heavy thrub, thrub; he heard a gurgling moan, something like the amplified sound of an underwater animal—liquids and gas moving in the system inside her. The nurse frowned, shifting the microphone across Allison's round belly. Suddenly she left, returning quickly with another nurse. They tried the same procedure, both frowning. The same slow thrub, thrub sounded, the same occasional gurgling growl— nothing else.

"What the hell is going on?" said Allison. "I have ears, dammit. Tell me!"

"We can't find the baby's heartbeat."

The doctor on duty came in, also frowning. He repeated the nurse's motions, holding the microphone at one location, listening intently, then shifting it quickly to another. "There was something," he said to the head nurse, "get a team together. We're going to take it."

"Howard!" she called. She thought about going into the darkness of anesthesia, while someone cut her belly open. She might never wake again. She felt him take her hand; his face hovered near, but she couldn't focus on either sensation. "Howard, I can't do this! Dammit I can't."

Before she called out for him, while the doctor was still frowning over Allison's belly, Howard had stood in the doorway. I'm a sinner, he prayed, I'll be a sinner my whole life, but please don't take this child from us. I'll give you my soul, my agency. He was flooded with peace, so when the doctor heard something, an echo of a heartbeat, he whispered, "Yes. Thank you, God." A nurse ran past in the hallway. Howard bent over Allison, almost afraid to touch her.

Before he could think of anything to say to her anguish, Dr. Perry walked up with a clipboard. His face was haggard as he led Howard by his elbow into another room, one with a couch and a low table but no hospital bed. "We're going to try a C-section," he said. "If there was no hint of a heartbeat, we'd deliver it naturally in order to prevent trauma to Allison. But since there's a chance, we'll take the baby as quickly as we can. If you agree, sign the papers."

"A C-section is more risky for Allison?" Dr. Perry nodded. Nurses and doctors ran past in the hall. Howard felt unreal, as if he were only watching a hospital drama. Soon he could walk away from the screen.

He took the clipboard and stepped into the hallway, just as a nurse wheeled Allison toward the operating room. He quickly explained the situation to her. "Sign, dammit!" she said. "I don't want to lose this baby after all we've gone through."

Howard turned back to Dr. Perry. "I want to be close," he said as he scrawled his signature. He thought that, if he could watch, God wouldn't dare go back on his promise, the peace Howard had felt.

A nurse helped him into some sterile clothing, green suit, pullover shoes, white mask; she showed him where they had taken Allison. The anesthesiologist put the mask over Allison's face. She ripped it off, her face distorted by terror. Then she lay back, waving for him to put it on again. From the doorway where he stood, Howard could hardly see her face under the equipment. A nurse swabbed Allison's belly. Someone else unfolded a green cloth which covered her everywhere except for her head and the swabbed area. The doctors bent low, and the arms and shoulders of the operating doctor were still in the way. Her voice was the only voice, speaking low to the nurse who handed her tools off a tray. Then she lifted the baby out, clipped the cord, and handed the baby to another doctor. Howard saw that the baby was so small and wrinkled it hardly seemed human. The skin was dark violet, the color of a bruise. Past the doctor he saw Allison's open flesh, as wide as the rib cage of a slaughtered animal. She will not survive, he thought. God, don't let her die.

The pediatric doctor and a nurse brought the child to an incubator near where Howard stood. He was certain they would revive the child. The Holy Ghost had spoken peace to his heart, but he had no such assurance for Allison, who might whirl off into darkness without him. They began resuscitation with a mask. Allison's doctor moved her hand rhythmically, stitching Allison together. When Howard turned back, the child had become pink. He said, "She's going to be all right."

"It's just the oxygen," said the nurse. "We still don't have any pulse or heartbeat." With his fingertips on the center of the baby's chest, the pediatric doctor gently pressed and pressed again.

By the time Allison was stitched together, the team had given up on the child. They left her lying in the incubator, and Howard watched as the pink flesh faded to purple again, as if from cold. He felt only a great weariness. He followed the gurney as they wheeled Allison to another room. She was still out, but when he bent over her, he was comforted by the sound of her breathing.

Around three in the afternoon, Allison woke. "Where is she?" she asked. Her words were slurred, as if she was drunk.

"Not alive," said Howard.

"I knew it," she said, blinking slowly. "I heard them saying there was no heartbeat."

"When she dropped, her skull compressed the umbilical cord against your pelvis."

Then she wept, great heaving sobs. Howard sat on the edge of the bed and held her shoulders and head. He worried that her spasms of grief were tearing out the layers of stitches in her belly and that she would bleed to death.

"They've stolen her," she said. "They'll give her to someone else."

"I saw her dead," said Howard. "Two doctors tried to revive her."

"You're lying. You always were a son-of-a-bitching liar." She lifted the sheet off herself and tried to swing her legs around. Howard held her down and buzzed for the nurse. The nurse attached a different sack to Allison's IV. Allison glared at him and the nurse. Howard wondered what he would do if she never returned from anger and isolation. Finally her eyes blinked, blinked again, and she slept.

Howard told God how angry he was at him for doing nothing to stop the child's death. "You told me it would be all right." Then he doubted himself, believed that he had felt nothing but relief that the troubled pregnancy was over.

When Allison woke, still slow from drugs, he called his mother and told her the child was born dead. The phone was silent. "This is too much," his mother muttered finally, "too much."

Where are the drugs for me? Howard thought. "They started artificial breathing, and the baby turned normal color. I thought she was all right." He sobbed once. "She almost died."

"Allison?"

"All through the winter," he said. "She was going to die and then she didn't."

"Howard," she said. "Howard."

"Oh," he said. "I almost asked you to drive out and tell Dad."

"Can you bear it?" she said.

"But he already knows."

He handed the phone to Allison, who started weeping as soon as she heard Emily's voice.

"Oooooogh, dammit," she said. "I didn't want to lose her."

"This wasn't what you planned," Emily said.

"I thought they'd stolen her. I called Howard a son of a bitch."

"He is one, " said Emily. "So was Walter. We just have to put up with it."

Allison laughed and then caught her breath. "I don't know if I can stand it."

"You just have to live," said Emily. "You just have to survive until your body learns how to deal with it. Like arthritis. Your body learns to live with it."

"Don't hang up," she said. "Talk to me."

Emily told Allison about the thaw in Rockwood; water stood in the streets and on the fields everywhere because the weather had turned warm so suddenly. The desert was covered with a sheen of yellow-green cheat grass. The bishop had helped her find a contractor who would repair the house according to state codes. She was going to save money by stripping the wallpaper in both halves of the old polygamous house.

Late that evening a nurse brought the child and laid her, wrapped in a receiving blanket, across Allison's chest. The baby's head was covered with profuse, silky black hair. Allison folded the covering back. The baby's arms and legs were heavy, substantial. The hands were wide for a child, the fingers strong. "Look at her," Allison said. "What a powerful creature."

Howard wanted to ask if she knew the child was dead. She still was so groggy and unstable that she might think any range of the impossible. When it was his turn, Howard lifted the child, which was cold and stiff even through the blanket. He placed his hand flat against the inert face. He held her as he'd seen his sister hold a new child, supporting her head with the crook of his elbow.

When the nurse took the child away, Allison sobbed and then wailed. She swung her head back and forth like a wild creature, someone foreign to him. He tried to touch her, but she thrust his hands back. The nurse came in and turned a knob on the IV. He thought about the drugs which muted Allison's sorrow. He moved to the edge of the bed and told her that the soul of the child still lived, that she had simply slipped into another dimension, and that during the Millennium they would have the chance to raise the child.

"Don't," she said. "You have no idea."

Soon she slept again, and Howard considered her anger. Belief in the resurrection took away the sting of death, people said. The resurrection was as real as his own breath, but how did that knowledge lessen the pain? Allison had keened like a primitive woman, realizing and releasing sorrow, passing through a fog of sorrow. He had said to her, Your child still lives, but elsewhere, where you can never see her, never touch or hold her, except in some impossible future.

He imagined the child, not as an infant, but as a girl of three or four, running across a meadow. Grandmother God sat on a boulder with Howard's father; they both watched the running child. "Walter," she said. "This one is for your care. Teach her as they would." Impossible vision, prompted by his longing to know the baby existed somewhere. Then he imagined Grandmother God smiling, despite Howard's despair at his daughter's death. Suddenly Grandmother God and Grandfather God both seemed creatures strange as aliens, creatures undisturbed by death, horrid, dispassionate creatures.

In the evening Allison woke up alone. Her body felt heavy with loss; a part of her body, a part that would have lived outside her, had been hacked away—no longer lived. Deep pain grew and faded in her belly, rhythmic as if someone had beaten her first with the blade and then with the head of an axe, destroying her nerves and cutting her muscle. Howard and the cold child seemed figures in a story that had nothing to do with her. The child had stopped existing—leaving Allison the biological urge to curl her arms around—nothing. At that physical register of loss, tears ran down her face, entered her ears. She shook her head. Impossible that the child had not lived, was not now in her arms. Not in her arms against her belly, mouth not like a bud against her swollen breasts, which didn't know the child was dead. Was not.

She imagined her own wrists slashed from palm to elbow, blood blossoming against the white sheets. Easy as breathing to slip into not. Easy as weeping. Water ran from her eyes and nose onto the sheet. She imagined a small being, tear-shaped, falling through space as dark as the water in the burial pool. Falling toward God's open arms. An impossible fiction. She knew that, even if the child had a soul that remained after death, she was lost still in the immensity of the universe, and Allison had no way of finding her.

She phoned her parents. "It didn't work," she said.

Her mother said, "He's gone back to the ranch?"

"No," said Allison. "The baby."

"Allison," she said. "You were almost full term. How could you do that?"

"You're not listening. It was full term. It was born dead."

"Why didn't they take it Caesarean?"

"They did take her Caesarean!" Allison shouted. "The doctor heard an echo. But it was our damn narrow pelvis. The umbilical cord was caught between her head and my pelvis." Then she lost it, sobbing into the receiver.

"Oh, Ali." Allison heard someone talking in the background—her father. "Stillborn," her mother said. "Allison, is he with you, Allison?"

"Yes." She looked at Howard, who sat, head down, in the chair next to her bed.

"Are they giving you something so you can sleep? Get off it soon, not now, but soon."

"Allison?"—her father on the other line. "Why are you so far away?"

"I'll be up as planned," her mother said. "I'll be there in three days."

"I'm coming too," her father said.

Her mother wanted to talk to Howard.

"Yes," he said, watching Allison stare at the ceiling.

"Don't leave her alone," said Lois. "Did she tell you I had a stillbirth—my first child."

"No," he said. "She didn't tell me."

"I would have hurt myself if I could. I didn't want to live."

"She's all right."

"You know nothing about it, so listen. She'll never get over it. I had Michael and Allison, but I've never stopped missing the first one, never stopped wondering what he would have been like."

"No," Allison sobbed after hanging up. "No, no, no. I can't." Then she became quiet, her eyes closed. Talking on the phone, she had seemed herself, then her face had dissolved into someone he didn't know.

He wondered if the stillbirth was God's way of breaking down her rationality, humbling her so that she would be open to matters of the spirit. "I hate you," he said to God.

"Howard," she said. "You think this was something I wanted? Something I did?"

"No," he said. "I wasn't talking to you." Grandmother God had not prevented the child from dying. Even Jesus, who was supposed to intercede, had done nothing. Perhaps Jesus' bargaining grace only concerned spiritual matters. Matters of the flesh were left to caprice. Then he wondered why his impulse was to debate matters of doctrine which were meaningless—the child was gone.

"Who?" she said.

"Nobody," he said. "I hate myself."

"Don't hate me, Howard. Don't say it or think it."

He couldn't open his mouth to say, couldn't think the first word.

It had been dark for three days, it seemed. The sun wouldn't rise for hours. By the faint light from the hallway, Allison watched Howard doze on the chair, which he had unfolded into a bed. She wished he'd leave, go home to sleep. Clearly now their only bond was sorrow. He'd felt angry too, had spoken out against her. Why didn't he just leave? Then she reached across and touched his face. He opened his eyes in the dark, she could barely see his lashes—shadows that twitched over his eyes.

The next morning Howard's sister-in-law Sherrie called. "Some spirits are given another chance if they didn't really get a first chance. That little girl could come back as your next child." Allison hung up. She gave the hospital operator a short list of people who could phone her.

Howard went home to gather his school books. When he returned, he had a large potted plant in each arm. One from Mark and one from the Relief Society in Howard's ward. Apparently he had called everyone he knew. He told her that someone had left dinner in a covered dish on their doorstep, even though he wouldn't be there to eat it. "There's more," he said. In several trips he carried flowers, all potted, up to her room. They caused the room to smell like a hothouse jungle, verdant and artificial. That afternoon Brother Yamamoto visited. He left Allison a tape of Japanese koto music, and sat while they listened. The odd harmonies soothed her greatly. His mouth was a thin line of sorrow. She was moved that he didn't try to say anything to her.

The bishop and his two counselors came to the hospital room—the short-haired man she'd met earlier, and two others, large as giants. She almost laughed—they looked like a comedy team—but then she saw their faces. They asked her if she wanted a blessing. "I'd like that," she said. Howard raised his eyebrows, but she did want one, couldn't explain it even to herself. They laid their hands on her head and promised her the knowledge that the child was hers beyond time and space, and that her despair wouldn't overwhelm her.

After the prayer they sat without talking for a few minutes. Then the bishop asked, "Do you want a small service?" Howard had told her that the Mormon church had an ambiguous attitude toward stillbirth. Life came with the first breath; had this child experienced life or had it never gotten that chance? They would be happy to organize a small meeting, which would give Howard and Allison the chance to voice their love to the child and to express farewell, although a temporary farewell, from their child. Allison's head started aching.

"No," said Howard, "we'll take care of it."

Then they asked about burial.

"Not here," Howard said, watching her face. Allison thought about the child laid in ground which would be frozen most of the year—small, stiff, and cold. She nodded. She knew that eventually she and Howard would leave Anchorage.

"Not Houston," she said. She felt no emotional attachment to the city she'd lived in most of her life. She hadn't thought it would matter where a body was buried, but she did care. She pictured a small grave in the salty mud next to the mineral pool, and she imagined coyotes streaming down the black ridge. Her body clenched with anguish. But it pleased her to imagine the small child in the Rockwood cemetery, where Emily would watch over it. "Rockwood. We'll bury her in Rockwood."

They talked with Howard in low voices, and finally stood to leave. "Thank you," Howard said. "I couldn't even start to think about those things."

In the end they decided simply to send the casket on the plane for Emily to receive. The mortuary would only keep it for a week and Allison was in no shape to travel. The day Allison was released from the hospital, they drove to the mortuary, where the mortician left them alone in a room with the casket. Howard said a long prayer in which he detailed what knowledge he wanted the child to gain. He reminded God that his servant the bishop had made a specific promise that the child would be theirs, that she would not be lost to them.

Allison thought the promise just raised a false hope, but then she started talking to the body, as if someone could hear. She told the child her dream of the three of them fierce as wolves; she told the child that she hadn't wanted to abandon her.

A week after the mortuary had sent the small casket to Utah, they received pictures in the mail: Emily, Belinda, Bishop and Sister Hansen and their children, Willey, and even Vernon Todd, stood around a small grave. The bright flowers looked strange against the dry ground.

For days Allison sat cross-legged on her bed and watched the clouds sweep across the inlet toward their cabin. The city was out of sight around the shoulder of a mountain. Even though below her spread the scattered lights of Eagle River, the cabin seemed as lonely as if it squatted on the moon.

She wept at odd hours. Howard held her in bed as her body was racked with sobbing. He felt that her sorrow was so immense that it overwhelmed his, made his insignificant. Howard vowed that like Job, he would face God at the judgment bar and ask him some hard questions. He imagined the child daily, still felt a load of sorrow that he couldn't release. They walked down the lane to Eagle River, up through the snow to where Emily had built the fire. Allison bled for three weeks. Several times he skipped classes, studying downstairs, listening for the sound of her breathing in the loft. Finally Dr. Perry said she should go back to work.

Nearly a month after the stillbirth, she suggested they drive to Wasilla to watch the start of the Iditarod. She wanted to take her skis along. She was still sore, and he said she was a fool to try it. She said he could stay home while she went. They drove north for forty-five minutes and then strapped on their skis. She skied slow and steady, knees bent as she moved down through the trees. They waited for half an hour, skiing back and forth to keep warm, stamping in place like deformed ducks. He watched her move, leaning into her skis as she stepped up hill or crouching on her skis as she swooped down. He thought, she is alive. The doctors had laid her on the table, used drugs to bury her consciousness so deep that she could drift, soundless, away (she had lived); they sliced nerve, vessel, and muscle, opened her belly; they drew the dead child from her body. She lived. He leaned against the tree and wept, watching her walk carefully on her toes up a hill, flicker back down through the trees.

Soon the first team of eager dogs passed, then another and another. The mushers leaned into the curve below Allison and Howard. The dogs were barely civilized wolves, running with their jaws wide as if they were carnivores of air.

Twenty

By March the structural repairs to the house were completed, and Emily had appointed a day when all her friends would come to paint and clean up the barnyard. A front had preceded Allison and Howard southward, and as they drove their rental car toward Rockwood, the desert was white with a half a foot of snow and another storm was coming, darkening the north sky behind them.

While Howard gathered their luggage, Allison ran inside. She found Emily, Belinda, Bishop and Susan Hansen all taping the windows and varnished hand rails. The walls were already sheet rocked and perfataped. "Someone is coming today to spackle it," Emily said. "They wanted us to lower the ceilings and put in smaller windows, but I refused. We want space in this house."

"Then we'll paint it," said Belinda. She shook Allison's hand and gave Howard a hug, which made his face flush red.

"I've rented a painting machine," said Emily.

"It's going to be like a new house," said Susan, the bishop's wife. She looked at him and smiled.

"Oh, no," he said. "We'd have to sell the farm to afford repairs like these."

"Now that's an idea," said Susan.

Allison glanced at Howard. He shrugged his shoulders and grinned, but she could tell the topic was still tender.

Bishop Hansen walked across the room and shook Allison's hand. "I've always wanted to hunt in Alaska," he said.

"You should come and stay with us," said Allison. "We could arrange a guide for you."

He shook his head. "Well, I'll have to think about it." But he beamed and glanced slyly at his wife.

"There goes the farm," she said and everyone laughed.

"The bishop has asked me to keep track of membership records in the ward," Emily said to Allison. "You're going to have to teach me how to use a computer."

"It's one of the hardest things I've had to do as bishop—find a safe calling for you."

Allison looked at Emily. Should she jump to the defense? Emily just laughed. "Giving me first crack at every new family in town," she said. "You think that's safe?"

"Luckily there are few new people in town," he said.

So Allison spent the day taping newspapers to windows and hauling junk to the dump. Howard worked at cleaning out the tool shed, sorting junk from what could be used by his mother or Brother Jenkins. Allison went out once to talk with him. "I grew up in that house," he said. "They're changing it. For the better I know, but a part of what created me is lost."

"Not lost," said Allison. "Reconstructed. Made useful."

That afternoon Emily, Howard, and Allison walked up to the cemetery, while a man from Hamblin spackled. They climbed through the fence which kept cattle and horses out. Snow covered the mounds and gravestones, the juniper trees and prickly pear. They found the mound, with the small marble stone Emily had ordered. Snow-covered flowers stood in a jar. Emily swiped snow from the small plaque, level with the ground, and read the inscription: "Emily Lois Warren Rockwood daughter of Allison and Howard."

"It was a nice ceremony," said Emily. "Bishop Hansen spoke."

Allison looked down at the mound and pictured the child lying in her crib, strong arms reaching for the faces floating above, sturdy legs kicking the air. Then she was a small girl, running up and down the stairs in the cabin in Alaska, in the new Rockwood house. She turned away from the grave. In another, better universe, it had happened. But nothing Howard did, no ceremony or profession of faith, could transform this part of their history.

The three of them talked late into the night. Emily told them that another girl had finally come forth with the same story about Samuel Fitch. She had been in the same Sunday school class. In March, just as the state people were preparing to act, Brother Fitch put his house up for sale and moved away. "They're still going to go after him," she said. "But they don't have much confidence." Then she talked about what she would do with the women: camping with them, working on the farm under Brother Jenkins's direction. Belinda would teach them art and music.

That night they slept on mattresses on the floor, the smell of new walls around them. Allison saw Howard leave the room in his white garments, heard him creaking down the stairs, wandering the house as if he were already a ghost.

The next morning Bishop Hansen, wearing a surgical mask, walked through the rooms, spraying the walls and ceilings with paint. Emily and the other two women went shopping for furniture in Salt Lake. Allison wanted to go with them, but Howard insisted that they drive west in the old truck to see the cattle. Crossing the pass, snow beat into the windshield. "Looks like the tail of a fox," Howard said. "At least, that's what my father said." Allison drove slowly so that they wouldn't slip off the road.

At the farm Howard disappeared into the swirling snow, and Allison took the car down to the pool. Leaving the engine running, she climbed out and stood at the water's edge, white snow, crust of alkali on gray mud. A wraith of steam hovered above the water. She bent and touched her palm flat to the hot surface. Flakes whirled above her like flocks of tiny birds. The wind shrieked through the squat brush. She almost heard the voice of her lost child, wailing. Teetering on the edge, she lifted her face to the cold flakes. She remembered Walter looking down into the water before he died. Had he seen his own future? It would be easy to follow. Life had become misery, death held no fear. She had stopped weeping every night, but she still occasionally broke down at work or in the cabin, and the pain grew deeper and blacker with time. Her mother had told her that eventually the pain would subside, but she had only hope, not belief, that it would happen.

She imagined those floaters, ankles bound, sunk upright in the deep water, waiting for passage back into the sun. Emily Lois lay in a casket on a dry hill. She, Allison, could leave the pool anytime she wanted, didn't have to remain as they had for year on year, century on century. She hadn't been compelled to follow. The steam was warm on her face, and she thought of the Goshute woman rising from the water, a child in her arms. Emily Lois in her arms. She would hand Allison the baby.

If only it wasn't a lie.

In September, two years after she and Howard first arrived in Anchorage, Mark announced that he was returning to Alberta. "I've listened to Lisa give one too many carrion-eater lectures," he said to Allison. "I want to go some place where the economy is vital."

"Calgary?" said Allison. "Might as well be Utah. Second Silicon Valley. You might find some new-wave Mormon woman, who's into pyramids, children in bakers' dozens, and bee pollen."

"After you, they'd all run second."

He wasn't joking. "You're a good friend, Mark," she said. "You like me even after I harmed you."

"No harm," he said, but she saw her own unsteadiness reflected in his face.

Lisa, who lived on the Hillside, threw a party. Everyone from the office and their partners stood on white carpet high above the dark city. Far out lay the inlet. Allison felt disconnected from the conversation.

"The entire program was junk," Nicole said. "He'd been working on it for six months."

"Must have been distracted by the ax at his back."

"I hit delete and started over."

A zydeco CD started on the player. Allison stood near the window, listening.

"We saw them running," said Howard. "It was cool."

"Three years ago," Mark said, "I made it over the Alaska Range. Then my dogs got sick."

"Poor babies," said Lisa.

"Alberta will be too tame after this," said Lisa. "You'll get bored as hell."

"What did you say it was," asked Nicole, "dairy farming?"

"A dairy co-op," said Mark. "They want to modernize. We'll computerize all the machinery as well as putting all the records into a program I've designed."

"I didn't know you wrote code," said Francine.

"I'm not just a pretty face," said Mark. "I have more talents than Lisa ever guessed. But I wouldn't be just writing code. I'd be assembling the team. Giving them the vision."

"I'm losing you to cattle?" said Lisa. "Damn."

"Call of the wild," said Nicole.

"Just like a Gary Larsen cartoon."

Allison faced the window; the city and the inlet spread below her. Howard, Lisa, Mark, and the others laughed out loud, the reflection of white carpet beneath their feet. The lights of the city shone through their bodies, stars grafted to their flesh. At the shore line, the lights stopped, as if past that limit lay the vacuum of space. During the earthquake, houses had slid toward the water, a whole neighborhood swallowed by mud. She wondered if the houses had been full of people, sliding toward drowning or suffocation, and she started to weep. She must have made some sound, because the room was suddenly silent.

"I want to go home," she said. She turned to Mark. "Sorry."

"You'll pull out of it," he said.

"No. Everyone talks about grief as if it's a stage to grow out of. It's not. I'm stuck forever."

Back at their cabin, Howard opened the flue and added more wood. He twisted the air vents open because he liked the crackle of burning wood. When she wept, as she did often, he didn't know what to say. In part, her easy expression of sorrow made him jealous. Sometimes she wouldn't even let him hold her, wouldn't let him close to her sadness.

"I can't think my way through this," she said. "I keep working it over like a problem with code, but it's not like that." He cranked the air vents back down and sat next to her on the couch. "She existed. I felt her kicking inside me. And now she's not. Sometimes I think about your idea that she still exists, and I get so angry with you I want to leave this house and you and anything that reminds me of her. You think that all this sorrow is useless. You admit none of it."

Howard took his heavy coat out of the closet and put it on, pulled on his ski pants and boots. The lights of Eagle River were scattered below him. He slid fast along the side of the road and then turned west, dropping ridge by ridge toward the river. When he came to the ice, he turned back and pushed himself up the hill, stretching his legs, feeling the burn. He smelled the sharp, evergreen odor; the air was so cold he could feel it. Soon the bitter air made his throat raw, and his nose and eyes run. He paused below the house, scent of wood smoke. He went inside, finding only darkness.

"Howard," she said from the loft. Soon his eyes adjusted to the scant, red light from the glass in the stove door.

"You're wrong about my feelings," he said. "You're wrong to think I didn't, I don't, feel sorrow. I read a story about a couple in New York whose child was killed at an amusement park. A year or two later, even before their suit against the park was settled, they divorced. Then they had a long court battle over who had sorrowed the most, because the one who sorrowed the most would get the biggest part of the settlement."

Her head, dark, appeared over the balcony, and he wanted to hold her. "Howard?"

He stood near the stove, held his hands to the heat. "I bury everything, but I still mourn. I imagine her with us in this cabin. We'd have to be careful of the stairs."

She walked down, wrapped in a blanket, and sat on the couch.

"You have no idea what I think or feel about Emily Lois," he said. "You remember when I prayed before we went to the hospital? Well, God spoke to my soul that everything would be all right. It was a lie. God stood by and let this happen."

"It was an accident," she said. "That's all."

"She turned a little bit and the cord looped beneath her head. If the cord had been an inch higher when she dropped, she would have been fine. All through the winter, whenever you had trouble, I prayed and she came back from the death, again and again. Why not this last time? A centimeter of pressure against a thin cord killed her. What if she hadn't turned? What if she had dropped slower? In the hospital I told God that if she was alive, I would turn over all my will to him. I would be totally his creature. He ignored me. I would give my life to have her back."

"Random chaos," she said, her voice thick with weeping. "An accident."

"What if you're right?" he said. "What if we will never have her again."

He moved to the couch, and she wrapped her arms around him. They rocked and held each other.

"Deja vu," he said. "Here we are again, dragging subterranean masses into speech." She snorted, and he couldn't be sure if she was laughing or crying, but, he decided, it didn't matter because both felt like communion. "We talk, don't we. All we can do. Like fish floundering on the bottom of a boat."

"Floundering sometimes helps," she said. "Sometimes it's all we can do."

"The bottom of God's boat, and he's grinning because he's got us on the line."

"That's not a healthy vision of your God," she said.

"Don't I know it," he said. "I return to that fearful image like a dog to his vomit."

"I could easily die," she said. "It would take no effort."

"When I'm sitting quietly and I let the knot of my thoughts untangle themselves, I know God is not grinning. Tonight skiing out there or whenever I pray, I feel that God is surprised and saddened by my sorrow. Then I receive a gift as clear as touching. It feels like the same comfort I felt when she was dead inside you, and we didn't know. The gods, mother and father, knew, but we didn't. They were helping me get ready for the sorrow. Telling me they loved me before the sorrow set in."

Allison looked at the crib they still hadn't hauled to the Salvation Army. "She would have been lying on a blanket in front of this fire. She'd kick her legs."

"I want her back. At the Judgment I'll face God and demand her back."

"You know I'll never really understand. It will always sound fantastic to me—this quick-and-easy transcendence."

"I thought you were dead," he said. "They let me stand in the door and watch. I knew that you couldn't survive what they did to you."

"You watched? I didn't know that. Why?"

"I thought everything would be all right if I was there. The baby was blue, and then she was pink. It goes over and over in my head, and I think that every second something different could have happened and she'd be here now. We could hold her."

Allison touched his shoulder. "I was wrong to say you didn't care."

"It's all right," he said. "I've felt like I couldn't say anything. I mean, she wasn't a part of me. I didn't have to suffer what you did." He told her again how they would have taken turns watching her. He would have shifted to evening school and would have found someone in the ward to take care of her during Allison's stints at the North Slope. Allison stood and moved to the crib. She lifted the clothing they had bought for the child.

"I'll mail these to Nan," she said.

"Nan's is a boy," said Howard.

"I'll mail them to Sherrie then. She'll never stop having babies. She's not superstitious about these things, is she?"

"She had a miscarriage once," Howard said. "She sorrowed forever over that."

"I want to feel finished with it," she said.

"Unless we forget her, it will never be over."

She looked at him.

"I hope," he said. "I don't know."

He opened the stove door and a puff of smoke came out.

"You always do that," she said. "Fills the house with smoke."

He shut the door and opened the flue another notch. Then he opened the door again. Firelight flickered in the dark room.

"I could be ready to move," she said.

He stared at her. "Now that we have a nice place?"

"Mark's smart. Not even Lisa can scrabble for work if all of it is gone."

"First, I finish my degree. Then I'd like to go to graduate school in marine biology. That means California."

"After that," she said, "the Philippines, Vietnam, Indonesia."

"As long as it has a shore," he said. "And a university where I can study."

"Yes," she said. "Plenty of places like that."

"We could have another child," he said and her body stiffened.

"Not yet," she said. "Not for at least fifty years."

"You'd be too old. You'd giggle behind your hand when I try to get you with child. My great-grandfather—"

"Stop! Not another word," she said.

"No," he said. "I won't stop talking. Only in hell can people avoid talk. Hell is when nothing moves anymore."

She knelt next to him.

"Fifty years is nothing to wait," he said. "You'll see. We're in it for a million. A million years of intense conversation, verbal and physical."

"My mind can't stretch that far."

"By then we'll manage ten or twenty planets," he said. "Make sure the oxygen nitrogen balance is right. Make sure the water cycle works smooth."

"The big ranch in the sky."

"Ten trillion spirit children. Ten trillion years of making love."

"Oh, Howard," she said, "a million years and I still won't be used to you."

He laid his head on her shoulder; she curled her arm around him and placed her palm on his cheek. She imagined leaving Anchorage on a jet, bound for Salt Lake or Indonesia or Kuwait. They would rise until the atmosphere was too thin to breathe. There would be limitless space above them and the solid earth below. Floating in a rare pool of air.